MISCREATION

By
Stefan Jakubowski

Published in 2008 by Zygmunt Stanley

ISBN 978-0-9554244-1-0

© 2008 Stefan Jakubowski

Cover illustration by Pat Moffett
www.illustration.gb.net

Cover and pages designed and typeset by
Rachel Loosmore
Absolute Design Solutions
www.absolutedesignsolutions.co.uk

Printed by Gomer Press, Wales

Special thanks to
Rachel Loosmore

THE AUTHOR

Originally from Reading Stefan Jakubowski moved to Wales in the latter part of the last century. (He wishes to point out that he is not as old as that makes him sound). Finally settling in Pembrokeshire where he has lived with wife Nia for the past nine years.

He has a cat called Peaches (whom he claims was already named) and has never owned a bicycle.

CHAPTER 1

'Bollocks!' said Musca under his breath, as he peered at the fire blackened valley that had once been his home. As he looked, he struggled with the horrible feeling that he was in some way to blame for the devastation. What *had* the alchemist said to him; add the saltpetre or don't add it? Musca thought hard but couldn't recall. Too late now, he supposed.

Musca, bedraggled lank hair, twenty-something, going nowhere fast, son of a chieftain, trainee to the late alchemist – at least he assumed he was late, he couldn't see him amongst the small gaggle of survivors milling about aimlessly at the foot of the hill he was standing on – and general standing joke in the village that was now no more, had a decision to make; take up his right as heir apparent to his late father now that the vacancy had suddenly arisen, or run like hell before anyone had the chance to point the finger; which would be a change from the other one fingered gesture that was usually directed his way.

He made his decision but before he had a chance to place one fleeing foot in front of the other destiny, with its middle finger pointing proud, intervened. Musca slipped on the rain sodden grass and careered towards the waiting gaggle below.

'Bol…locks!!!'

CHAPTER 2

We must now leave Musca for the moment and do a bit of travelling of our own. Travel backwards. Back in time; back to the very beginning.

There was a world
There was a bit of a cock-up
There was light
There was life

The creator of this insignificant speck of dirt suspended in space, which he named Apomas, was hungry. It seemed light years since breakfast and he had for the moment had his fill of making mud balls. Why couldn't he have been assigned to the Black Hole department? Now there was a job you could get your teeth into; and lose, if they weren't fitted properly.

The creator's mind wandered back to happier days when he had been making suns; an altogether satisfying job and a warm one at that; no rheumatism slowing you down there. The creator rubbed an ancient joint for good measure. Anyone could have made the mistake, he thought ruefully. What's a nought anyway? A nothing, that's what. What difference did a nothing make?

As it happened quite a lot when you were working in trillions. He had got a right dressing down when they had all failed and had to be replaced. Twenty million stars. It had been quite a bang. Of course it wasn't that easy and not all could be replaced, some had to stay put; luckily for him.

The creator looked at the lump of spinning mud he had just created. He supposed he was lucky. If a couple of the suns hadn't become anomalies he may well have been facing the likelihood of being reduced to an Inkling (a sort of labourer to the Creators) and a lifetime of pea creating or something just as obscure. He shuddered, when your lifetime spanned eternity that would be an awful lot of peas. He was lucky. Creating the Brown Dwarfs – they were named after him, Brown not dwarf – had been a stroke of good fortune and had saved him. Once you had created something the Chief Creator hadn't thought of, you were in the mainstream for ever. Not everyone had agreed of course, saying it was an accident and thus not a bona fide creation. That he shouldn't be let loose in the universe. But rules were rules and whatever anyone said or thought he Creator Brown was here to stay; besides the Chief Creator had come to his defence, placating the doubting masses. Creator Brown could remember every word as if it were only yesterday. 'What can possibly go wrong with mud balls?' The Chief had said.

Creator Brown poked a finger into the mud ball one more time for effect before packing up his gear and heading home for lunch, leaving a spinning Apomas suspended in space's cold lonely void.

Time passed and Apomas span happily, doing what mud balls in space did, which generally speaking was nothing, for quite a little while before anything else was added to that particular part of the cosmos.

Then, just as Creator Brown was sitting down to lunch, a large sun popped into existence. This ordinarily should have had little or no bearing on the mud ball Apomas, but Apomas you see was just a tad, no, a smidgeon, no, a nought, further away than it should have been, consequently it wasn't going to be a barren world as was ordained. And as Creator Brown picked up his knife and fork some strange and wondrous things were already taking place on its surface. A primeval sludge had appeared and was gurgling happily. Apomas was no longer going to be the planned mineral stopping point for intergalactic explorers who had slopped from their own primeval soup millions of years before to find and to mine. And if that wasn't problem enough, to make matters worse, as Creator Brown prepared to break bread, an object of intense brightness, a comet, its tail a trail of glittering particles was winging its way through the cosmos, heading for the solar system Apomas called home.

No larger than a family sized saloon car the comet sped at incredible speed through space's endless void on a journey set to last an eternity of never ending flight.

What is a nought anyway?

CHAPTER 3

The gaggle of wet, smoke blackened refugees crowded round as Musca landed in a mud covered heap; they shuffled over to him.

'Ah-ha... hum,' said Musca, trying desperately to get to his feet.

'Do you need a hand?' enquired a voice.

'Well...'

'Well you can't 'ave one, but yer can 'ave me finger.' The statement was followed by guffaws of laughter as the voice demonstrated.

Musca finally got to his feet and faced the gaggle. Looking at them he knew he had to think quickly or things were going to get ugly. 'I...' he started. Musca raked his lightweight brain. 'I have something I would like to say... if I may?' There was unease in the way the gaggle moved, even disdain, but they stayed quiet. Musca cautiously threw back his shoulders. 'I feel... that as... er... huh... I am now the new...' Musca stopped talking as the gaggle shifted again. This was going to go so wrong, he just knew it, but he had nowhere to run so he continued, 'the new chieftain.' There he had said it.

The uproar Musca had expected surprised him by not materializing, instead there was a silence so quiet for a moment he thought he had gone deaf. The gaggle just stared at him, their eyes set deep in dark and sore sockets; they were thinking; digesting his words. Did they want him as their new chief? Not if they could help it. His father wouldn't let him play with anything sharp so why should they?

Shaking just a little Musca decided to chance his arm and push ahead, after all no one had actually said no; not as yet that is.

'As my father was our great proud leader,' – no one could argue with that – 'I feel that, considering our predicament, I should now take up that mantle,' – they could with that – 'and lead you to...'

5

Lead them where? Musca was suddenly out on a very precarious limb; the gaggle moved restlessly. He had to say something quickly. 'To... to... a wondrous new land.' Where the hell had that come from? He eyed the gaggle nervously.

The gaggle shuffled some more and formed a ragged circle. Musca could hear hurried conversation and the occasional argument. Again Musca looked for a way out; still he drew a blank. The circle became a gaggle again.

'Where?' asked a suspicious face.

'Where?' Good question. Where? Think Musca boy, think. Then it came to him in a sort of flash. He had heard his father speaking of it many times but always in a hushed voice and always through wattle walls. A secret place Musca thought. One his father never spoke of in public. He had almost forgotten about it these past couple of years since moving in with the alchemist. And his father had only spoken of it when he had returned from long journeys. The place was obviously far, far away.*

'To Ohm of course,' said Musca with a dramatic sweep of his arm that pointed to no direction in particular. The gaggle each turned in different directions to see what the idiot was pointing at but said nothing.

'To Ohm,' said Musca, sweeping his arm again, trying to drum up any vestige of enthusiasm that might be lurking. This time the gaggle didn't even bother looking away. 'Well?' said Musca, a feeling of desperation creeping over him.

'Well what?' said a voice as dispassionate as a dish rag.

'Are you with me or not?' said Musca putting all his eggs in one basket; the only basket.

'Didn't his dad try to have him adopted when he was born?' said a voice ignoring Musca and striking up a conversation in the gaggle.

'Ay, but the other chieftains said it couldn't be done, 'ad to keep the eldest. They 'ad their 'eads screwed on right they did; 'ad an eye on the valley.'

'No good now, ha-ha.' Giggles erupted in the gaggle.

Musca could feel his basket rapidly unravelling.

* Aren't they always? *SJ*

6

'Er-hum,' coughed Musca trying to get the attention back on him.

'And you know where this Olm is?' said someone.

'Ohm,' Musca corrected before he could stop himself. One thing the gaggle didn't need was aggravating.

'Well?' All eyes were back on Musca.

For the umpteenth time Musca looked for a way out. He needn't have bothered. Time to act like a chieftain or at least try. The thought "die trying" flashed into his head. Musca shook it. That's all he needed, his own mind turning against him.

Chieftain time. 'Have I not the blood of chieftains running through my veins?' said Musca. He had to give himself credit it sounded convincing so far; to his ears anyway. 'The strength of champions. The guile of the alchemist.' Was that right? Maybe he shouldn't have added that one. 'The...'

'Bull of Taurus?' added someone helpfully.

'Who said that?' demanded Musca, who had started to believe his own speech.

The gaggle remained silent, an aura of innocence radiating.

A small piece of respect growing, thought Musca kidding himself. Light at the end of the tunnel. Musca was the only person Musca could kid. Musca ploughed on.

'Now if I may carry on.'

'Will it take long?' This time there was a face to the voice that spoke. A rotund bearded one that belonged to Cetus and the rest of his rotund body. He was also the closest thing to a friend Musca had; that is Cetus could stand him if food wasn't anywhere in the equation. He was also very hungry. He found standing for long periods had that affect on him, as did sitting too long, walking too far, etcetera, etcetera. 'Because if it is, could I trot off and forage for nuts and things before you start?'

'Ha-ha, ol' blubberguts wants to trot. That'll be a first,' taunted the village drunk, who was beginning to feel the worse for being slightly sober.

'And what would you know about trotting or even moving eh Pistor? You old sot,' Cetus retaliated.

'Sot eh? I'll give you sot.'

7

Things were starting to get out of hand so Musca, his own words still ringing in his ears, pushed between the warring factions where he managed to stop a flailing fist with a bravely positioned nose. Musca went down like a sack of spuds but to his credit got straight back up again. 'Stopth thit,' he blubbered in a dazed sort of way. Why did everything end like this? Spinning, pain, disorientation.

The argument, now looking on the verge of turning into a free for all melee, was suddenly cut short as a calm but authoritative voice rang out stopping everyone in their tracks.

'Have you quite finished?' demanded the voice.

The gaggle, arms falling quietly to their sides reminiscent of a group of naughty children caught doing something they shouldn't be, nodded dutifully. This was a voice they all knew and if you wanted to survive you listened to.

'Good. Now, Musca, come over here and take your thumb out of your mouth.'

Avoiding eye contact Musca did as he was told and sheepishly walked over to where Fornax was standing.

Fornax, for all her faults, and there were many, was everything you would imagine a budding female warrior to be; beautiful, tanned, firm physique bordering on perfection – to the men who worshipped her, which was everyone bar Cetus for some reason, the wonder and dismay as to how it managed to stay within the confines of what little she wore was a constant bane – and long flowing locks of the fieriest red. She was also known to maim first ask questions later; if there was someone left alive to question that is, hence the quiet obedience currently on display.

The small gaggle of survivors shuffled nervously and then shuffled some more as the ones at the front tried unsuccessfully to merge with the ones behind.

'Now,' said Fornax, causing a few in the gaggle to wince and one or two to check for accidents, 'tell us more of this mysterious land you call Ohm.' Her emerald eyes flashed with green fire as they bore into the small watery pools for eyes that were the entrance to Muscas' soul. Damn the man, she thought as she looked at his pathetic frame, she loved him, she knew not why and would, one day profess that love openly, but for now, as it always had been, it

8

would be her secret, especially as the arsehole needed one hell of a lot of work doing.

Musca bravely puffed out his pigeon chest, threw back his coat hanger shoulders, looked deep into those eyes of living green fire, and squeaked.

'Sorry?' said Fornax; managing to quell a stirring of giggles with one carefully aimed don't you dare stare.

Musca felt his face redden and tried to pull himself together. It was hard to breathe let alone talk when you were this close to Fornax and her... he tried not to think about what he was so close to. 'Er... Fornax?'

'Yes?' she said.

'Could you move your sword, it's... well... poking.'

'Sorry.'

'Thank you,' said Musca, some of the pressure on him lifting. He now felt able to continue. 'Well,' he croaked, his voice ready to crack at any moment, he not far behind it. 'I... well...' he stammered, trying to conjure up a backbone was harder than he thought. 'The story goes...' He was wilting and he could tell Fornax, who didn't know the meaning of patience, was fast loosing whatever it was that was in its place.

The gaggle became a shuffling nervous entity with the sole purpose of looking for somewhere safe to hide.

'Well?' said Fornax, fiddling with the pommel of her sword.

The gaggle stopped dead, then quickly grouped in a tight protective huddle; the old and infirm pushed to the outside.

With a sound akin to the clucking of a chicken who has happened on a fat juicy worm, Muscas' backbone at last snapped into place, albeit uneasily.

'Ohm,' he said slowly, 'Ohm is where the heart is.'

The gaggle stopped looking for somewhere to hide and looked with puzzled faces at each other. Surely he didn't mean what they thought he meant.

'Yes,' continued Musca, ignoring the looks and getting a full head of steam on, 'Ohm is a place hidden from the evils of the world in a valley of peacefulness and plenty,' – he was rallying like a good 'un – 'and only kings and great chieftains can find this enchanted land,' – engines full ahead, – 'and although this happy, mysterious land is far far away, I Musca will lead you all to it and we will once more become a great nation.' It was there that he began to lose his audience. For one they hadn't the faintest idea what a nation was, and surely there was a perfectly good valley not some ten minutes down the old well beaten track.

One of the gaggle, Bootes the old herdsman who had lost all his sheep in the devastation, thought he might mention it so put his hand up. 'Oi, wot about the green valley down the ol' well beaten track? Surely we can live there? Sheep'll love it.'

'No,' Musca responded stoutly, 'I have heard my father proclaim often that there is no place like Ohm and as the green valley is much like our own was, then that cannot be Ohm.'

There was a certain amount of pondering on what Musca had said amongst the gaggle as well as a pronounced nagging feeling that sort of nagged that something obvious was being missed by the great chieftain. All eyes done with pondering looked to Fornax.

Fornax meanwhile, mesmerised by the sudden change in Musca, decided there and then that she would follow the idiot, her idiot, to the ends of the world if need be, and any inconsistencies could, for the moment, be forgiven. It was also in her blood that a chieftain was just that and was he who was to be obeyed; but she was no lemming. Fornax stared hard at the gaggle who instinctively knew when their safety was in question, and that any further questions would further put that safety in jeopardy. A line had been drawn and only an idiot would cross it. The gaggle took a precautionary step back and gave their full attention to Musca, to see what the idiot was going to do next.

'So,' said Fornax, 'when do we go?'

Musca, confidence now brimming like a bucket full of fools' gold, suggested that they set off with the next day's sunrise; if that was all right with everyone else. It wasn't, but no one was brave enough to mention it.

* * *

Not so far far away, as democracy was thrust firmly into a back seat, a solitary dark figure watched with keen interest at the goings on of Musca and his newly acquired gaggle of subjects; an interest that was heightened by the explosion that was the cause of the valley's devastation.

The figure had been watching and waiting for just such an incident for years, centuries, for longer than he cared to remember. Watching and making notes. Watching and waiting for the sign the Dark One said would come to pass, and now that time had come; the explosion, the fire, the culprit. At last he could report back to the Dark One with the news that the prophecy had been fulfilled.

Slowly the small shadowy figure capered stealthily from his hiding place with a gladdening heart; today would be the happiest day of his sorry existence. The prophecy was true, there was now a chance he would be going home, and best of all, if he was lucky and the Dark One was feeling benevolent, maybe, just maybe, he would get his tongue back. Oh happy day!

CHAPTER 4

'What do you mean, slowing down?' growled a large, sweaty creature with horns and red scaly skin. Sweaty because he'd spent the best part of two millennia encased in an object half his size (something to do with special distortion) that travelled at way beyond what was physically possible; horns and red scaly skin because it was the look.

'Well Sire, your Mighty Worthiness of never…'

'Cut the crap and explain,' demanded the large creature, stopping his smaller travelling companion in mid grovel.

'Well your Stupendous Master…'

'STOP IT!' roared the creature raising itself up to full height to bear down on the diminutive groveller. 'WELL?' said the towering creature, lowering its face to meet that of the other and displaying an impressive set of razor sharp teeth which glinted menacingly in their blood red gums as he spoke.

The small figure cowered at the sight and stepped backwards into the other three quieter passengers of varying shapes and sizes that also occupied the special distortion who quickly followed suit.

'I'M WAITING.'

The smallest of the four cowering in the large creature's shadow, the one that had done all of the grovelling to date, was gently if not a little forcibly pushed forward. His eyes rolled in their sockets as he desperately looked for a way out of his predicament; there was none. He tentatively opened his mouth, 'Please Sire if I may be so bold?' The silence that met his question, though menacing, was encouraging none the less. Feeling a little more confident, the small creature with the sly look of a snake that had just come upon rodent with a broken leg, chanced his arm. 'Stupendous Warrior Lor…'

A glare that could turn you inside out and back again but with your eyeballs left on the inside just for fun stopped the sly one in his tracks before he could go on.

'Creator Brown,' whimpered the sly one.

'What about him?' said the large creature, his curiosity aroused. Everyone who was anyone, or thought they were, knew of Creator Brown and his short comings.

'It is rumoured, Sire, that it was he who worked out our trajectory*.'

Another menacing silence filled the air this time accompanied by a thoughtful look which gradually turned into the sort of grin that would have had the bravest of warriors looking for a change of underwear and calling for his mummy.

'You have done well, Lyra. You will have the skin torn from your back by a thousand lashes.'

'Thank you, your... Sire. May your warts forever rub,' said Lyra, gleefully rubbing his greasy little hands together and slyly glancing at the others. He may only be an imp but he was Serpens' favourite.

The comet they were travelling in had slowed considerably during the question and answer session and was now banking sharply. A small brown planet that shouldn't be where it was came into view. A small brown planet that would soon not know what had hit it.

The comet's occupants watched with saucer eyes, or plates as was the case with one of them, as it plummeted at a frightening velocity towards the ever closing surface of the planet, the surface of which was rapidly changing from dismal brown to hues of blue and green.

'It's quite pretty isn't it?' said Lyra wistfully.

Three sets of saucers and a set of dinner plates turned as one, the saucers aghast; the dinner plates glaring.

Slow as he could be Lyra instinctively knew that he was no longer Serpens' favourite.

---

* He hadn't but as fate would have it... *SJ*

'Sorry Master, I don't know what came over me,' spluttered Lyra who would have been shaking in his boots if he'd been wearing any. He began to babble, 'I must be ill. That's it, I'm travel sick. I won't do it again. Just a slip of the tongue. You know how it is on long journeys.' Lyra tried to become as small as possible as Serpens stared at him with all the ferocity of a nuclear blast.

'Maybe you would like to pick flowers and make a nice chain of daisies when we land?' hissed Serpens, fiery spats of spittle spewed from his lips that burned like acid where it landed.

One of the other occupants, a changeling and part-time werewolf called Lupus was obviously overjoyed and honoured to have some of the master's body fluid land on his humble body and danced and jigged with a smile on his face as he sort something cold and wet to soak part of his more important anatomy in.

'Why yes Master,' answered Lyra, who wouldn't know sarcasm if it bit him, so for an insane micro-moment had helped himself to a large portion of self deluding relief. Serpens' eyes grew so big they looked as if they might explode. It was this, and the snarl, and the protruding talons, and the fact that all of those not frantically dousing their private parts had rammed their hands in their mouths and looked away, that gave Lyra a clue that all was not well. 'No I mean,' gulped Lyra, starting to backtrack so fast he was beginning to smoke, 'I was jesting. A little light relief as we land. Seat belts everyone and please stow any loose objects.' But Serpens wasn't smiling. 'And talking of loose, that's just what my tongue was. Sometimes I don't wonder if the damn thing hasn't got a life of its own.' The hole Lyra was digging was nearly ready. 'Why if I could I would bite the troublesome thing off and put it where it could do no harm.' Lyra grinned manically and looked around for support. Lupus was still rubbing his groin but the others, Draco, the whatever he was and Ophiuchus, Serpens' right hand ogre, were staring at him in open-mouthed disbelief. Lyra suddenly became horribly aware of his mistake.

'That will do nicely!' boomed Serpens. 'And when I think you have served me well enough to deserve its return you shall have it back.'

'But... I...' protested Lyra. But it was too late Serpens had him by the throat and was squeezing mercilessly. Lyra's tongue started to bulge from his mouth. He blacked out.

When he came to the comet was ploughing through the planet's upper atmosphere. He didn't feel well, he was hot and dizzy. He started to slip back in to unconsciousness but before he did he saw Serpens and caught a glimpse of something familiar hanging limply from the belt round Serpens' waist. Lyras' head slumped to the floor with a smile on its lips; he was Serpens' favourite imp again. He missed the landing.

Serpens' voice boomed across the massive crater that housed what remained of the comet. 'WHAT DO YOU SEE DRACO?'

Draco and Serpens were the only ones to survive the impact in one piece. Draco had been sent to investigate what lay beyond the crater's rim; one that stretched for miles.

'Dust, your Most Hideous High One,' reported Draco.

'WHAT?' Serpens' hearing had been temporarily impaired during the impact.

'Dust!'

'WHAT?'

'Oh for Creator's sake,' said Draco under his breath. He was fast losing his patience which was a dangerous thing to do considering what his master would do to him if he had the slightest notion that he was being shown disobedience.

'WHAT DID YOU SAY?' growled Serpens, sensing rather than hearing dissent amongst the troops. 'YOU SNIVELLING BREATH OF A DEAD DOG.' Serpens' repertoire of oaths and curses were almost legendary if not a tad inane.

'Dust, Sire. Nothing but dust,' said Draco, hoping his momentary transgression had passed unnoticed. He scrambled down from the crater's edge and quickly made his way over to where Serpens was waiting, his eyes drawn to Serpens' belt and the grisly reminder of how insolence was dealt with. Draco bowed low and crossed his claws for luck. Luck though had seen the look on Serpens' face and had just remembered it had a pressing engagement elsewhere that it just couldn't miss.

Serpens immediately lashed out with his foot catching Draco full on his backside. Draco sailed through the air to land upside down amongst the mangled pulsating heap that was the remains of the others. He watched nervously as Serpens approached, not daring to move, even though one of Ophiuchus's claws had lodged itself where the "sun don't shine".

'Remember who I am, insolent one!' snarled Serpens, his eyes glowing like two fiery pits.

Draco wasn't sure if it was a question or not but answered anyway. 'Yes, Master,' he said, eager to cover all bases.

Serpens pushed his face close to Draco's and suddenly Draco was glad the claw was where it was, any sudden involuntary and embarrassing noises could well have dire consequences on his ability to see any future plans he may have through. Serpens pushed his face closer, his foul breath turning the swirling dust between them into a gagging fog.

'Then remember this also, NO ONE IS INDISPENSABLE! Do I make myself clear?'

Draco nodded, which was quite difficult considering all his weight was resting on his neck.

Serpens' face hovered for a moment or two studying Draco, wondering, then it was gone from Draco's view as Serpens stood up. 'Good,' he said, the fire in his eyes subsiding a little. 'Now put those balls of slime back together again.'

Draco nodded again.

'NOW!'

Draco didn't need telling twice, removing the offending claw that made an unpleasant slurping noise as it was freed, Draco quickly set about the task at hand and started to scrabble amongst the pulsing body parts, carefully placing each piece in three separate piles.

Serpens watched for a moment then turned away. 'I need to think,' he said to no one. He had plans, big plans, plans that had been put on hold for too long, and being marooned on a dusty planet wasn't one of them.

CHAPTER 5

Outside the confines of the comet and away from the timeless domain the Creators and Inklings existed in, time would drag slowly for Serpens and his minions and apart from the occasional insect that buzzed or chirped from the surrounding vegetation it seemed they were alone on the Creator forsaken planet. This of course made them the only intelligent life forms on Apomas. This of course also meant they were in deep do-do.

It was another hot and humid day as the changeling Lupus rose lazily from his midday siesta to get a drink from the lake that was once the crater the comet had created. These days (and there had been thousands since the crash) Lupus preferred to stay in the form of a wolf, its thick fur a defence against the numerous blood thirsty flies that had sprung to life some hundred years or so ago.

Parting the green slime that now seemed to cover most of the lake's surface Lupus prepared to indulge in a long cool refreshing guzzle. Instead he stopped short and puzzled at his reflection. There was something strange about it. My, what big eyes he had. Lupus took a closer look. His reflection started to blow bubbles. Lupus instantly recoiled at the sudden realisation that all was not as it should be and as he quickly back peddled he fell over the sleeping bulk of Ophiuchus waking him. Ophiuchus, not the most civil of creatures when waking, did what all self respecting ogres did when finding a buttock resting on his face, he sank his teeth into it.

'OwwOOO!' howled Lupus.

This woke Lyra and Draco who quickly scrambled from their respective slumber to see what was going on. It turned out that the most exciting thing since the landing was in progress. Lupus and Ophiuchus rolled across the dusty ground biting, clawing and generally ripping bits out of each other in the process.

'Go on, bite his gonads!' yelled Draco, who had lived a comparatively sheltered life and thus didn't really know what gonads were.

'Yeth!' agreed Lyra, who did.

'WHAT IN THE NAME OF ALL THINGS BLACK AND TWISTED IS GOING ON HERE?' thundered Serpens, appearing between Draco and Lyra and shoving them to the ground.

Draco and Lyra exchanged identical grubby looks and made merry haste for the nearest available boulder large enough for them to take shelter behind. Serpens was well pissed and that meant trouble with a capital T-R-O-U-B-L-E!

'WHO DARES AWAKEN THE DARK LORD FROM HIS BEA- SLUMBER?!'

Safely ensconced behind a few feet of solid rock, which was more than a few feet away, Draco gave Lyra a puzzled look.

'Never heard him call himself that before,' whispered Draco.

'Ofiurth-Oafpiurth,' attempted Lyra, unsuccessfully getting what was left of his tongue round Ophiuchus's name. 'Bollockth.' He had been a good imp, he didn't deserve this, he thought. He tried again; slowly. 'Theth... ogreth... seth... heth... thaw... thim... pothing... byth... theth... laketh... athmiring... hith... reflecthion... ath... heth... trieth... outh... newth... nameth...' managed Lyra, giving Draco the look of one who knows.

'What?' said Draco.

'Nether mindth,' Lyra sighed, peeping around the rock to gaze longingly at his errant mouth muscle that still hung limply from Serpens' belt.

'WELL!' roared Serpens, raising his voice high enough to cause ripples at the lake's edge.

Away from the shore something near to being a sonic blast struck into the grappling minions splitting them apart. Lupus was first to his feet ears ringing and groggy but confusion was soon forgotten when he spied the look on Serpens' face. Whining pitifully his tail dropped down between his legs. Ophiuchus, not as groggy as there was a lot less to addle in his skull, took a while to realise what was happening but when he did.

18

'It was him,' said Ophiuchus pointing an accusing stumpy finger.

'*It was him,*' mimicked Serpens, sneering horribly. 'YOU ARE SOLDIERS OF THE DARK FORCES. MEAN BASTIONS OF ALL THAT IS EVIL. NOT SNIVELLING INKLINGS! THIS IS WHY YOU ARE HERE.'

This came as a bit of a surprise to those listening as they were under the impression that they had been expelled – at some considerable speed – from the Hall of the Creators for evolving first vegetables and then animals and humanoids into amusing forms that resembled people's naughty places. The vegetables had been sort of okay, even the Chief Creator had had a bit of a giggle at those, but the others were classed unacceptable, a definite no-no, one step too far. There were standards to be adhered to, codes to be observed. There had been warnings but to no avail. The last straw had been the quarantining of a planet so that the humanoid eating pussies* could be discreetly rounded up and removed. And even though there had been no animals hurt in the making of these creatures or rude shapes involved, enough was enough. Things were getting out of control and one certain inkling it was felt, the ringleader, was starting to act way above his station. The result had been inevitable.

Steam was still coming from Serpens' ears and his talons were still glinting steely in the noon sun, but something had changed, the rage was starting to subside, replaced by a faraway look forming in his eyes. 'You are the chosen minions of the cause.' His voice had become softer almost tender. 'And together we shall go forth as one to meet our destiny.' Serpens was now pointing with some poignancy at the sky while wiping at a non existent tear on his cheek. 'Together we will rule the universe.'

The minions, who had started to have serious doubts about their leader's sanity even before their expulsion, regarded this latest outburst as a large weight of evidence that went a long way to confirming their suspicions. In short, it was as they thought; the boy was stark raving bonkers.

* Please! They were nothing more than cat shaped carnivorous cacti.*SJ*

Serpens continued to stare into space for a full minute before snapping back into the here and now.

'But it was still him that started it,' said Ophiuchus, regarding, ill advisedly, the lull as an opportunity to again plead his innocence. Beside him Lupus growled under his breath.

With a strange lopsided smile on his face Serpens walked to where Ophiuchus was standing and pushed him over. He then swiftly grabbed Lupus by the throat.

'Pray tell Lupus, what was so important that you felt you had to put your miserable pitiful pelt of a life on the line by waking me so?' The smile changed sides.

Lupus hung from Serpens' fist like a new born kitten from its mother's mouth.

'The... the water,' Lupus managed as the skin around his throat tightened. He pointed to the lake.

'What about the water? Scared of your own reflection?' Serpens laughed out loud at his attempt at a jolly jape and looked at Ophiuchus who started to laugh, nervously at first, as well. Draco and Lyra quickly stumbled from their hiding place and joined in. After all didn't the old saying say, "when Serpens laughs the whole world laughs with him or you get it in the neck"?

'Haw haw,' laughed Ophiuchus.

'Hee hee,' chuckled Draco.

'Arth arth arth,' barked Lyra somewhat like a performing seal. It was at times like this he really, really, wished he could have his tongue back.

Serpens held Lupus eyeball to eyeball.

'See how ridiculous we all think you are? Good. Now go and think about what you did.' A flick of Serpens' wrist sent Lupus hurtling towards the lake where he landed with such force the splash sent a shower of water and green slime high into the air. 'Now I will return to my slumber while you reflect...' Serpens paused a moment to titter at this, joined of course by his minions, before finishing, 'on how lightly you have been let off.'

As Serpens turned to return to the cave he had commandeered as his bedroom something wet, slimy and thoroughly unpleasant to the touch slapped unceremoniously between his horns and onto his head.

'What the…?' said Serpens, reaching up with the growing notion in his mind of ramming whatever it was down Lupus' throat but then the whatever it was went; 'Gloop!'

Serpens looked at the thing in his hand. Two large round eyes looked back at him. The thing went 'Gloop,' and then 'Gloop Gloop.'

The look of anger on Serpens' face rapidly subsided to one that could be loosely associated with glee.

'In the lake?' said Serpens to Lupus who was struggling ashore covered in green slime. Lupus nodded and Serpens began to laugh again. 'At last,' he roared. Then, without uttering another word he returned double quick to his cave. He left behind four bewildered minions. Three of whom were laughing but didn't have the faintest idea why.

It was the middle of the night and the stars shone in their heaven down on a certain quartet of minions huddled together mulling over the day's events. Serpens hadn't been seen since his dramatic exit.

'Ow… ong… oo… oo… ink… e… er… oing… oo… e… ere?' asked Lyra who had decided to drop his "th's" in an effort to get himself understood.

Blank looks were exchanged.

'Personally I think it's all quite exciting,' said Draco, ignoring Lyra's question.

'How's that?' asked Lupus who was still finding the odd piece of slime secreted about his person.

'Well,' said Draco with a conspiratorial air. He drew closer to the others. 'Serpens was our team leader at the Hall of Creators.'

'So?' said Lupus as he gingerly licked the slime to see if it had at least one redeeming feature going for it. It didn't.

'Well I think that there's more to his expelling than meets the eye,' said Draco knowingly. He sat back looking extremely pleased with himself.

A trio of vacant looks.

'Oh for goodness sake,' exclaimed Draco, sitting back up again, 'haven't any of you noticed the change in him since we got in the comet?'

More vacant looks.

'The horns? Red scaly skin? Pointy tail? He wasn't like that when we left.'

Ophiuchus shifted to one side as if to speak.

'At last,' said Draco, 'go on Ophiuchus, what do you think?'

'Could everyone call me Bob?' said Ophiuchus leaning to one side thus heralding in his thought with a not so sly passing of wind.

Draco rolled his eyes to the heavens and his nose to more personal space.

'I-o, I-o,' said Lyra moving away from Ophiuchus, 'ee eems oo ee ettin…' There was a slight pause as Lyra's itty bitty mind struggled with the pronunciation of his next word; he decided he needed to revert back to using his "th's" 'narthtier anth morth ethil.'

'There!' said Draco. 'Thank you Lyra. At least one of you has still got the brains you were born with.'

Lupus stopped his quest for slime and stared at Draco, a look of horror etched on his face. 'Hang about; are you trying to tell us what I think you're trying to tell us? You think he might be the...' His voice trailed off, afraid to say what he was thinking.

'Yes Lupus,' said an increasingly excited Draco, 'I think Serpens is the *ANARCHIST*! Won't that be fun?' Draco in his naïvity had no idea of the enormity of what he was suggesting. To him it was just a name. To the others though it was the equivalent of a hot sharp stick poked into a sensitive place.

'Do you know what you're saying?' said Lupus, trying to get his head around just what Draco was saying.

'It's obvious.'

'But the Anarchist is just a myth. A tall tale told to frighten tiny inklings. I can remember being told that if I didn't eat up my liver I'd grow up to be just like the Anarchist, the most stupid evil creature that ever lived.'

'Just my point,' said Draco smugly.

'Bollocks,' said Lupus quietly.

'Yeth, ollockth!' agreed Lyra, dropping his "b" with fear.

Only Ophiuchus remained unmoved by Draco's suspicion.

'Ophiuchus?'

'Er… if not Bob, Stan would be nice.'

A perfectly aimed rock took Ophiuchus out of the discussion leaving the others to contemplate their, would be, predicament. It was going to be a long night.

When Draco awoke next morning he was alone. He got up, stretched, breathed in the new morning's air and started to hum to himself as he looked around for the others. Ophiuchus was nowhere to be seen, but Lupus and Lyra were standing down by the lake. They were talking.

'Do you think Draco's right?' said Lupus, staring at his real reflection in the lake.

'I on't o,' said Lyra dropping his "th's" again.

'If he is we could be in big trouble.'

'I o,' said Lyra, who had found a new friend in the shape of an interestingly shaped stick; he was poking the green slime with it.'

'If he is you know what that makes us?' Lupus checked to see if there were any "Gloopers" around, there wasn't so he chanced a quick swig of water from the lake, he wasn't a big one on things slimy; especially after yesterday.

Lyra didn't answer as he was too engrossed in retrieving the stick he'd just dropped in the water.

'It means that we're the legion of the damned, or at least the start of it.'

'O', said Lyra as he balanced precariously on the edge of the bank. He was more intent on getting his stick back than listening to anything Lupus was saying.

Lupus dipped his head for another drink.

'Good morning,' breezed Draco as he joined them, 'and how are we this fine and wonderful day?' He sounded certifiably cheerful.

'Why are you so happy?' said Lupus, not bothering to turn round.

23

'Weren't you listening last night?' said Draco, taken slightly aback by Lupus' attitude. 'We are the chosen ones. We are the minions of the Anarchist.'

'That's Dark Lord to you.'

Draco turned to find he was enveloped in shadow. It was Ophiuchus, only he was somehow different, bigger; massive. Also he was wearing armour so dark a hue it seemed as if it was sucking the surrounding light into it. For a moment no one said anything; couldn't say anything, it was as if they were spellbound by the new and forbidding apparition that stood towering above them. Then there was a splash and a yell for "helpth" and all returned to normal, or as normal as was when one of your fellow minions had been transformed into an armoured goliath.

'I am Ophiuchus,' said Ophiuchus as he advanced to within a few feet of the others.

'I am Ophiuchus,' he repeated.

'Yeah we gathered that,' said Lupus, not quite sure what to make of things.

A large fist shot out at terrific speed but missed its intended target and sent Draco sprawling.

'Listen,' barked Ophiuchus, seemingly oblivious to his mistake, 'I am Ophiuchus, bearer and herald of the Dark Lord. You will listen.' He rummaged under his massive breastplate and pulled out a scroll of parchment which he unrolled. 'Serpens the Dark Lord does so order his dreaded minions of darkness to report this instant to stand without comment before him.' He read this with monotonous exactness. He then saluted, turned smartly and marched at the double to the cave Serpens called home.

When Lupus was sure Ophiuchus was well out of earshot he turned to Draco. 'I hope you'll still be thinking today's so wonderful when we get to the cave,' he said grimly.

'Of course it will,' said Draco reproachfully. He brushed away the twigs and dirt that had clung to him after his unexpected meeting with the ground. Doubts though were beginning to leak into his mind. It was one thing being a mischievous whatever he was minion but a "dreaded minion of darkness" had an altogether different ring to it; one that didn't sit well in Draco's belfry. He hoped he wouldn't be called upon to do anything really bad. Feet unconsciously dragging he started towards the cave.

Behind him Lupus had helped Lyra from the lake and was following suit. With apprehension forming about their minds in big dark clouds the three dreaded minions of darkness reached the cave and peered inside.

'Enter!' ordered Ophiuchus.

The three entered in Indian file and were met by an eerie reddish glow that appeared to be emanating from the cave walls.

'It'th eepee,' said Lyra, the last to leave the natural light of day behind.

'Quiet,' ordered Ophiuchus, 'and stand before the great Dark Lord Serpens.'

The minions shuffled forward, their eyes gradually growing accustomed to the strange glow, until they stood before a terrible sight. Sitting on a huge stone throne was Serpens; a Serpens that had changed almost beyond all recognition. The pea-brained team leading bully from the Hall of Creators had gone. Muscles now bulged where there were no muscles before. The pigment of his skin was no longer a common or garden red but a deep crimson, the colour of blood and the horns that had been naught but nubs when the comet had crashed were now magnificent menacing black horns the like of which any prize bull would have been proud to call their own. Serpens was terrifying; awesome to look upon.

The hapless minions bowed low, partly as duty, mostly through fear; bowed as low as they could. They could feel Serpens' gaze burning down on them.

Serpens rose from his throne. 'BEHOLD ME!' he ordered, his voice reverberating from wall to wall, ceiling to floor. 'HAVE YOU EVER LOOKED ON ANYTHING SO MAGNIFICENT?'

The minions slowly straightened.

'WELL HAVE YOU?' bellowed Serpens before they had a chance to answer.

'No, Master,' gulped Lupus, his ears flat to his head. He honestly hadn't.

'Nor me, Master,' agreed Draco, as humbly as he could. He told no lie.

There then followed an ominous silence. Draco and Lupus chanced a quick glance at Lyra to see why.

Lyra was stood, eyes rolling in their sockets, staring at Serpens with his mouth hanging open. Draco and Lupus knew this look; it was dangerous; Lyra was thinking. Knees began to knock.

Serpens stepped down from his throne and stooped in front of Lyra. He bent further forward until his nose and Lyra's snout were almost touching.

'WELL!!?'

The question was spat with all the ferocity of a hurricane and crashed against Lyra almost tearing skin from muscle; Lyra landed on his backside with a solid bump. Beside him Lupus and Draco were beginning to have problems of their own.

Fear had taken hold and Lupus had started to change so uncontrollably from one shape to another he was having trouble remembering which part of his body belonged to which shape. Draco meanwhile was fighting a losing battle with his bladder and thinking that maybe Lupus had been right; it wasn't going to be such a wonderful day.

Lyra lay stunned, gathering his wits. Above him Serpens was glowering and towering, his fangs, usually white as death, now looked as if heavily bloodstained as the red glow from the cave walls danced on them.

Lupus lost all cohesion at the sight and collapsed to the floor in a formless, colourless but not odourless puddle. Draco sadly created a puddle of his own.

Serpens reached for Lyra but just as it seemed all was lost for the hapless imp Lyra at last spoke.

'Ou ook thupendouth, Mathter.'

Serpens hesitated; a compliment was a compliment; even from a dolt like Lyra. His lips reluctantly slid back hiding the grotesque glistening fangs, his jaw, a second ago set on mayhem, gradually relented then slackened and finally closed.

From horror to immense relief to a dangerous flower of misguided confidence growing within, Lyra scrambled to his feet and opened his mouth. Beside him Draco and Lupus, even in puddle form, instantly knew that Lyra was about to put one of his big, ponderous feet into his equally big mouth.

'Whyth arth ou wearinth thath thilly oo oo, Mathter?'

'What did he say?' said Serpens.

Draco and Lupus looked at each other in horror (as much as was possible when one was a puddle) and then at Serpens who was glaring at them, luckily Ophiuchus came to their rescue; answering with the unerring innocence and assurance of the brain dead lackey that he was.

'He said,' – at this point Draco passed out and the clear puddle that was Lupus changed to an ominous straw colour before trickling down the nearest convenient deep crack in the ground – 'why are you wearing that silly tutu, Master?'

Now some things are meant to be ignored; left unsaid. For instance: you don't inform the mugger who is about to shoot you that his gun is pointing the wrong way, or point out to Mr Know-it-all-pain-in-the-ass that the stile he insists is the way to go is in fact disused and now presides over a sheer drop of a thousand feet or more*, or "yes your bum does look fat in that," and you most *definitely* do not ask the Anarchist, the most viciously pernicious vain and stupid being in the entire universe why he is wearing a silly tutu; you admire, not ask. Not if you don't want something terrible to happen to you that is. Some things you just don't do or say.

Steam, actual steam, started to pour from Serpens; from every orifice; dampening his tutu. The veins on his head began to stand from his temple looking like rivers on a Martian map. He opened his mouth to speak but no sound except that of escaping steam ushered forth. Serpens took a couple of steps back then stopped, his eyes bulging from their sockets.

A confused Ophiuchus, no longer under the Dark Lord's control, was cautiously backing out of the cave when Serpens exploded. Not angrily, with a tirade of verbal abuse but actually, physically. As the cave suddenly filled with little pieces of Serpens, Ophiuchus found his steady retreat immediately hastened.

* Okay maybe you should. *SJ*

27

Propelled backwards at incredible speed he ended up embedded in a small hill half a mile away.

In the cave a terrified Lupus, quivering in his crack could only watch as Draco became a spinning blur, a blur that gradually corkscrewed into the ground. Lyra however had amazingly escaped the carnage and was still standing in the same spot as when he'd asked his killer question. He now stood in the aftermath of Serpens' literal outburst surveying his surroundings with the countenance and stance of a dazed shell-less shell-shocked tortoise. Here and there the sound of something gory plopping to the ground could be heard. His gaze eventually fell on Lupus emerging from his crack. Lupus, sensing the storm was over changed back into his more familiar shape of the wolf.

'Oopth,' said an utterly bewildered Lyra, 'wath ith thomethinth I thaid?'

It was quite some time before the four dreaded minions of darkness were able to relax a little and discuss the day's events. Draco had been the hardest to free, him being screwed up to his neck in the ground like that, but with a little ingenuity plenty of grunts and the odd sharp stick Draco had been released. Ophiuchus thankfully had returned to normal size and the hill he'd crashed into was mostly chalk making the rescue that much easier. The chalky white indentation which was left had thrown up a question or two though, especially as to why the chalk Ophiuchus appeared to have more than two legs. Further investigation was promptly shelved when realisation dawned. Discussions quickly moved on and away.

All but one of the dreaded minions returned to the edge of the lake where Draco reclined against a handy termite hill and popped the first termite that made the mistake of coming to investigate, into his mouth.

'So,' said Draco between termites, 'what do you think happened to his high one then?'

As Ophiuchus had returned to normal and was staring blankly ahead, his sudden rise through the ranks of intelligence evaporating along with his black armour, and Lyra having skipped off to the cave this left Lupus as the question's only able recipient.

'You tell me,' said Lupus.

'Look like we'll be stuck on this rock forever,' said Draco, idly popping another termite into his mouth.

'Nothing changed there then,' said Lupus.

'You think we should maybe build a shelter and look for wood?' said Draco, angling a claw between his teeth in an attempt to release the twig he'd just mistaken for a termite.

'Why?'

'How should I know?' pouted Draco, 'I thought it was the done thing when you're marooned.'

'Hello? Anyone in?' said Lupus, tapping Draco in the centre of his forehead. 'We've already been stuck here for over a thousand years, give or take, I think.' None of them were totally sure how long it had been since the crash.

Draco sagged and his eyes glazed over as his wonderful day crashed around him. It seemed such an adventure when they had set off. Even though they had been cast out into the universe forever Draco's naïve optimism had seen him thinking that any time now the creators would rein them back and everyone would have a good laugh about it. Now though, and as it looked like Lupus wasn't wrong as to how bad Serpens really was, which meant that maybe the creators had been dead serious about the whole episode, things were looking extremely bleak. To cap it all their best means of getting off the planet, that large red scaly homicidal insane creature, now lay in pieces scattered across the cave. Oh woe was he. What would become of them? Draco's mind was only inches away from the cliff of despair's edge when he was suddenly brought back from the brink by a muttering from Ophiuchus.

'The Dark Lord,' muttered Ophiuchus sternly.

Lupus and Draco jumped, hearts pounding, to their feet expecting Serpens to be ranging over them but the coast was clear and Ophiuchus still sat in the same place with the same stupid expression on his face. Lupus and Draco exchanged relieved looks and quietly sat down again. It appeared Ophiuchus hadn't yet fully thrown off the yoke of Serpens' mind control and the odd echo was still swimming in the space he called his brain. It had been seriously unsettling though, so a well aimed rock again sang lullabies to Ophiuchus as it made contact with the side of his head.

Sure they would have no more interruptions from "Bob" Lupus re-started their conversation.

'You back from la-la land then?'

Draco nodded.

'Good, I was beginning to think I was the only one left with a functioning brain.' Lupus stole a glance towards the slumbering Ophiuchus. 'I don't know whether I prefer him stupid or intelligent.'

'I know what you mean,' agreed Draco, feeling much better for having thrown the rock.

'You know what? I think I'll join him and have forty winks myself. It's been a long day.' Lupus leaned back against a boulder.

Draco agreed and as he made himself comfy on the termites' nest – who were slightly quicker on the uptake than Ophiuchus and had now vacated the hill as being terminally dangerous – he let his mind fill with the delusion that tomorrow would be better.

Lyra took one last furtive look over his shoulder and entered the cave. Inside it was as quiet as the grave.

Cautiously tiptoeing amongst the strewn body parts so as not to step on anything that might belong to him, Lyra surveyed each piece carefully before moving on, eventually as the gloom lifted from his vision – the red glow no more – he spotted what he was looking for. Hanging from one arm of the great stone throne was Serpens' belt. Caution thrown to the wind Lyra quickened his pace and quickly squelched his way over to it.

'It'th mith tongth,' said a delighted Lyra as he prepared to scramble up onto the throne's seat.

'Ow,' said a voice from somewhere underneath one of Lyra's feet, stopping him in mid climb.

Lyra, hardly daring to breathe, looked down to see part of Serpens' face glaring up at him.

'Well don't just stand there you dumb cluck, get off my face.'

A small shudder racked Lyra's small gnarled frame but he did as he was told.

'And if you want to leave the same shape as you came in I suggest you remove your other foot from my groin.'

Lyra did a quick two foot shuffle and chanced a peep towards the cave entrance.

Realising his mistake and just how helpless he was at the moment Serpens quickly changed tact. 'Thank you my favourite imp,' said the face trying to smile but failing miserably. 'As you can see I am in a bit of a pickle and only your help will suffice in getting me out of it.'

'Thuffith?' said Lyra, his face now expressing interest.

'Do…'

'Oo whath?'

'Sorry?'

'Oo saith oo,' said Lyra.

'Oh for badness sake, will you please get your tongue and put it back.'

Lyra didn't need telling twice.

'There's a good imp,' said Serpens, while thinking something totally different.

Lyra was over the moon as he re-attached his wayward member but not only because of the reuniting, it sounded like he was *numero uno* with the master again.

'Thank you, Master. Thank you,' extolled Lyra, while bowing and grovelling in the finest imp fashion.

'Very good Lyra, my friend, now if I…'

But Lyra wasn't listening; he was at that moment fast approaching a utopian state of ecstasy. He called me his friend, sighed Lyra in his mind. I'm his friend; the thought running through green meadows hand in hand with the madly grinning Lyra. All thoughts of the real Serpens lost in a mist.

'Lyra?'

Maybe we can pick flowers together, thought Lyra.

'LYRA!'

Lyra at last came down from the ceiling.

'Yes, Master. Thank you, Dark Lord. I am your obedient servant and here to do your bidding.'

Serpens was glad to hear it; he would have to remember the friend thing for future use, but at the moment, 'Good. Now I've a little job for you.' The face of Serpens attempted another smile but the nature of the beast changed it into a grotesque sneer.

If Lyra had noticed he would have been afraid; trouser filling afraid.

The first rays of the morning sun cleared the distant mountains and spread a sheet of sparkling light across dew laden meadows, heralding the beginning of a brave new day.

Draco and Ophiuchus were still dozing as the sun reached them but Lupus had risen early and was down by the lake lapping at its cool waters as the temperature already had began to soar.

He felt the first day of the rest of his life was just starting and he felt great. All right his bunion was playing up for no good reason but he could live with that; now that he was free.

Lupus finished drinking and ambled back – in his own time – to the clearing in the rocks where he gave Draco a gentle shake.

'Er – wuz up?' muttered a sleepy Draco.

'Nothing,' enthused Lupus, 'and you should be awake to enjoy it. Life's wonderful.'

Somewhere in his sleep addled mind Draco recalled hearing that before, but he made an effort and sat up.

Lupus left Draco rubbing his sleep encrusted eyes and steered a "good to be alive" course to an exotic orchid that struggled to catch the early sunlight in the shadow of Ophiuchus's massive bulk. Lupus bent down to sniff its exquisite scent just as the shadow moved.

'Bloody battlegrounds!' screamed Lupus, as Ophiuchus sprang straight to a standing position, startling him. He screamed again, this time with pain as Ophiuchus landed with all his weight on the innocent orchid and his enflamed bunion. 'Get off! Get off my foot you great oaf!'

Draco jumped to his feet as the screaming chased away any remaining remnants of sleep. What he saw didn't fill him with anything near a wonderful day glow. Ophiuchus was again twice his size, standing to attention, saluting and covered once more in the mysterious black armour.

'Ophiuchus?' whispered Draco, afraid to venture anything louder. There was no response. Ophiuchus just stood there stock still, staring at Serpens' cave. Draco felt a cold chill course through his body as his attention was drawn to the cave entrance where something was emerging from its shadowy depth.

At first the image was blurred a little by heat shimmer but gradually it sharpened into stark focus.

'Pssst – Lupus,' hissed Draco urgently but also half-heartedly, in his mind a hope that what he was seeing might be encouraged to go away if he didn't give it sufficient credence.

Lupus didn't hear Draco at first; being otherwise occupied with his own problems. All his efforts, including screaming, were now focused on getting his numb foot from under Ophiuchus. This included battering Ophiuchus on the chest with the nearest rock he could reach.

Draco tried again to get Lupus's attention this time finding his voice. 'Lupus!' yelled Draco, a little too loud for his own liking.

'What? Can't you see I'm a bit busy?' Lupus stopped his battering, which didn't appear to have made much impression – on Ophiuchus or his armour – and wiped at his sweaty brow. 'You could at least give me a hand.'

But Draco wasn't listening, instead he just pointed, his mouth open wide; the look of a fool.

Lupus often wondered if he was the only one of them with a smattering of brains and it was moments like this that confirmed it. Even so, Lupus turned to see what Draco was pointing at. He promptly dropped the rock on his other foot, but this time he didn't feel a thing.

The image stopped short of the clearing; a signal for Ophiuchus to snap into life.

'I am Ophiuchus, bearer of the Dark Lord and herald elite.' Both Lupus and Draco briefly shared the same experience; déjà vu. 'Pay homage to your leader: The Dark Lord,' announced Ophiuchus, finishing with a complicated flourish of hands and the bonging of a small gong.

Together a shaking Lupus and Draco bowed as low as was physically possible. Serpens entered the clearing complete with tutu.

'I see from your faces you never thought to see me again,' said Serpens, 'yet here I am and as you can see I've managed to pull myself together again.' There was a pause; Serpens seemed to be waiting for something.

Right on cue Ophiuchus gave a polite chuckle.

Lupus and Draco deemed it wise to follow suit.

'Good – thank you my minions but enough, I have decided from this day forth my energies will not be wasted on such futilities so I have therefore taken steps to curb my temper, as magnificent as it is, and hence forth not permit myself to go to pieces at the slightest problem.'

Draco's polite laugh was rewarded with a smack on the back of his head by a heavily armoured arm.

'I am Ophiuchus and you will only laugh when the Dark Lord jests. I heard no such jest,' said Ophiuchus sternly.

Draco staggered to his feet and apologised.

Serpens for his part did look to have his anger under control. 'As I was saying,' he continued, 'things have changed since my little mishap in the cave.' He paused again and nodded at Ophiuchus who immediately responded by giving Lupus and Draco slaps across the head. They seemed preoccupied and he wanted their undivided attention; what he was about to say was very important.

Lupus thought of pointing out that his foot was still beneath the bearer's size forty-fours, but thought better of it.

Sure he once again had control over the floor, Serpens announced his big news. 'I have discovered a way to escape this misbegotten dirt-ball.'

Hope suddenly somersaulted into Draco's and Lupus' eyes. They couldn't believe what they were hearing. A chance to escape. Their minds started working in unison; even maybe the chance to escape the clutches of Serpens and start afresh somewhere. Who knows, perhaps they could find forgiveness with the creators. Putting peas in pods was not all that bad when you really thought about it. Anything had to be better than being stuck for all eternity with Serpens.

'And now Lyra will explain fully.' Serpens stepped to the side, hands on hips with his favourite faraway look on his face.

Lupus and Draco looked on anxiously. They waited. They all waited. Serpens shifted his weight from one leg to the other. Still nothing. Serpens started to look agitated; the moment was passing; his moment. It passed; head down.

'Lyra,' snapped Serpens, with slight irritation – anger was a no-no. 'Explain the meaning of this!'

Together Draco and Lupus took a precautionary step backward.

'LYRA!' roared Serpens, 'I COMMAND YOU TO SHOW YOURSELF!'

A very faint and muffled voice could now just be heard.

'What?' said Serpens peering over his shoulder, puzzlement replacing the slight irritation.

Lupus just managed to dodge the powerful arm that came winging his way as Ophiuchus pointed behind Serpens. Serpens twisted sideways.

'Oh,' said Serpens quietly. He moved his belt so it faced back to front and Lyra came swinging into view; he was tied to the belt by his tongue. 'Ahem,' said Serpens, sounding a tad embarrassed. He began to tug at Lyra but with no success.

Ophiuchus stepped smartly forward brandishing a fearsome dagger which he offered, handle first, in Serpens' direction. Another day Lupus would have marvelled as to where all this stuff was coming from but for the moment he was just glad to have his foot back.

'Good thinking that, ogre,' said Serpens, gratefully receiving the proffered instrument.

That must be a first, thought Draco.

'NOTH!' screamed Lyra when he saw the size of Serpens' weapon. He began to struggle violently but to no avail, the weapon did its job and Lyra slumped to the ground in a dead faint.

Serpens handed the dagger back to Ophiuchus who saluted, turned on the spot, returned from whence he'd come, turned again and snapped to attention.

'Lyra,' said Serpens moving the little imp with his foot. Lyra stirred and started to come round. 'Come now, the dreaded minions of darkness wait for your words.'

Two certain minions didn't even bother looking at each other this time.

Lyra tentatively flicked open an eyelid and peered up at his lord and master to see what he thought he would see in his hand, instead Serpens held nothing but the remains of the leather binding that had held him to his master's belt. He felt inside his mouth; it was still there.

With a burgeoning glee that bordered on happy insanity Lyra sprang to his feet and prepared to tell it as the master ordered.

'Onceth...' Lyra gave a small cough; he wasn't used to having his tongue back quite yet. 'Thorry... I mean sorry.' Lyra concentrated as hard as was wise for him.

'Please carry on,' urged Serpens, trying hard not to grind his teeth.

Lyra relaxed a little, gave another cough and tried again.

'Well it's like this init.'

'No-No-NO!' yelled Serpens, his poise and pose beginning to falter. 'Tell it like I told you.'

'Yes, Master. Sorry, Master,' said Lyra shrinking under Serpens' glare.

Happier, Serpens calmed down and regained his composure.

'The Dark Lord, our great leader,' started Lyra; behind him Serpens extended his chin in a jutting masterly way, 'has devised a wonderfully clever plan.' So far so good, thought Lyra, but now comes the hard part, he could already feel the embarrassment welling up. 'Once upon a time, a long time ago...'

'A long, long time ago,' Serpens corrected, without moving his lips.

'A long, *long* time ago,' echoed Lyra.

Lupus and Draco pinched themselves hard; it wasn't a laughing matter.

'There was a great and noble warrior leader called…'

And so Lyra went on aided by the occasional prompt and gesture from Serpens until, just after noon, the tale was told.

Ophiuchus started to applaud and was hurriedly joined by a thoroughly bored Lupus and then Draco who had been asleep on his feet and was only roused from it when the clapping started; survival instinct had thankfully kicked in as Draco hadn't the slightest idea where the hell he was.

'Well done Lyra,' said Serpens, grabbing Lyra by the neck and re-attaching him to his belt. 'Now any questions?'

'Yeth, Mathter,' said Lyra.

'Anyone else?' Serpens surveyed his dreaded minions of darkness. 'Not one? Good – then I take it you were all duly impressed by my plan.'

'Of course, Master,' said Draco, frantically looking to Lupus for some clue as to what had been said. Lupus just shrugged. He'd lost the plot somewhere around the theory that the "big bang" was nothing more than a bad case of colic.

'Good. Then you both agree to the sacrifice?' An evil glimmer shone in the corner of Serpens' eye.

All of a sudden it felt as though the bottom had not fallen, but jumped out, carrying with it the only available parachute from Lupus and Draco's world. Serpens snapped his fingers and Ophiuchus hauled them both from the ground by the scruff of their necks.

'You *were* both listening I take it?' said Serpens, glowering at them.

They nodded the best they could.

'Good. It's agreed then.' A smiling Serpens snapped his fingers again and Ophiuchus immediately obeyed, dropping the two to the ground. 'Tomorrow the four of us will succumb to a long sleep while Lyra here,' he swung him into view, 'will stay concealed keeping a vigilant watch on the lake until the creatures that dwell there have developed sufficiently, as I predict they will, to be of use to me. Whereupon this happening Lyra will awaken us from our slumber.'

The next day Lyra was alone. The others holed up in the cave warm and snug while he stared despondently at the lake.

Nothing much was happening.

He wished he'd been allowed to keep his tongue.

Bubbles started to rise at the lake's edge.

He wouldn't be so lonely.

A pair of bulbous eyes followed by flippers and a slimy body appeared.

Sometimes he liked to lick things.

The creature gave the landscape the once over then flipped ashore.

He was bored already.

A large noisy burp emanated from the slimy one's mouth.

Still, he did still have his stick.

Other slimy ones appeared at the water's edge.

CHAPTER 6

The gaggle, ragged band, whatever you want to call them, that followed Musca – through fear more than any feeling of camaraderie – had been sullenly walking Indian file for two days following a dirt track with barely a rest when the heavens opened up again.

Black clouds that had hung menacingly in the sky all day, teasing, waiting for just the right moment to unload their burden, decided now was a good time; when all below had finally managed to dry and shelter was nowhere in sight.

Thoughts raced through Muscas' troubled mind as the rain lashed at him. He had to find shelter and quick, somewhere they could get a good rest, it was a chieftain's duty, was it not, to look after his people; but where?

As Musca frantically scanned the landscape for suitable refuge Fornax, a pace or two behind him, had thoughts of her own as her eyes bored into the back of his head and they weren't what you would call friendly. Skinned alive and used as a tent was one of the ideas bouncing around in her head, and Fornax wasn't one to trifle.

On they trudged; wet, cold, tired and begrudgingly.

Cetus came next, his mind, like his stomach, rumbling with the thought of where his next meal was coming from. Behind him and following very closely in his footsteps was Equuleus, the youngest and driest – thanks to Cetus' bulk – of the survivors and by this virtue was still able to think of all that happened and was happening as an adventure.

Still they trudged.

Next in file were the twins, brothers Hydra and Hydrus. Two peas in a pod have never looked more alike; that is if you forgive the fact that Hydra, the eldest by a matter of pushes, was a good foot taller. This had been known to cause the occasional havoc especially when it involved girls and the twin's favourite game of changing places. One poor girl was never the same again and was still receiving therapy.

Last but not least, lagging somewhat behind, was old Bootes – more affectionately known as smelly ol' Bootes to his friends and just about everyone else who had had the misfortune to come into close contact with him – dragging his feet as his thoughts remained with the loved ones he had lost in the fire. There was little Lottie who used to follow him everywhere. Millie and her sad three-legged gambol. Poor old blind Silvey and of course his favourite, old Nob the ram. Bootes managed a smile as he thought of old Nob, with his twisted horn and shaggy matted coat, forever scouring the fields looking for his oats.

Bootes gave out a deep sad sigh as he resigned himself to the sadness of not seeing them again, but then dug deep and found solace in the words of ol' Grandpa Bootes. 'Don't ya be worrying boy. There be plenty more sheep in the sea,' he often said, tapping his pipe on a young Bootes' head as he did. Bootes had never fully understood what the old man was going on about but smiled all the same. He then took consolation that maybe there would be sheep in the valley the idiot child Musca was intent on taking them to. Bootes, a little happier at the idea, rummaged through the bag he had slung across his back and took something from it. Another sigh and a sniff as eyes filled with water and his nose started to run. Never see them again. Bootes took a huge bite from the charred leg of mutton he had in his hand whilst wiping away a tear with his other hand. Not in one piece that is. 'Gud ol' Nob,' said Bootes quietly, tears now flowing freely. He began to chew.

Finally there was Pistor, painter and village drunk, lurking not at the end of the line but somewhere ahead; sent by Musca, with the help of a glance from Fornax, to scout. Pistor had discovered to his joy a new and alcoholic use for the humble potato but now all that lay in ruins, his secret potato patch, his still which was hidden behind the alchemist's, was lost, consumed by the fire; gone in a very big flash; except that is, for what was left in his hip flask or in Pistor's case thigh flask which he always had strapped to his leg under his trousers for emergencies. At least he could dampen his sorrows if not drown them.

Pistor loosened his trousers and slipped his drinking tube into the top of the flask. The strong liquid slid down his throat doing a fine job of warming his cockles. A couple of sips would have to suffice for now though, thought Pistor, wondering when and if he would be able to make more. The thought depressed him but for now he would have to lump it. He took in his surroundings. It was a small enough cave but it would do, it was lucky he had found it before the rain had started. Pistor looked at the rain bucketing down and gave thought to the others. Should he go and look for them? He decided it would do no one any good going out in that, especially him, he may not be able to find the cave again for one; besides, the others might this very moment be sitting in their own snug warm cave somewhere. Pistor took another sip and chuckled to himself, he doubted they would though, not with that idiot leading them. Still chuckling Pistor found a mossy corner and settled down to wait for the rain to stop.

Struggling to keep his feet on the now treacherous track, the incessant rain turning the dirt into ankle deep slippery mud, Musca called an abrupt halt. A couple of steps ahead the track ran down and away from him at a steep angle; tricky in the conditions but not impassable; they would have to be careful so as not to slip straight down. It was then that Musca saw it as he carefully peered down to where the track levelled out again at the bottom; an immense cave mouth looming dark and menacing. Musca immediately felt the pit of his stomach lurch uncomfortably. He had a fear of such things; he had a fear of most things.

Behind Musca nearly all the Indian file had become a queue, all pressed against each other wondering why Musca had called a halt. Behind them Bootes, chewing noisily on what was left of gud ol' Nobs' leg, had remained oblivious to the situation up ahead and thus merrily ploughed into the back of the stationary Hydrus. The reaction was that of an inverted domino effect, each slipping backwards as the feet of the following took away the feet of those in front. Musca, knocked onto his backside, didn't even have time to scream as he joined them, hurtling towards the edge of the steep slope like a human log flume. Down they went, careering helplessly in a mass of arms and legs, not stopping until they reached the bottom of the slope.

'I should hang you upside down and leave your scrawny body for the crows!' bellowed Fornax as she emerged from the melee of mud covered bodies squirming for footholds. Her anger vented at Bootes who she suspected was the guilty party behind this latest mess – she had an uncanny sixth-sense when it came to sensing the guilty. 'Where is he?' she demanded, her hand hovering above her sword. But Bootes was nowhere to be seen; a wise move on his part.

Frustrated by the lack of a culprit to harangue Fornax took her temper out on the nearest thing to hand, the mud clinging to her hair throwing it in clumps to the ground with all the contempt she could muster until most of it was removed. When it was nearly all gone she started to calm a little using the rain that showed no signs of stopping to wash the rest from her hair and body. At last satisfied she was as clean as she was going to get her mind turned once more to the chore of finding shelter again and in turn to the cave mouth she now noticed for the first time.

The cave mouth was all of fifty metres across and the same high; it gave the impression of a giant mouth hungry to be fed. Fornax shuddered; whether it was the cold of the rain trickling down her back or the cave's appearance she didn't know but dry was dry to her. That will do, she thought, wringing water from her hair.

Thoughts of Bootes fast receding and ignoring any misgiving she may have felt at first glance Fornax entered the cave and disappeared into its shadows.

'Ooof! Get off me!' wailed a mud covered body that could have been just about anyone, in this case though it was Hydrus that Musca was using as a stepping stone to reach more solid ground. Musca scraped as much of the mud as he could from his face and watched as the rest struggled clear one by one until only Equuleus remained. Steadying himself against an outcrop of rock Musca leaned forward as much as he dare and stretched out a hand. Equuleus managed to grab it first time and was hauled up and away from the quagmire the simple dirt track had turned into. Someone could drown in that, thought Musca, watching the water from the track above cascade down the slope to the track below, a churning mass intent on turning the quagmire into a swamp. Musca shivered; it was a horrible thought.

'Is everyone all right?' shouted Musca. Bedraggled voices answered. Two, three, four replied. Four plus him, five counted Musca. Five? Three missing. No Pistor was somewhere else; found somewhere to hide no doubt the selfish -. But that did leave two missing. By the Stars, thought Musca, panic slicing into his heart. Where's Fornax?

Leaning forward again Musca scanned the mud for life. 'Fornax!' he shouted, his heart beating as if it were about to explode.

Beside him Equuleus put a hand on Muscas' shoulder; he was pointing. 'She went in there,' he said. 'I saw her go in but then that fat oaf Cetus rolled over me nearly squishing the life out of me.' Equuleus glared across to where Cetus was sitting. Cetus didn't notice; his thoughts elsewhere.

'In there?' said Musca. His heart did a sort of flip as it jumped from one horror to another. He turned to Equuleus. 'She went in there? Are you sure?'

'I'm certain,' said Equuleus, his mind wandering to those wonderful moments as he watched her washing the mud from her body; her wonderful, wonderf-. 'Ah-hem… certain.'

Musca gave Equuleus a queer look then started to cautiously edge his way to the cave mouth.

It looked as forbidding as when he'd first seen it from above but now it was ten times the size and ten times as menacing.

He reached the edge of the opening and peeped in, behind him Equuleus had been joined by the brothers.

'What's going on,' whispered Hydra.

'Fornax went into the cave,' explained Equuleus.

'Shit,' said Hydrus, making a face.

'Sssch,' said Musca, 'Fornax, you there?'

No reply. The cave stood silent as a graveyard, the graveyard playing through Muscas' head; his imagination starting to take the helm. Musca called again. To the others behind him the call lacked the conviction of the first; no surprise there. Not a sound, it was as if the cave had swallowed her up. An idea squeezed through before Musca could stop it. Perhaps he should wait; wait until the cave spat her out of its own accord, he thought.

Coward, cowardly, cowardly custard! Musca turned sharply and looked at the others.

'What?' frowned Hydra, puzzled by the expression on Muscas' face.

It wasn't them, thought Musca, quickly turning back to the cave. Which meant. Why now? Why did his conscience pick now to prick? He loved her sure but that didn't mean he had to put himself in danger. Did it? She'd understand. No she wouldn't. Who said she was in danger? His imagination took time out to tap on the inside of his skull; it made a hollow sound.

Musca tried to get a grip. There was nothing to say there was any danger other than maybe the odd spider or two, or three. And that didn't mean anything – unless – they were giant spiders. Two or th-.

'You going in or what?' said Hydrus, looking over Muscas' shoulder, 'Looks nice and dry.

Aha! thought Musca, the perfect ploy to lure us in.

'Well I don't like the look of it. The place doesn't smell right,' said Hydra, who was seldom wrong where his nose was concerned.

'I think he's right,' agreed Equuleus, 'don't ask me why but it smells of evil.'

Without realising it the four of them had inched into the cave's shadows, they now inched back again; the rain and mud not seeming so bad now.

'But we can't just leave her,' protested Musca, inching back slightly faster than the others.

'We could wait outside until she calls,' suggested Hydra, 'you know how she hates to be disturbed.'

There was an awful lot of good reasoning in that statement, but...

'What if she's lying naked and afraid, not able to call out for help, her captors holding her down, threatening her,' said Equuleus with a faraway look in his eye.

No one knew or wanted to ask where the naked bit had come from but he had a point and the retreating slowed a little.

'What now?' said Hydrus.

'I think... I think we should do what Hydra suggested and wait outside, you know how she gets,' said Musca, his imagination swaying back in favour of the dark, horrible and dangerous and away from anything enticingly lustful. 'Over there, against the rocks behind those bushes, that looks a nice spot. We should be safe there. From the rain,' he quickly added. 'And if she comes running chased by who knows what – his imagination still heavily at work – we can pounce on her pursuers as they appear and save her.' Even though the bushes lay some forty feet away no one argued.

Once safely ensconced Musca took on his mantle of chieftain again and explained the plan to Cetus who'd been looking on and then joined them by scrambling over the track on a small precariously placed tree trunk. Men deployed, or at least those he could find; Pistor and Bootes would have to wait, Musca settled down behind one of the thicker bushes and waited with fingers crossed for nothing to happen.

The rain had stopped and the first rays of morning sun were starting to stretch and spread across the land when Musca woke with a start from a dream involving the odd explosion, pointing fingers (at and middle), pickles for some reason and a very sharp sword he hadn't liked the look of. It was this very sword that had woken and now confronted him; its cold tip pricking his Adam's apple. Gulping wasn't an option.

Musca slowly followed the length of the sword to its hilt and its owner. Arriving at the top the sight that met his gaze instantly set differing signals scampering down his spine. Most were attributed to fear and travelled down well worn routes as far as

Muscas' body was concerned, their targets the bowels, bladder etc; the usual suspects when embarrassing moments were called for. One though, a big smile spread across its face, headed for Muscas' loins.

Above him, her feet either side of Muscas' chest, stood Fornax. Terrifying yet oddly arousing as she looked down at him past her heaving breasts, her red hair glowing copper in the sun, moving slightly in an early morning breeze.

'Glad to see you're awake,' she said, 'I'll have someone to protect me now, won't I?' Her tone was dry her face impassive.

Surely she couldn't know, could she, thought Musca, about last night? She must. Musca went to gulp but thought better of it. The signal, the one that had moments ago been grinning from ear to ear, suddenly lost all momentum and slowed to a limp before disappearing completely.

The sword against Muscas' throat relaxed a little to give him a chance to reply.

'I... well we... that is all of us decided that you, as the only female,' Musca could almost feel the corner he was backing into, 'should have the safety of the cave while us men protected you from any intruders.' Musca tried to smile, but it barely registered as such before dying on his lips. He'd been too much of a coward to enter the cave and see if she was okay. It was hopeless and he knew it; she knew and she knew he knew she knew he was a worthless wimp and trying to worm his way out of things as usual.

He was right. Fornax had been closer than he and the others had realised and had overheard everything that had been said but what should one do in a situation like this? When the snivelling, lying coward, sprawled at your feet was the man you inexplicably loved with all your heart. Forgive and forget she supposed returning her sword to its home. Besides, one of them had been right, she wouldn't have liked being disturbed. Oh, and she had spent the last hour or so honing her sword's edge to razor perfection; shame to waste a good sharp edge. Still though, she didn't think he should get away scot-free.

Thanking Musca for his thoughtfulness she carelessly stepped back to where the smiling signal had been heading, accidentally twisted her heel as hard as she could, then apologised before nimbly sauntering away in the direction of the cave.

'Nuts!' groaned Musca, cradling his family jewels.

'What?' said a sleepy Cetus, stirring from dreams that contained food and nothing but food so help him any deity; especially those that could provide more. 'Did someone mention food?'

It had been awhile since they had eaten, Bootes being the exception, who'd only chewed on his meat when no one was looking (no one was going to chew on his Nob but him), for Cetus that was the equivalent of half a lifetime ago.

'You were dreaming,' said Musca through waves of pain. He rolled on his side away from Cetus. 'You always dream of food. Why don't you have a scout about, there must be something growing somewhere that you can eat.'

'You all right?' asked Cetus, noticing Musca didn't seem to be himself. Using the rock face behind him as leverage Cetus got to his feet and waddled over to where Musca lay. 'You don't look too good.' Cetus reached out a hand and noticed Musca's eyes looked even more watery than usual; he thought it better not to mention it.

'Yes, fine. Must have slept awkwardly,' said Musca accepting the outstretched hand.

Pulled to his feet and trying hard to ignore the messages coming from his nether regions – thanks a lot stupid – got any ice? – Musca gathered his wits together the best he could – a supreme effort at the best of times – and turned his attention to his followers who were beginning to stir. What was needed was a plan of action; something he remembered his father once saying. Sadly Musca hardly learned anything after that; how or what it took to be a great chieftain, as two days later he had been introduced to the alchemist as his new apprentice.

Shrugging off those thoughts of happy days Musca steeled himself for the unnatural and began to take charge and put the action into his hurriedly formed plans. Cetus would do what came naturally to him and look for food. Hydrus would go with him to make sure at least some of it found its way back.

'Equuleus.'

'Sir,' said Equuleus, getting into the spirit of things.

'I want you to see if you can find any sign of Pistor or Bootes,' Musca was beginning to feel he might actually be able to pull it off; be like his father; be a great chieftain. Equuleus saluted and scampered away across the tree trunk. 'But don't go too far or take too long. We don't want to have to come looking for you too,' Musca shouted after him.

To Musca's delight Equuleus turned and saluted again. He had never been saluted to before. Musca was beginning to feel like a real chieftain.

'What about me?' asked Hydra as the others disappeared on their merry ways.

'You can come with me to the cave and see if we can find Fornax,' said Musca with an air of bravado. Bravado now that he knew there was only Fornax waiting in the cave.

Hydra nodded and for some reason unbeknown to him saluted. Embarrassed and wearing a puzzled expression on his face he quickly removed his hand from the side of his head and followed Musca.

It wasn't far to the cave, forty feet, but thanks to Musca's aching gonads it took twice as long as it had the night before to reach it.

'You all right?' asked Hydra, who received a grunt for his trouble. If Musca heard one more person ask that he... he'd... he didn't know what he'd do. Explode probably.

Finally, after much hobbling and cursing, they got there and peered inside. To their surprise they could smell smoke. Musca hobbled inside. Hydra, who didn't know what Musca knew cautiously hung back.

Through the gloom Musca thought he could make out the outline of someone or something standing silhouetted against an eerie glow. He stopped in his tracks and shivered even though he knew what he knew, the hairs on the nape of his neck standing up, packed, and ready to go at a moment's notice. Behind him Hydra,

48

plucking up courage even as his heart beat like a thing possessed, sidled up beside him.

'Fornax?' whispered Musca; half afraid the someone or something wasn't her. His heart decided to join Hydra's in an impromptu duet.

To the duo's relief it was Fornax's voice that answered. 'Over here, but careful you don't trip on the bones.'

'Bones?' said both Musca and Hydra together.

Gradually, as their eyes grew accustomed to the lack of natural light, they began to take in their surroundings. The walls of the cave were your usual run of the mill kind of walls; grey and damp with the occasional trickle coming from who knows where and going to who cares where. It was the floor that was different.

From a distance of twenty feet from the entrance it was as you'd expect; soil and rock, some scattered and loose. It was after this that it got interesting, interesting in an "I don't really want to be here" kind of way. At first glance an array of greys browns and whites gave the impression of some intricate mosaic. A second closer look, helped by the illumination from the fire Fornax had built, told a different story.

Musca and Hydra carefully picked their way across the carpet of bone and hide to where Fornax sat warming her hands.

'So glad you could make it,' said Fornax, a wry smile on her face. 'Didn't think you would for a while; the way you were limping back there.'

Musca blushed and the pain, forgotten but not gone as he'd made his way across the bones, returned as a deep dull ache.

'What is this place?' asked Hydra, the looks between Fornax and Musca missed as he scanned what he could see of his surroundings. His eyes eventually settled on a large shadowy object a little way behind where Fornax sat. 'And what's that?'

'At a guess I'd say it was a throne,' said Fornax turning to look at it, 'and we're sitting in the throne room.'

The throne was massive, at least twenty feet tall at the back and five feet from floor to seat.

'I think we should get out of here,' said Musca, his eyes glued to the throne.

'Why?' said Fornax.

'Look at the size of that thing. It's massive,' wailed Musca, 'who or whatever sat in that might be back any moment.'

Fornax smiled and pointed at the floor. 'Calm yourself Musca; I'm sure we're safe. Look around you.'

'Bones, bones and more bones is what I see, oh that and the odd piece of torn hide.' Musca was edging towards hysteria. 'Bones and skin of very dead things probably killed and ripped apart by whatever owns that throne.' A "whatever" better suited Musca's now racing imagination. 'And a very big whatever at that. I don't know about you but to me that sounds a good enough reason to leave and pronto.'

Musca started for the exit but Hydra was already ahead of him – hysteria was easy to catch when sitting near Musca for too long. But he only managed a couple of steps before he came face to face with Fornax, her hand resting on her sword.

'Going somewhere?' she asked.

'I… er… I thought,' mumbled Hydra avoiding eye contact.

'Well-well one of you boys having a thought. Now there's something new.'

Hydra now had another thought. Sitting by the fire wasn't such a bad idea after all. Behind him Musca had had time to reflect on his actions.

'Shame on you, Hydra. If Fornax says it's safe then it –'

'Cut the crap Musca and sit down,' said Fornax firmly, cutting him short with the precision of a surgeon, a withering look sending him scurrying back beside the fire.

'Now,' said Fornax joining them, 'if you boys are done shaking in your boots take a closer look about you and you'll notice that the bones you are so worried about are picked clean.'

Both Musca and Hydra stared at her with blank expressions. Fornax rolled her eyes upwards and sighed. 'It means that even the flies have long lost interest in them. This cave has been deserted for I don't know how long. We'll be safe enough sitting here waiting for the others to come back as anywhere.'

Somehow this didn't quite fill Musca and Hydra with the confidence Fornax seemed to possess. She had been known to be wrong in the past but no one had had the courage to point it out to her. So they sat there beside her, the minutes dragging, to wait for the others to return.

At first to take his mind from the surrounding carnage Musca took to picking the dried mud from his clothes. This though proved a thankless task and he soon grew weary of it. Hydra on the other hand, made drowsy from the heat of the fire, had fallen asleep. Musca decided he'd give it a try, if his mind would let him that is, and did manage to doze for a little while before waking with a start to discover to his dismay that Fornax had wondered off.

Musca suddenly felt very alone even though Hydra was by his side snoring his head off. Musca gave him a sly kick but he didn't stir. How he wished he was as brave as he sometimes pretended to be. He began to nervously twiddle his thumbs as the light cast by the firelight danced and contorted the shadows into hideous writhing shapes. He tried to ignore them, but beads of sweat were starting to form on his brow as his imagination took hold. His thoughts turned to Fornax again.

'Fornax?' he whispered nervously into the darkness beyond the fire's reach. When there was no answer he tried again, this time louder, 'Fornax!' The result wasn't as he expected though and her name came out in a sort of forced squeak.

Trembling slightly Musca got to his feet and tried to see if he could see her. He couldn't, his eyes too accustomed to the light of the fire. He had to move closer to the darkness. As he edged forward a thought from his childhood sprang to mind; something his mother had said to him. "Don't worry son. Fear is just the body's way of giving itself a head start should danger appear." She had also told him that being frightened was nothing to be ashamed of and that everything would be all right. He wished he could believe her. He wished she was here now.

Musca inched his way through the bones and hide, his eyes never leaving his feet in case he should disturb something real or imaginary. He whispered Fornax's name again when he decided he'd travelled far enough away from the fire. When nothing more than his own voice softly echoing from the closest rocks responded he looked up to check his bearings. To his surprise and undoubted

51

relief he found he wasn't where he thought he might be, but was within spitting distance of the soft earth and loose stones that welcomed you when you entered the cave's mouth. The mouth itself looked bright and inviting with its daylight backdrop against the gloom in which he stood. He had almost forgotten it was still day outside. Musca went to take a step towards it but stopped. He thought he could hear voices. He listened. It was voices, but not from behind him, they were coming from outside. It had to be the others. But what if it wasn't and there was a giant amongst them, hungry and angry from a failed hunt. Musca turned and ducked into the shadows not far from the entrance.

From his hidey hole Musca strained to make out if the voices were friendly but they were to far away to identify. He began to think, if not entirely coherently, as to what his options were. He could never hope to beat the giant in combat. He'd never beaten anyone in combat. He'd never been around long enough to engage in combat*. His body with its overpowering sense of self preservation had seen to that. Musca sank deeper into the shadows, his arms around his knees hugging them. His mind continued to play its games. But if he didn't do something the creatures would surprise the others and do unspeakable things to them.

Musca stood up, then sat back down again; his mind in a quandary as to what to do. He'd never been brave before. He didn't know how to do it.

'Musca?'

The sudden sound of Fornax's voice snapped at Musca like a whip cracking across his back draining the colour from his face. He would surely have to do something now; the creatures would have heard her for sure. He thought he could hear them running. He imagined them charging in; grotesque and writhing; squirming with glee as they sought out and pounced without mercy on her heaving, defenceless body.

He could take no more, but while his heart said, charge to the rescue, his legs, weak and wobbly pleaded they be stretched

---

* Not counting that time with the rabbit when it took him by surprise; so he says.

far and away from here. He sat there, head and heart throbbing; legs and bladder voting for release. Something had to give. Then without warning Musca stood up, drew his sword and leapt from his hiding place.

CHAPTER 7

'Are you certain it happened as you say?' asked Serpens, hardly able to contain his excitement and his surprise that his prophesy had actually come true and so quickly. He had dashed to the scene of the crime as soon as he had heard, but Musca and the others had long gone.

'Yes Master. I saw it with my own eyes,' said Lyra, who then added without thought. 'May they be pulled from my head.'

Both Lupus and Draco winced and wondered if the stupid little imp would ever learn?

Serpens plucked Lyra from the ground and expertly issued just enough pressure against his head to pop an eyeball from its socket, which he deftly yanked free with a sickening twang. Luckily for Lyra, Serpens was in a good mood and only took one.

'Go on, tell me again,' said Serpens, dropping the luckless Lyra an arm's length away.

Lyra picked himself up and stepped backwards until his remaining eye was able to focus completely on an eager Serpens who was busy looking for a place to keep his new toy. Lyra, good imp that he was, waited patiently until Serpens was ready and then started to relate for the third time – Serpens had seen fit to give Lyra his tongue back when the first telling looked as if it would take forever – all that he had seen in the time that had passed since Serpens and the others had hidden in the cave to wait for the prophesy to come true.

'So where is this child now, this monkey man, this maker of grand devastation?' Serpens demanded when Lyra finished.

Lyra shrugged and blinked his one eye nervously.

'You don't know?' snarled Serpens, his skin turning an angry shade of puce.

'Breathe.'

'WHAT!'

'Breathe, Sire. You told me to tell you to take deep breaths if you changed colour, Sire,' said Ophiuchus, his face devoid of expression.

'Ah – right,' said Serpens, his eyes narrowing; looking for any sign of dissent, the slightest snigger, from his minions. He took a deep breath, his colour returning to a dark red but the anger could still be seen bubbling away just below the surface.

'Two, three -.'

'Don't push it Ophiuchus,' growled Serpens.

'Sorry, Sire,' said Ophiuchus, his features still blank.

Almost back to his normal colour and resigned to Lyra's stupidity, Serpens turned to one of the other minions. 'Change into something that can find the monkey man's trail,' he ordered.

Lupus obeyed, changing into a bloodhound; extra-large, and bounded in the direction of the blackened valley.

Ten minutes later he bounded back.

'Well?' said Serpens impatiently.

Lupus started to bark, saw that Serpens had started to tap his foot and hurriedly changed back to his familiar werewolf form. 'Sorry, Master. A group of humanoids, almost simian, left the valley three days hence.'

'Which direction?'

'Towards the cave, Master.'

Serpens smiled and stroked his chin thoughtfully; a pose he'd been practicing.

'And towards the sea.'

The smile dropped, the pose faltered. 'Two groups?' said Serpens, puzzled.

'Yes, Master,' said a very wary Lupus.

'LYRA!'

His goldfish mind devoid of any past or impending terror, Lyra capered and sidled within Serpens' reach.

He knew it would surely be a hopeless task but he asked any way. 'Why didn't you mention there were two groups?' said Serpens. 'Well?'

'I don't know,' said Lyra honestly.

Serpens was right, but he couldn't help himself from continuing. 'You don't know. Why not?'

'Breathe.'

'What?'

'Sorry, Sire, I forgot myself,' apologised Ophiuchus.

Serpens returned his attention to Lyra. 'I'm waiting.'

'I forgot. My mind must have gone blank or something.'

Draco smiled as he thought even Serpens would have trouble finding that and removing it.

'You forgot?' said Serpens, wondering why he was even bothering. Enough was enough he decided. 'Lupus.'

'Yes, Master?'

'Any idea in which group the monkey man is?'

'The one heading for the cave, Master,' said Lupus confidently, if somewhat chancing it, as he only had Lyra's description of the man to go on. A coward's scent was always stronger than the man himself.

A smile once more crept across Serpens' face. Things were looking up. 'At last we seem to be getting somewhere,' he said. 'Now, gather round and listen carefully to my plan.' Serpens straightened his tutu as his minions did just that.

'So,' said Serpens, when all had been divulged, 'I hope you all realise how important it is we find this particular monkey man?'

'The cowardly one?' said Lyra.

'Yes Lyra, the cowardly one,' reiterated Serpens for the umpteenth time. 'The cowardly one holds the key to us getting off of this Creator forsaken planet. Do…you…understand?'

Lyra nodded, his lone eye wobbling in its socket.

Sighing deeply Serpens turned to Draco. 'But first we must split up, you Draco shall fly high and shadow the larger group, reporting to me at intervals of their movements.'

'Fly high?' said Draco, not certain he had heard Serpens correctly.

'Yes Draco, that is what I said. Now of you go unless you have a problem with that.'

Draco did. He didn't know how to. 'Surely, Master, begging your pardon, you mean run after them and watch from a great height?' said Draco, doing a great job of cowering.

It was then, in that defining moment, that Serpens felt he knew why he had been lumbered with these four imbeciles to work with. He could hardly conquer the universe, or anything else for that matter, with minions that counted so few brain cells between them. But he would show them. Show the creators that he meant business and would win through no matter what they threw at him. He glowered down at the cowering Draco as one day he meant to look down on the creators.

'Do you know what you are Draco?' said Serpens, his resolve already being tested.

Draco looked to Lupus who could only shrug.

'You are a dragon, Draco. A fearsome, fire-breathing worm, that leaves death and destruction behind wherever he steps.' Idiots, thought Serpens, I'm surrounded by idiots.

'Oh,' said Draco. Because no one had told him what he was he had assumed he was an imp with an impressive party piece.

'OH!' thundered Serpens.

'Breathe-!' Ophiuchus started, but he didn't get the chance to finish. His feet leaving the ground as an immense bolt of energy hit him square in the chest sending him cart wheeling towards the valley at great speed.

Serpens grabbed the cowering Draco and lifted him into the air by an ankle. Upwards he marched, carrying his struggling minion, until he stood at the edge of a crumbling cliff that edged the valley. He peered over and spied Lupus and Lyra way below looking like minute insects.

'Now Draco, your first flying lesson,' said Serpens, his grip loosening on Draco's leg.

Draco looked down. He didn't like what he saw. He didn't like heights for one thing. If he was a dragon he was going to be a low level sort of one. Serpens let go and made his way back down again as Draco's screams echoed in his ears.

* * *

'I'm sure he'll get better the more he practises,' said Lupus, eyeing the crumpled heap at the foot of the cliff.

'He had better,' growled Serpens, looking around for his remaining minions but not seeing hide nor hair of them. 'Where are the others?'

Lupus pointed to a large ancient oak tree some distance away that no longer possessed branches; its bark blackened and twisted by fire. Ophiuchus lay in front of it, his head buried deep in the thick trunk.

'Oh yes,' said Serpens, 'and Lyra?'

'He's under Draco, Master,' said Lupus, wincing; preparing for an outburst.

It didn't come. Serpens let out an almost imperceptible sigh and looked thoughtful for a second, his eyes wandering from the stricken Draco back to the prostrate Ophiuchus. He just couldn't bring himself to ask why.

Lupus felt compelled to explain though. 'Lyra thought Draco's shadow was a hole opening up in the ground and went to investigate,' he said.

'Ah,' said Serpens, somehow managing to keep calm without Ophiuchus' help. He again looked thoughtful. 'I'm going to sit awhile and think and I don't want to be disturbed until you've retrieved your fellow minions. Oh, and when Draco comes round tell him to keep up the good work.' Serpens shuffled away; he had a lot on his mind. His most immediate thought; how was he ever going to conquer the universe when his minions of darkness demonstrated all the prowess of a peashooter pitted against armoured cohorts? A peashooter that, he doubted, could muster a single pea between them.

Many hours of painstaking chopping, rolling and digging later the minions reported for duty.

'Good,' said Serpens, glad to have his mind released from thoughts of the seemingly hopeless task ahead, 'we shall now set forth for the cave to find this monkey man and the secret he holds.'

Serpens snapped his fingers and Ophiuchus, who was now once again almost doubled in size and clad in the dense black armour, bent onto one knee with his back facing his master. Serpens then clambered aboard a makeshift wooden throne constructed from the remains of the oak tree that was strapped to the ogre's back.

Sitting comfortably Serpens bade his minion onward. 'Forward Black Knight!' he commanded.

When, what seemed an incredibly long and embarrassing moment had passed by, Serpens tried again. And again. *And again.* Looking seriously grumpy Serpens was about to try once again when Lyra sidled up with a whispered suggestion. Serpens frowned but tried anyway. 'Giddy-up,' he said quietly. Ophiuchus immediately rose to full height and started toward the cave.

'Wait!' Serpens ordered suddenly, bringing the march to an abrupt halt. He turned to Lupus who had been following just below him. 'Draco?'

SPLAT! The noise of Draco hitting the ground reverberated through the valley.

'Still practising, Master,' said a grimacing Lupus.

'Ah-ha… Good.' Happy that at least something was going as planned Serpens settled back in his throne. 'Then onward Black Knight! Onward to meet our destiny!' It took a moment. 'Oh for badness sake, go on then, giddy-up.'

CHAPTER 8

'You took your time didn't you?' said Fornax, who was standing way above the cave entrance. She had found a small tunnel, like a chimney, that had led up and out through the caves roof. When Musca hadn't replied to her calling she had decided to explore it on her own to see where it led. She now looked down on Hydrus and Cetus who were looking puzzled as they peered into the cave. 'Up here,' she shouted. Acknowledging their waves as they looked up and saw her, she began to climb down the outside of the cave to where they were standing.

As Fornax reached the bottom she, Hydrus and Cetus were joined by Equuleus appearing from behind the bushes. 'It was Pistor,' he explained, 'he was drunk and it took us ages to drag him out of his hiding place.'

'Yeah,' laughed Hydrus, 'thought we were robbers trying to steal his booze. Put up one hell of a fight.'

'Where is he now?' said Fornax.

'He's sleeping it off in there,' said Equuleus pointing to the bushes, 'Cetus sat on him.'

'And he survived?' smiled Fornax.

Cetus laughed and threw his bag to the ground. 'A couple of bruises, that's all. He'll survive,' he said as he spread the bag's contents for Fornax to see, 'and food aplenty for us for a couple of days.'

'And by the stains on your face there could have been more,' Fornax joked, happy inside that the hardship of the last few days were forgotten for now. And talking of hardships, thought Fornax, where was that perpetual thorn in her side Musca?

Cetus looked up and grinned before packing what he had found back in the bag. Watching closely to see that all went back in was the ever vigilant Hydrus.

Leaving them to it Fornax thought she had better see what Musca was up to; no doubt nothing and still huddled witless by the fire, but she felt she had better check. Equuleus joined her as she made for the cave.

'Bootes?' she asked, suddenly remembering the smelly old fool had also gone missing.

'No sign,' said Equuleus.

'Not to mind,' said Fornax sensing a tinge of sadness from the boy, 'he'll turn up; just like one of his lost sheep.' She gave Equuleus a hug, a small brusque one; she couldn't have people think she was going soft in her old age, but a hug all the same.

Equuleus looked as if he was going to say something but it stayed on his lips, as a fearful Hydra rushed to greet them.

'Quick, it's Musca. Something's happened to him.'

Sword drawn and her femininity once more packed away into the part of her brain that rarely saw the light of day, Fornax hurriedly entered the cave.

Not far in from the cave mouth she found Musca lying on the ground, his hair matted with blood from a nasty looking gash that lay deep across his skull. Fornax replaced her sword and told Equuleus to summon the others. She felt Mucsa's pulse; he was alive, but the pulse was weak.

Grabbing arms and legs they managed to carry Musca outside without too much blood loss and laid him in the shade of the bushes along side Pistor who still languished in a boozy stupor.

'What happened?' asked Cetus, dabbing at Musca's wound with a piece of cloth dampened from a pool of rainwater amongst the rocks.

'I think he was attacked,' said Hydra, not really sure what to think, but going by the evidence before his eyes, 'hit from behind.'

Drawing her sword, Fornax motioned for everyone to stay where they were. Knowing better than to try and argue, they obeyed and watched with a rising feeling of dread as she headed back to the cave.

With movements a wild cat would be proud to boast of Fornax stealthily inched her way to where Musca had lain. All seemed quiet enough, but Fornax crouched and waited until her sight grew more accustomed to the gloom. She now looked for a sign of a struggle but the immediate area showed nothing. The thought that Hydra might be right about Musca being attacked from behind entered her mind and she moved to where she thought Musca may have been standing when it had happened.

With a wary eye on her surroundings, Fornax slowly rose and went to edge her way across. Something caught her eye, something alien to the rest of the cave's interior. Sword now raised, she headed for it. Something glinted. She took the last couple of steps at a leap; ready for anything. But when she landed all there was to meet her was Musca's sword wedged between two boulders. A mixture of relief and disappointment coursed through her at the realisation. Fornax took the sword's handle and pulled; it wouldn't move. She sheathed her sword and tried from the other side of the boulders. Still it held, stuck fast. Fornax climbed on the boulders and pulled with all her might. The sword at last came free and Fornax went flying through the air, almost landing in the same spot as Musca had lain. Above her, nasty looking stalactites stared down at her. Another couple of inches taller and she would have had a nasty cut across her head. As she lay there regaining her wits a sudden suspicion flashed into her mind; Musca was taller than her; a couple of inches; he may have fallen differently. He certainly didn't have the sword in his hand and if he had been trying to release it he may have fallen as she had.

Fornax got to her feet and examined the cave roof where it curved to become the wall. She was drawn to a patch, darker than its surroundings. The patch looked wet. Fornax ran a finger across it, it was sticky. She held the finger with the sticky substance on the tip to her nose and then licked it. It was blood. Her suspicions were right. The wound was self inflicted. The idiot had knocked himself out. No doubt while in hiding for one reason or another. Smiling grimly Fornax headed out to give Musca one hell of a piece of her mind. He'd pay for worrying her so.

Outside though things were in turmoil and as the fuming Fornax emerged expecting to roast Musca over the coals she was met by worried looks and what felt and sounded like a minor earthquake.

'What's going on?' she yelled, as the noise slowly grew in intensity.

'Something's coming,' Hydra replied, pointing in the direction they'd come the night before.

'What is?' said Fornax, noticing that even Pistor was moving and looking alarmingly sober.

'No one knows, but I've a horrible feeling it might want to sit in that chair.' Hydra nodded towards the cave, his face white, his eyes wide.

Fornax seriously doubted the throne's owner had arrived; just a tremor, common enough, but as she thought of complacency as an enemy she decided she would laugh at turning tail later, when the tremors had stopped.

'What about Musca?' shouted Equuleus. Musca, his head now bound with the rag Cetus had been using, was still unconscious on the ground.

Anger for now lost amongst the noise, Fornax brushed past Equuleus and in one movement picked Musca up and threw him across her shoulder. 'Now quickly,' she said, urgency in her voice, 'head towards the mountains.' Giant or no giant she didn't want to be buried alive in an avalanche; better to find open ground somewhere.

They moved as fast as they could, avoiding the quagmire path until it grew drier up ahead and then joining it as it wound its way towards the mountain range that loomed large before them. As they ran they knew not what manner of creature was behind them or even if it was only their minds playing tricks with them or even as to whether they were heading in the direction Musca would have led them. All they knew was that they didn't want to be anywhere close if something that could make the ground shake like that was coming to call.

* * *

The journey to the foot of the mountains was only short but the path had risen steeply from halfway and had narrowed considerably. All struggled as they coped with the rise, negotiated patches of slippery mud and dodged boulders loosened by the constant shaking of the ground, until the path came to an abrupt end under a multitude of fallen rocks almost as high, it seemed, as the mountains themselves.

'What now?' gasped a profusely sweating Cetus.

The way forward looked impossible but the noise behind them sounded ominously closer.

'We climb,' said Fornax without hesitation. Her earlier fears of avalanche were confirmed but her thoughts changed as to its cause. The tremors had gone on too long now for it to be an earthquake.

'But I'll never make it,' wailed Cetus, face raised, but unable to see the top.

'Of course you can,' Fornax reassured, 'just don't look down.'

'I'll go first,' volunteered Pistor to everyone's surprise. But sadly he had only looked sober back at the cave and his bravado had been further fuelled by the odd sip of liquor he had imbibed on the way up. Pistor staggered forward, attempted to find a foot hold, saw two, went for the one that didn't exist, missed it and span hopelessly away before disappearing from sight into the ground.

'Not again,' groaned Cetus, as the twins dashed to where Pistor had been. They found a hole; its edges giving evidence to the twigs, moss and dead leaves that had been hiding it.

'Pistor!' shouted Hydra, into the hole.

The call echoed somewhere down in the darkness but there was no answer from Pistor.

'What are we going to do now?' said Hydrus, turning to Fornax. The rumbling sound they were running from was sounding closer by the second.

'We follow Pistor, we have no choice,' said Fornax coming to the edge of the hole. She had no way of knowing what was down there, but by her own admission they had little choice.

With the help of the twins she swung Musca from her shoulder and lowered his limp body into the hole as far as was possible until they had no option but to drop him. Fornax was quick to follow, shouting as she dropped for the others to follow suit. The twins did, quickly sliding feet first into the hole, leaving just Equuleus and Cetus to come.

'We don't know what's down there,' cried Equuleus, as he paused at the edge.

Cetus grabbed his arm. 'The others for one,' said Cetus, all for the down rather than up solution.

'But we could break something.'

Just as Equuleus made this point the rumbling stopped leaving in its wake a thunderous silence.

'I don't think we have a choice any more,' said Cetus, afraid to look behind him; afraid of what could be standing watching them. Without warning, he threw his bulk into the hole, his trailing right arm grabbing Equuleus as he went, his weight giving the youngster no time to respond.

Down they all went, tumbling and moaning, their curses echoing in the dark as the shorter than expected drop bruised them before the tunnel that it led to meandered them away with it, winding them round and round as it spiralled at a gentle downward angle until finally levelling out at its musty damp nadir.

As bodies groaned below him, Equuleus gingerly reached out an exploratory hand only to instantly pull it back again when it plunged into something warm moist and hairy. His life suddenly flashed before his eyes.

'Oy!' growled an angry voice, 'who put their hand in my mouth?'

'Is that you Cetus?'

'Who do you think it is the bone fairy?'*

Equuleus relaxed and thanked the stars, 'Sorry.'

'When you two have finished your bonding maybe you can pass me that rope you have secreted around your person, Cetus,' said Fornax from somewhere in the dark. Typical that Fornax was already on her feet and typical that she knew about the rope Cetus had hidden around his middle in case of emergencies.

---

* An old folk legend. It was said that warriors of old returning from battle would place a retrieved lost limb under their pillow at night and wake up to find a piece of silver in its place. Heads didn't count. *SJ*

Without a "how", Cetus fumbled for the rope. Freed from his waist it was promptly snatched from his hands.

'Where are we?' said Equuleus.

'In a hole,' said Fornax, her answer honest, not glib, 'but there is light some distance ahead. She tied the rope round her waist and handed the rest to Cetus. 'Pass it along to the others and then give me a hand with Musca, he's getting heavier with every step.'

The going was to prove harder than the slope to the rock fall above, mainly to the darkness of the tunnel and its closeness.

'How much further?' asked Hydrus from somewhere behind.

'I don't know,' said Fornax, struggling with Cetus to keep from dropping Musca, 'just keep moving.'

Hydra reassuringly patted his brother on the back and pushed him gently forward. In the distance, the pinprick of light Fornax had found was at last growing. Though not quick enough for some, it was encouraging none the less; renewing lost vigour. But if this was not enough to entice the weariest among them to step quicker, the sound that now echoed through the tunnel surely would.

'AAAOOOooooo!'

The ghostly echoing noise brought the line to a stop.

'Did you hear that?' said Equuleus, who was bringing up the rear. The others could feel his shakes travel the length of the rope.

'Nought but the wind,' said Cetus, though the air was still.

'Keep moving,' ordered Fornax.

With the pace somewhat quicker now they continued towards the ever growing light, but twenty paces along the eerie noise of before again brought them to a halt; this time it was accompanied by the sound of a sword being unsheathed.

Leaving Cetus to take the full weight of the unconscious Musca, Fornax moved slightly ahead. She whispered a warning, 'Keep close, I think the noise is coming from up ahead.' But if truth be told none of them could put hand on heart and swear exactly from where it came.

The next couple of minutes were tense as they waited for the sound to come again, when it didn't Fornax pushed ahead; the opening ahead was now double the size of Cetus. Signalling for the others to wait, Fornax crept closer until she stood only inches from the light that pooled in; all appeared quiet; the light natural. Fornax stepped into the streaming daylight and, senses telling her the way was likely clear of ghosts or ghoulies or whatever it was that had made the noise, continued outside.

As if waiting right on cue the noise started again the very second Fornax stepped outside. Fornax ran back in. The sound was behind them for sure and very close.

'Outside quick!' shouted Fornax, her sword ready to smite down anything that came after.

With Musca safely propped against a boulder, Cetus, the oak staff he always carried gripped tightly in his hands, and the others joined her facing the shadows whence they'd come. The twins, their matching swords drawn and ready, adrenaline pumping, stood beside him. Equuleus, pushed slightly but gently behind them by Fornax, held out his knife as his father had taught him, in his other hand a sharp stone.

They waited, breath bated. Something moved inside the tunnel. Bodies grew tense as a dark shape slowly detached from the shadows at the tunnel's mouth. Swords, knives, sticks and stones were raised, ready to rain down on whatever foul creature daylight was about to reveal.

'Hello,' said the shape.

'Pistor!' exclaimed Fornax. 'I thought...' Fornax took a quick glance behind her to double check it wasn't some Pistor doppelganger standing before them. 'I thought you were with us. Where the hell were you?'

'I fell down a hole – Hic,' said Pistor taking in his surroundings for the first time. 'It's a bit bright isn't it?'

Weapons were relaxed as Pistor staggered forward.

'Next time try and let us know where you are,' said Fornax angrily.

'Yes, and you nearly scared us shitless with your wailing,' added Cetus, wondering if he should still use the staff.

'Whaling?' puzzled Pistor, 'Aren't whales a bit big to be in there?'

'Not whales you idiot, wailing, AAAOOO,' said Cetus, mimicking the sound from the tunnel.

Pistor gave thought to what Cetus had said, the puzzled look not leaving his face. 'I didn't – Hic – call out. I thought it was – Hic – you lot.'

Hands renewed their grip on their weapons.

'I think we may have outstayed our welcome,' said Fornax, looking past Pistor into the tunnel. 'I think it best we be on our way.'

Facing them now was a choice. Two paths led away from where they stood. Fornax, not big on discussions, took the reins and motioned to the one on her right.

'Lets hope it's the right one this time,' said Equuleus, his remark light-hearted. But the joke seemed lost on Fornax and the stony look thrown in his direction brought colour to his cheeks.

Fornax hated that she had done it; they were looking to her to lead them, but hard times she felt were not over yet. There were hard lessons to be learnt for some and the place for levity was not now. Now was for getting as far away as possible from here and help for poor Musca. Those were her priorities. 'Cetus – Hydra, carry Musca between you?'. They took an arm each. 'Equuleus,' Equuleus shifted his gaze from the ground, 'you go on ahead, but be careful.' A faint glimmer of a smile returned. 'I'll bring up the rear.'

'What of me and Pistor?' asked Hydrus.

'Pistor can look after himself,' Fornax shot a glance in Hydrus' direction; 'but keep an eye on him.'

Without another word they set off along the path Fornax had chosen. Would Ohm be at the end of it? If it was, it was a thought none were thinking. Nor did they spare a thought for their home and what they had lost. Now was now and they were in danger.

Fornax held back, waited Sure she'd heard something; heard a voice calling from somewhere deep in the tunnel as they prepared to leave? Bootes perhaps? No, not Bootes. The sound she thought she heard hadn't sounded of this world. She hovered awhile caught betwixt and between, listening; then shivered deep inside. She decided to wait no longer.

CHAPTER 9

'AAAOOO!' The sound reverberated down the hole.

'AAAOOO!' It repeated a little while later.

'What's he doing?' asked a frowning Serpens, as he watched Lyra poke his head down the hole where Fornax and the rest had recently fled.

'Shouting,' explained Lupus.

'What's he shouting?'

'Who, Master?'

Serpens turned his frown to Lupus.

'Hello, Master,' said Lupus quickly.

'Hello Master?' queried Serpens.

'No, Master. Just hello,' said Lupus, feeling a nervous giggle trying to surface, he pinched himself hard on the buttock.

'Still got his tongue though?' said Serpens, checking his belt.

'Yes, Master. He sometimes forgets.'

'Bring the idiot to me.'

Lupus saluted, a gesture he'd learnt went down well with his disturbed and fickly dangerous master, and went to get the imp.

Serpens nudged an elbow into Ophiuchus' back. 'To the cave,' he ordered.

'Ah, home sweet home,' mused Serpens, as his obedient ogre carried him into the cave, 'but not for much longer, eh Ophiuchus?'

'No, Sire,' Ophiuchus agreed, though whether in his present hypnotic condition he knew of what Serpens was talking about was anyone's guess.

'Down,' ordered Serpens.

'Sire.'

Stepping from the back of the kneeling Ophiuchus, Serpens swapped one throne for another. The cold stone felt good against his back, so much better than the wooden one. It was a shame it had to be left behind but it was necessary; they needed to travel light. 'Now leave me and wait outside for Draco's return,' growled Serpens.

Ophiuchus saluted, turned smartly and ambled outside to wait, his fixed gaze turned in the direction from which they had just arrived.

Meanwhile Lupus had arrived with Lyra.

'Step forward, idiot,' said Serpens.

Lupus automatically stepped forward.

'Not you,' sighed Serpens, 'the other one.'

Apologising profusely Lupus, head bobbing, returned to Lyra's side. Lyra meanwhile was now facing the wrong way, his one eye appearing to be frantically searching for something.

'Now what is he doing?' groaned Serpens.

Lupus grabbed Lyra by the shoulders and spun him round to face Serpens. 'It's since the incident with Draco, Master,' said Lupus, wishing he was anywhere but where he was right now, 'he's not been himself.'

Shifting forward on his throne, Serpens leaned across and with a gleaming outstretched talon gripped Lyra under his chin and pulled him to him. Serpens glowered into Lyra's tiny upturned face. 'Do you know who I am?' he asked.

Lyra, his eye dodging furtively in its socket, gave Serpens a momentary faraway look before answering. 'Yes, Master,' said Lyra, bringing a huge uncontrollable sigh from Lupus, 'The Dark One, Master.'

'Well done,' smiled Serpens, relaxing his grip momentarily before re-establishing it. 'NOW TELL ME WHAT YOU SAW AT THE HOLE!!!' The skin on Lyra's face was forced so taut by Serpens' blast, his ears almost touched at the back of his head.

'Humanoids,' whispered Lyra, through lips stretched to snapping point.

'WHAT?'

'Humanoids, Master.'

'Humanoids, Lyra? And would I be right in thinking that they would be the humanoids we are looking for? The group of humanoids travelling with the monkey man we so desperately need to have words with?' said Serpens, his head cocked at a grotesque angle looking at Lyra as a preying mantis may look upon the hapless prey that's wandered unknowingly within its reach. 'The monkey man that may well be our only chance of escaping this rotten planet?'

Now dangling helplessly a couple of feet off of the ground from Serpens' talon, Lyra opened his mouth to say something. Watching, with a certain amount of desperation in his eyes, Lupus wondered if he should stay or should he go? And if he did, would Serpens notice? Oh be sure he would. He stayed put; he'd found his feet weren't working that well anyway.

'Yes,' said Lyra, his eye settling like a ball at the end of its roll in the roulette wheel.

'And you said, "HELLO"?!'

Lupus wanted to shout "breathe", but he also wanted to stay in one piece. Lyra, regaining a smidgeon of sanity; perhaps more than he'd been blessed with when hatched, started to wriggle and shrink back from Serpens' growing ire. Alarm bells ringing in the fog he called his mind.

Serpens continued even though the anger he was trying to hold back swelled upon a wave of fury. 'And you thought this was a good idea, to announce our presence just as we had them, him, in our grasp?'

Don't answer that, thought Lupus, knowing full well Lyra would; good stupid imp that he was. Lyra nodded, changed his mind and then shook it furiously, but it was too late. The line broke, the anger gave way to the fury and its wave of tidal proportions broke against Lyra who flew through the air and out of the cave. Lupus lost his grip and liquefied to become a damp patch on the ground.

As Lyra flew out, Ophiuchus' voice drifted in. 'Breathe,' it demanded.

His hands crushing the arms of his throne, Serpens intent on finishing the job this time, shortage of dreaded minions of darkness or no shortage, tried to ignore the command. His temple fit to burst, as the veins protruding from it swelled to breaking point.

71

'Breathe, Sire,' repeated the command, this time quieter; soothing.

Blinking, as if trying to recall something he was supposed to do, Serpens slowed, but didn't cease in his intent. The soothing commands kept on coming though as he moved on, until outside Serpens' pulse had slowed and he was calm once more and breathing regularly. He took one last deep breath and sneered across at Lyra lying broken against the rocks across from the muddy path Musca and the others had been struggling in the day before, before glancing in Ophiuchus' direction. Ophiuchus, his lips moving, remained oblivious to his master's presence or to the words he had said and was still whispering. Serpens snapped his fingers and the words stopped.

Serpens had thought it better this way. It had been all too easy to ignore and rebuff Ophiuchus when he was just following orders, but this had been a master stroke; planting a safety valve in his own mind, linked to the fool's subconscious one, so that the words could not be stopped so easily. It was lucky he had or someone may have got hurt. As he headed back to his throne he laughed at his little joke; a sound so cold it would have had the hottest flame shivering amongst its coals. But hilarity aside he had to plan his next move.

A couple or so hours later Serpens called for Lupus. Lupus strode in. He wasn't happy. It had taken him almost an hour to get his body back together again; for some reason parts of it had frozen while in liquid form. The rest of his time had been spent reassembling Lyra. Something had to be said. He knew it would be a dangerous thing to do but he was angry and he had set his mind to tell the Dark Lord so.

'Ah Lupus, good of you to come so promptly,' said Serpens, sounding in a surprisingly good mood, which wasn't like him at all.

'Master, I wish to say something,' said Lupus, his heart in his throat; another reason he wasn't happy.

'Do you?' said Serpens, his smile wavering just a little, his eyes narrowing just a little. He leaned forward, elbow resting on what was left of the throne's arm, chin in hand, 'Go on.'

'Well it's…' muttered Lupus, the weight of Serpens' stare resting on his every word.

'Yes,' encouraged Serpens. Serpens' smile regaining its composure.

'The hopping, Master,' said Lupus, his words rushing from his mouth as if they were a piece of rotten meat he wanted to spit out. There he'd said it.

'Hopping?' said Serpens, straightening up.

'Yes, Master. I think it was why we missed the monkey man.' Lupus didn't like the way Serpens was looking at him but he was determined to say his piece. He tried to rid his thoughts of vicious looking talons and ripping noises. 'I don't think Lyra was to blame.'

'Then,' said Serpens slowly, 'pray tell who you think is at fault?' Serpens casually scraped a talon along the arm of the throne.

The noise of talon on stone set Lupus' teeth on edge. Bitten off more than he can chew; would seem likely. Harbouring a death wish; you'd think so, but Lupus carried on regardless. Something had changed in him since arriving on this rotten planet; for the better he thought. He felt it was time he stood up for himself and for others weaker than him.

'Ophiuchus could be heard for miles around. It was that that alerted the humanoids and set them running. At least Lyra found where they had fled to.'

Serpens suddenly leapt from the throne and landed inches from were Lupus stood. 'ARE YOU BLAMING ME, LUPUS?' he thundered, causing Lupus to take an involuntary step or two back, 'BECAUSE IT WAS I WHO ORDERED OPHIUCHUS TO DO SO!'

Lupus, verbally at least, stood his ground. 'If the cap fits,' he heard himself say. In his mind's eye he now clearly saw his demise and it wasn't pleasant; not pleasant at all.

Shaking with rage, Serpens towered over a now cowering Lupus. Lupus could feel his body starting to unravel. In a matter of seconds he would be nothing but a puddle again. A puddle Serpens would soon be happily splashing about in. What happened next took Lupus completely by surprise.

It wasn't rage Serpens was shaking with, it was laughter. 'Ha-ha-ha,' cried Serpens, 'you know what, I like you Lupus.' Serpens carried on laughing.

'You do…?' said Lupus, waiting for the punch line; or punch as may well be the case.

Gradually the laughing subsided and Serpens gently lifted Lupus by his shoulders until they were facing each other. Serpens studied him for a moment and wondered. The wretch had guts and more than a spark of intelligence. He could prove handy to have around. He would also have to be watched.

'Do you know what, Lupus?' Lupus shook his head, fearing something psychopathic. 'I think you might be right.' Serpens returned the shaken Lupus to the ground. 'I also think you may have a bright future in my army of dreaded minions of darkness.' Serpens' eyes sparkled insanely as he spoke, 'Well done.'

'Can I go know?' said Lupus, sensing it might be a good idea.

'Of course,' said Serpens.

Lupus saluted nervously and prepared to leave but Serpens wasn't quite finished with him.

'Haven't you forgotten something?' said Serpens, stopping Lupus in mid turn.

'Master?' said Lupus, one leg wavering in the air.

'I called for you.'

'Yes, Master. Sorry, Master,' apologised Lupus, his airborne limb returning to terra firma.

'How is Lyra?' asked Serpens, his hands clasped together beneath the concerned look he had managed to create. It had just dawned on him that he couldn't remember why he'd called for Lupus.

'Fine, Master, he'll be as right as rain as soon as I find his spleen,' said Lupus, not sure where all this was leading.

'Splendid,' said Serpens, clapping his hands together, his concern replaced by a huge plastic grin.

'Is that all, Master?' asked Lupus, eager to be on his way.

'There is one more thing.'

Here we go, thought Lupus.

'If you value your miserable little hide don't ever blame me for anything again,' snarled Serpens, returning to his old self, 'do I make myself clear?'

Lupus gave a stiff nod.

'NOW GO!'

Lupus' body tensed at the first hint of inflection and was out of the traps and flying by the exclamation mark.

Alone again. Serpens quite liked being alone. There was no one trying to undermine his authority. He would never admit to it but he was a tad insecure. He also had another reason to want to be alone. He had to do something he didn't like doing; something he wasn't very good at; making plans. Serpens had always relied on bullying and brute force to get him what he wanted. This time he would have to think, and think hard. Serpens sank back into his throne and rummaged through his tutu. He found what he was looking for and pulled out a faded tatty piece of blanket, the corner of which he placed in his mouth. A fretful Serpens began to suck.

CHAPTER 10

Fornax cursed as the path she had chosen gradually became a steep and narrow gully with a mountain face to their left and a rising wall of rock to their right. At some time, before the warm age, it had been an escape for water flowing from melting snow caps above to the foothills below. She prayed it led to the other side of the mountains. To anywhere, as long as it wasn't back to the noise she'd heard coming from the tunnel. It had chilled the marrow in her bones to the core. Going back wasn't an option she'd like to entertain.

Night was falling fast and Fornax, now leading the way, found her warrior breeding coming to the fore, readying for what creatures of the dark hours might be lurking. Each shadowy niche could prove their downfall; each a potential ambush; hiding places for robbers or worse. She had lost count of how many times her hand had sought the hilt of her sword since the start of the path. And now the sky was darkening and a layer of clouds were forming between them and the stars. There would be no guiding light that night. Fornax would have to find somewhere safe to rest before every turn turned into a dark rocky arbour filled with potential danger. Fornax called a halt and called the twins to her.

Hydra, with the help of Cetus, eased the still unconscious Musca to the gully's floor and joined his brother at Fornax's side.

'I want you to scout on ahead for a place to rest but don't go too far; within shouting distance,' said Fornax. The twins nodded and set off along the path. 'Be careful,' she whispered to their backs.

'What about me?' said Equuleus, 'I can use a sword.' He was carrying Musca's.

Fornax gently took the weapon from him and smiled. 'I need you as a runner Equuleus, the sword will only weigh you down.'

Equuleus looked puzzled. 'I can run like the wind, but where do you want me to run?' he said looking from the gully's sheer sides to the sky above.

Fornax actually laughed at this and relaxed a little. 'No Equuleus, I do not want you to run to the stars,' she teased, 'just to the brothers and back. And when I say run, I mean be a messenger. Run here in the dark and we may well end up carrying you as well as Musca. You could easily turn an ankle or worse break a leg.' Equuleus was thankful for the deepening darkness as his face reddened. 'You shall lead the rest of our party and I will return to the rear. She then spoke to Cetus. 'How are you faring Cetus, my round friend?'

Cetus was sat beside Musca, glad of the rest, his breath coming in rasping pants. 'Just give me a few moments more and I'll be ready as I ever will,' he answered wearily. In all the years he had known her he could not recall her showing a single semblance of compassion. Maybe she was thriving in her new role. He hoped it boded well for them.

'And you, Pistor, you drunken sot, how are you?' Fornax asked.

Pistor was leaning against the rock wall, head in hands. When he looked at Fornax it was through bloodshot eyes. 'I'll be all right once the fog clears and the lead weight in my brain stops rolling back and forth.'

'Good, you will have to give Cetus a hand with Musca. Do you think you can manage that?'

Pistor nodded and then wished he hadn't..

Affording herself another smile as Pistor groaned, Fornax turned to Equuleus as the sound of Hydra's voice carried down the gully. 'Your first job, Equuleus. Go see what the twins have found. If they are just calling for distance sake tell them to stay quiet, we don't want to draw the attention of anything that may be lurking. Otherwise tell them to stay put if they find a place to rest and to come back if they find trouble.'

'Yes, Sir – I mean, Ma'am,' said Equuleus, eager to please.

'Fornax will do,' said Fornax, 'now go as quickly as is possible and report straight back.'

As the eager Equuleus disappeared into the lengthening shadows ahead Fornax, with help from Pistor, grabbed an arm each and hauled Cetus to his feet. It was time to move again.

Darkness finally arrived. They had travelled an hour; two perhaps, with the occasional stop for Cetus and Pistor to get their breath back; Musca was heavier than he looked. With each stop Equuleus was sent to tell the twins to also rest and wait until Fornax gave the word to continue. The weight of Musca also pressed heavy on Fornax's shoulders but in a different way. She worried for him and cursed herself for doing so, but surely he should have come round by now?

With the darkness came the decision to rest again, perhaps for the night as the gully had levelled out for the last hundred yards or so and looked in no hurry to change up ahead. But to be sure Fornax would need to speak to the twins to assess the real lie of the land ahead. She asked Equuleus to take word to the twins to rejoin the group. If they did stay guards would have to be set, both forward and in rear.

A few minutes later an excited Equuleus came rushing back, his face flushed, his chest heaving.

Fornax instinctively went for her sword. 'What's wrong?' she said, expecting bad tidings.

'It's the twins,' gasped Equuleus, 'they've found something and said you should come straight away.'

'Did they say what?' said Fornax.

'No, I met Hydra on his way here.'

Sword now drawn, Fornax told Cetus to stay but be ready with his staff. She handed Pistor her dagger.

'Stay and wait for Equuleus' word and watch your backs,' said Fornax, gesturing back the way they had come. 'Now young Equuleus lets see what awaits us up ahead.'

When Fornax and Equuleus arrived they found the twins laying across the path their heads missing from their shoulders. For a moment Fornax feared the worse but released a relieved sigh when Hydra's head appeared from where it had been hidden. She could now make out a dark gap to her right in the gully's wall.

'What's so important that you have us scurrying in the dark?' said Fornax, happy all seemed well, but slightly angry that she had wasted energy worrying about nothing. 'I thought something had happened to you both.'

'Sorry,' said Hydra, realising his meeting with Equuleus earlier could have been less dramatic; he could have told him what they'd seen, 'but I felt it was important and you would want to see this.' Hydra pointed to the gap.

Fornax put her sword away and took his place at the gap, what she saw through it had her sending Equuleus back to the others at haste to tell them to hurry along and join them.

At the sound of fast approaching footfalls, Pistor and Cetus did what all the guilty did when faced with surprise; they were caught out. When Equuleus appeared Pistor was busy arranging his trousers and Cetus was still attempting to wipe away any incriminating tell tale liquid from his lips and chin.

'You shouldn't be doing that,' said Equuleus, alert to what had been afoot, 'it'll make you go blind. Fornax wouldn't like it.'

'Don't you worry yourself about that,' said Pistor quickly, 'it was only a quick one. Wasn't it so Cetus?'

Feeling as guilty as he looked, Cetus could only agree and cover his tracks best he could. 'I don't think Fornax would begrudge me one small one, especially with the baggage I've had to carry.' Cetus struggled upright and hoped the boy would agree. The last thing he wanted was to be held in Fornax's bad books. To his relief Equuleus shrugged his shoulders and supposed it would be all right.

'Our little secret boy, eh Cetus?' said Pistor conspiratorially.

Cetus did his best to ignore him and with a little help from Equuleus hauled Musca into a standing position. Pistor took an arm and gave Equuleus a sly wink.

On the way Pistor badgered Equuleus as to what he thought the twins might have found. Equuleus explained he didn't know but Pistor still continued pushing until they drew within sight of Fornax and the twins. At the sight of the gap he thrust Musca's arm onto Equuleus' shoulder and darted forward.

'What's the hurry,' said Fornax, grabbing Pistor by the arm before he could get there, 'and why is Equuleus doing your work?'

'The boy offered, didn't yer?' said Pistor, another oily wink shot Equuleus' way.

Equuleus looked uneasy about his answer, but said that he had agreed.

Fornax glanced at Cetus, but he avoided her eyes. She decided something was up but felt it wasn't the place or time to kick whatever it was into the air for open discussion. Instead she relaxed her grip on Pistor and spoke of what the twins had found.

It appeared a part of the gulley wall had collapsed at some time to leave the gap the twins had discovered, beyond it a dark void. Nothing interesting you would think but far away, down and in the distance a fire was burning; a campfire.

'So?' said Pistor, fast losing interest.

'If I'm right, it lays somewhere along the path we would have taken if the landslide hadn't blocked our way,' said Fornax, 'at a guess I'd say it lay three to four miles away.'

'I still don't see what all the excitement's about?' said Pistor, finding somewhere to sit, 'it's not as though we'll be seeing the fire's owners sometime soon.'

'Sooner than you might think,' said Fornax, 'I think the rope will just be long enough. We dropped a pebble over the side and there's solid ground somewhere near.'

Cetus nearly dropped Musca with shock. 'You're not saying what I think you're saying, are you?' he said, looking with dismay at the gap and more so the dark nothingness beyond.

'We have to think of Musca,' Fornax said, moving to take Musca's weight from Cetus. 'Someone down there might be able to help.'

'And who's going to help us if we fall?' spat Pistor.

'And what if we find what's below is just the top of something high and sheer?' groaned Cetus, not liking the idea one iota.

'We cope with that when we meet it.' Fornax sounded determined and they all knew that that meant there was little point in arguing with her. Moving Fornax with her mind set was like trying to lead a mule somewhere it didn't want to go. But Pistor wasn't giving up without a fight.

'And what if we do get down safely,' argued Pistor, 'who's to say the fire doesn't belong to bandits, or worse.'

'He's got a point, Fornax,' said Cetus, gripping with desperation to Pistor's argumentative shirt-tails.

Fornax ignored Cetus and rounded on Pistor. 'If he dies,' she said, pointing at Musca, 'we may never find this place he was leading us to, this Ohm, and I like the sound of it better than the thought of wandering the roads like homeless beggars. So if there is the slightest of chances that he really knows something I say we take that chance.' In the dark her eyes blazed like beacons.

Pistor stepped away and leant against the mountain. He supposed Fornax was right; who knows what was waiting for them along the gully path? Perhaps it just went on and on until you reached the top and then they would have to turn back again. He didn't like it, being told what to do; especially by a woman, but this wasn't any ordinary one, this was Fornax; shewolf some called her. For now he had little choice, it was a case of stand up and put up or go on alone. He had to admit he didn't much like the sound of that.

Happy she wasn't going to hear any more arguments from Pistor, not for now anyway, Fornax demanded the rope. Cetus duly obliged.

'How far down do you think it is to the bottom?' asked Equuleus, peering over the edge.

'I'd guess about thirty – forty feet, give or take,' said Fornax, securing one end of the rope to a sizable rock. She tugged on it; it appeared it would more than hold their weight when the time came.

'Forty?' said Cetus, doing a quick calculation in his head; one that didn't add up. 'But the rope's only about thirty feet long. Some of that you're tying round that rock.'

'I said thirty to forty,' said Fornax, throwing the rope's length into the darkness below.

'But –.'

'Now,' said Fornax with cold determination, stopping Cetus before he could further work himself up, 'who's first?' Cetus became quiet.

Hydrus volunteered, but Hydra was having nothing of it. He argued as he was a foot longer he would have less to drop and before anyone could say anything he was through the gap and hanging precariously above the invisible ground below. Fornax just had time to wish him good luck before he started his descent.

From below Hydra could just make out two or three faces, grey-white against the night, peering down at him. He guessed he had come maybe twenty feet or so. Seven feet later he was at the rope's end. Hydra looked down to see if he could make out anything to aim for, or anything he should equally avoid, but the night was too dark to give him any clues. He dangled for a moment then, praying to the stars, let go of the rope.

'Hydra!' shouted Fornax, as the rope went slack, 'Are you all right?'

There was for a moment, a moment filled with fear and dreaded thoughts, silence, then Hydra's triumphant voice carried up to them. 'All's fine,' he yelled, 'the drop's not too bad if you land feet first.' Above him more than a few sighs were issued, and at least one prayer was answered as the clouds thinned and starlight for the first time that night managed to break through and illuminate the ground below.

The area around Hydra was now visible and he had been lucky. To his right, the other's left, lay a lipped ravine that stood deep and dark. Dropping into this would surely be the end for the unwary traveller. To Hydra's left, the ground lay wild and equally dangerous as the right, but with formations of sharp rock jutting skyward; jagged teeth almost as tall as Hydra himself. The ground beneath Hydra's sandalled feet lay smooth, eroded perhaps by water from above, but narrow, no more than six or seven feet at its widest.

The rope now snaked its way back to the gully above, Fornax pulling it up ready to make it ready for the next descent.

'Now,' said Fornax, keeping eye contact with the obviously apprehensive Cetus, 'when the rope reaches its full length you must pull on the end to release the knot. You must be ready to drop when you do it. Do you understand?' Cetus couldn't speak so nodded. 'Ready?' said Fornax.

Ready or not Cetus knew he had no choice and allowed Fornax to lead him to the gap's edge. Below, he could see Hydra looking up. The ground looked a long way away. Cetus cautiously placed a foot on the edge and turned, gripping the rock; he then gradually climbed down until he was clinging, with all his might, to the floor of the gully. He was in the hands of the others now and slowly, bit by bit, they lowered him over the side.

The drop at the end wasn't as bad as Cetus had feared it would be, but he had landed on his bottom and wouldn't be sitting easy for a few days. Still, he had thought, it could have been worse and he was down now.

Next came Musca, Equuleus with him to release the rope. 'I'm undoing it,' he called. The rope loosened and Musca was released to waiting hands. 'Have you got him?'

A sound akin to a head striking a feather filled pillow, but the head and pillow in this case a lot bigger, drifted up followed by a laugh.

'Hydra?' said Equuleus, now hanging, ready to drop, 'is everything all right?'

'Yes,' laughed Hydra, Cetus caught him – sort of.'

Equuleus landed nimbly to find Cetus on his back with Musca stretched lengthways atop him; like two lovers in an embrace.

'Well don't just stand there grinning,' groaned Cetus, now thinking he may not be able to stand let alone sit, 'get him off me.'

As Hydra and Equuleus struggled to oblige, Hydrus landed beside them.

'Just in time, brother,' said a grinning Hydra.

When Fornax, the last to descend, dropped from the rope, Cetus and Pistor had already resumed their role as Musca's bearers, his weight distributed between them. The twins, a little ahead, stood surveying what awaited them. Equuleus greeted her.

'Hydra says the way looks fairly straightforward.'

'That's good news,' said Fornax. She knew her decision to climb down could have had dire consequences; they had been lucky. 'And all are unhurt?'

'A few scratches and bruises,' Equuleus showed her a small cut on his wrist, 'but all well otherwise.' He then grinned, 'but I don't think Cetus will be sitting comfortably for a while.'

In the distance the campfire burned brightly. All they had to do now was reach it without incident and hope the natives weren't hostile when they got there.

CHAPTER 11

'Got it!' The triumphant shout came from Lupus as he retrieved Lyra's lost spleen from the jaws of a large rat. The rat didn't go to waste. Chewing on his unexpected snack, Lupus inspected and dusted down the elusive organ. It would do, a few scratches but they would heal soon enough once back where it belonged.

'There,' said Lupus, patting Lyra on the head, 'as good as new.'

There was a bit of the old sparkle back in his eye as Lyra came to. 'What happened?' His speech was normal at least which was a good sign. It seemed the break, or several, as had been the case, had done him the world of good.

'You upset his Lord and Master again,' said Lupus, casually hooking his snack's tail from between his fangs and flicking it away.

'Oh,' said Lyra, a little of the sparkle fading.

Lyra did try to be a good imp, but he wasn't what you could call consistent. Sometimes he wanted nothing more than to curl up and die, but being immortal had its drawbacks. Sometimes he wished he was back in his old job, the one he had before the secondment to Serpens' section. He and Lupus sat down together and started to reminisce about old times.

'You know what I miss?' said Lupus.

'What?'

'A moon. Nothing better than a good old fashioned full moon,' said Lupus wistfully. Lupus loved the full moon. The way it pulled at the mind. The baying. He could howl anytime he wanted, but there was nothing like a full moon to bring out the best in him, a true blood-curdling bay that sent creatures for miles around scurrying for their lives. Above him, the clouds Fornax had worried about, were fast obscuring the millions of stars; stars but no moon. What he'd give for a quick bay at a shiny full-bodied moon.

Lyra's thinking was elsewhere. His fondest memories were of the mischief he had been responsible for when doing what he had been hatched for. As a member of the Imps Collective it was his duty and the duty of imps everywhere to cause a little chaos in an otherwise well scripted universe. The creators knew of them, they had created them just for that reason. Lyra smiled when he recalled the good old days. Moving this, hiding that, watching as someone swore that the object they were now seeking had been where they had left it. The puzzlement. The frustration. Simple, but fun times. He then remembered his own personal *pièce de résistance*. It was what got him shipped in disgrace to his present detail; what got him into the mess he was now in.

He had swum for hours with that iceberg. But it was worth it for the look on the captain's face as his "indestructible" ship – against anything but icebergs, well you'd hardly expect one where he was – was broadsided and holed. The other imps were impressed and had pressed him until he left to tell them how he had done it. But the secret went with him and to this day no one but he knew how that iceberg came to be floating two miles above a planet's surface and lying in the flight path of that ill fated interstellar cruiser.

It was to prove a step too far for Lyra. Imps were supposed to be nothing more than troublesome little creatures with a natural penchant for the merest levels of naughtiness. Lyra had overstepped the mark big time and had wandered into Fate's domain. Needless to say the creators weren't happy about it and he was put where he could be watched.

The daydreaming and reminiscing may have gone on well into the night but for Ophiuchus sounding the alarm.

'Someone comes,' he announced in the monotone speech of someone heavily subdued and controlled.

Brought abruptly back to reality, Lupus and Lyra quickly scrambled to where Ophiuchus was standing.

'Is it Draco?' said Lupus, peering into the distance but seeing nothing.

'No.'

The imp and changeling exchanged puzzled glances before scurrying into the cave. A second later they reappeared and dragged Ophiuchus in with them.

'Who do think it is?' whispered Lyra.

'Don't know,' said Lupus, 'do you think we should wake his Lordship?'

Away in the cave's interior slumped on his throne snored Serpens, his security blanket billowing with each exhaled breath.

'I think you should wake him,' said Lyra, a slight twinge in his spleen airing caution.

Lupus wasn't all that keen either, especially after the latest confrontation but, 'Master,' he whispered, moving closer but not within reach.

Serpens stirred but didn't wake; he was in the middle of a lovely dream.

Lupus was just about to chance his arm again when Ophiuchus took matters into his hands, thanks to Serpens' control. 'Sire!' hailed Ophiuchus.

On the throne Serpens turned away from the sound and muttered in his sleep. 'Thaz it,' he groaned, 'just a little higher. Use the sharp end.'

'SIRE!' Ophiuchus repeated. It had the desired effect.

Serpens' eyes flickered open. 'What? Where am I?' A dribble of saliva trickled from the corner of his mouth and dropped silently into a fold of his tutu. Then, as though introduced to an electric shock, he sat bolt upright and shouted at the top of his voice, 'I LIKE MY BUN STICKY!!'

The cave fell as silent as any run of the mill sepulchre.

It was Lupus that broke it, 'There's… er… someone coming, Master.'

Serpens rubbed his eyes and looked for all the world to be anywhere but with it.

'Master?'

'Stranger you say?' said Serpens, squinting in the general direction of whomever it was speaking.

'Yes, Sire,' said Ophiuchus.

'Stranger than what?' Serpens was still struggling with his wrench from the land of nod.

'No, Master,' said Lupus, hoping this wouldn't be seen as a contradiction, 'not stranger, *a* stranger; heading this way. Ophiuchus said.' It wouldn't hurt to pass the blame now he felt, should there be call for it later.

At last the right nerve was hit and Serpens responded with the speed of a coiled snake. He grabbed Lupus, who was a little slow off the mark, by the scruff of the neck and strode over to where his other minions were congregated. Arriving, he dropped Lupus and pulled the other two into the shadows and out of view. 'We will wait here and stay hidden until we discover what manner of creature approaches,' he said with all the air of an actor with the opening line in some amateur dramatics production.

Lupus and Lyra raised eyebrows, exchanged shrugs, then vied for a view round Serpens' legs at whatever it was that was stupid enough to be heading their way.

'Phoo-phoo. Phoo-phoo-oo.' Heralded the arrival of someone on whom the concept of whistling was sadly lost.

As Serpens and his minions watched, the owner of the dubious aural onslaught appeared at the cave entrance. All inside took a step back as a dark figure hesitated on the threshold.

'Na,' it said, 'could be bears.' The figure moved away and began foraging amongst the bushes.

'What's it doing?' whimpered Lyra who'd become wedged between the cave wall and one of Serpens' legs.

'Ssssch!' said Serpens, reaching down and squeezing Lyra's mouth shut.

The figure stopped his foraging and started to arrange what it had gathered into a neat pile. When it had finished it started to vigorously rub two sticks together. Smoke appeared then a lick of yellow flame flickered into life. As the flame multiplied and became a fire the light from it revealed the dark figure to be a gnarled old man with a fleece about his shoulders. He began to sing, badly.

'Me name is Bootes
An' I don't gives a hoots
'cause me little Lottie's dead.
Millie 'as gone Silvey too
It's all such a shame
But I still got a bit o' me Nob.'

The occupants of the cave grimaced. They'd not heard a noise like that since Creator Brown spilt hot primeval soup onto the Chief Creator's lap.

Lyra, who had lost out to Lupus in the viewing stakes, looked worried. 'Do you think he's one of those homosexuals? You know, like on that world where they all became extinct because of their goings on.'

Blank looks all round until the penny dropped. Serpens slapped Lyra hard on the back of his head, 'You mean Homo sapiens, idiot,' said Serpens, as Lyra tumbled away, 'but you're right. There was a world where the Homo sapiens became extinct, but it wasn't the fault of homosexuals; ran out of fossils or something for their fire; so the story goes.'

'I heard it's because their genes were too tight,' said Lupus.

'Whose genes?' said Lyra, disentangling his limbs from the bone pile.

'The Homo sapiens,' said Lupus.

Serpens had had enough and this time clipped Lupus smartly behind his ear. 'Quiet, the humanoid's lying down. I think he intends to sleep.'

Taking advantage of the prostrate Lupus, Lyra nipped in and pinched his place.

'Master,' he said when he got his first look at the stranger, 'I think he's one of *them*.'

Hand raised Serpens was about to give Lyra another backhander when the imp quickly elaborated.

'No Master, not one of *them*, one of those,' he pointed away to where the hole in the ground was, 'the ones that went down the hole. He's the shepherd I told you about.'

Serpens' hand dropped to his side. 'Shepherd you say?'

'Yes, Master.'

'Lupus.'

'Yes, Master?'

'Come here. I have a plan.'

Next morning Bootes was awakened by the biggest sheepdog he had ever seen.

'Wha-!' shrieked Bootes as the sheepdog's massive tongue threatened to engulf his face for the second time. 'Wha... wo... whoa.'

Lupus stepped back avoiding the old man's flailing arms.

Bootes struggled to a sitting position and wiped saliva from his eyes so he could see what was attacking him. When he did his eyeballs nearly popped from his head.

'Where did you come from boy?' said Bootes, clearly delighted. He rifled through his bag and pulled a bone from it. 'Would yer like a bit of me Nob?'

The question was innocent enough, but Lupus stepped back all the same. Homo sapiens, if that was what he was, had a history of not being trustworthy.

'Here boy, have a lick.'

'Wha-?' said Lupus, unable to stop himself in time. In the cave a large red forehead was being slapped.

'Yer spoke,' said Bootes, scrabbling backwards on his bottom.

'Woof,' said Lupus.

'Yer did. I knows yer did.'

Lupus threw a glance towards the cave. Two large red dots glowed angrily like hot embers in its depths. Serpens was watching and he wasn't pleased.

'Woof woof woof!' barked Lupus earnestly.

Still sitting, Bootes ran grubby fingers through long thin grey strands of equally grubby hair. 'Dang it,' he said, scratching at his head thoughtfully, 'mayhap it's me ol' ears playing up.'

'Woof,' agreed Lupus.

'Not as young as I was,' Bootes drivelled on. Lupus wasn't really listening; he was more concerned with what he saw from the corner of his eye. He was relieved to see the glaring red dots were fading.

'Woof,' said Lupus, his tail managing a wag.

'Well ne'er mind,' continued Bootes, ''ere boy 'ave this.' He threw a bone with a bit of gristle left on it Lupus's way.

Gingerly sniffing at Bootes' offering, Lupus wondered across to it when the scent of mutton filled his nostrils.

'Gud boy,' Bootes extolled. He had never owned a sheepdog before, well not a real one, his 'ol Da' wrapped in a blanket and making yapping noises didn't really count he supposed. He leaned across and stroked Lupus who immediately recoiled; he wasn't sure about this touching business.

'It's all right boy,' soothed Bootes, 'yer in safe 'ands now. I'll look after yer. Why yer can 'elp me find me friends so yer can.' Bootes gave Lupus an almost toothless grin.

If Lupus had been able he to would have grinned along with him, or at least smiled a relieved smile. Serpens' plan looked like working. The first part at least. Finding and capturing the monkey man might be a different kettle of fish.

'Now eat yer breakfast an' we'll be on our way.' Bootes kicked dirt on the ashes of last night's fire and wet a finger, this he held in the air. He had no idea why, but it was a family tradition of sorts. Bootes studied his finger then decided he would head back the way he had come the night before.

'An' we'd best be sharpish,' said Bootes, stuffing his blanket back in its bag. 'I don't think winter'll allow autumn much of a look in this year. At least that's wot me ol' bones tell me.' The seasons on Apomas were slightly erratic, autumn the worst, if it wasn't careful winter had a habit of nipping in uninvited before it.

A wayward winter aside, Lupus had a problem of his own, how did he get the old man moving in the right direction; to the hole? He didn't have to look to know the red dots were back and glowering at the back of his head; he could feel them.

'Woof!' said Lupus, hoping he could somehow draw the old man's attention.

'Wot's it boy, a coney?' said Bootes, looking around.

Lupus wondered where the old man got that idea from. Still, when in doubt go for the one with gout, thought Lupus. He decided he hadn't time to wonder where he dragged that up from. 'Woof,' he repeated and set off at a fair pace towards the hole. Bootes, curiosity getting the better of him, fell in behind.

It took a while, but Lupus finally managed to cajole Bootes to the rock fall and the opening in the ground beside it. It would be only a matter of time now, he thought. How wrong can you get? Bootes completely missed it, trundled past it, and now stood looking bewildered at the grounded avalanche.

'Looks like yer coney got away,' said Bootes, hands on hips trying to see if he could see the top of the rock pile.

Either the old fools' half blind or he's stick stupid, thought Lupus, tail dropping between his legs. He plumped for the latter. Perhaps he should just push the old idiot down it, he'd notice then. That wasn't part of the plan though. He had to earn the old fools' trust, blah-di-blah-di-blah, why him? But Lupus knew, the others could hardly do it, he couldn't imagine Lyra, or even Serpens trying to befriend the shepherd, the old fool would have keeled over right there and then on sight. They would have scared the living shit out of him. Lupus gauged the situation. It was time for a more direct approach he decided; push the old man to the edge, stopping short of actually tipping him into it of course. That or throw himself totally into his new shape. Lupus again decided the latter.

'Woof,' woofed Lupus, his massive paws hanging over the edge of the hole, his great fan of a tail wagging as if there were no tomorrow.

Bootes' attention was drawn. 'Wot 'ave we 'ere then boy?' Bootes got to his knees after a fashion and peered into the hole. 'Looks like an 'ole,' he said.

It was an effort, but Lupus managed to keep his tongue in check.

''Ello,' cried Bootes, craning his neck so his head all but disappeared into the opening. The similarity between the old man and Lyra was there for all to see. Lupus held back a groan.

'Woof,' Lupus encouraged; any minute now.

'Do yer know wot boy?' Bootes mused. Go on, thought Lupus, you're nearly there. 'I don't think yer coney went this way, 'oles too big.'

Praying for strength Lupus flopped to the ground and dropped his head between his paws. It was then that he saw it. A rag of some description caught just below the hole's edge. Lupus sniffed, it had a strange scent – if Lupus had had knowledge of such a substance he would have likened it to meths – but also an underlying humanoid scent, not the monkey man's but surely one belonging to one of his companions. He reached down and gripped it in his jaws. Perhaps now? But he wasn't holding his breath.

'Woof,' Lupus invited, laying the rag at Bootes' feet.

'Wot yer got there boy?' said Bootes, brushing dirt from his bony knees. 'Well I'll be,' he said taking the piece of cloth and sniffing it, 'smells like Pistor.' He peered into the hole again. 'You know wot boy, I think me friends might 'ave gone down yon 'ole.' Halleluiah! thought Lupus, sadly jumping the gun. 'But yer won't find ol' Bootes going down sum dirty creepy ol' 'ole. No siree dammit. Tell yer wot though, I can't keep calling yers boy can I?'

A dazed Lupus was only half listening.

''ow 'bout Lassie?' Bootes bent forward and peered between Lupus' hind legs. 'Nope, yer all laddie, can't call yer that, wouldn't be right now would it?' Bootes continued, oblivious to Lupus who was equally oblivious in his incredulous state. ''ow's about Shep? Naw can't use me ol' Da's name 'e'd turn in 'is grave. I know,' Bootes sidled over to Lupus' side, catching him unawares, and ruffled his hand in Lupus' deep pile fur, 'Fluffy! That's wot I'll call yer; Fluffy.'

This snapped Lupus back from wherever it was his mind had lingered. Enough was enough. Ears pricked he took a single bound to where Bootes stood, caught him full in the midriff with his big fluffy paws and sent him backside first down the hole. Lupus stood at the hole's edge to admire his handy work, down below he could hear Bootes groaning and cursing; he didn't sound too badly damaged. It was his turn now, but he paused and listened, his sharp hearing picking up something. He turned from the hole and scanned the path leading from the cave. He saw nothing but that didn't mean there was nothing there. From the hole Bootes was now calling.

'Fluffy! 'ere boy!'

Lupus took one last look at the path, it was still empty, but then he didn't expect to see anything, and then dropped to his new "master" below. As he did the noise he thought he heard earlier rang in his ears again. This time it was clearer and he swore it sounded like laughter.

CHAPTER 12

More cuts and bruises where gathered, none serious, from stones and thorns hidden by the night and ready to surprise along the way, but now they were within hearing distance of the campfire. Fornax signalled for quiet before stealthily moving forward on her belly, beside her crawled Hydra.

'Gypsies,' whispered Hydra spying a couple of wagons on the far side, one plain the other appearing, as far as he could make out in the light afforded him by the stars and fire, to be ornately decorated.

Around the fire people, silhouetted by the flames, stood or sat. To the side and luckily down breeze from them a couple of oxen and an ass were idly grazing.

'How many?' hissed Fornax, wanting to verify her own count.

Hydra's count tallied, but he pointed out that more could be in the wagons.

Doubting there would be, or if there were they would perhaps be children, Fornax decided a face on attempt to ask for help would be best called for. She had never had problems with gypsies in the past and had always found them a cautious people, but helpful when contacted direct. Skulking in the grass and spying on them was not going to earn their trust. Fornax told Hydra her plan and together they started back. But halfway there her plan hit a snag.

'Shit!' cursed Fornax as an almighty burp filled the still night air.

'Pistor or Cetus?' said Hydra.

'I don't think it matters.'

Behind them the camp had suddenly sprung to life accompanied by the glint of steel in the firelight as swords were unsheathed. 'Who's there?' demanded a male voice. 'Show yourselves murderous scum or die like the slithering cowards you are.'

There was as usual no choice, they would have to do as asked and hope for the best. Swords held above their heads for all to see Fornax and Hydra steadily rose from the long grass they were hiding in. 'We mean no harm,' said Fornax taking a step forward.'

'Hold where ye are,' ordered the same male voice, 'ye slide through the grass like snakes yet beg to mean us no harm. It sounds like the voice of a sorceress who would lull us into false trust.'

Whispering for Hydra to stay where he was, Fornax took another step forward.

'Hold I say!'

'But we are in need of medicine,' said Fornax, risking another smaller step. 'One in our party is badly injured and all we ask is for a moment of your time to see if you can help us.'

Hurriedly exchanged words drifted from the gypsy camp. Fornax thought she could hear a female talking, but she couldn't quite make out what was being said.

'Step forward then, but on yer own woman and with yer sword kept high where I can see it.' The male that spoke clearly didn't agree with what he was saying.

Slowly but surely Fornax made her way into the clearing that surrounded the campfire. What she saw there all but stopped her breathing. Her heart even skipped a beat. The male who had threatened her now stood revealed. He was Musca, but muscled. He was Musca, but bronzed. He was Musca, but rugged. He wasn't Musca, he was gorgeous. A warrior yang to her yin. She stood opened mouthed, gaping like a fool.

'Speak then woman,' he said, 'or has a cat got yer simpleton tongue?'

The brusqueness of his tone snapped Fornax back to the here and now. With it came anger, some for the man, some for the way she had felt; mostly for the way the man had made her feel. How dare he, this stranger, cause her to have such feelings; like a stupid love struck child.

The mood became dangerous; exciting, a spark, not from the fire, crackled between them. What would happen next lay with the stars and the intervention of an old woman who appeared from one of the wagons, the ornate one.

'Why am I wakened?' demanded the woman.

The man broke from Fornax's stare as one would from a dream. He put away his sword and spoke, 'It would seem we have visitors.'

The woman was old and made heavy weather of walking down the steps that led from the rear of the wagon. As she drew closer Fornax could see that she had an ancient look about her, small and shrunken, her face lined dry like a fruit left too long in the sun; the look of a wise woman. Hope for Musca rose in her breast.

'Come forward girl, let me see who wakes an old woman from her dreams,' said the old woman. Warily replacing her sword Fornax did as she was bade. The old woman studied Fornax hard with piercing blue eyes then hobbled to the fire where she stopped and rubbed her rheumy hands together against the heat 'Speak.'

Fornax looked from the old women to the handsome male and back again before answering. 'We need your help,' she said, simply.

'Yet ye creep upon us like robbers.'

'We had to see if it was safe.'

'Ye say we, how many?'

'Seven, there was eight.'

'Dead?'

'Missing.'

The old woman drew a breath, 'I believe what ye say. Call your band forward and take the ailing one to my wagon.'

'But Corvus,' objected the young man that could have been Musca but wasn't, 'we know not enough of them. They slither like snakes so why not talk like one, with two tongues?'

The old woman said nothing and dismissed his objections with a wave of her hand. 'Don't mind him,' she said to Fornax, 'Aquila has the head of a rock and the caution of a fox.'

'But,' said Aquila.

'Enough,' snapped Corvus, 'when they come make them welcome and give vittels and drink enough to fill them.'

Fornax called to Hydra, who was still standing where she left him, to fetch the rest. Cautiously they approached; a sorry bedraggled sight, until they stood in a group in the clearing before the fire.

The old woman Corvus whispered something and a young woman stepped from the shadows of the plain wagon. 'This is Columba,' Corvus introduced, 'she is deadly shy, but will tend to yer wounds and make room in the wagon for yon ailing one. She will tend him there and see what can be done.'

With Musca comfortable and tended in the wagon and appetites sated and thirsts quenched the night became late and events took a turn to talking. Fornax told their story and the gathered gypsies listened with varying degrees of surprise, belief and dismay. When she finished the old woman gave a loud sigh. The gypsies, she revealed had been on their way to Musca's village to perform and ask shelter from the coming winter.

'Where will you go now?' asked Fornax, her question for general answering but hoping the reply would come from Aquila; she had hardly been able to keep her eyes from him all evening. He didn't. Keeping the silence he had kept since their arrival in the camp.

'To the edge of the desert where the snows won't venture, then west I fancy,' said Corvus, 'ye may travel with us if yer travels take yer in that direction.' The old woman had taken a pipe of tobacco while they talked and now spat juice into the flames. Fornax chanced a quick peek in Aquila's direction, then a quicker one to see if anyone had noticed her doing so. She wouldn't want anyone to get the wrong idea. She felt safe no one appeared to have. 'As for this Ohm ye speak of,' the old woman said, her eyes suddenly bright, 'I have never heard of it, so I can't guide ye on, doesn't mean it doesn't exist o' course, but,' here she paused, 'I have heard of a special tree that is said to walk and talk, and know things, some things not of this world.' The old woman spat again into the fire; the gob landed and sizzled on a blackened branch.

'Tell me of this tree,' said Fornax, her interest in Aquila eclipsed by what the old woman had said.

But Corvus declined to say more, until morning that is. It was late and all needed rest. She pointed with her pipe to Equuleus who had curled into a ball on the ground.

'Get blankets,' said the old woman.

Dawn, though dismal, was met by the usual noisy ensemble of birds and insects happy to be alive to see another day. The gypsies, even though the talking had gone on late, were already packed and ready to move on; winter would soon be in the mountains, best be where they wanted to be before it claimed the lowlands.

Amidst the turmoil Fornax regained her waking senses and sprang to her feet her hand going to her sword.

'Fear not warrior woman, yer belongings are still with yer.' Aquila sat on a log smiling at her, his frosty stance from the previous evening somewhat thawed.

'The old woman, where is she?' demanded Fornax, failing to reciprocate in any way shape or form the man's obvious attempt at fellowship.

Aquila's expression changed and the grimness of their first meeting returned. 'She said ye would be impatient when ye woke but I have still to treat ye as a guest.' He bowed formally and gestured to the plain wagon where Musca lay. 'Corvus says yer friend needs more attention than she first thought,' Fornax looked worried prompting Aquila to drop his grimness and talk a little softer, 'but ye are not to worry, she says she will speak with ye when yon friend shows signs of improvement. Meanwhile ye and the rest of yer companions are welcome to travel with us until our paths split.'

Fornax looked past him at the wagon. The old woman was wise and it was best, she decided, that her words be heeded for now but she wanted to know more of the tree she had spoken of; she felt it could be important.

'I accept,' said Fornax now looking straight at Aquila. By the stars he was handsome. 'But I must ask about the tree she spoke of.'

The smile returned to Aquila's lips 'I would help if I could, but Corvus keeps her own council on such matters. I only know shallow rumours and these I'd be bound would hold little truth. This much I can tell ye, the road to the tree is on the way.'

This time Fornax returned his smile. After all he had only acted last night as she would have done in his place. 'Thank you,' she said, averting her gaze from his. Stars! He acts and speaks as a prince. Why did he stare at her so? She giggled inside. As if she didn't know.

'Then if I cannot help ye for now I will take my leave of ye and return to my chores.' Aquila nodded curtly and went to tend to the oxen. Fornax, her heart beating a little fast, went to rouse her companions.

The day wore on, but there was no sign of the old woman. Nor was there the next day or the next or the next after that. And each time Fornax asked to see the old woman she was told the same, "she will talk to yer when she has something to say".

Soon a week had passed by. Then, two days into a second, an hour or so after stopping to make camp for the night the old woman appeared at the wagon's door. Fornax didn't need telling, she was there as soon as the door moved a crack.

'How is he?' she asked, peering into the wagon.

'Come see for yerself,' said the old woman brightly. Her face though held grim.

Inside Formax found Musca lying calmly as if asleep in the wagon's cot.

'He is over the worst,' announced Corvus, following Fornax in, 'his delirium has left him, but I am at a loss as to when he might wake.'

Fornax gave the old woman a puzzled look.

The old woman explained the best she could. 'When he hit his head blood had thickened beneath the bone. I released the pressure and used special herbs to heal the wound but he has not recovered like I thought he might.'

'*When* he wakes –.'

'That is the problem, he should already be awake. I should have said if he wakes.'

The blood in Fornax's veins ran cold when she heard Corvus' words.

'You must be able to do more,' said Fornax, 'he's our leader; (regardless of what was thought) he's the only one who knows where Ohm is.' If it was to be admitted, Ohm had been far from anyone's thoughts the last few days as suspicion turned from tenuous friendships to something fuller amongst the gypsies and their guests; Fornax included. The old woman shook her head; it was out of her hands now.

'Here, take this.' The old woman removed something from a cupboard and gave it to Fornax.

Fornax looked at the vial of clear liquid she had been given. 'Will this help him?' she said.

'It's for ye, not him. It will steady your nerves and set ye seeing clear.'

At first Fornax objected, but with gentle persuasion she drank. The liquid had an instant warming effect relaxing her; soothing her.

'Come,' said Corvus. The old woman held out a hand and slowly led Fornax to the campfire, which was now burning and bright, where they sat.

Her mind in turmoil Fornax asked about the special tree, the walking talking one. Perhaps it could help them; help Musca? But the old woman had other ideas.

'We will talk of that later,' she said, 'but first I wish to know ye all better. Stuck in yon wagon I've not yet met with ye properly. Your name Fornax, it interests me. It is a name I am familiar with. Some time distant, way distant, I believe yer people and mine may have been kindred. Do you know where it comes from?'

'Yes,' said Fornax, the liquid she'd drunk now working its magic; relaxing her completely, 'it's from the stars.'

'Aye,' said Corvus, 'but do ye know what it means?'

'No.'

By now the campfire had become crowded; all knowing Musca's fate because of word from Columba. It was her that had ushered everyone to join Fornax and Corvus.

Cetus was intrigued. 'Do you know the meaning of mine?' he said.

The old woman chuckled. 'Aye,' she said, smiling.

'And mine?' said Equuleus, eager to hear.

'Aye, all of your names, but hold and I will reveal each in turn.'

'I asked first,' said Cetus.

'Ye name is Cetus, yes?'

'Yes.'

'Whale,' said the old woman, her smile broadening.

'What?' said Cetus, colouring at the laughter that followed and wishing he had not been so keen to ask.

'Then I did hear one back in the cave,' laughed Pistor.

'And your name laughing man?' Corvus enquired.

'Pistor,' said Pistor, who had been sober now for over a week, but obviously not as clear of head to remember his own name.

'I confess I haven't heard of this name before,' said Corvus, mystified.

'That's 'cause it isn't his name,' said Cetus, diving in quickly, hoping to take some heat from his situation, 'it's Pictor.'

'Ah,' said Corvus, 'I know of the name Pictor, it means artist.'

This revelation brought further laughter. From the gypsies because Pistor forgot his own name, from his companions because of how apt it was.

'Ha, Pistor artist,' laughed Cetus, heat he felt now well away from him.

'Whale!' taunted Pistor.

'Enough,' said Corvus, 'refresh me ye name boy?' She pointed at Equuleus with the stem of the pipe that had somehow magically appeared in her hand.

'Equuleus.'

'Little horse.'

Equuleus appeared happy with that.

'Mine's Hydra.'

'Water snake.'

'Hydrus.'

'Lesser water snake.'

Hydrus wasn't so happy but it was better than whale; to his mind anyway.

'And me?' asked Fornax, not to be left out.

'Aye,' said Corvus, 'drawing on her pipe for the first time that evening, 'the best for last. Furnace it means; one of fire. Your parents named ye well.'

Fornax felt pride at that, but she wasn't last was she? What of Musca; poor Musca. He wasn't here to ask. She decided she would ask for him and tell him when he woke. He was going to wake. 'What of Musca?' she asked, 'what does his mean?'

The old woman got to her feet as if to leave.

'Corvus?'

The old woman took a pull on her pipe. 'Tomorrow ye will leave us. The path to the talking tree is now only half a day away. I will show ye the path. He is yer way now.'

Puzzled by the old woman's sudden change Fornax also stood up. 'Is there something the matter?' she said, concerned.

'Nay,' said Corvus, lying, 'but the night grows late and I don't grow any younger.' The old woman started for her wagon, the ornate one. 'Sleep calls.'

Fornax let her walk a few steps then set after her. 'Tell me,' she said, her voice quiet, but adamant.

The old woman stopped and half turned. 'It's yon lad,' said Corvus, 'he in the wagon; his name.'

'What about it?'

'It is a jinx name.'

'What do you mean?'

'It means fly, and nothing good comes from where the fly lands. I thought it wise not to mention this before the others.'

Why she felt so she didn't know, but she was staggered. Surely it was all just a game these name ideas. Wasn't it?

The old woman shook her arm free from Fornax's hand, a hand Fornax didn't realise until then she had placed on Corvus, and continued to her wagon. Fornax didn't follow. An old woman's folly, that is all.

Aquila appeared by Fornax's side. His words were soft and soothing. 'Do not take too much heed of what the old one says,' he said, his eyes finding hers, 'but she is right that ye must seek the talking tree tomorrow. It may be yon friend's only chance.' He then took her arm and led her back to the fire. There they sat and differences cast aside sat talking into the early hours.

The morning came all too quickly as did the journey to the path that supposedly led to a walking, talking tree. Provisions, as much as the gypsies dare share, were provided along with a stretcher of strong wood and reeds for Musca to lie on. Goodbyes were exchanged, some with heavier heart than others. Some would have jumped at the chance to stay. Why look for fools' gold when…? Musca had earned a modicum of respect since they set out, but it seemed not enough for some.

Fornax for her part had fallen in love and through it she realised her mistake; her love for Musca was that of a sister for a brother, nothing more. She felt torn inside as they stepped towards the path they must now travel on, but she knew her duty was to her kinsmen.

With scarcely a look back, for fear they wouldn't leave if they did, they set off to find the talking tree and the silver cave it was supposed to live in. Aquila had come forth with that piece of information as they were leaving; "just a myth, but…" he had said.

They had travelled less than five minutes, enough time to adopt out of sight out of mind, when they discovered someone was missing. Fornax called a halt; it was Pistor. Now what's he up to? She sent Equuleus, about the only one not sick for staying so the safest option, back to find him. He didn't have to go far.

Around the next corner Equuleus bumped into Pistor struggling with a huge sack.

'What's that?' said Fornax, when they caught up.

'Insurance,' said Pistor, grinning ear to ear. He put the bag down and some of its contents spilled to the ground.

'Potatoes?' gasped Cetus, his mind already working hard as to the best way they could be used. It was close between baked and mashed.

'And they're mine,' growled Pistor, seeing the way Cetus was looking at them.

'Oh no you don't,' said Fornax, not having any of it, 'you take them back where you got them from.'

Pistor's face changed. 'But they were a gift… from Aquila. We wouldn't want to upset our new friends would we? Besides, I thought we could put them on the stretcher with Musca.'

Fornax glared at him. She knew he was lying; he'd stolen them, but time was short and Musca wasn't getting any better.

'Some of them?' Pistor pleaded.

'If you want them you carry them, but if you start slowing us down may the stars help you.'

'Not a problem,' said Pistor, a cautious smile returning to his lips.

Fornax ushered everyone to move on, but instead of joining them she stopped where she was and stole a quick glance in the direction they had come. She couldn't see the gypsies, the bend in the path obscured her view, but she imagined them trundling towards the desert, her heart going with them. Fornax then had a thought, silly for her; she realised she hadn't asked Aquila what his name meant. Perhaps one day. Fornax turned, smiled sadly, then, romantic notions locked away, hurried to catch up.

CHAPTER 13

The path that led to the walking, talking tree – if it actually existed – started at the foot of yet more mountains, their peaks disappearing into the clouds that had hung ominously in the sky for the past couple of weeks. The way this time was easier than the last path and good time was being made as it meandered gently upwards.

Fornax, thoughts of Aquila pushed aside, strode on ahead; ever vigilant; watchful for a sign of the tree creature the old woman had spoken of. In the rear struggled Pistor; his sack of potatoes now lighter by the odd spud dropped along the way. In between the others took turns carrying Musca. Fornax called a halt.

'What is it?' said Cetus, nervously scanning the way ahead.

'The clouds,' said Fornax, looking skyward, 'what do you think?'

Faces lifted to the heavens. The clouds are getting darker,' said Cetus.

'I fear winter is almost on us,' said Fornax grimly, 'and up here that means snow. We can't afford to dither; our lives may depend on it.'

'And if we don't find this miraculous tree soon?' Cetus asked.

It was a question Fornax had been waiting for. 'We'll deal with that when we're forced too.' But what then? she thought.

Onward they continued, mostly in silence, onward and upward, stopping where they could; eating with restraint their meagre rations, always on the lookout for some sign.

Two, three days they continued like this, the air getting colder the higher they climbed. The clouds growing darker, heavier; carrying a burden they wanted to share with the world. The next day things changed. Now the air itself felt heavy; thick with expectation; a metallic, almost electric taste to it. Evening drew in and a halt for the night was called.

The blankets, thin summer ones; all they had at hand, were proving less and less of a barrier to the increasingly cold wind that occasionally picked up and whirled about their heads. Equuleus shivered beneath his, his thirst for adventure slowly ebbing as thoughts of home and what he had lost finally started to haunt him.

The fire they built, mainly made from small faggots of kindling donated by the gypsies – wood was scarce, almost non-existent on the path – hardly warmed.

'How much further?' said Hydra, poking the fire to keep what there was of it alive. His voice was dull, tired. The question however sat in everyone's mind and on everyone's tongue; all listened expectantly, waiting for the answer.

'All I know is what I've been told,' said Fornax, what she possessed of patience frayed almost beyond repair, 'what I've told you all numerous times. We follow the path to its end then follow the sun from midday to its setting.'

Murmurs and grumbles came from everyone but Pistor. Pistor was looking forward to seeing this silver cave – not so much the tree, that could go hang as far as he was concerned – but the cave intrigued him; his greed. In his mind he saw a huge cavern made of the precious metal and dripping with jewels; rubies, diamonds. The thought made his mouth water. Silver, jewels and potatoes; what could be better?

When morning came no one could imagine following any sun to anywhere with the cloud so thick. Yes they could roughly guess its path, but no one had said if it was a winter sun or a summer or spring sun. How would they know if they were on the right track? How would they know if they had walked straight past it without realising? Would the walking, talking tree come forth and greet them with garlands for all to wear or would it just watch as yet more pilgrims wandered aimlessly by? What if it was only a myth?

They set off, each, apart from one; his greed carrying him forward, with a grave sense of foreboding tugging at their hearts. Pistor smiled as he hauled his sack onto his back. Potatoes, jewels and silver. The thought gave him strength as he tagged on behind.

The days that followed grew harder as the higher they travelled, the colder it became; the nights even harder. The faggots were now exhausted and what little warmth they found at night came from huddling close. The clouds above a seamless grey blanket filling the sky; a winter blanket ready to cover the world.

Now wrapped in their own blankets during the day their steps slowed to a tired plod, only Equuleus still possessed a modicum of spring in his step; the day a relief to him, a break from maudlin thoughts. Thus it was Equuleus, walking on ahead despite warnings that it might not be safe, that discovered the track's end.

'Fornax,' squealed Equuleus, running for all he was worth, 'Fornax!'

Fornax drew her sword as Equuleus came running, sure her cautions had borne fruit and some ogre now chased the boy. When he reached her he could hardly speak.

Ready for whatever monster it was chasing him, Fornax grabbed Equuleus by the arm. 'What is it?' she said, knuckles white.

'It's – it's...' was all Equuleus could utter as the cold air, now bitter, grabbed at his tongue.

'For the stars sake spit it out,' snarled Pistor, 'what have you seen.'

'It's – it's the end!' Equuleus finally managed to blurt.

Hearing this Pistor dropped his precious sack and started to yell at the top of his voice, 'I knew it! I just knew it!' He kicked at a spilled spud with as much venom as he could muster, 'I knew we'd end up dead or worse following that useless skinny fool.' Pistor waved a hand towards Musca, 'and you're all as bad. Taking advice from a wizened old crone with all the wits of a toothless bab. A walking, talking tree, my backside!' Despite his raving he still held out hope for a silver cave.

Fornax ignored Pistor's tirade and lowering her sword spoke quietly to Equuleus, trying to calm him, 'What do you mean, end?'

'The end,' Equuleus repeated. He now looked at the others as if they were stupid. 'The end of the track!' he said, laughing.

Comprehension dawned.

'How far?'

'Not far,' grinned Equuleus, wriggling free from Fornax's grip, 'come on.'

There appeared a renewed spring in the step as the dour pace of earlier now quickened at the thought that an end to their quest at last beckoned.

'Nothing good will come of it,' grumbled Pistor, calling after the others as if he didn't give a toss while retrieving the spud he had kicked. The beating of his heart if heard would have told another story though. Pistor picked up his spud and saw when he stood up his grumbling had fallen on deaf ears. The others had already disappeared around the bend ahead. He sneered after them and grumbled under his breath. He had plans and they didn't involve a skinny no good kid and his loser friends. Pistor hefted his sack onto his back and followed at his own pace.

The end of the path levelled out and opened up onto what could be best described as a huge black shiny elliptical bowl; its edges almost polished as if glazed by some great heat; its length indeterminable merging as it did with the arriving dusk. Left and right two narrow tracks the width of a man skirted its edge, the right one ending abruptly some eighty or ninety paces distant against a dead end of rock, the left disappearing into the distance.

'It's almost as big as the valley,' gasped Hydrus, when he got his first sight of it.

'And deep as a lake,' said his brother.

'What do you think made it?' said Equuleus, venturing near its edge.

Swift as a snake Fornax grabbed his arm and pulled him back. 'I don't know,' she said, her eyes exploring the glassiness of the hole's sides; she didn't fancy the look of it, 'but I think it best not to go too close.' Fornax particularly didn't like the look of the white objects lying at its bottom. She also wondered why it *wasn't* a lake. With all the rain that had fallen recently they should have been able to swim across. She shivered, the place felt unnatural.

Equuleus went to heed Fornax's advice, but at that moment Pistor arrived, his sack of potatoes his main concern so giving no notice to how short the distance from the end of the path to the crater. He bumped into Equuleus who was stepping back.

For a brief second Equuleus teetered precariously on its edge. If Fornax had still held his arm he wouldn't have fallen, but she had released her grip as Pistor appeared. Equuleus lost his fight against gravity and fell screaming into the crater's depths.

Fearing the worst Fornax carefully peered over and called his name. She could see him below, amongst the white things; he wasn't moving. Cetus called. This time there came a response.

Stunned but unhurt, the fall had turned into more of a slide when he hit the crater's side, Equuleus shifted his weight until he could see Fornax looking down at him. 'I'm all right, I think.' Equuleus ached but nothing felt particularly bad. Gingerly he picked himself up.

'Do you think you can climb up?' shouted Fornax, thinking she already knew the answer.

Carefully stepping over the – he now knew what the white things were – bones once belonging to a multitude of unlucky creatures, Equuleus tried to climb. But, as Fornax had guessed, it was useless; the sides of the crater were like glass.

'No,' Equuleus confirmed.

Fornax had an idea. She told the others to hand her their blankets and began tying them together. She hoped they would be long enough to reach, but she wasn't confident. Although she didn't think as Hydra had that it was as deep as a lake, not ones she knew of, but it was certainly deeper than a good sized village pond. Finished she threw the knotted blankets over the edge. Below, Equuleus prepared to catch hold.

'Can you reach it?'

Equuleus tried, but the blankets lay some twelve feet above him.

'What about standing on those white things?' suggested Hydra, joining Fornax at the edge.

'They're bones,' shouted Equuleus.

Hydra shot Fornax a worried glance.

110

'It's all right,' assured Fornax, 'they won't bite.'

This didn't instil the greatest of confidence in Equuleus, especially when he found what he was sure was a human rib cage, but he began to gather a pile together. It was still short though when he had finished and to make it worse when he climbed on the pile it crumbled beneath his weight.

'It's no good,' shouted a despondent Equuleus, 'the bones keep breaking.'

Up above Fornax had another idea; if Equuleus couldn't come to them then one of them would have to go to him. 'Equuleus?'

'Yes?'

'Is your blanket in one piece?' He shouted that it was. So far so good. Fornax then told Hydra of her plan.

'Will it work?' said Hydra when she finished.

'As long as you don't fall off the end.'

'I'll try not to, but you hold on tight up here, I don't want to join Equuleus at the bottom.'

'I'm sure we'll manage,' said Fornax. Hydra smiled grimly and swung his legs over the crater's edge. Behind him, Fornax, Cetus and his brother prepared to take the strain. Pistor had done enough for one day.

The idea Fornax had come up with had Hydra climbing to the bottom of the blankets where hopefully Equuleus would be able to throw him his blanket. Hydra would then attach it to the end of the rest. Once tied Hydra would climb down it and become the final link; hopefully holding on as Equuleus clambered up and over him. It was dangerous, but their only hope.

At the second attempt Equuleus managed to grab Hydra's feet, but a twinge in his right arm told him he wouldn't be climbing anywhere. 'I think I've pulled a muscle in my arm,' he shouted, 'I won't be able to climb with it.'

There was no panic from above. Fornax told him to hold tight and they would pull them up. Pistor was called upon and together the four of them heaved on the makeshift rope.

It was hard work, but they managed it and Equuleus, a little frightened, but none the worse for the experience, apart from a pulled muscle that is, now lay on the path getting his breath back.

'What now?' said Pistor, spending little time retrieving his blanket, 'I'd guess it's way past midday.'

The sky was darkening above them. Late afternoon perhaps? Either way they couldn't go on. The only clue they had as to what to do next was what the old woman had told them; follow the midday sun to its setting. Fornax calculated the distance somewhere between fifteen to thirty-five miles (six to twelve hours give or take if all went well) yet to travel. It was argued that if that was the case they didn't need to wait for the noon sun; not that they could see it anyway. It was all hit or miss so sooner better than later. Ordinarily Fornax would have been the first to agree, but argued that perhaps there was some reason they had to travel at that time? In the end it was decided to wait until morning and decide then..

Yesterday they had been met by a greying blanket of a sky; today part of that blanket was falling gently around them. The first of the winter snow was introducing itself. Soft, gentle and sparse; soon it would be coming thick as sheep wool.

'I said it before and I'll say it again, what now?' said Pistor, wrapping his blanket tighter.

The man was a pain and Fornax would gladly leave him behind given an excuse, but he was right, a decision had to be made. Fornax stood up and shook her blanket; it had started to snow before anyone had woken. There would be no sun so what was the point of waiting for noon? There could be a reason for waiting, but a better one for going was falling from the sky. To stay where they were could be suicide. The path along the crater was narrow, it wouldn't take long for it to become impassable. One choice then, or was that no choice? Time to move and hope for the best. It wasn't ideal, but what was?

'We move on, Pistor. Gather your sack and follow, but remember this, if you lag behind don't expect us to come looking for you.'

Pistor grunted something no one could make out and picked up his sack.

As expected the weather worsened, but luckily not as badly as it could have. The path remained clear; little of the snow settling enough to stay. On they marched. To their left, sheer rock, to their right the crater continued; no longer a bowl, but a giant meandering ravine. Equuleus cautiously leading, a lesson learned, behind him Fornax and Hydrus taking their turn with Musca then Cetus, Hydra and finally Pistor. Pistor managing to stay with them; he didn't want to miss anything should they happen on the silver cave.

Five hours later winter decided it had had enough of dallying. An icy bitter wind picked up from nowhere and the snow that had been teasing in varying degrees, threatening heavy and then thinning to almost nothing, suddenly turned into a full blown blizzard. Underfoot the snow began to pack quickly making movement more and more difficult. An hour later they were in deep trouble.

Taking her turn carrying Musca, Fornax tried desperately to keep the snow from covering his face, ahead of her at the other end of the stretcher Hydrus, tired and near frozen to the bone, was struggling to keep his feet. Things were looking bleak. And all the time they could sense the crater beside them; inviting them to stumble, to join and become as one with the piles of white upon white at its bottom. Then the worst happened. Hydrus, his legs knee deep in freezing snow, discovered they no longer obeyed his wishes. He pitched forward unable to stop himself and crashed face first to the ground taking the stretcher with him. Musca slipped feet first from it, landing on top of him. Behind them Fornax shuddered to a stop her weight snapping one of the wooden support rails.

'Help me!' screamed Fornax, trying desperately to pull Musca away and free Hydrus.

Cetus appeared by her side, a living snowman. With what strength he could muster he hauled Musca from the stretcher and dragged him free. Hydrus didn't move.

'We can't go on,' yelled Cetus, trying to be heard above the thunder of the wind.

'We've got to try.' Fornax reached for Hydrus, but found her hands too numb to hold him. 'Help me.'

'It's no good Fornax, I've got to rest.' Cetus felt suddenly weak. The exertion of lifting Musca had taken the last of his strength. He also felt very, very tired. 'If I can just sit for just a moment or two I'll be all right.' Cetus leaned back against the rock face, Musca beside him. 'A couple of minutes rest and I'll be as right as rain.'

'You can't.' Fornax went to shake him, but again her hands let her down; all feeling had completely left them. She needed help. Fornax turned, the full force of the storm blowing in her face, stinging her, the cold burning her eyes. But there was no one else. She knelt beside Hydrus and tried to wake him. As she did she heard a voice. She couldn't see anyone, then realised the voice was in her head. It was telling her that resting might not be a bad thing after all. That if she did sleep all would be well in the morning. Fornax tried to argue but in vain, the voice was persuasive, too persuasive. Perhaps resting wouldn't be that bad. Fornax reached for Musca's blanket and pulled it about her. Her eyelids flickered for a few moments then closed. Rest now, said the voice, tomorrow will bring a better day.

As Fornax slipped into unconsciousness she didn't know that one of them was still pushing on. Hydra was oblivious that he was now the only one moving; he had left an exhausted Equuleus to wait for the others and knew nothing of their fates Pistor having been the first to succumb to the weather moments before Hydrus had collapsed. Hydra struggled on. But for how much further was the question?

Half blinded by the snow, all but completely numb from the cold, Hydra finally dropped to his knees unable to travel further. It had been a miracle he had got as far as he had. Kneeling there eyes barely open something caught his attention. Hydra tried to blink away the snow so he could see more clearly. There was something there; he was sure, moving towards him. Hydra tried to call out, but the words stayed in his throat. He had to get their attention. Hydra tried to get to his feet, but his legs were having none of it. His eyelids grew heavy, too heavy to keep open. He tried. The shape was closer. It couldn't be, could it? No it wasn't, his mind decided. The walking, talking tree was nothing but an old woman's fancy. No… it was just his mother; coming to say goodnight.

CHAPTER 14

'Well Fluffy, me boy, I jest don't know,' said Bootes, scratching his head. The trail had ended abruptly and Bootes was a puzzled man. Adding to his woes daylight was fast fading. 'There's only one way to go on this track and that's up,' he muttered, 'unless they 'as started walking backwards.'

This train of thought seemed perfectly feasible until he realised they would have had to have passed him at some time. He thought hard about this for a minute: nope, he couldn't recall it happening.

Bootes squatted on his haunches and inspected the footprints. He had always prided himself on being "one darn fine tracker" but this time he had to admit he was stumped. Nothing he could do about it now though. Best wait for morning and try and pick the trail up again then.

It didn't take long for Bootes to visit the land of Nod and he was soon happily snoring away beneath his blanket. Beside him Lupus aka Fluffy flipped open an eye as soon as it started. He edged closer and sniffed at the old man; something he wouldn't recommend even to his worst enemy. Trying desperately not to gag, but happy he was well and truly out for the count, Lupus carefully got to his massive shaggy paws and tiptoed quietly away.

When he felt he was far enough away from the old man Lupus whispered into the darkness, 'Lyra?' Lyra was supposed to follow and make contact when it was prudent to do so. Lupus just hoped Serpens had got it through the imp's thick head that being prudent had nothing to do with certain strained fruit. 'Lyra?' he repeated. Where was the idiot?

Lupus moved further down the slope sniffing and investigating each shadowy niche he came across.

'Lupus.'

At last, thought Lupus, looking around, 'Where are you?'

'Up here,' came a reply from on high.

When Lupus looked up he was astonished to find Lyra casually hovering in the air some six feet above him.

'How are you doing that?' asked the mystified "canine".

'Serpens did it,' Lyra explained, as he gently came in to land. 'And that's not all,' said Lyra bowing, 'I can think cleverly too.'

Lupus frowned at the grotesque face smiling up at him. Lyra flying, he could just about cope with, but Lyra with intelligence? That was going to take some getting used to. If Serpens had indeed pulled that one off he truly was someone to fear. Lupus looked closer. There was something different about Lyra and he didn't mean the inane smiling look on the imp's face. Some things couldn't change. On closer inspection Lupus discovered what it was that was different with Lyra; he appeared to have something hanging from his nether regions. A tail, but he had a tail; a short stubby one. This was another, longer and had ribbons tied at intervals along it.

'What's that?' said Lupus, trying not to sniff it. Did dogs have to sniff at everything?

Gathering it in his stubby little hands Lyra proudly announced that it was his new improved tail cum communication link.

'How long is it?' asked Lupus, sniffing at it and following it back until it disappeared up up and away into the cloudy night sky. They did have to sniff at everything it seemed.

'Master says it's infinite,' Lyra informed proudly.

'How does it work?'

'That's easy. If you were *a* intellectual like me you would understand, but I'll try to explain the best I can in layman's terms.' Lupus decided he didn't like the new improved Lyra very much. 'If I have an important message for the Master I concentrate,' Lyra pulled a strange face, 'rise into the air,' he didn't, it was only a demonstration, 'and pull on it.'

'Pull on it?'

'Yes, like this.'

Before Lupus could stop him Lyra gave his new tail a sharp tug.

'Seeeeeeeee!!!' screamed Lyra as he careered at breathtaking speed up the mountain side and into the night.

Lupus was alone again and apart from the odd muffled scream in the distance as Lyra hit the odd immovable object all was quiet again. Obviously the kite idea still had a couple kinks that needed ironing out and Lupus was sure that Lyra would be when Serpens got hold of him. If dogs could smile this one was literally grinning.

Padding quietly back to where Bootes slept he stopped to check it was a deep one. Satisfied the old man would sleep through a planet quake, Lupus trotted over to the gap in the gully wall. The rope the monkey man's friends had used to climb down was still there swaying slightly in a breeze somewhere below. They weren't far ahead, maybe a day or so. He turned when Bootes let out a *pardon me* beneath his blanket. It wasn't going to be easy. The old fool would be hard pressed to find his own belly button. He was going to need more help. With that in mind Lupus changed form into that of a large monkey and clambered down the rope. Better to do it now than attempting it in dog form tomorrow. Once down he changed back and curled up on the ground to wait for morning.

'Fluffy!' shouted Bootes, 'where is yer boy?'

Down below Lupus flicked open an eyelid. It was morning; time to get going. 'Woof!' he said.

Up above a confused Bootes scratched his head and rubbed his chin. He could hear him, but he couldn't see him. Several barks later Bootes happened on the gap and rope.

'How'd yer get down there?' said the bewildered *numero uno* tracker. He was looking at the rope. Did dogs climb? Hang about, I recognise this rope. It's valley's rope. The others must have come this way. Darn I'm good. Quickly gathering his meagre belongings together an excited Bootes prepared to get back on track. 'Watch out below!' he shouted, throwing his belongings down. His spindly legs followed them over the gap's edge. He sat there a moment staring down at Lupus. 'See boy,' he said, grinning, 'alls it needed wuz a good night's sleep to rediscover me

117

ol' tracking skills.' Lupus rolled his eyes in exasperation. The old man was unbelievable.

Somehow Bootes managed to descend the rope – crippled crab had come to Lupus' mind – and now stood surveying the options. 'Wot yer think boy?' said Bootes, wetting his finger and holding it up. When this proved as useless as he was Bootes thought it a good idea to close his eyes and spin round three times. Lupus only just saved him from dropping into the ravine.

'That way it is then,' said Bootes, at last pointing in the right direction.

Lupus barked a sigh of relief and fell in behind as Bootes ambled forward, happy for the old man to lead, but ready to administer the occasional nudge in the right direction when necessary.

Mid afternoon and the odd deviation later Bootes and his faithful dreaded minion of darkness, Fluffy, stood inspecting the remains of the gypsy camp Fornax had seen from the gap and the wagon tracks leading away from it. Lupus had a good sniff about, as was his want in the current guise, and came up smiling; he'd found a good length of stale but edible sausage lying discarded by a wheel rut.

'Wot yer got boy?' said Bootes coming over, 'dinner eh? Think I'll join yer.' Bootes sat on a handy rock, removed his pack and took out a rather sorry looking piece of Nob. 'Winter'll be early, I can feel it in me bones,' he suddenly announced to no one in particular in between mouthfuls of gristle, 'wouldn't wannerbe in the mountains when it comes.'

Swallowing the last piece of his sausage, Lupus gave the sky a thoughtful look. The idea didn't sound all that good to him either. But he had a feeling in his bones; call it intuition, that that was where they would be headed. Lupus licked his lips and gave the old man the old up and down once over. And when they got there, there was the question of food. Serpens would be far from ecstatic if he found out one of his minions had eaten the only link to the monkey man. The old man didn't look as if he had much meat on him; Lupus imagined it would be tough and stringy if he did. Then again, if he was that hungry, who knows? A frail old man climbing mountains could have an accident. Serpens couldn't blame him for that. He'd be suspicious, but he wouldn't be able to prove anything. Lupus was absentmindedly licking his lips again when Bootes' voice snapped him from his daydreaming.

'Cum on Fluff,' said Bootes, checking to see if he had managed to get every last scrap of marrow from the bone, 'best we be making tracks. I got friends to find.' He aimed a playful kick in Lupus' direction, hitched his pack and started to wander away from the direction the wagon tracks led. Lupus huffed, got up and with a little persuasion coaxed Bootes the way of the wagons.

The next few days were exhausting. Each passing day the old man would grow slower. Each night Lupus would gently grab the sleeping Bootes by his collar and drag him along to make up for lost time. The old man was right; winter was coming and Lupus didn't want to be in the mountains when the snows hit.

When they finally arrived at the final campsite Bootes' friends and the gypsies had shared, Lupus took the chance to collapse in an exhausted heap.

'Look 'ere,' said Bootes, checking the ashes. Whether he knew why he was doing it was neither here nor there. 'Looks like they stopped 'ere and moved on again,' he cleverly concluded. 'I think they went this way.' Totally ignoring the six sets of footprints heading away to the mountains he started to follow the wagon tracks again.

Here we go again, thought Lupus peering at Bootes from between his paws. But enough was enough. He wanted to rest. As far as he could make out they had made, no thanks to the old man, good and steady progress since the climb from the gulley. Lupus rolled onto his side and stayed put.

Bootes had gone on twenty or so steps before he realised his best friend wasn't with him. He turned and placed hands on hips. 'Tired eh boy?' said Bootes; what with the ashes he was on a roll, 'You should get yer 'ead down more like I do.' He didn't hear the heavy groan Lupus released. 'But maybe yer right; mayhap we'll make camp and move on the morrow. Figure we've made good time.'

Fluffy wagged his tail happily. *Lupus* wondered what the hell was going on with that part of his body.

119

A couple of hours later Bootes had a good fire going and was rummaging in his pack again. ''ere boy,' he said, tossing a bone to Lupus. Lupus sniffed it. There was nothing there; apart from bone that is. The old man had sucked it dry. Bootes took another bone from his bag and started to gnaw on it. From where Lupus was lying it didn't look any better.

He would have to do something or the old idiot would starve. There followed a brief double take as Lupus played what he had just thought through his mind again. What the hell was he thinking? What did it matter to him if the old fool keeled over? This was worrying. Nevertheless Lupus raised his aching body from the ground and prepared to go hunting. Why? It was the right thing to do under the circumstances; that's why. Console yourself with that if you want Fluffy, thought Lupus, but he wasn't so sure. As he bounded from the camp before the old man could object Lupus thought he might ask Lyra what he thought was going on; sad times. Half an hour later he returned with a couple of good sized coney in his jaws.

The old man was over the stars when Lupus returned and it wasn't long before a full tummy, old age and a bone warming fire took its toll, Bootes wrapped tightly in his blanket slipped into a deep and contented sleep.

A couple of feet away a wide awake Lupus, waiting for the first noisy snore of the night from Bootes, was wondering how long he had before the darkening clouds made his tracking a nigh impossible task. Snow would hinder them if not stop them completely. Perhaps Serpens would be thwarted in his scheming if the monkey man was caught out in the open in the mountains. Not much could survive up there.

The first snore duly arrived, announcing it would need a thunder clap somewhere in the vicinity of the old man's ear to awaken him, and Lupus knew he could leave camp undiscovered. He needed to speak to Lyra. Lupus trotted back the way they came, he hadn't seen the imp since the gulley, but he sensed he would be lurking somewhere close by.

He found Lyra sitting on a rock looking extremely sorry for himself. 'What's wrong with you?' asked Lupus.

Lyra held up his left arm; it was handless.

'Serpens?' It was a stupid question.

'He said it would make me think twice before jerking too soon,' said Lyra, 'he said I should only tug when necessary.'

It wasn't a laughing matter, but all the same Lupus found it hard to stifle the smile that wanted to spread across his snout.

'So what do you want?' said the little imp, his lower lip sticking out, 'something to report?'

'Not as such. I want to pick your brains.' There he had said it.

Lyra instantly brightened up. In all his miserable little life he had never expected to hear those words – except perhaps from an over-eager carrion crow. Maybe Serpens wasn't such a bad guy. Lyra went to wipe away a small tear that had appeared at the corner of one eye. He tried again with his remaining hand. Maybe?

'What can I do for you?' said Lyra, furrowing his brow. If he possessed a pipe he would be filling it.

'It's… I've…'

'Spit it out man,' said Lyra, the pensive look he was trying to achieve somewhat let down by his wobbling eyes.

He hated to do this, but, 'I've got feelings,' said Lupus reluctantly, grimacing.

Lyra nearly fell off of the rock. 'For me?' he said, steadying.

Lupus looked aghast. 'What? No… I mean not that your not…' What was he going on about? 'The old man.'

Only slightly crestfallen; story of his life, Lyra did his best. 'Ahem… Love; what is love.'

'Not love you idiot,' snapped Lupus, horrified, 'I feel sorry for him. I got dinner.'

'And?'

'And what?

'And how did you feel when you took him to dinner?'

'I didn't take him. I got a couple of coney.'

'Ah.'

'What do you mean, ah?' Lupus didn't like the sound of this.

'I believe you might have feelings for him.' Lyra was now holding a make believe pipe and chewing on its stem.

Why had he bothered? 'That's what I said,' said Lupus, 'I've got feelings. What do I do? I mean how do I handle it? What the hell's happening to me? He's a humanoid.'

Taking a good long look at his non-existent pipe, stump on hip, Lyra gave Lupus' problem a serious looking moment's thought then, 'Beats me,' he said, sticking the non-existent pipe back in his mouth. 'Got any messages for the big man?'

'Who?'

'Serpens. Got anything for me to tell him?'

Lupus shrugged his shoulders. 'Tell him we're on the monkey man's track but we may have a problem with the weather.' Lyra had been no help at all, he would have to sort out his own problems; he daren't tell Serpens.

'We're?' said Lyra, giving Lupus a funny look.

'I mean *I'm* getting closer,' said Lupus, and as an afterthought, 'you won't tell Serpens about what I told you, will you?'

'Any of it?'

'You can tell him about the monkey man bit.' Obviously, thought Lupus, the shelf life where Lyra's enhanced intelligence was concerned was a short one; probably had to be topped up from time to time

'Okey-dokey,' said Lyra tapping his non-existent pipe on the rock where he was sitting, 'I'll be off then. See yer later allegory.' Lyra tugged on his tail; the new one.

Wincing, Lupus could hardly watch as Lyra, forgetting to hover, skidded across the ground at great speed, tore through a nasty looking blackthorn, crunched into and bounced from vicious looking rocks and finally soared into the night sky and away. Perhaps he should have that tail looked at, thought Lupus, seems a tad too long. Maybe someone should tell him. Lupus padded back to where the old man lay, still snoring heartily.

Next morning they set off following Musca's trail into the mountains. Bootes had his blanket pulled tightly round his neck. The day had started cold and with the clouds the way they were, hanging low and dark, it was doubtful it would be getting much warmer.

Lupus sniffed at the air; snow was on the way. There was little he could do about that. He just hoped he would find what he was looking for before that happened. The chance though looked as bleak as the weather.

A day and a half later the cold and tiredness were starting to take its toll on Bootes. Lupus sensing the old man's distress tried to gently edge him on. 'It's no gud boy,' whispered Bootes, 'I gotta sit down.'

Not long ago Lupus had eyed the old man as nothing more than nourishment should the situation be presented. Now though, he was concerned and thought he now knew why; apart from the Chief Creator only this wretched creature had shown any sort of kindness towards him. And perhaps it was just a dog thing. Why, at times he had even wanted to lick the old man; self preservation of the tongue had dissuaded him against doing so.

'I gotta rest.' Bootes sounded tired and drawn.

Lupus had an overwhelming urge to speak words of encouragement but commonsense and the thought of Serpens' wrath stilled his tongue.

As Bootes slumped to the ground his old pigeon chest raising and falling in wheezy rasps the first snowflake drifted past his head unnoticed and landed at Lupus' paws. Lupus started to bark. They couldn't stay where they were it was too open. The snow started to fall with more purpose, but Bootes just sat there, eyes closed oblivious to it; to Lupus' warning.

Lupus decided to take his life in his hands and licked the old man across the face. Still no response. Lupus tried again, but realised it was no good the old man had slipped into a deep sleep.

The snow now came thick and fast and Lupus knew he would have to do something quickly or the old man would surely die. He started to change shape; Lupus the dog becoming Lupus the man. He would have preferred the shape of an ogre, bigger, but if the old man were to wake; better this way. Lupus wrapped the old man tightly in the blanket and threw him over his shoulder.

As the path wound higher the snow grew thicker and the wind increasingly bitter. No mortal man could have walked naked and endured what nature was throwing at Lupus, but he kept doggedly on even though the snow was building past his knees and all around him the world was a swirling white canvas. But Lupus knew he couldn't go on much longer, not if the ragged bundle he was carrying was going to live.

Snow now waist deep, the way ahead impassable in the form he had adopted, Lupus decided he would have to try something drastic or the old man would surely perish, but what? Lupus collapsed against the rock wall and racked his brains.

The first thought that sprang to mind told him to leave the old man and head back to Serpens or contact Lyra; he was bound to be somewhere close; they didn't really need the old man. But that was the old Lupus. He had to admit that he was different somehow. Something inside of him had changed. The old man didn't deserve to die like this. If he hadn't pulled the old man during the night he wouldn't be here, he would still be on the grasslands. Even the old man wouldn't have been so stupid as to venture further when he saw that the mountain tops were turning white. No, he had to do something; change.

Lupus laid Bootes on the snow and started to do just that. His body grew larger, thinner, stretching until he was near transparent. It folded in on itself, meeting, engulfing Bootes until Bootes was the equivalent of a yolk in an egg the size of a horse. There he nestled as the snow deepened and slowly buried the egg. Gradually his breathing returned to normal; the snow and Lupus insulating him from the cold. Lupus, satisfied his plan would work, sent a small hollow tendril skyward, its job twofold; supply just enough air for Bootes to survive in his present condition; Lupus didn't want him waking until he was ready, and to give him the heads up when it was safe to move on.

As Lupus congratulated himself on a job well done a small figure, hovering unseen amongst the falling snow, watched. He watched until the egg was all but covered then tugged on his new tail and was gone.

CHAPTER 15

'Mother?' whispered Hydra, as he came round. He reached out, but stopped short of touching the blurred image standing beside him. It wasn't his mother. 'Who?' He attempted to reach again, but his strength failed him.

The reply was thick, as if its owner had a heavy cold. It told Hydra to be still and save what strength he had. Hydra lay back, confused. He then remembered the others.

'What of the others?' he asked anxiously.

The image didn't reply immediately but hurried away returning seconds later with something in its hands. 'They are fine,' the image said taking Hydra's arm. Hydra felt a momentary coldness pressing against him just above the elbow, this was succeeded by a spreading warmth. 'Now sleep.'

But Hydra didn't want to sleep. He wanted to know about the others; where he was? What was...? His eyelids grew suddenly heavy. Who was...? The sedative he had been given took effect; Hydra slept.

Once Hydra was comfortable the anonymous administrator of drugs scurried away, muttering to itself, wobbling from side to side akin to a robot propelled by buckled wheels. It then left the room to attend to more pressing matters.

Some considerable time later, six sedated bodies awoke simultaneously to a wondrous, but puzzling sight.

The room in which they lay dazzled in a profusion of silvers. Silver beds, sheets, blankets, walls, ceiling and floor. Even the light that emanated from numerous tiny stars set in the ceiling shimmered and shone with an easy gentle silverness.

Equuleus was the first to fully regain his wits. 'Where are we?' he gasped, senses reeling. He looked from the others to his hands; everyone's skin had a silver sheen. 'We're silver!' he exclaimed.

He lifted the blanket that covered him and took a peek below. 'No we're not,' said Equuleus, a little disappointed. Beneath the blanket, which had a dull grey underside, he could see his legs were still a dull old pink. Second to fully recover was Fornax who leapt from her bed, as all good warriors do, to search, in vain, for her sword. All of their belongings it seemed were gone. Even the clothes they had been wearing, as Equuleus testified to his dismay. 'I'm wearing a frock!' he observed.

By now all in the room had a fair idea things had changed dramatically since last they had been conscious.

'I don't like this,' muttered Pistor, looking under his bed for his drink, 'they pinch an honest man's drink and potatoes, then they have you wearing a dress.' There was something else wrong too; apart from him thinking he was honest that was; Pistor could sense it, but couldn't quite put his finger on what it was. It would be a while yet before he recognised his own sobriety.

'They?' said Fornax.

'Whoever?' shrugged Pistor, slipping from his bed.

The amazement at their surroundings and to their whereabouts and howabouts masked the single most obvious thing; one of their number was missing from the merry reunion of the conscious. Cetus, wondering amidst all this wonderment when he might be able to partake of his next meal, discovered the lack when he decided to whisper to Musca to ask his thoughts on his comestible quandary. 'Where's Musca?' he said. It wasn't panic but more on the lines of low key alarm that ensued.

All but one were now up and off their beds.

'We have to find a way out of here,' said Fornax, searching the silver walls for a means of escape. She was joined by all but Pistor who remained seated, but apart from small portholes dotted along its length the walls were smooth and seamless and gave no indication that a doorway existed. Equuleus tried to peer through the portholes but they were covered on the outside by a white curtain of snow. After a while of fruitless toing and froing, Fornax stopped and slumped dejectedly on the nearest bed at hand. She knew what was expected of her when faced by an enemy, but this was beyond her. The place was a devilment. Grim thoughts pervaded her mind. What if they were the prisoners of some evil warlock? Musca could this very moment be someplace near, fearing for his life; their turn next. Worse; he could have been left for dead, frozen beneath snow and ice. Or perhaps he had survived and they were dead; this place she sat in, the afterlife amongst the stars. Fornax stood up, sat back down again. Whatever, there wasn't much it seemed she could do about it, except wait that is, for whatever to appear; she felt sure in her bones something or someone would.

'What do we do?' said Equuleus, still looking for a way out.

'We wait,' said Fornax grimly.

'For what?' said Pistor, making his presence felt and as usual in the negative.

Fornax glared at him, but any further discourse between the two was brought to an abrupt halt as a disembodied voice sounding thick with nasal congestion echoed throughout the room.

'Tidings,' said the voice, and after a brief pause punctuated by the odd um, it continued, 'welcome to my humble abode.'

Like a cat falling on its prey, Fornax leapt to where she felt the voice had emanated, demanding to know what was going on.

The voice remained silent until Fornax had finished, then continued as if nothing had occurred. 'And now if you would be so kind as to form an orderly queue, please follow the green footprints to my private chambers where I will be pleased to meet you in person. Thank you.' The voice cut off as abruptly as it had arrived. Then as if by magic a gap appeared in the wall not far from where Fornax was pressed against it.

First instincts told them it was a trap, but after cautiously peeping through the gap for any nasty surprises that may be waiting for them and seeing none, obvious ones at any rate, Fornax tentatively led the way through. Beyond the gap was a long silver corridor, walls and lighting the same as the room they had just left, on the floor three sets of footprints; one set blue, one red and the green set they had been told to follow. With a deep sense of trepidation gnawing at each of them they set off along the corridor until they came to a junction with similar corridors leading away left and right. The green prints carried straight on, the blue and red ones going off left and right respectively.

A halt was called by Fornax. 'I think we should split up,' she whispered giving the new corridors suspicious glances.

Pistor didn't agree. 'You heard the voice,' he remonstrated, 'follow the green prints it said.'

'I know what it said,' said Fornax, turning on Pistor, 'but if it's a trap who is going to find Musca? He's the only one that knows for sure where Ohm is.'

'So he says,' said Pistor sneering.

'What's that supposed to mean?' said Fornax, close to losing her temper.

Cetus stepped in. 'I think Fornax is right,' he mollified, 'if it is a trap at least we wouldn't all be caught. The others would then have a chance of rescuing them.'

It made sense and eventually everyone agreed. Cetus and the disgruntled Pistor went left, the brothers right and Fornax, accompanied by Equuleus, headed straight down the middle.

The corridor stretched out before them unchanging until the outline of a door, standing slightly open, came into view directly ahead. Fornax gestured for Equuleus to be quiet and together they inched forward. As they drew closer they saw the door stood before another three-way junction.

'Someone's coming,' whispered Fornax, spreading flat against the left wall. Equuleus quickly followed suit. They could now hear, but not make out to any degree, the sound of a whispered conversation approaching from the left hand corridor.

The whispering stopped, but the plod of footfalls continued, slowly getting closer; almost creeping. Fornax tensed; this wasn't the steps of someone wanting to greet openly; it was the sound of someone ready to pounce. Well, she thought, two can play at that game. Fornax waited. The footfalls stopped short of the junction. Did they sense something? Waiting, Fornax decided, was over and she flung herself bodily around the corner raising her foot in a kicking motion as she did.

'Aaargh!' yelled Fornax, adopting full battle mode, red mist swirling in front of her eyes. Her foot hit home. There were two of them, the first catching the full force of her kick in the groin. As he fell to his knees screaming her fist caught the second full on the chin sending him crashing to the floor like a sack of spuds. With fists and feet preparing to do further damage Fornax suddenly found herself restrained by three pairs of hands. She struggled. Someone was shouting at her to stop. The red mist gradually thinned as the words began to register.

'Stop it Fornax,' pleaded Equuleus, 'it's Cetus and Pistor.'

The mist now cleared sufficiently for Fornax to make out the squirming body of Cetus at her feet, beside him lay Pistor, dead to the world, the smack to the jaw knocking him clean out.

'But...?' stuttered a stunned Fornax, 'how?'

'It looks as if all the corridors lead here,' said Hydra, releasing his hold on her.

Fornax dropped down on her knees beside the groaning Cetus who had tears streaming down his cheeks. 'I'm sorry Cetus,' she said with heartfelt regret, 'I didn't know it was you. Here give me your hand.'

Even though the pain he was feeling kept him doubled up Cetus still managed a rueful smile. 'Give me a minute,' he wheezed, 'feels like a whole army just marched over me.'

Nodding, Fornax turned to see how Pistor was; funnily enough she wasn't having the same feelings of regret where he was concerned. 'How is he?' she asked anyway.

'Nothing broken,' said Hydra, 'but he'll have one hell of a headache when he wakes up.'

'Nothing different there then,' said Fornax. She stood up, 'Cetus?'

'Nearly there. Going numb, thank the stars.'

Fornax offered her hand again and this time Cetus took it. Fornax hauled him upright.

'Just one thing though,' said Cetus, grimacing a little as he straightened his legs, 'remember I'm on your side next time.'

Smiling, Fornax reached and gently squeezed his shoulder, 'I promise I shall try.'

'Look,' said Equuleus, 'the door's gone.'

In the melee the door had been completely forgotten, but now it had disappeared, propelled into the wall by a silent hydraulic system leaving a gap the same as the one that had mysteriously appeared in the wall of the room they had come from.

'What do we do?' asked Hydrus.

'I think it's time we found out the identity of our host,' said Fornax. She checked once more that Cetus was all right then strode with purpose across the door's threshold and into a large space beyond.

'Ah, good, you've finally arrived,' said the owner of the nasally speech, stepping forward to greet them, 'come in come in.'

They had heard the stories of the talking tree but it was still a shock to say the least when faced with the realisation that they were true. Pistor who was just coming round between the supporting arms of Hydra and Hydrus was suddenly forgotten and dropped as the brothers looked on in jaw dropping awe. He landed face down with a jarring thump; his light that had flickered briefly going out again.

After a lengthy period of stunned silence where gawping was the name of the game, Fornax finally managed to string some words together and asked the second question on her mind. 'Who are you?' she said, unable to hide her astonishment.

The tree creature shifted uncomfortably from foot to foot before answering. 'Shouldn't that be, "what are you?"' it said.

'I… er,' said Fornax colouring slightly. The creature had read her mind somehow.

'But never mind,' said the tree creature, wobbling away to a panel of glowing red squares which he reached up to with a degree of difficulty, 'I get it all the time. At least you had the decency to save it for your second question.' The creature waved a withered hand across the panel. 'There,' it said, as the squares turned clear. 'Some of my instruments are slightly off.' He proceeded to punch a button here and there until he was happy with the result then turned back to his guests. 'It appears I was getting a little ahead of myself.' He gave a muffled sort of laugh that sounded more like a cough and moved forward holding a withered hand out before him, 'Let me introduce myself.'

'Stay back,' warned Fornax, now recovered from numbing first impressions and retreating a couple of steps.

The creature stopped and placed a thoughtful hand on his chin. He'd come across just such behaviour before. It was because he was different. Strange race; hated anything that was different to them, but if there was trouble and they needed help who they gonna call? He stifled a giggle and moved to a console on his right.

'It's not my fault you know,' said the creature, as he stood on tiptoes so he could see the console, 'planet wasn't where it was supposed to be; not by my charts anyway. Didn't want to show myself either, but my ship sustained a far amount of damage when I crashed so had no choice. Fat lot of good that has done me.'

His explanation, if that was what it was, drew only blank looks.

He continued anyway, 'I don't look like this normally; it's the gravity on your planet; heavier you see.'

Of course they didn't, they just pulled closer together, eager to get Musca and be on their way from this, this, whatever it was.

'I suppose you would like to see your friend now and be on your way, correct?' Behind him five pairs of eyes widened slightly. 'This way then.' Without looking at them the creature waddled across the room and pressed a button on the far wall whereupon part of it slid away to reveal a sleeping Musca lying on a silver bed much the same as the ones they had woken up on.

Fornax dashed across to him, but was instantly thrown to the ground as she reached the bed.

'Oops, sorry,' said the creature, shuffling into the room past the prostrate Fornax, 'forgot to turn the force field off.' He flicked a switch. 'You will be all right now.' He quickly shuffled out again.

It was Cetus' turn to help Fornax up. Together they cautiously approached the bed.

'If you've hurt him I'll...'

'Wuz up?'

'Musca.'

The creature lingered a moment in the doorway before tutting and leaving them to their reunion muttering as he went, 'You'd think you'd get the odd thank you for saving him, but oh no. But then what did you expect?' He stopped beside Pistor who was snoring nosily. 'And I suppose you need dealing with.' With the merest of effort the creature leaned forward and lifted Pistor from the floor. 'And if any of you are interested,' he shouted, 'I've prepared food.' The creature waited for a reply, but when none was forthcoming he tutted again and left with Pistor tucked beneath one of his arms.

'What is he?' asked Hydrus when the creature had gone.

'More to the point,' said Fornax, 'can we trust him?'

A moan from the bed drew their attention back to Musca who was trying to sit up. 'Where am I?' he quizzed when succeeding.

The room instantly erupted into a cacophony of noise as everyone tried to talk at once, each trying to outdo the other. Fornax, wet eyed, simply hugged him. Musca at this point began to wonder if there was something he should know; especially as everyone appeared to be pleased to see him; something as alien to him as the tree creature in the next room was to the rest of the planet.

Hugging over, tears blinked discreetly away, Fornax called for hush and got down to answering Musca's question; filling him in at the same time as to the whys and wherefores of how they were where they were and the nitty-gritty of the here and now as she knew it. When she had finished, the simple truth was short and succinct; no one knew.

Legs now hanging over his bed, Musca gently suggested that perhaps they should have a chat to this tree creature thingy. To his surprise they thought it a good idea.

'Ah,' said the creature as Musca and the others trooped through, 'come and eat.' The creature gestured to a table fairly sagging with foods and drinks of all descriptions. At it sat a recovered Pistor, his mouth crammed full, grease running down his chin. 'And when you've had your fill we will talk.'

A suspicious Fornax looked from the creature to the table and back again, but any suspicions she harboured of duplicity on the part of the creature were in part allayed by the marvellous smells drifting to her from across the room.

'Please eat before it gets cold.'

A slight hesitation from Fornax was evident but it was nothing more than that, she knew she wouldn't be able to resist the wares on offer. Jaw jutting she joined the others who were already stuffing food in their faces. Besides, she thought, as a piece of chicken melted in her mouth, if the creature wanted to harm them surely he would have done so before now.

The signal that announced feasting was at an end came via a satisfied burp that emanated long and hard from a now reclining Cetus. The tree creature who had removed his presence several times through the course of the meal to escape just such noises tutted in disgust – he thought himself cultured and above such boorish behaviour – but waved for them to join him on a semicircular seating arrangement placed in the centre of the room.

When the creature felt everyone was sitting comfortably, Cetus had managed to roll backwards off of the backless seats when first sitting, he pressed a button on a small handheld console. A panel in the wall slid open and a large rectangular box glided from it. Hovering inches from the floor it made its way to where the creature was sitting and settled at his feet. Another button pressed and the top of the box folded away to reveal its contents.

The tree creature reached inside and pulled from it something small and furry, he held it up. 'Whose are these?' he said waving them.

'Mine,' scowled Fornax, snatching her bottoms from the withered hand that held them.

'Ah-hum,' said the creature with what could have been taken as having a bit of a twinkle in its tiny little eyes if anyone had taken the time to notice. He continued to pull things out of the box until the contents were exhausted and all had been reunited with their belongings, including weapons. Well almost all. Pistor, hugging his clothes, looked on with mounting despair as the box gradually emptied with no sign of his beloved potatoes or his drinking tube. 'There,' said the creature when finished, 'all washed, mended and sharpened.

'What about me spuds?' said Pistor, peering into the empty box.

'Ah,' said the creature wriggling from his seat, 'I'm afraid they were damaged by the extreme cold,' Pistor took on a crestfallen look, 'but I managed to save what I could and, well, I think you may appreciate what I did with them.' Pistor perked up as the creature reached behind the seat he had been sitting on and reappeared with his drinking tube in his hands. 'It's my own recipe,' said the creature, handing it to Pistor.

Pistor uncorked the tube, fixed the drinking tube to the top and took a tentative sip. 'Phew-waa-ha!' exclaimed Pistor, gripping the seat for support.

The creature tapped the side of his knotty nose. 'I'll share my secret with you before you leave,' he said.

Standing, Pistor gave out a bellow of laughter and slapped the poor creature on the back, sending him sprawling. 'I'll remind you,' said Pistor, taking another sip then quickly plopping back onto his seat before the effect of the drink did it for him.

Musca went to the creature's aid.

'Thank you,' said the creature, brushing himself down, 'and now, as I said earlier, I think we should talk, but first let me introduce myself properly, my name is Heterosis, but my friends call me Tee Hee.'

Fornax, who had been watching the creature intently* since the brief matter with the briefs, had come to the decision that, whilst there was a lot she didn't know about this creature, what she did know of him gave her the impression that he was harmless or at least friendly enough to trust. On that assumption Fornax decided to let down her guard; slightly.

'That's a good sounding name,' said Fornax, tracing a fingernail down the edge of her sword to check its keenness, 'does it come from the stars?'

'In a way, yes I suppose it does.'

* Perhaps someone had noticed the twinkle.

'Good. What does it mean?' asked Fornax, licking a globule of blood from her finger; the sword would do, 'My name is Fornax and it means fiery furnace.'

'Well-er-hum, I'm afraid mine means nothing as grand as that,' said Tee Hee. Fornax beamed. 'Heterosis, as I'm a scientist, has a significance… what I mean to say is…'

'Not that one,' said Equuleus interrupting, 'the other name. The one your friends call you.'

'You don't want to know that,' said Tee Hee, suddenly coy, but throwing Fornax a wrinkled glance.

'Why would we not?' said Fornax.

'Oh all right then,' laughed Tee Hee, 'but you won't understand.'

'Try us.'

'It means…' Tee Hee could feel his face growing hot. Privately he loved the nickname but he didn't really like talking about it; it embarrassed him. Especially when someone as beautiful as Fornax was in earshot and staring at him in the way she was.

'Go on,' Fornax prompted.

'It… it means terribly heterosexual.'

The explanation was met with silence and blank faces until Equuleus ventured another question, 'I understand the "terribly",' he said, 'but the second bit… does it mean ugly?'

Tee Hee attempted an explanation but it was useless, as soon as he had finished the room erupted in laughter. He threw his arms up and waddled over to the wall where he pressed a button. A drawer appeared from nowhere. Tee Hee removed something and waddled back. On the seats his laughing guests were trying to understand just how a small shrivelled tree creature could remotely be described as sexy.

'Look,' said Tee Hee, holding something out in front of him, 'this is what I looked like before I had the misfortune to bump into your planet.'

The laughter subsided as Fornax and the others stared at the object in wonder. It was a model of a man, about eight inches high. But not just an ordinary man, the most physically perfect man any of them had ever seen before.

Fornax couldn't believe her eyes. She cast a glance at Musca; nothing. She thought of Aquila; a bit of a twinge. She returned her gaze to the statuette; oh mamma! 'This is you?' she drooled, half in disbelief, half in hope.

Tee Hee managed a nod.

'What happened?'

Now that he had regained their attention Tee Hee told his story – in a way they would understand. How he left his own home planet, many years ago. His job to interact with new species – people – plant his genetics – get down to business with as many females as was humanly – alienly – possible. About the crash landing of his spaceship – starship – silver sky chariot – on their planet – world – country – homeland. Finally, the toughest, his predicament when the pressure fell in his ship and how the heavier gravity of their planet caused the strange condition he was now having to cope with – there is more rain on your planet so he shrank a little.

By the time he had finished, apart from the occasional burp from Pistor, the room had fallen silent.

'I see you finally believe me,' said Tee Hee.

It was Fornax who broke it. 'I believe your story, even the silver chariot that floats amongst the stars, but I cannot believe that this is you.' She still held the statuette in her hands, 'It does not seem possible.'

Tee Hee was about to try to explain again when Fornax's caressing fingers found and accidentally pressed a secret button. The small figure immediately lost its modesty which landed around its ankles and revealed another secret. Tee Hee smartly snatched it away from her.

'Sorry about that,' said the flustered Tee Hee, 'just one of my friend's little jokes. It's supposed to pee-pee but I've removed the liquid.'

On the semicircular seat Fornax was no longer listening. What she was doing was wondering if the little statuette had been built to scale.

The conversation was taken up by Hydra who wanted to know if Tee Hee would ever be the same again.

136

Tee Hee waddled back to his seat and struggled onto it; he looked thoughtful. 'I hope so,' he said, 'in fact I've been working on getting the gravity re-stabilised on the ship.' Hydra frowned at him. Tee Hee tried again, 'I think I've found a way of drying myself out. I was in the process of adapting a spare chamber when the radar picked you up.'

The faces had grown blank again. Those that were still listening. Cetus was back at the food. Pistor had rolled off his seat and was happily sat on the floor sipping at the drink with his back to everyone. Only Fornax appeared to be showing real interest.

'And in this room you will be exactly as the doll?' she asked, holding out her hand for the statuette.

'A bit older, but yes,' said Tee Hee, handing it to her.

Fornax took it and, still looking at Tee Hee, searched for the secret button. No one seemed to notice apart from Tee Hee.

'Everything the same?'

'Yes.'

The evening wore on. More questions were asked. More chat. Misunderstandings. Explanations. Until the rigours of the previous days began to take their toll and one by one they made their excuses and retired to the silver bedroom; Pistor with the help of the brothers. Eventually only Musca and Tee Hee remained. Musca wasn't as tired as the others and besides had questions of his own. Questions for Tee Hee's ears only. Ones he didn't want the others to know about.

An hour later Musca stood up and said goodnight. To his dismay Tee Hee hadn't been able to throw any light as to the whereabouts of Ohm, leaving him as clueless as when he'd left the valley. But one thing nagged at him as he followed the footprints to join the others; a feeling that Tee Hee wasn't to be trusted. He thought back to the way Tee Hee had looked at Fornax as she played with his toy. Musca shivered. He was beginning to feel uneasy. As soon as he got to the room he would talk to Fornax about it.

Musca reached the room and stepped inside. The others were asleep, only Equuleus not snoring. He glanced at the huge lump that had to be Cetus: didn't take long for him to fill out again.

137

The door closed silently behind him. Perhaps he should wait until morning? Let Fornax sleep. No best not, something was up; best say something now. He looked from bed to bed and back again. Alarm bells started to ring somewhere in the recesses of his mind. Two empty beds and five full ones.

He started to pull back the covers on each to the annoyance of those ensconced below. Fornax wasn't there. Musca turned meaning to go back and demand to know her whereabouts, but there was no sign of the door, just an endless seamless wall.

Tee Hee dressed in a robe much too big for him, rubbed his withered little hands together and hurried off to another room along the corridor. There he paused composing himself before opening its door. Ready, he opened it and stepped into a small chamber boasting just one piece of furniture; a large padded armchair-like contraption with seatbelt type straps in the centre of it. Tee Hee climbed into it and clipped the straps across his body. The room began to pulse with a soft light. Tee Hee closed his eyes and tried to relax.

The process took no time at all, but to an impatient Tee Hee it felt like ages. At last the lights began to dim and a muted buzz sounding in his ear announced the process was complete. Tee Hee removed the straps. Had it worked? Of course it had. Tee Hee got up from the chair and breathed deeply. He was back to his old self again, six feet six of rippling muscle.

In front of him was another door. He paused again before pushing a button that opened it. Beyond was another larger chamber. Tee Hee stepped in and gasped.

Ahead of him floated Fornax, her hair in a cascade about her naked shoulders and breasts, a small smile on her lips. She was the most beautiful humanoid he had ever seen.

'Well?' said Fornax, her smile growing.

Tee Hee returned her smile and disrobed.

'*Oh mamma!*' said Fornax.

CHAPTER 16

'What do you mean an egg? Explain yourself,' growled Serpens at a beleaguered Lyra. He was furious. Not only had they lost the monkey man's trail but it would seem Lupus was now masquerading as an egg.

'It's the snow, Master,' Lyra tried to explain, as he shrank out of reach the best he could without making it obvious. There was always the hope that Serpens, who looked fit to bust a gut, would vent his frustration in some other way than through violence. He was to be disappointed.

'SNOW!' roared Serpens, lashing out.

Lyra was catapulted across the cave coming to rest on a far wall where he dribbled down it like a raindrop down a windowpane; slow at first but then gathering speed and landing at the bottom in a messy splodge.

At that moment a huge dark shape loomed in the cave entrance. 'Breathe,' it said.

Serpens turned with such ferocity the ground beneath his feet blackened and burned. His eyes glowing like the pits of hell. 'BREATHE!' he spat. 'BREATHE!'

'Breathe,' repeated the emotionless minion of darkness.

It was all too much for Serpens who gave out a bloodcurdling yell of fury and charged at Ophiuchus who remained where he was, unmoved and unmoving. Serpens rammed the full length of his arm down the poor minion's throat, grabbed, twisted and pulled. Ophiuchus' legs buckled beneath him and he fell to the ground.

Serpens glowered triumphantly at the massive pair of glistening lungs that he held in his fist. 'And let that be a lesson to you,' he growled at the crumpled Ophiuchus, 'when I tell you to do something, you ask me first.'*

* ? *SJ*

139

His anger subsiding Serpens clipped the set of lungs to his belt and turned his attention to Lyra who was still spread-eagled on the ground. He slipped a talon under his chin and lifted him up.

He wasn't into cosmetic treatments but Lyra could do nothing about the face peel he was undergoing as Serpens' caustic and not too fresh breath caressed his skin. But that was really the least of his problems. Any second now he was sure one of his organs would be hanging beside those of Ophiuchus' and he had a clear idea that he needed all of them.

But that second passed and so did a few more. Lyra hung; waiting. Serpens stared. Lyra gave a little cough. Not that he wanted to encourage his own mutilation you understand; he wasn't stupid you know; him now being a intellectual an' all. It was the talon. It was starting to irritate in a sharp painful way. Lyra politely cleared his throat again.

Serpens reacted. 'What's that?' he said.

'What's what, Master,' replied a puzzled Lyra.

Serpens poked at one of Lyra's eye sockets, 'That.'

'An everlasting gobstopper, Master; a proper one; none of yer modern rubbish,' said Lyra brightly.

Deep down Serpens suddenly had a very bad feeling. 'I can see that oh simple one, but what's it doing there?'

Forehead wrinkling Lyra gave this some thought and as he was now *a intellect* it didn't take him long, 'I think you gave it to me Master, back in the days when I was stupid.'

'Me?' said Serpens with some uncertainty. In his stomach a small Mexican wave of bile was building.

'Yes, Master,' said Lyra nervously, 'I didn't think it important to say at the time, but then I wouldn't have as I was stupid.'

Serpens began to fumble at his belt with his spare hand. He found what he was looking for and produced a ball of blue tissue paper. 'And this?' he said, showing Lyra its contents.

'That's easy, Master. That's my eyeball.'

The Mexican bile wave suddenly grew. Serpens turned green and not just his face. He relaxed his grip on Lyra who slipped to the ground. 'Take it you… ugh… can… ugh… go,' said Serpens, trying hard not to let the gagging in his throat turn into full blown vomiting. It was going to be a close one.

Lyra snatched the tissue paper and its contents, hesitated then thought better, seeing the colour Serpens was turning, of asking if he wanted the gobstopper back and ran from the cave.

Slumping onto his throne Serpens had three things on his mind, four if you counted the effort that was going into not being sick. One: The monkey man. Two: His tutu which had been badly stained by Ophiuchus' lungs. Three: The gobstopper/eyeball incident, which really encompassed thought four to be fair. He sat and pondered each in turn. He pondered the circumstances he now wallowed in. What was the meaning of life?

He decided it didn't matter a whole lot about the tutu; he wasn't that keen on primrose anyway. The blood and gore had in a way added to it; giving it a certain *je ne sais quoi*. That left one and three. Bile, for the moment suppressed; but there was no guarantee it would stay that way, Serpens rose from the throne and began pacing the cave. Thoughts of the gobstopper eventually pushed aside he began to mull on the monkey man situation.

One hundred paces or so later he had it. He, personally, would have to go after him. As went the old adage: "If you want something done, kill everything in your way." Serpens vowed that that would be his motto from now on.

'Ophiuchus!' roared an excited Serpens, eager to get things moving. 'Ophi-oh bugger!' Serpens unclipped Ophiuchus' lungs and replaced them. 'Ophiuchus?'

'Yes, Master?' said Ophiuchus from his prone position on the ground.

'Are you all right?'

'Yes, Sire. Why shouldn't I be?'

Serpens ignored him and concentrated on telling Ophiuchus his plan.

Not long after Ophiuchus was outside, the wooden throne strapped to his back. Inside Serpens was feeling a lot better and a lot happier. 'It won't be long now,' he muttered, gleefully rubbing his hands together, 'soon the monkey man will be mine, all mine and I shall learn his secret.' Hands still rubbing together Serpens went out to join his minions. He climbed aboard his throne and gave Ophiuchus the order to giddy-up.

Now, as he was carried away from the cave, there remained one last thing unresolved; the matter of the gobstopper. Where the hell was he going to get another one?

CHAPTER 17

Warm sunshine poured through the small portholes dotted along the silver walls and bathed the room in glorious sunlight.

On one of the beds a nose twitched, eyelids fluttered; their owner in that place between sleeping and waking. There had been dreams, bad dreams, where he had almost suffocated in a sea of white. Where small spindly creatures, like twigs, had detached themselves from a larger tree like monster and had tried to carry him off. The worse though involved his love. She had been taken away from him to who knows where. He turned on his side. Fornax! He had shouted. Fornax where are you?

Fornax! Musca woke with a start.

It all suddenly came flooding back. Fornax wasn't with them. He had to do something. He had to find her. Musca sat up and lay straight back down again. His head swam but he knew he hadn't had that much to drink. He tried again and this time managed to balance on an elbow. Here he stayed, blinking in the sunlight, until the swimming eased enough for him to try again.

He went from elbow to sitting from sitting to sliding, feet first from the bed. Standing, he was to find, was a whole lot harder. They weren't his own he was sure of it. That or they were rebelling against something and had voted while he slept for independence. Hands taking his weight on the edge of the bed he tried again, but his legs still wobbled and shook though there was feeling coming into them that he recognized; pins and needles.

Grimacing, his face a mask of pain, Musca decided to hurry the process along and attempted, with some success, to stamp his feet on the floor. At last he was standing, but nausea threatened to take control. Musca fought it and managed to stagger over to one of the portholes. Outside, the world had changed considerably.

Musca was shocked. Gone was the snow that had built up past the portholes, in its place a meadow sloped gently away bordered by rock, verdant green, dotted with a multitude of colourful flowers. Musca recognised some of them, but others he thought native to the mountains. Above and beyond, a cloudless blue sky framed the scene. Confused he turned away. How could there be snow deeper than a man one day and the next nothing? His head pounding he reacted to a murmur from one of the beds. Cetus was sitting up and rubbing his head with his hands.

'How much did we have to drink last night?' he said, squinting around the room until he found someone else awake, 'my mouth's as dry as a dead man's armpit.' He unsuccessfully tried to moisten his lips as if to prove the point.

'Something's wrong,' said Musca.

'You're telling me,' said Cetus, still holding his head whilst slipping gingerly from the bed, 'but a hair of the dog should put that right.'

The room began to fill with moans and groans as the rest started to surface.

'There's something wrong with outside,' said Musca, 'take a look.'

His legs going through the same processes as Musca's had, Cetus struggled across the room to see what all the fuss was about. When he got there it took a moment or so for it to sink in. 'What the hell?'

'What do we do?' cried Equuleus on the verge of tears. He had suffered most from whatever had happened to them and the hair that broke the camel's back for him was to hear that Fornax was missing; probably kidnapped by the tree creature, Tee Hee.

'Yes, oh great warrior king, what do we do now?' sneered Pistor, sarcastic as ever. Worse perhaps because he was totally sober.

Musca, staring at the vista beyond the portal, ignored him. He didn't know. One day in a winter wonderland the next who knows where; another country for all he knew. Perhaps one of those other worlds Tee Hee had spoken of.

'Well?' pushed Pistor. 'Or did you secretly get yer little friend with the twigs to take us to this imaginary Ohm you keep spouting about and any moment you're gonna shout hurrah and surprise us?'

Pained expressions suddenly flickered with something else, hope perhaps. Musca meanwhile again said nothing, but a small ember of anger had started to glow within.

Pistor laughed. 'What am I asking you for anyway? You don't know where we are now, let alone Ohm. You have enough trouble sorting yer arse from yer elbow.'

Equuleus stopped his sniffling and looked to Musca, 'Tell him, Musca. Tell him where Ohm is.'

All eyes were now on Musca whose slowly smouldering ember was beginning to glow white heat and burn his gut.

'He can't,' sneered Pistor, 'he doesn't even know where his girlfriend is.' With Fornax out of the picture Pistor was taking full advantage. 'He's all bluff and wind.'

Enough was enough. The white heat became an inferno and with tears pouring down his cheeks Musca erupted like a volcano and like lava poured over Pistor, knocking him to the floor.

The two rolled grappling and punching across the floor, heading towards the part of the wall where the door would have been had it not just opened. Without realising it they rolled out into the corridor and into the stumpy legs of a waiting Tee Hee.

'So this is how you repay my hospitality, brawling in my home like ungrateful barbarians!' snapped Tee Hee, his tone sharp. The effect of it stopping Musca and Pistor in mid brawl. But before either could get their wits back about them Tee Hee spoke again. 'Now follow me I have something to show you.' He started down the corridor without waiting for a response.

Shocked by the sheer temerity of the creature in not offering an explanation for the change in surroundings or Fornax's disappearance, but instead to berate them, a dumbfounded Musca untangled from Pistor and simply forgetting their argument did as he was told and followed lamely behind; the others who were equally dumbfounded tagged along.

They were led back to the room where they had eaten and bade to sit down on the semicircular affair. Still in a daze they sat and said nothing as Tee Hee turned about face and waddled out again, the door sliding closed behind him.

'What in the stars is going on, Musca?' whispered Cetus, the first to find his voice.

Musca glared across at Pistor who was sitting opposite him and for once Pistor found nothing to say. Musca looked down at his feet his mind in a whirl. He didn't know. If he was honest with himself he didn't know a lot about anything. The question went unanswered and the room fell quite.

After what seemed like ages the door slid open again. Heads looked up but any questions that had been building, any queries needing resolving, were suddenly and swiftly forgotten. Standing in the doorway was Fornax her head adorned with a circlet of silver, her hair shining like a living fire. She glided towards them with an exquisite grace. The dress she wore matched her eyes, the colour of emeralds, yet in another light clear as an icy mountain stream. Yet it wasn't her awe inspiring beauty or the simple fact she was there that took their speech and breath away. It was what she was carrying.

For the second time that day Musca's brain decided enough was enough, but this time it took the decision to disengage itself and he dropped to the floor in a dead faint. Cetus attempted to catch him, but his legs acted otherwise and stayed rooted to the spot. Pistor and the brothers just stared open mouthed. Equuleus, who didn't know why, wept.

CHAPTER 18

A large wet warm tongue swept across Bootes' wrinkled old face. Bootes didn't stir. Lupus spat the taste of this latest attempt and tried again. Bootes twitched and made a face, but still didn't wake.

It had been two days since Lupus had resumed the guise of Fluffy and after numerous unsuccessful attempts at waking Bootes he was getting worried. The last remnants of the snow were still visible on the higher peaks where the warmth of spring and summer rarely reached, but here, where Lupus fretted, the snow had at last melted away. Lupus had no idea exactly how long he had been a cocoon for Bootes but hazarded a guess at months. He also hazarded a guess that Serpens would not be a happy bunny.

While wondering what he should do next a familiar voice popped into his hearing from directly behind him.

'Why don't you drag him into the sunshine,' it suggested.

Lupus spun round but there was no one there. He growled low and menacingly; he wasn't in the mood for games.

'Looks like he could do with a bit of a warm to me,' said the voice which had moved behind Lupus again.

Spinning back to find he was still alone Lupus began to wonder if Serpens had made the little idiot invisible.

'Up here!'

Lupus looked up and found Lyra sat above him perched on a rock. He was grinning like a grotesque hairless caricature of the Cheshire cat who in turn had swallowed a gallon of cream.

'What are you so pleased about?' growled Lupus, who couldn't be described as been overly overjoyed on seeing his fellow minion of darkness again.

Carefully clambering down, being careful not to snag his special tail, Lyra landed besides Bootes and stared into his face, 'Learned to throw my voice while you were pretending to be an

147

egg, it's wonderful being *a* intellect. He don't look too good does he.'

'When I want your advice I'll pretend okay. What do you want anyway?'

'The Great Dark O wants to know when you are likely to move on again.' Lyra paused a moment, then added with a confidential tap of the nose, 'Between you and me I think he's getting a tad tetchy.'

'Dark O*?'

'Says it's classy. Says it gives him a touch of ineffable mystery.'

'An ineffawhat?'

Lyra gave a shrug of his bony little shoulders and stood up. 'Dunno, but Serpens says I am to be his Major-Domo when he takes his rightful place as Master of the Cosmos.'

'Good for you,' said Lupus, pushing past Lyra and grabbing Bootes in his powerful jaws. He proceeded to drag him into sight of the sun where he nudged at him with a paw. A sudden dank aroma, not unlike stale boiled cabbage, wafted from Bootes' nether regions and gripped Lupus' snout like a long lost friend. Lupus recoiled and rubbed at his nose. It would seem the warmth of the sun had set something in motion; Bootes was on the way to being his old self again.

'And,' said Lyra, who hadn't yet stopped for breath in his eagerness to bestow on everyone and everything in earshot his imminent rise in status and importance and was pushing his pigeon chest out as proudly as he could, 'he promised that I was to be responsible for mistakes.'

Lupus cocked an ear at this and shook his head. 'Do you understand what he means by that?' he said, wondering if Lyra's intelligence wasn't selectively bestowed.

'Of course I do,' said Lyra pouting indignantly, 'Serpens said I am to be the Butt where everything stops and,' here Lyra took a dramatic stance; hands on hips etc, 'also said it was the most

* There's a ring in all the best books and films.

148

important position he could think of for me and no one, no one he said, deserved the position of Butt more so than me.'

As Lyra finished, a tumble weed rolled past and in the ominous silence that followed Lupus was sure he could hear laughter of the darkest kind echoing somewhere far and away in the deepest recesses of his mind. But he didn't have time to dwell on it as a groggy groan announced the introduction of Bootes arriving back in the land of the living. And if Bootes was coming round Lyra would have to go.

'Do you still tug when you want to go back?' asked Lupus innocently.

As Lyra nodded Lupus leapt at him and tugged. Lyra rapidly faded into the distance.

On the ground Bootes was sitting up and looking extremely puzzled.

Inside Lupus something strange was again happening as he watched the befuddled old man sat on the ground scratching his head. He felt a sort of twinge, something odd, something alien, a strange tugging deep in his chest. A feeling almost the same as the ones he had been feeling before they had climbed into the mountains but stronger. It felt unnatural

Bootes struggled upright staggered a couple of steps then plopped back down on his backside. Lupus ran to his side, a worried frown on his shaggy face.

'Gud boy, gud boy,' said Bootes, ruffling Lupus' fur, 'I'm okay, me legs a bit shaky that's all.' Lupus was relieved and his tail had started to wag; equally unnerving to him.

They sat and rested waiting for the strength to return to Bootes' legs. The sun went down and night passed.

Next morning Bootes tried again and this time he stayed up. He gathered his meagre belongings together and squinted up at the cloudless morning sky.

Where the clouds had gone he didn't have the faintest idea. And why it was so warm? It was more like spring than winter. Who knew? He was alive and that was all that mattered to Bootes. Why's and wherefores had never played a large part in Bootes' life. What was there was there and what wasn't, well, didn't matter

149

much. He stretched and creaked some, hefted his belongings over his shoulder and was then ready to continue where he had left off. He had a track to follow and friends to find.

'Right boy, we better be moving if we're gonna catch the others before winter *really* sets in.'

Lupus barked in agreement and smiled to himself as he gently nudged the old man in the right direction.

CHAPTER 19

Someone was saying something to him. Whispering in his ear. The words were soothing and reassuring. They were asking him something. What was that?

'Wake up Musca.'

The words oozed between his unconscious and conscious self, gently easing them apart. Musca murmured something.

'What did he say?'

For an instant the soothing voice had an edge. 'Be quiet Pistor, let him speak,' it said.

'I was dreaming,' Musca managed through reluctant lips. 'Dreaming about Fornax.' His eyes stayed firmly shut but a faint smile crept upon his lips, 'We were to be wed.'

Pistor, who had been hovering outside the main ring of people around Musca, stood up, 'I've had enough of this I'm going. He's as stupid asleep as he is awake.'

A sharp glance from Fornax sent him scurrying from the room quicker than he had intended.

'Come on Musca,' urged Fornax gently as she cradled his head in her arms, 'it's time to wake up.'

Musca's eyelids fluttered for a moment as if he was about to wake, but instead he curled up into a ball. Fornax glanced anxiously at Cetus. 'I think he's in shock,' she said.

'You could be right,' Cetus agreed, 'but what can we do about it?'

'I know.'

The huddle around Musca turned as one and looked up at Pistor who had returned carrying a bucket.

'I thought I…,' said Fornax, but before she could finish a deluge of icy water aimed at Musca drenched them all.

'Why you…' Fornax reached for her sword but it wasn't there. She stormed towards him anyway; her fists would have to do, 'I'm

151

going to break every bone in your rotten drink soaked body.' Pistor backed away as she bore down at him, but as she prepared to land a fist Musca, fully awake thanks to the water, intervened.

'No Fornax, leave him to me.'

At least it sounded like Musca but not the one she knew. Fornax stopped short and turned. Musca was dripping from head to foot. He walked forward, the stoop he always carried, gone. A different Musca indeed.

Musca reached Fornax, smiled the briefest of smiles and walked on by until he was standing face to face with Pistor. 'I want to thank you Pistor,' he said, 'you've brought me to my senses.' Pistor relaxed a little. 'But,' he continued, 'if I am to lead you all to Ohm then there must be only one leader.' He suddenly swung a fist catching Pistor by surprise and on his chin. Pistor went down like a sack of his favourites. Rubbing his bruised knuckles Musca faced the others, 'Do you agree?'

At first there was only stunned silence, but gradually smiles appeared followed by nods.

'Hurrah for Musca!' shouted Equuleus.

'Thank you Equuleus but now I think we,' he gestured towards Fornax, 'need to be alone. We'll meet here in an hour.'

Cheeks flushed, Equuleus vacated the room with the others, Hydrus and Hydra dragging Pistor. At the door Cetus stopped and looked back. He wondered how Fornax was going to explain the baby. Across the way Fornax was thinking the same thing. She looked Musca squarely in the face and began. It was going to be a long hour.

With the exception of Pistor who had mumbled something under his breath before sloping away on his own, the others waited patiently outside the silver cave with the sun warm on their backs. Two hours had elapsed since Tee Hee had stopped them from going back to the room holding Fornax and Musca. He had explained a few things as he had led them outside. Most they hadn't been able to grasp; the long sleep for one. Fornax and the baby another, though mostly because they had tried to blank that conversation. But he had shown them the way down before leaving them. It was at the start of the downward path that they now sat waiting for Musca to join them. Nothing had been said officially but none expected Fornax to be travelling on with them.

Half an hour later Musca appeared. With him to everyone's surprise was Fornax but the momentary flash of hope they felt dissolved as quickly as it had appeared as they each decided she was only here to say goodbye.

Musca spoke. 'Tee Hee has generously provided provisions for the journey down,' he said, 'I suggest we start.'

Expecting Fornax to begin her goodbyes the others hesitated then looked puzzled as she, without a word, walked past them and started down the path. They turned to Musca who paused just long enough to tell them explanations would have to wait as they aimed to get as far as possible along the path before night fell. His voice held an uncanny calmness about it and for a change his word was their command. They collected the supplies together and silently did as he asked. No one looked back, but all wondered where the baby was.

The rest of the day was one of easy, albeit steep, downward marching, not a taxing descent but all the same everyone was feeling tired and drained. Questions, weights in their minds, adding to the fatigue,, and when the days journey came to an end they were all more than ready to unload this burden.

They stopped, Fornax always a distance ahead, calling a halt in a small clearing, which by the dark scarring on the ground had seen many campfires over the years. As they prepared to make their own Musca offered up an explanation for the scorch marks.

'Visitors to the silver cave,' he said, pointing to the marks, 'this is where Tee Hee meets and vets the people before allowing them to move on.'

It was all very interesting, but there were more important questions that needed to be answered; answers that would have been pursued had it not been for the quiver and tone of Musca's voice. A brave face was definitely being put on.

Thinking better of asking, Cetus let the question on his lips lie and spoke to Equuleus instead, 'Come Equuleus, let's gather firewood.'

When they returned the others had already set their blankets on the ground. Cetus got to work and soon a good fire was burning. Musca handed out bread, cheese and cold meat. They sat and with the stars burning brightly in the night sky they ate, drank and pondered in silence. Each encapsulated in their own world and thoughts. Fornax hadn't joined them, instead wrapped in her blanket she lay some way apart from them.

The meal finished, the fire burning low; the night was warm there was no need to feed it further, Musca at last started to talk. His voice, almost a whisper, was low so as not to wake Fornax. Fornax though was not asleep, only feigning it. She didn't want them to see her crying; her tears were her own affair.

It was hard for Musca, they could see he hurt, but he told what he knew. What had happened to them while they had slumbered like bears through the winter. Some facts they already knew, but they still uttered sympathetic noises when it was needed. He then started on what they didn't know, how Fornax had fallen for Tee Hee when she saw him in his true state, that of the doll and how she unexpectedly fell with the child. It wasn't meant to happen; it was nothing but a fling. Fornax had meant to join them in their slumber but the pregnancy had changed everything. She couldn't have joined them, the baby wouldn't have survived. And so, as it is with those of Tee Hee's kind, the pregnancy was short and the baby arrived not long before they had woken.

'Why hasn't she brought the baby with her?' whispered Equuleus.

'I'm coming to that,' said Musca, resting a hand on Equuleus' arm.

The baby would not survive long unless it stayed in a special room in the silver cave. Sets of eyes were filling, some leaking onto their owner's cheeks.

'Then why didn't Fornax stay with the baby?' asked Hydrus, a little louder than he had meant it to be.

Away at the edge of the clearing Fornax stirred and spoke. 'Because,' she said, 'I am a warrior and a warrior's life holds no place for a child.' In the dark away from the glow of the fire's dying embers, no one could see her red eyes and puffy cheeks. 'Now

154

I suggest we get some sleep. We still have a full day's walking ahead of us before we reach the desert.' Fornax turned her back to them and pulled her blanket back about her ears.

Desert? But nothing more was said that night. Nestling beneath their blankets, each with only their thoughts for company, they slowly drifted into sleep.

Above them, sometime after the last had succumbed to sleep, the stars witnessed something strange travelling across the sky. A streak of light travelling at speed flew over the sleeping travellers then abruptly stopped and hurtled to the ground. No one heard the crash, a few nocturnals perhaps were sent scurrying for cover, but in the camp all were oblivious to it. As they were to the flash that lit the sky as it hit the silver cave.

CHAPTER 20

As usual Serpens wasn't happy. This time it was finding his latest plan wasn't going to be as easy as he thought. Because of his size there were no handy holes or gaps for him to travel through which meant time lost travelling around the mountains. There was also the matter of Lyra who had arrived back encased in a dead, well on its way to becoming petrified, tree. He vowed he wasn't going to ask.

'So, Lupus is no longer an egg?' said Serpens, pacing.

'No, O Dark O,' said Lyra, from within his tree.

'And he is now back to being a dog and the old man still lives?'

'Yes, O Dark O.' Lyra felt uncomfortable and that was more to do with Serpens pacing than the tree, but he stood to attention the best he could.

'And that is all you have to tell me?'

Was this a trick question? 'Er – yes, O Dark O.'

'So,' said Serpens, stopping his pacing a moment, 'Lupus is no longer an egg, you will stop me if I get anything wrong won't you?' Lyra nodded best he could, 'and he is now a dog again,' Serpens resumed his pacing, 'and the old man is still alive, yes?'

'Yes, O Dark O,' said Lyra, a trifle confused and more than a little worried as he couldn't see Serpens, but could feel him breathing down his bark.

'Good. I would hate to miss something of importance that you would regret later,' said Serpens, reappearing.

Lyra gulped and thanked whatever deity it was he thanked at times like this, that his master was such an understanding soul.

'AND THAT IS ALL?!!' bellowed Serpens suddenly, eyes glowing, his tenuous patience unravelling from its tether.

'Breathe,' whispered Ophiuchus, bang on time. Serpens' stare immediately dimmed a little.

Face screwed up tight, Lyra waited for the crunch but it never came. Cautiously chancing a peep through a couple of branches he saw Serpens was standing inches away from him taking deep breaths. He let out a sigh of his own, the sound of which snapped Serpens back to the here and now.

'And that is all?' said Serpens, as if his earlier outburst hadn't happened.

'Yes,' said Lyra, puzzled, but relieved.

'Then it's time to make my move. We will catch up with Lupus and I shall take the matter into my own hands. The sooner we find this monkey man the sooner I will be Supreme Ruler of the universe.'

Lyra gave a tentative cough.

'Yes?'

'Will I still be your Butt O Dark O?' queried Lyra.

'Of course,' smiled Serpens.

Happy he was still going places, Lyra decided to offer his services and grovelled, as far as the tree would allow, humbly before his master. 'And shall I fly after him again O Dark O?'

Serpens gave this some thought, 'No, you travel with me for the moment. I need some light entertainment for the journey. Now go tell Ophiuchus we are ready to depart. I want to be back in the saddle as soon as possible. Oh… and drop the O. I've decided I prefer Dark One; more substance.'

Lurching over to Ophiuchus Lyra wondered what Serpens had meant by entertainment. He couldn't dance, except that one time, but he *was* on fire. He couldn't sing, except that one time, but that was soon stopped due to the loss of ornithological life. Still, as long as the master was happy.

A short time later Ophiuchus with Serpens on board and the tree wrapped Lyra trailing behind set off. The going was hard especially for Lyra, but Ophiuchus, thanks to the trance he was under, found it easy. His eyes, ever alert for a glimpse of Lupus or the return of Draco, continually scanned the surrounding terrain. On his back Serpens, enjoying the sunshine, idly flicked his wrist and thought good thoughts. He smiled as he flicked his wrist again. It was so good he would have to give it a name.

Several thoughts later, 'What do you think of Ooh-Ooh?' said Serpens, the question directed at Ophiuchus.

Ophiuchus gave it careful thought and, as it summed up the essence of the recreation at hand, agreed.

Several flicks later Serpens wasn't so sure. He decided to seek further ideas.

'What about you Lyra? What do you think would be a good name?'

Lyra attempted a reply, but it wasn't easy as he was getting a tad dizzy. 'W-ell Mas-ter,' he managed, before he was propelled out of earshot. Seconds later he returned, 'You-you-ouuu...' but shot skyward before he could finish.

Serpens sat upright in his throne. He liked it. 'You-You, I like it. Well done Lyra.'

Lyra tried to look pleased as he shot back and beyond the mirthful Serpens.

'You'll like this, Lyra. I shall call it "walking the deadwood",' enthused Serpens. With a complicated twist of the wrist the string that was Lyra's special tail grew taut and both Lyra and the tree he inhabited rolled back along the track they were travelling.

And on they journeyed. Ophiuchus clothed in shiny black armour winding his merry way along the track that skirted the mountains, on his back his master sitting on his throne. Serpens, his worries and woes forgotten for the moment as he happily flicked his new toy, his You-You, back and forth and at anything and everything; twice or thrice if it squeaked on contact. And Lyra, more than happy in his ignorance; and why not? He was back in favour with the Dark One who was enjoying his company and who had thoughtfully let him keep the tree. Although deep down he suspected it wouldn't last; novelties never did. The bumping would end, wouldn't it?

CHAPTER 21

Musca held his hand aloft and called a halt. Spreading out as far as the eye could see was the desert; an endless sea of gold. He leapt onto an outcrop of rock and shielding his eyes from the setting sun surveyed the vast expanse.

'What do you see?' asked an eager Equuleus, clambering up the rock to stand beside Musca.

'Nothing, Equuleus. Nothing but sand,' he said grimly. He climbed down and faced the others, 'Well we've made it to the desert. Now all we have to do is cross it.'

'How far?' said Cetus.

Sliding his pack from his back Musca avoided Cetus' gaze, but he couldn't avoid the question. 'I don't know,' he admitted, laying the pack on a patch of scrub grass. Pistor mumbled something. 'But I do know roughly how long it will take us to cross it and what lies beyond,' he continued, ignoring Pistor. He asked them to gather round so he could disclose the rest of the information he had been able to glean from Tee Hee before they left.

The journey across the desert was going to take at least five days and nights depending on how fast they moved. Once across, the vista would change to a half day or so of barren rocky terrain. They would also have to travel mostly by night starting that night. There were a number of discontented murmurs which Musca did his best to ignore and carried on with what he had been told.

'And once through the jungle at its furthest edge we will come to a sea. Tee Hee has heard its name is Oarllat and I and Tee Hee believe Ohm is somewhere across it.' Finished, Musca sat back to let it all sink in. He anticipated a deluge of questions but was happy that he would be able to answer them, especially as he now felt he had a plan and some semblance of direction.

Everyone sat quietly digesting what they had been told. The obvious came to mind: Did they have enough food? Enough

Water? What did they do when they reached Oarllat Sea? Finally the first question came, but it wasn't one Musca expected.

And it came from Pistor. 'What more do you know of this lost city Tee Hee spoke of?' he asked.

'Nothing. As I said we use the well and leave. We leave everything else alone. We seek Ohm, nothing else.'

'What of the screaming spirit he said protects it?' Pistor persisted.

'It's what Tee Hee was told. He doesn't know if it's true, but if it is, it could be dangerous so we don't want to upset it if it exists.'

'But what's it protecting?'

'The city I suppose, but it's not our concern, do you understand?'

Expectant attention turned to Pistor to see his reaction, but he just nodded and unrolled his blanket.

'Good,' said Musca, relieved. The last thing he wanted was another argument. 'Now, are there any other questions?' To his surprise none were forthcoming. 'Right then, I think we should follow Pistor's lead and catch some sleep if we can. We'll need all the rest we can get.'

Night came soon enough and as they prepared to move a cold wind blew from the desert. Fornax shivered as she arranged her pack.

'Are you all right?' asked Cetus, reaching out a concerned hand that gently brushed against her shoulder. It was something he would never have dared do back at the village. She nodded and gave him a faint smile, but Cetus felt she wasn't; who would? It would have to do though, he wasn't about to push his luck. Besides Musca had taken his first step onto the sand; it was time to move.

Midway through the sixth day of their journey, that consisted of skin searing hot days and mind numbingly cold nights, an end to their ordeal finally came in sight.

Hydra, standing at the top of a sand wave, a dune more than twenty times his height, brought the others clambering and scrambling to its peak with a triumphant shout. Ahead, perhaps another half days trek away, stretched what looked, at first glance, like an immense shadow. This shadow was in fact the rocky terrain some of the party were beginning to think they would never see.

'We've made it! We've made it,' squealed Equuleus with delight, his blisters temporarily forgotten as he jumped for joy.

Even Fornax expressed emotion, the first sign of any for days, as a look of relief registered on her face.

Relief for Musca too, who danced with glee at the distant sight. 'Tee Hee was right,' he grinned, 'we should be there by tonight; tomorrow morning at the latest.'

Only Pistor, his brooding darker by the day, remained silent.

'Come on, Pistor,' said Cetus, slapping him on the back, 'surely even you can afford a smile? We're nearly out of the desert.' Since leaving the village Cetus had noticed the gradual change in Pistor and was worried. Not that Pistor was ever the life and soul of the party, but he did smile sometimes. Back then they had been friends, of sorts. More your food and drink buddies. The closest Pistor had to one, but he was becoming more and more withdrawn as each day passed; darker almost by the hour; worse since the mention of the city in the jungle it seemed. Cetus had decided to keep an eye on him.

'I'll believe it when I'm sat in the shade of a tree and not before,' replied Pistor, scowling.

'You old grouch,' laughed Cetus, 'when will you ever be happy?' He went to playfully pat Pistor on the back again, but Pistor shied from his touch. A nasty glint shined in his eye for an instant that would have worried Cetus further if he had noticed.

'Maybe when I'm under that tree,' said Pistor, 'and that sandstorm coming our way has passed.'

Cetus stopped laughing and followed Pistor's gaze. Sure enough there was a cloud of something some distance away but it was no sandstorm. Something was travelling hard and fast in their direction and kicking the sand up behind it as it went.

A short and hurried discussion later they were on the move again. The general consensus was that whatever it was coming their way could be purely coincidental, but to be on the safe side they wouldn't stop until they reached their goal.

Wary, to being on the point of paranoid, they moved as quickly as possible, but when night came again it appeared the worrying had been for nothing. They were still in the desert, the journey to its end further than appeared, but there had been no sign of whatever had kicked the sand up. The party relaxed a little but moved quicker, there was now a grim determination amongst them to leave the desert behind as soon as was possible.

Just before dawn, as the cock would have been preparing to crow, they reached the first clue that they were at last coming to the end of their sand adventure. Rocks, small at first, started to appear. The pace picked up. Then bigger ones, rising like islands in the sand, until all of a sudden the desert was no more and they were standing on solid ground. But that wasn't all. In the not too distant distance as the first light of day threw its cloak around them, they could make out the odd smattering of greenery. Surely a hint that the jungle they were heading for wasn't far away.

Like bedraggled survivors from a shipwreck thrown up on some foreign beach, they scrambled forward and slumped exhausted to the ground. No one said a word as they lay there, chests heaving, getting their breath back.

They lay like that for perhaps an hour before the heat of the day, rapidly rising, started to impose itself on their tired vulnerable bodies. It was time to move and use what strength they had left on a mission to find somewhere more hospitable to rest and possibly escape the midday sun. Tee Hee had reckoned the rocks lasted only a half days march. If they pressed on, it might be possible to reach the jungle before the hottest part of the day.

Press on they did, but the sun was in no mood to give quarter as they stumbled across the rocky domain. Sweat pouring, mouths dry; the water reduced to the odd mouthful when desperate, they struggled on. In the distance the promise of green shade beckoned but never seemed any nearer. Then, when the weaker among them may have called enough, the first tree; stunted and browner than it was green; more a bush than a tree, standing as proudly as its surroundings would allow greeted them, encouraging them.

More stumbling, more single trees; bushes but no respite from the heat of the rising sun; none sadly able to offer much in the way of shade. Thirst was now on every mind but none wanted to stop. At last they came to a small cluster of trees that stood defiant against the elements; safety in numbers perhaps. Not much taller than the rest that had been passed, but together they formed an umbrella of welcoming shelter.

They thankfully dropped beneath the intertwining boughs. Water was sought, found and eagerly received, then minds turned to rest. But not all minds. From where they sat the main canopy of the jungle could be seen and Pistor, sitting away from the others as was usual now, eyed it thoughtfully. He had a plan, and a secret, neither of which he intended to share. He swigged greedily from his leg flask as he imagined within all that greenery a lost city dripping with gold and precious jewels. He replaced the cork and loosened the cords around his pack. Inside was the secret. Three secrets really, but only one that needed kept so. He rummaged in the pack and produced the largest potato he had ever seen; a present from Tee Hee. A secret, but no big deal. He replaced it and pulled out a clear bag made from a material he hadn't seen before, in it another gift; the secret smelly stuff Tee Hee had used to produce the large potato. Each of these he eyed with glee but they weren't the main secret. He put the smelly stuff back and with a sly look to see no one was looking pulled out his prize; his "gizmo". This, Tee Hee didn't know he had.

When Pistor had gone back to the silver cave while the others were outside waiting, he had overheard Tee Hee telling Fornax about it. How it could make certain things bigger or smaller or destroy them. Pistor hadn't entirely understood what he was hearing, but gathered it was a weapon of some description and had peeped around the door to get a look at what they were talking about. It was, he decided, something that could prove handy to someone with a plan. And as the gizmo had fitted his hands perfectly when he had slipped unseen into the then empty room a little later, he decided it was obviously meant for him.

Satisfied with his haul he stuffed it back into his pack and fastened it tight; you couldn't be too careful. He then lay down using his pack as a pillow, his back to the others. Soon, he thought, he would be rich beyond his wildest dreams, but sooner still exhaustion overcame him and he drifted into sleep; a sleep of many other stranger dreams.

CHAPTER 22

Trotting alongside Bootes, Lupus felt amazingly good in himself. The sun warmed his back. His belly hadn't had cause to groan for quite a while thanks to the abundance of rabbits popping up on the way and to cap it all, he was certain the old man's friends weren't too far ahead of them.

Marching full steam ahead, Bootes had found a new energy surging through his body since his long sleep, they had made good time; stopping only when it got dark.

'Okay boy,' said Bootes, 'time fer grub.' The sky was just beginning to fill with stars.

As the old man searched for firewood, Lupus set off to find dinner. It didn't take long to spot. He bounded after it, but just as the rabbit prepared to travel to the great alfalfa patch in the sky, Lupus stopped pre kill and, ears pricked, cocked his head skyward to see a streak of light speeding across the heavens. Moments later it seemed to stutter then fall; a loud crash and a huge flash signalling its landing.

The rabbit, frightened as it was, saw a heaven sent opportunity to escape and took it, scampering for its life down the nearest hole.

Distracted, but not by the flash or crash, Lupus hurried back. His sharp hearing had picked up a cry for help. Bootes was in trouble.

Retracing his steps as fast as he could, he was soon back where Bootes had called a halt for the night but there was no sign of him. Lupus started barking, but there was no reply. Lupus decided to put nose to floor and after a couple of false starts – Bootes' "scent" was after all somewhat all consuming at close quarters – he managed to latch on to a trail.

Wiping running eyes with his paws, Lupus didn't need to be a detective to know that he was getting close. He stopped, it was pretty obvious that the old man had been seriously frightened, and he licked at his nose; it didn't help. He continued on, a few steps perhaps, then stopped dead. He became aware that something was dangerously wrong, call it instinct, call it the fact he was waving a paw over thin air. So intent on nose down tracking, Lupus had nearly missed the huge crater directly in front of him. He sniffed at the lip of this sudden nothingness and gasped; this was definitely where Bootes had gone after his fright.

It took a couple of barks before Lupus got an answer. It was weak and sounded far away, but it did mean the old man was still alive. Lupus gave a howl of joy.

Now all he had to do was rescue the old man. Carefully putting a paw over the edge, Lupus dragged his claws over the surface, testing to see what sort of grip he would be able get. The answer was none. It was like ice. Climbing down was not an option, he would have to change. Below, a pitiful voice reached his ears. 'It's no gud Fluffy boy,' wailed Bootes, 'I can't get out. I'm too old. It's too slippy.'

Spurred on by the pitiful sounds reaching him, Lupus racked his brains. He'd often thought how handy it would be to be able to change into inanimate objects; a rope would be handy right now, but he couldn't – so, something living? Something long? Then in a flash of inspiration he had it. He'd been thinking fauna, but why not flora?

Eureka! He thought. 'A vine! Why not?' he blurted.

Bootes' voice floated from the pit, 'Who yer got wiv yer boy?'

'Bol…woof!' said Lupus, flattening his body on the ground. Bootes called a couple of more times, but Lupus thought it best to ignore him hoping the old man would think he had imagined what he had heard.

After a while the pit grew silent. Lupus, who had decided it might be better to wait until the old man was asleep before attempting a rescue, lifted his head and pricked his ears. A snore from below. Another one. He gave a tentative bark. No reply. To be on the safe side he decided to wait a little longer.

With more snores, deeper now, Lupus decided it was time to put his plan into action. A couple of squelching noises later, a thin tendril slipped over the edge of the crater. With no sense of smell or sight to guide it the tendril slithered down relying on touch alone. It reached the bottom and slid over the cold bare bones of long dead creatures. Probing here and there it searched amongst the remains until at last it found the only living warmth. Carefully and very gently it wound around the sleeping Bootes and drew taught. Lupus, in two minds on the best action to take next; a quick tug or a gradual pull, decided on the latter and started to drag Bootes from the crater inch by inch. But if Lupus was hoping Bootes would sleep through it, he was going to be disappointed.

A sudden sharp pain shooting the length of the tendril to the heart of the blob that was Lupus, signalled all was not well. It was quickly followed by another and then another. In the pit below Bootes was screaming, 'Run, Fluffy! There's a ruddy monster down 'ear. Fluffy? FLUFFY?' His voice suddenly filled with terror as the realisation hit that perhaps he wasn't the monster's first victim. 'FLUFFY!'

Up above Lupus was in a panic. Another shooting pain coursed through his body. He would have to send another tendril down. This one when it arrived found a leg and tugged on it.

'No yer don't, yer sodding dog killer!' yelled Bootes. 'Take that!'

Lupus screamed as only a plant can, as agonising pain shot up through the second tendril.

'Ha-ha,' cried Bootes, maniacally, 'try to take us in our sleep, ey?' Thumping and thudding rang from the crater. 'You'll 'ave to be smarter than that to catch an ol' shepherd, so yer will, yer manky cowardly bag o' crap!'

As Bootes was going off on one, Lupus was trying to pull the second tendril from whatever Bootes was doing to it.

'Oh no yer don't!' yelled Bootes, 'if yer going so am I.'

The pain eased as Bootes clung for dear life to the second tendril. The plan was going to work, but not quite how Lupus had envisaged it. He loosened the grip he had with the first and pulled

Bootes up. What he was going to do when the old man arrived was something he wasn't clear on.

Up came the squirming Bootes and appeared at the edge gripping and cursing with all his might. 'Where is 'e? What 'ave yer dun wiv Fluffy, yer great ugly whatever yer is?' It was fighting talk and Bootes was living up to his name and well and truly putting the boot in to the tendril that had carried him up. He then dived on it and sank what teeth he had left deep into it.

Lupus was desperately trying to shake the old man off without hurting him so the tendril could join the rest of him hiding behind a handy boulder. Once achieved he could then change back without giving the old man a bigger shock than he already had, but the old man only sank his teeth in deeper and harder the more Lupus struggled.

'Having trouble?'

Lyra. What the hell did he want? Couldn't he see he was a tad busy? Still in blob form Lupus managed to form an eye and a mouth.

'Pith oth!' said Lupus, his mouth not perfect.

Lyra was sat on a branch of a small gnarled tree Lupus couldn't remember seeing before. He was no longer encased in a tree – to Lyra's relief he had thankfully been right about the You-You being a one minute wonder – but was now wearing a garish combination of purple tutu and sandy coloured short camouflaged combat jacket that finished just below the armpits.

'What do you think?' said Lyra, performing a somewhat nimble pirouette, 'It was Serpens' idea. Wanted to dress me up. Said that as I was an upper echelon dreaded minion of darkness I should dress as one. He said khaki was so passé.' Lupus let out a groan as Bootes did something nasty. 'I could go if it's a bad time.'

Lupus could hardly believe what he was hearing. Either Lyra was suddenly alive with sarcasm or he was doubly as stupid as was normal. Either way he wasn't in the mood for guessing games and lashed the first tendril at Lyra and grasped him by the throat.

'I'mth gothing tuth… buggeth.' Lupus put a bit of effort into arranging the mouth but oaths and threats were discarded as more urgent matters were in order. 'I'm going to drag you over to those rocks. When you get there bark like a dog. Do you understand?' The tendril was tightened as encouragement.

Nodding the best he could, Lyra was swiftly dragged by the tendril to rocks some thirty feet distant.

Meanwhile. 'I'll not ask yer again,' threatened Bootes, 'so help me, yer'll lose this… this… thing. I'll bite the flipping thing orf.'

Now would be a good time, thought Lupus, giving Lyra his cue with a helpful squeeze.

'Wuf-wuf.'

Bootes stopped in mid bite and looked up.

'Wuf… wuf… wuf.' Rang out from behind the rocks, this time a little louder and if Lupus was hearing right, just a tad sarcastically. It was still a pathetic attempt, but it was music to certain ears and for differing reasons.

'Fluffy boy. That you?' Bootes fell from the tendril and started for the rocks. 'I'm coming boy. Ol' Bootes is coming.' In his wake the tendril made a hasty exit. This was heard by Bootes who turned with a face like thunder and a warning, 'If yer's 'urt me dog I'll be back,' he threatened.

The tendril disappeared. It was swiftly joined by the other one while Bootes' attention was elsewhere.

'Fluffy! Where is yer boy?'

'Waf… wif,' said Lyra, trying his best.

With Bootes now only a few feet from making a brain numbing discovery, Lupus completed his change back to Fluffy and emerged barking from his hiding place. 'Woof woof,' he said.

Bootes span on his heels with surprise.

'Woof,' Lupus reiterated.

'Well blow me,' said Bootes, 'I thought yer wuz over there. Must 'ave been an echo.' Bootes crouched down as far as his old knees would allow. 'Come 'ere boy.' Bootes spread his arms wide.

Running over, hobbling really as his two front paws happened to be heavily bruised, Lupus sped towards the old man. But as Bootes went to hug him Lupus took a side step and ran straight past and over to the rocks where Lyra was hiding.

Lyra, looking like the happiest, yet ugliest gargoyle in the entire universe, was sat on his haunches grinning from ear to ear. 'How'd I do?' he grinned. But Lupus had no time for praise or idle chit chat and instead made straight for Lyra's tail and pulled on it. Not even a thank you.

'Noooooooooooooo!' wailed Lyra, but it was too late.

Hobbling quite badly, Lupus came out from behind the rocks to be greeted by a puzzled Bootes. Inside him a feeling was welling up that he couldn't quite put a dewclaw on.

That night neither Lupus nor Bootes got much sleep. Lupus too sore to rest properly, spent most of the night licking his wounds and wondering where the strange feelings he kept feeling were taking him. Bootes was too excited to go straight to sleep after vanquishing, single handedly, the monster from the pit.

When morning came, more warm sunshine came with it. Bootes, waking with an eagerness to get going, was first up and about. After going back to retrieve his belongings, he gently roused Lupus who was soon reminded of the previous night's exploits.

'Time to move, Fluffy,' said a smiling Bootes.

"Fluffy" wasn't so sure. His front paws and legs hurt like hell, but the old man was positively brimming so what could he do but give in and get up.

With a resigned sigh Lupus trailed behind Bootes as he led the way, his pigeon chest stuck out so far his shoulder blades were in danger of crushing his spine. Luckily for Lupus there was only one path to follow so there was no chance of Bootes needing the usual directional nudge. They moved on. Bootes was fairly floating on air feeling he could take on the world; a warrior capable of ridding the world of all monsters that should be foolish enough to stand in his way. Lupus, on the other hand, had his paws firmly and painfully on the ground.

The going was slow, nothing to do with Bootes this time, this was a situation contrived by Lupus. There was something worrying him. Not long after they had set off, a scent had come to him from up ahead; one he thought he recognised. He wasn't sure though. It was faint, mixed with sulphur; which was throwing him

170

and wasn't it an alien planet? It could have a few of its own; which he doubted, but he wasn't going to take any chances until he had a better idea of what or who he might be dealing with. So Lupus played on the old man's sympathies. A pitiful whine here, a groan there, usually saw the old man come running when Lupus felt he was moving too far ahead.

The further they went the stronger the scent. Lupus was certain now. He could smell Draco. But he was still puzzled; if he could smell Draco, why couldn't he smell Serpens? And why would they be ahead? Another change of plan by the great pretender perhaps? He was sure he would find out soon enough and if he could smell Draco, Draco would certainly be able to smell him. Nose working at one hundred per cent capacity, Lupus marched on and straight into the back of Bootes' legs. He hadn't noticed the old man had stopped. Bootes wobbled for a second, but held his ground pointing ahead.

'Look boy,' said Bootes, wonderment literally dribbling from his lips, 'a big silver something.'

Lupus looked. It was an amazing sight, but it wasn't the massive silver saucer that lay half embedded at the end of the crater that had his jaw dropping. Lupus was looking up, up above the saucer, where a hot and bothered Draco, silhouetted against the now night sky, hovered blowing the occasional blast of sulphurous flame out through his nostrils. He now looked every bit the fire breathing dragon of lore. Lupus made to edge closer, but Bootes restrained him.

The old man had seen Draco. 'Wait boy!' said Bootes, firmly, 'I knows wot manner of beastie that is,' Lupus cocked his head in a do tell kind of way, 'me mammy tol' me 'bout them when I wuz a sprat.' Lupus narrowed his eyes, waiting. 'It's one of them there monster fire flies.'

Lupus looked at the hovering Draco who had not seemed, as yet, to have noticed them. Well he can certainly fly, thought Lupus.

At which moment Draco manoeuvred his hovering in their direction. Sensing danger, Bootes pushed Lupus away from him; at least attempted to and produced a large thighbone that had not belonged to poor old Nob. It was what Bootes had used to do the damage to Lupus. He held it ready. 'This one's mine,' he announced.

Caught momentarily off guard by the sight of Draco actually flying, Lupus had momentarily forgotten the danger Bootes may well be in. Bootes for all his bluster would be hard put to beat a carpet let alone a fire-breathing dragon; however new Draco was to it. There was only one thing for it. With a sweep from one of his massive paws Lupus caught Bootes squarely on the back of the head. He hated doing it but…? Bootes crumpled and lay still as Draco appeared overhead.

'Can I help you?' enquired a very civil Draco.

'It's me, Lupus,' said Lupus.

'Sorry?'

'Ah,' said Lupus, remembering he was still in Fluffy mode, 'there,' he said back in the more familiar guise of a wolf, 'it's me, Lupus.'

But all he got in return was a blank look. 'Perhaps the master knows you. Please follow me and er… please bring your baggage with you.' Draco turned and floated away.

Strange, thought a mystified Lupus. Master? Did he mean Serpens? He didn't think so; he would have been able to sense him. And why didn't he recognise him? Perhaps he wasn't in a position to do so. Stranger and stranger. Anyway he would find out soon enough. Grabbing Bootes in his jaws; the baggage, as Draco had referred to him, Lupus did as asked.

Draco stopped just short of the saucer. 'I have someone to meet you,' said Draco, to no one Lupus could see.

Dropping Bootes to the ground, Lupus waited anxiously for this master to show himself.

Where are you? thought Lupus, as he scanned the immediate area for a sign of this mysterious master.

'Over here,' answered a voice in his head. A startled Lupus looked to his right; nothing there. 'Please step into my craft.'

It would appear the master, who or whatever he was, was a telepath. Lupus decided he would have to guard his thoughts.

Gripping Bootes again, he headed for an opening that had appeared in the side of the saucer. Inside he wondered what next?

'Please carry on along the corridor with green prints,' said the voice, dead on cue, 'I'll be with you in just a moment.'

Not sensing any immediate danger Lupus gave the air a sniff. He didn't smell any either. He felt it was safe for the moment to do as was asked and started down the corridor, dragging Bootes with him. At the end of it he came to a junction where a door automatically slid open at his approach.

'Please come in.'

Lupus held back and sniffed. Again there appeared no obvious cause for alarm. Even so, Lupus allowed himself a cautious peep before entering. Judging it safe enough he entered; the door sliding effortlessly closed behind him. He stood for a moment, blinking as the lights in the room dazzled against the silver interior. The voice again entered his head, but this time through the usual channels; his ears.

'Please make yourself comfortable. It's the first time I've had the privilege to meet a shape changer face to face.'

Dropping poor old Bootes to the floor, Lupus made his way over to where he was sure the voice had emanated from, but the only other thing in the room, apart from the furniture and Bootes and him, was a shrivelled tree. A shrivelled tree he suddenly recognised. And this time it wasn't supporting that idiot Lyra, but was reclining somewhat clumsily on a semicircular couch.

'You're the one that's been talking to me?' said Lupus, a little surprised.

'Yes, and please excuse the subterfuge. I had to be sure you could be trusted.'

Trusted? Lupus guarded this thought.

'And may I say what a pleasure it is to meet someone with obvious civility.'

Civility? Him? What was the creature going on about?

'It is a little tiresome continually coming down to the level of the locals when called upon to do so.' The tree creature sat up. 'But please, where are my manners? Let me introduce myself. My name is Tee Hee and this is, sadly for now, my home.' Tee Hee waved his arms.

Lupus decided the creature believed him to be a higher life form than others he had met; someone more on the creature's level. This, he decided, made the creature a galactic snob. But as he returned the formal niceties of introduction, he couldn't help but feel at ease in the creature's company. This felt, he was certain Tee Hee wasn't a danger; not to him and Bootes that is, although, on another level, he felt it best not to be too relaxed and to keep his mission and his relationship with Draco hidden; for the moment anyway.

Tee Hee continued, explaining his situation and eventually coming to Draco. Lupus, not meaning to, straightened at the mention of his friend's name. Tee Hee didn't appear to notice and explained how Draco had fallen from the sky but a night or two ago and was now helping him to free his spaceship. Sadly the dragon – Tee Hee said the mythical word without falter – had lost all memory but that of his name when he had crashed. Lupus wondered how much Tee Hee really knew. Then Tee Hee mentioned Bootes' companions. Lupus pricked up his ears, a gesture that this time didn't go unnoticed.

It was Tee Hee's turn to show interest, sitting forward on his seat. 'Please pray tell your interest in these natives?' he said.

Under a scrutinising stare Lupus, reluctant at first to admit he knew anything of them, but then thinking better of it, told a sketchy story, excluding anything that he felt Tee Hee didn't need to know, of helping Bootes find his lost companions. Tee Hee listened intently.

'And what will you do when you find them?'

This question caught Lupus slightly off guard. Either the creature hadn't been listening or he was a lot brighter than Lupus thought he was.

Tee Hee stood up before Lupus could answer. 'I don't think you have told me everything Master Lupus,' he said, waddling across the room, 'but I think you have good reasons not to do so and a healthy conscience that will see you well, so I won't press you further. It is good that you care enough to want to help the old man. I wish you good luck.'

Lupus was further taken aback. Conscience? Care? What the heck was he going on about? Then things started to fall into place. Perhaps Tee Hee had seen further into his mind than he had realised. Had delved deep into places and knowledge yet unknown to even him. But surely not, he was a… a? Lupus' shoulders suddenly slumped. It would explain a lot. The strange feelings he had been having. Helping another soul out of the goodness of his heart. Grief! What if Serpens found out? That would be bad. Very bad indeed. He stared at the strange creature as it shuffled towards a new opening in the wall and wondered.

Reaching the gap, Tee Hee turned and beckoned for Lupus to follow. He spoke, his voice suddenly tinged with sadness, 'Please come with me I've something I want to show you.'

On the floor Bootes was still out for the count, Lupus went to pick him up, but Tee Hee stopped him. 'No… just you.'

CHAPTER 23

The giant potato, a sinister gleam radiating from its numerous eyes, towered over Pistor. In its shoot like arms it held Pistor's favourite bottle upside down, emptying its contents onto the ground. Below, cowering from the razor sharp teeth the thing bared at him, Pistor shook with fear. The giant potato let forth a hideous scream of delight.

He had to get away. Pistor tried to get to his feet, but they wouldn't move. The massive potato gave out another delighted scream as Pistor looking down at his feet discovered they were no longer flesh and blood, but stringy brown roots.

Laughing hysterically the potato spoke. 'It's too late for you, Pistor, you can't get away. Did you really think you would get away with the jewels from the lost city? They're mine and now you're doomed to spend the rest of your miserable life as a potato!' More hysterical laughing.

It was Pistor's turn to start screaming.

The potato waddled forward. 'A potato forever!' it taunted.

'Nooo!' shouted Pistor, as the world started to spin around him, 'Nooo!'

'No!' Pistor opened his eyes, he was covered in sweat.

Gathering his wits; he was not a potato, nor did he have roots, he sought his bottle. It was as he had left it. Pistor gave a sigh of relief and took a swig. It had just been a dream; a nightmare. He gave out a laugh. And now it was morning. He had slept longer than he should; a whole night and part of the day. He took another swig and replaced the cork. Another laugh. Sometimes even Pistor felt how good it was to be alive. Not to be a potato. He placed the bottle down his trousers and packed his meagre belongings. His thoughts turned to food and the others.

But as he entered the small umbrella of trees where the others had taken shelter all he was met with was eerie silence. The place was empty. He placed a hand on an indent in the grass where someone had lain; it was cold. They had left without him and a while ago it would appear.

Anger began to bubble in Pistor's mind and breast. 'So that's their little game is it?' he spat, 'Leave me behind, ol' Pistor, the troublemaker and have the gold and jewels for themselves.' Grinding his teeth together Pistor glared with murderous eyes at the jungle. They wouldn't get away with it, oh no, he thought, there was going to be a price to pay. Cursing vengeance as he went Pistor headed for the greenery.

But as he went, blinded to all by his rage, Pistor failed to notice the glint of something amongst the grass and ferns. An object discarded, reflecting the rising sun's rays on the edge of the shelter. It was a sword; Fornax's sword.

CHAPTER 24

Just managing to duck in time and avoid the speeding low flying Lyra, Serpens barked an order. Ophiuchus immediately stuck out a massive, well placed hand. Lyra stopped dead on impact and dropped like a stone to the ground. Serpens casually clambered into his throne and gave the flattened Lyra a thoughtful look.

'Welcome back,' said Serpens, chewing on a talon belonging to one of his little fingers, 'though a tad quicker than one would have expected.' Lyra scrambled to his feet and performed a sort of untidy curtsy. 'I suspect you must have something vitally important to tell me judging by the urgency of your return.' Serpens narrowed his eyes, 'Pray tell.'

Lyra straightened his dress and coughed nervously.

'Come now, Lyra,' said Serpens, transferring his razor sharp fangs to another talon, 'we are all friends here and... come closer.'

'Well,' said Lyra, shifting uneasily as he stopped just short of the base of the throne. It then all came out in one huge blurt, 'Lupus was a great big plant and I had to bark a lot.' And that was that as far as Lyra was concerned. He now cowered as low as he could.

It wasn't low enough. One of Serpens' feet, the one with the verruca problem, was raised high, ready to strike. 'You had to bark! A plant!!' howled Serpens, as he thrust his foot downwards. Again and again his foot crashed down on the hapless Lyra. Then, as it hovered for the umpteenth time, something strange happened.

'Sire! I have had a vision,' announced Ophiuchus.

Foot still raised, head turning slowly, a surprised and puzzled Serpens stared curiously at the ogre. This was new. 'Well?' he said intrigued.

Spreading his hands before him in a slow sweeping gesture, a serene look on his face, Ophiuchus spoke in a long forgotten

Oriental language, 'They sleep amongst the trees, Master. They rest after a long journey through massive sands.'

'Say again,' said Serpens, 'and this time in Inkling'.

Ophiuchus said again, in Inkling.

'Who does?' asked Serpens, not quite sure what to make of it all just yet.

'They, Sire. The ones we seek.'

Still not sure what was going on Serpens decided to play it by ear.

'Massive sands you say?' said Serpens, 'Do you mean a desert?'

'Yes, Sire. A place of sand as high as hills.'

This was a turn up for the book; old Ophiuchus being able to… to… Serpens didn't know what Ophiuchus was able to do, but whatever you called it, it sounded very useful, very useful indeed. Serpens started to pace back and forth, rubbing his massive palms together.

'What else do you see?' said Serpens, cocking his head at Ophiuchus.

'Sand, Sire.'

Serpens stopped his pacing, 'apart from sand?'

'A lovely blue sky and a few wispy clouds,' replied Ophiuchus, his face a mask of inner serenity.

Serpens' face on the other hand was twisted in despair as the feeling that, as always, things were going to prove too good to be true.

'No you dolt. What else do you see surrounding the monkey man? Where exactly is *he*?' But much to Serpens' consternation Ophiuchus just stood there, silent, staring trance like, as if into some other world. Then, as Serpens began to curse everything he could think of, Ophiuchus sprang back to life.

'A sack, Sire,' said Ophiuchus, his eyes narrowing.

It took a moment. 'A sack? Did you say a sack?' said Serpens, midway through a curse on all things bigger than him.

The serenity was back. 'Yes, Sire,' purred a calm Ophiuchus. 'One moment the monkey man was amongst the trees and then he was amongst a sack.'

179

It was almost too much to bear. A plant. A sack. Barking. Amongst a sack. Could you even be *amongst* a sack? Serpens dragged his hands down his face and groaned. How the hell could the monkey man be in a sack? Serpens started to bemoan his fate. Why him? Why was it always him?

Face free of hands Serpens tried again, his voice almost beseeching, 'Anything else?'

'No, Sire. Not at this moment. I'm experiencing slight interference.'

'Aaargh!'

'Breathe, Sire.'

Hands returning to stifle another groan, Serpens wandered back to his throne slumped into it and exhaled a deep, agonised sigh. He glanced over to where Ophiuchus was standing staring blankly into nowhere. Serpens sank deeper into his throne and rested his head in his hands. If he didn't get off this stupid lump of spinning rock soon he would go mad; if he hasn't already.

'Mathter.'

Serpens, wanting nothing more than a small respite from the madness surrounding him and, if the Gods saw fit, another gobstopper, peeped through his fingers. There was no one there. This was it, he *was* going mad.

'MATHTER!'

Hands dropping, Serpens was sure he had heard something that time.

'Downth hereth, Mathter,' said a helium voice.

Peering down from his throne, Serpens saw what could only be described as a flattened Toby jug. It was in fact a Lyra plate. Lyra was blinking up at him through his large boggle eyes. A gurgle welled in Serpens' throat as he entertained the idea of shrieking hysterically.

'It'th meth, Mathter, Lyra,' squeaked Lyra, 'I'th anth ideath.' Lyra tried to smile, but unfortunately he failed and the look he achieved was that of a half finished fried breakfast of two eggs, sausage, mushrooms and baked beans that had been half-heartedly, yet savagely toyed with.

Managing to quell the need to shriek, the slouching Serpens pushed on the arms of the throne and sat upright. This needed thought. Composure was called for. He then heard his own voice asking what the idea was. He slumped again. Had it really come to this? Asking an ugly plate for advice? An ugly plate, that just happened to be one of his, the Dark One's, dreaded minions of darkness. He suddenly had a vision of leading a massed dinner service, backed by mounted cutlery, into battle for the cosmos. He now felt the need to sob. He reached in his tutu for his rag.

'Wellth, Mathter ath youth athk. Perhapth Ith coulth floatth inth the thky andth perhapth thee the thith ofth the lanth. Thee thith dethert Ophiuchuth thaw.'

Serpens sat up, rag forgotten. 'Run that past me again,' he said, suddenly brightening. 'No – hold that thought, I've an idea.' Serpens leapt from the throne, spirits spiralling upward, 'I'm going to fly you high in the sky so you can see the lie of the land. Perhaps you will see the desert that fool Ophiuchus was banging on about.' Serpens felt better. He didn't need a cracked piece of crockery telling him what to do. He had a mind of his own.

As Lyra watched his master dancing round the throne he couldn't help but feel a burst of pride. Fancy that, he thought, a mere underling like me having the same idea as the mighty Dark One. He was still harbouring that same thought a second later as he soared, saucer like, into the deep black yonder.

*　*　*

'Anything?'
　'Nope.'
　'Anything?'
　'Nope.'
　'Anything?'
　'No – wait… nope.'

It had gone on like this all night and the best part of the morning; Serpens impatient; Lyra himself.

'Anything now?' said Serpens, his mind entering the weird and wonderfully empty head of Lyra for the umpteenth-plus time.

181

Lyra scanned the horizon for the umpteenth-plus time. As usual nothing on it and nothing in it.

Serpens was getting impatient; surely they should have seen something by now, he was coming to the end of his tether or rather Lyra's. He let a little more slack into the air. 'Surely you can see something now?' he said in Lyra's mind, 'Some indication.' There was no response, 'Lyra?'

'Nope.'

Something wasn't right, Serpens could feel it in his bones. He gave the rope a shake, still no response. This time Serpens tugged violently on it. An instant later Lyra was floating eye to eye with him. The still flattened Lyra swayed uneasily. Serpens looked closer, deeper into Lyra's eyes. 'WELL!!' Vacant, Lyra blinked. 'You've forgotten, haven't you? Forgotten why you were up there.' Serpens pointed to the now deep blue yonder.

'Breathe.'

Reluctantly Serpens counted to ten. He may as well. He could see that shouting was going to have little effect on the imp. No point in giving him another beating either, he was already an omelette. Obviously the previous stomping had had some sort of delayed reaction on the idiot's senses. Serpens looked into Lyra's eyes. They appeared to be staring at each other. A different plan was called for.

'CAN... YOU... HEAR... ME?' said Serpens, tapping the imp on its skull.

A slight blink. Serpens took this as a yes.

'Good. Now take this up with you.' There was a small pop and Serpens handed Lyra one of his eyeballs. 'Hold it like this,' he explained, turning the pupil away from Lyra's grubby palm, 'and don't drop it. Remember, I'll be watching you.' Serpens waited for a reaction, but the pun was lost on the imp. A sigh. 'Now go.' Lyra rose into the air and was gone.

Once high enough, Serpens began surveying the area but there was no sign of desert or monkey man. After further fruitless searching, mainly due to Lyra's somewhat erratic manoeuvring, Serpens decided enough was enough and entered Lyra's mind. He was going to take the controls; which in Lyra's case was akin to those of the fairground dodgem. Serpens was going to extend the search area to beyond the horizon. Forward a stabilised Lyra glided, in his grubby little hand Serpens' eye swivelling and darting for all it was worth.

But as the area covered grew larger and larger with no result Serpens started to lose heart and curse his trust in Ophiuchus. How could he have ever believed the big useless dolt to be anything else but…? He started to slow and was all for cutting his losses when three small dots appeared in the distance flying above the edge of a great sea. He decided to investigate. He didn't have anything else to do. Serpens steered Lyra closer.

At first, and logic bore this, Serpens thought the dots to be some sort of sea bird. Perhaps the sand Ophiuchus had seen was a beach. He now turned his attention to the sea to look for it, but as he drew past the dots that were now large enough to identify, he realised his serendipidus mistake. The dots were not sea birds, but vultures, hovering high on drafts of warm air. The sea, a shimmering desert. He was sure he had at last found what he was looking for.

Delighted with himself Serpens speedily returned his mind to his body and reeled Lyra in. Recovering his eye he gave the order to move.

Back on his throne, it gently swaying to the plod of Ophiuchus' movements, Serpens watched as the flattened Lyra struggled to keep up. Soon the monkey man and his secret would be his and then his dream of conquest would become reality. He afforded himself a discreet chuckle. Soon he would be master of all.

CHAPTER 25

Quiet, infidel!' ordered a gruff strange accent. It was smartly followed by the thump of wood on sacking.

Inside the sack, Musca ruefully touched the back of his head; he could feel a lump swelling already.

'Any more of your noise and by the sands and the Seven Sacred Scarabs we will leave you all in the desert and let the sun bleach your worthless bones!' threatened the same voice.

Rubbing spittle onto his lump, a woozy Musca wondered what the hell was going on. The last thing he remembered was being rudely awoken by a huge hand wrapping itself roughly across his mouth.

As Musca lay there wondering, sweating, rubbing, suspended in his sack and pondering his fate, five similar sacks, housing equally bewildered occupants and not that far away, quietly rocked and rolled as the beasts that carried them strode through the hot desert sands to their waiting destination.

The camels were brought to a standstill and the ropes securing the sacks cut sending them to the desert floor.

From behind him Musca heard a female voice let loose a tirade of expletives; at least Fornax was with him. He twisted at his bonds, but the more he struggled the deeper they bit. He felt the need to go to her aid, but it was no good. He couldn't even shout support; a combination of a dry throat and the fear of another lump saw to that. Other voices did answer her, ones with the strange accents and gradually Fornax quietened down.

Now someone else entered the fray; this one spoke in high strained tones as if the owner was hanging by his nose from a clothes peg. 'Bring them! The High One, Fatidic, will see them now.'

The order was obeyed without question and the sacks were hoisted up and over shoulders and carried a short distance before being unceremoniously dumped on the ground once again. This time though, light crept in through the top of the sacks.

Realising the sack was now open Musca quickly wriggled free of it and found he was no longer in the desert. Below him a threadbare carpet, above him canvas. Hands and feet still bound, Musca struggled to his feet and looked about him, blinking as he did against the harsh sunlight flooding through the open tent flap.

'Come forward, all of you so I can see you clearly,' said someone hidden amongst shadows on the far side of the tent.

Musca looked round to see the others were with him. He struggled forward, his heart a little lighter.

'That's close enough,' announced the shadows, 'I am Magus Fatidic, the Lord of all planes and the Seer of all things. Welcome to my humble abode.' His accent differed from the rest.

From out of the shadows strolled the tallest man any of them had ever seen. That was until he stood in the light from the flap. Then they saw that he wasn't tall at all, but was the smallest man they had ever seen wearing probably the tallest hat that they had ever seen. The little man clicked his fingers and as if from nowhere half a dozen swarthy, weather beaten men appeared carrying the cruellest looking curved swords.

Musca could feel his legs jellifying as the nearest headed for him, sword held aloft. With two swift strokes Musca was on the floor.

'What's wrong with him?' asked the Lord of all planes and Seer of all things.

'I think he's fainted,' said Fornax, rushing to Musca's side. She removed the sliced bonds from his wrists and briskly rubbed his hands.

'Wha...!'wailed Musca, coming round, 'I'm too young to die.'

'Musca, it's me Fornax.'

An eye partially opened and looked at her. 'I'm not dead?' said Musca.

'Not yet, but I wouldn't wager against it happening soon.' Fornax smiled grimly and pulled Musca upright.

Once up, Musca's cheeks coloured as he realised what the swordsman had done and avoiding eye contact kicked away the loose bonds from his ankles. Across the tent Cetus smiled, happy to see his old friend showing signs of his old self again.

'Good, good, all is well then,' said Magus Fatidic, moving closer. He clicked his fingers once more and a large man with rotten teeth and pitted features appeared by his side. 'Akneed here, my captain, will show you to your quarters where you will be fed and allowed to freshen up.'

'But?' said Fornax.

'Later,' said Magus Fatidic, and with a dismissive wave of a hand was gone. In his place the six swordsmen reappeared. It was obvious there was little choice but to do as the little man had commanded.

'This way,' said Akneed, leading the way to the tent flap. The swordsmen followed on behind.

Outside the sun was dazzling. Shielding their eyes Musca and the others were led to two tents set on the edge of the main encampment. They stopped outside the first one.

'Please to enter,' said Akneed, pointing at Fornax, 'you men to the other one.' It was pointless arguing as the tips of six razor sharp swords were making a point against it. They did as they were told. 'Please to make yourselves at home. I will have fresh garments sent to you once you have eaten.

Left alone in their tent, a worried Equuleus whispered to the others. 'Where are we?'

Cetus moved to the tent flap and attempted to push it open, but a sharp rap on the knuckles persuaded him otherwise. Rubbing them he turned to Equuleus, 'Well I think we may well be back in the desert, but other than that, your guess is as good as mine.' Something behind Equuleus caught his attention and thoughts of whereabouts were instantly replaced with signals coming from his stomach. In the centre of the tent were benches surrounding a table loaded with food. 'But for now I think we should take advantage of our hosts' hospitality while we can.' Cetus moved to the table, and eyeing its wares greedily, began to eat. It didn't take long for the others to join him.

An hour later when the tent flap opened the food and drink was but a memory. It was the captain.

'Good. I'm glad to see our guests have enjoyed their meal,' said Akneed, winking slyly to the guard accompanying him. 'Now to please freshen up and slip into something more comfortable.' He threw an impressive looking pile of grandiose robes and garments onto the tent floor. 'We only want the best for our *guests* during their stay.'

Musca got up from the bench he was sitting at and made a bee line, not for the clothes lying on the floor, but foolishly perhaps for Akneed. The knuckles of the guard whitened as his grip on his sword tightened.

'Why are we here?' Musca asked boldly, stopping well out of sword's reach. Behind him Equuleus covered his eyes.

Akneed raised both hands, one to Musca, the other to the guard staying his hand. 'Please, young Master, all will be revealed tonight at the grand feast to be held in your honour.'

'But...?'

'Tonight, Master.' Akneed bowed his head and was gone leaving behind him frowning foreheads and puzzled looks.

'I don't like this one little bit,' said Cetus, who had decided that now the food was gone it was time to worry. 'First we're bundled up in smelly sacks without so much as a by your leave, then we're dragged off to goodness knows where in the middle of the desert. And now there is to be a feast in our honour. It doesn't ring right so it doesn't. It doesn't ring right.' He started pacing back and forth, fretting as he went. 'And where's Pistor? Trust that sot to go missing.'

Cetus wasn't the only one worrying. Musca too had a head full of doubts. More so now that Cetus was acting as he was. If the big man wasn't excited by the promise of more food, then something was terribly afoot. Musca joined Cetus in his pacing, but from the other direction. They paused only to dodge from each other's path.

'Maybe they think we're princes from the stars.'

Cetus and Musca ceased their pacing and stared at Hydrus.

'It was just a thought.'

Hydra placed an arm round his brother's shoulders and led him away to the benches. The two worriers continued their pacing.

The day was late when Akneed returned to check on the guests. 'Ah you are dressed; I will take your dirty clothes away.' He started to collect the discarded clothes.

'Why have we got to wear them? I'm cooking,' complained Hydrus, pulling at them.

Akneed ignored the question, as he had ignored all the rest.

'You can't keep ignoring us,' said Musca, rounding on Akneed with his armful of clothes, 'we demand to know why we are prisoners?'

Turning to face Musca, Akneed blew a shrill whistle through his large rotten teeth. Two guards instantly entered the tent swords drawn. Musca stepped back and grew silent as the rays of the setting sun glinted evilly on the edge of their weapons.

'Please do not be a feared, young Master,' sneered Akneed, showing his teeth in all their glory, 'these men are here to keep danger out, not you in.'

'Then why don't you let us go?' croaked Equuleus, his voice shaking with emotion.

Akneed smiled, his teeth as black as his heart. 'Oh, but we will. As soon as the sun sets you will all be taken from the feast and you will be set free of all worries.' No one liked the look of the glint in his eye. 'Soon all seven of you will be on your way.' He turned to leave. 'I will have your friend sent to you before the feast begins.'

So Pistor is with us, thought Cetus. 'You mean friends,' said Cetus. 'You said seven of us.'

'He's right,' agreed Musca, 'Fornax and Pistor?'

The smug grin that perpetually clung to Akneed's face faltered. 'All but the woman are here,' he said, but the statement carried a lack of conviction. He began to frantically scan the tent. There were five, there should be six. 'Aha!' he suddenly shouted, spying

188

a bundle of clothing lying in the shadows. 'You try to make a fool out of Akneed. Guards! Seize that man.' The guards rushed past him. 'Bring him to me.'

But the guards returned sheepishly carrying a set of clothes the captain had thrown in earlier. Akneed grew deathly white.

'But there was seven of you,' said Akneed, dropping the bundle he was carrying. 'I counted you as you left the desert.' There was now a look of horror spreading across his face. 'Get Ramblest!'

One of the guards hurried out of the tent and returned moments later with a huge man, who in the dark could easily be mistaken for a camel. He grinned inanely at Akneed.

Grabbing the newcomer by the arms, Akneed spoke slowly to the man, 'Ramblest, where is the other infidel?'

Shrugging his massive shoulders, the big man stared at the tent's captives. 'Ramblest count on hands like you tell me; one hand and two fingers.' He held the two fingers proudly aloft.

Akneed's heart sank. 'Ramblest, I want you to think carefully before you answer. Which hand did you count on first?' There now lingered a surreal calmness about Akneed; a fate already accepted?

The big man thought deeply, then thought some more. At last the strain slipped from his face and he spoke. 'This one,' he said, holding it triumphantly.

His fears now proven Akneed stared dumbly at the hand; the one with the thumb missing.

'Ramblest count good. This hand is five and two fingers is seven.' He shoved them proudly under Akneed's nose.

Akneed couldn't ignore the obvious and looked to verify his own stupidity. 'And how many infidels are there in here?'

Ramblest looked at his hands, then at the group of infidels and then back to his hands. He then proceeded to hold up his thumb less hand, fingers splayed to his face. Once Musca, Cetus and the brothers were blotted from view by his huge digits he started to laugh out loud. 'Yes they are my hand,' he shouted. 'They are five and one more, the young one,' he blotted Equuleus from view with a finger from his other hand, 'is six and girl is seven.' Ramblest laughed out loud again.

'Good Ramblest, you can go now,' said Akneed, feeling the world's worries settling heavily on his shoulders.

'Ramblest do good?'

'Yes, Ramblest do good,' agreed Akneed, nodding glumly.

As Ramblest happily ambled outside, the guard who had brought him in whispered something under his breath; something along the lines of "camel with dung for brains".

Akneed exploded with rage. 'If you speak of my brother so again, I shall personally flay you alive and roll you in salt.' The guard shrank away nodding profusely and reversed very carefully from the tent. Akneed turned to Musca and the others, his grin back, but unsteady. 'There appears to have been a misunderstanding. The feast may have to be postponed for a while.'

Outside a small commotion was raising momentum. A certain guard had been quick to spread the bad news and a shrill voice was calling for Akneed. The colour that had began to reinstate itself in Akneed's cheeks quickly drained again at the sound of it.

Akneed hurried from the tent with the horrible feeling the feast wasn't the only thing in danger of being cancelled.

CHAPTER 26

Lupus had been struck speechless; he hadn't known what to say. The Tee Hee creature had been in obvious distress when he had left and soon he would be back; wanting an answer. Lupus prowled the room, sniffing at this and that, thinking about what Tee Hee had asked of him. It was something new for him; someone wanting his help, unconditionally trusting him. He stopped and gave Bootes a gentle nudge. The old man was still out cold. Lupus left him to his dreaming and continued his wandering and thinking. He didn't know what to do. If he helped and Serpens found out he would make his life a living nightmare, but on the other hand if he didn't at least try to help he couldn't help but feel this new conscience thing might turn out to be just as uncomfortable.

The door to the room slid silently open and Draco entered. 'The Master has instructed me to see if there is anything you need and to enquire whether you are comfortable yet.'

Lupus, who had decided not to pry into Draco's mind to see what he was playing at, studied his blank stare and wondered about the dragon's last remark. Was this Tee Hee gently pressuring him or was he flirting with paranoia?

'Tell your master that, yes I am comfortable and that I will see him when he is ready.' Lupus had made his decision.

Draco nodded and left. As the door closed a moan filled the room.

'Ooh, me 'ead,' said Bootes, trying to rise.

Lupus went over to him and with a swift flick of a paw sent Bootes back to dreamland. He was sorry for doing it, but now wasn't the time for complications. He expected Tee Hee any moment now. Right on cue the door slid aside.

Standing in the doorway Tee Hee spoke to Lupus telepathically, 'You have made a decision.' It wasn't a question, more a statement.

Lupus didn't reply, he felt he didn't need to. Tee Hee smiled his grainy smile and stepped inside. He sat himself in a seat and started to converse normally. 'I'm glad you have agreed to help me. Now, please be seated, we need to talk further.'

Lupus sat on the floor and listened intently to what Tee Hee had to tell him. When Tee Hee finished, Lupus asked for a moment to play it over in his mind.

'Well, Master Lupus, what do you think?' said Tee Hee, when a polite amount of time had passed.

'Sounds fine to me,' said Lupus, looking up, 'when do I go?'

Tee Hee rose from his chair, wearing a smile that looked hewed by an axe it was so wide. 'Excellent,' he said, clapping his hands together, 'as soon as possible. I go to prepare.'

Tee Hee left, leaving Lupus pondering his choice. Was it the right one? He lay down to wait, head between his paws, thinking. He supposed, right or wrong, he would no doubt find out in due course.

CHAPTER 27

The going was tough, but as the saying goes; Pistor's saying: when the going gets tough, take another swig from the bottle; which is what he did as he eyed, with growing trepidation, the savage greenery surrounding him.

He had been travelling for hours in the humid heat of the jungle and all he wanted at that moment was to find a clearing big enough to sit in and rest awhile, but the jungle was being uncooperative.

Pistor took another swig from his bottle, then stuffed it back down his trousers. The drink helped ease the aching in his weary bones, but did nothing to allay the uneasiness as he headed deeper into the jungle's depths. There was also something else the drink couldn't help him with; a feeling he had harboured since awhile back, after his anger, fuelled by revenge and greed, had wilted in the heat; that he may have been wrong about the others abandoning him. Which if right meant, and this left him cold inside, he was all alone in this hostile place. Alone and lost.

With sweat running riot from head to toe, Pistor pushed on, dodging best he could, the hidden creepers and tree roots that wanted to trip him and the plethora of insects of all colour and size that were queuing to bite and drink deep of the intoxicating fluid that ran through his veins. The temptation to sit and rest grew heavier with each step, but was outweighed by the undoubting knowledge he would find it hard to rise once he did, providing an unconscious ready meal for whatever predator may lurk and crawl beneath the undergrowth.

On he went, backtracking when the way proved too dense. Cursing his fate, the trees, the insects and the others, when scraped or scratched. Then, when he thought it could get no worse, came the howling.

Neck hairs bristling, Pistor struggled on; where could he go? Still, he told himself, whatever was howling couldn't be any worse than the insects that were trying to eat him alive. He hoped.

The howling grew louder, the hairs on Pistor's neck were trying to uproot. He stopped and crouched low; the howling was just ahead and if he was right, it now sounded human. He pushed on, but crouched again when other noises reached his ears. Lower, intermingled with the howls were growls and roars. Not loud roars, but those roars that said the owner was triumphant. Now he could clearly hear a man's voice shouting. Pistor swallowed hard and started crawling towards a dense clump of undergrowth through which he cautiously peeped.

The sight that met him had the hairs on his neck looking for somewhere to hide. Not far from him, no more than thirty or so yards, in a clearing, stood the most ferocious, yet magnificent beast, he had ever seen. It was covered in golden fur and around its neck a majestic mane of gold and black framed its regal head. A head with jaws as large as the mouth of a well, gaped open. Its teeth, the size of a large man's fingers, shone white and menacing in the sunlight that managed to perforate the dense canopy above. It stood growling in a spotlight of gold. A king, thought Pistor in a daze.

He may well have stayed like that admiring the beast for a year and a day if the suddenness of a massive roar hadn't brought him to his senses.

Well, thought Pistor, you've found your clearing, now what?

For now though, he watched, as the great beast became quiet and swayed its head back and forth. Then he saw the man. It had to be the man that had been shouting and howling. He was lying beneath the beast, pinned by its massive front paws, but still struggling; frantically pulling and tugging at its mane.

Pistor suddenly saw a way out from his jungle hell. He would have to save the man. It went against the grain, but what choice did he have? Save the man or stay lost; perhaps until he died. Even worse, if there could be anything worse, the beast might pick up his scent when it was finished here and follow him. Seconds! No, he did have a choice; die lost or eaten, or die saving the man.

He needed a drink. With a swig from his bottle for courage and another for what the hell! Pistor took a deep breath and made his choice. He burst from the undergrowth screaming and cursing and with arms waving about like a deranged windmill, charged at the beast.

In the clearing man and beast stopped their struggling and stared at the crazy creature racing headlong towards them. Arms swinging, spittle splattering, mouth screaming, hair flowing. It was all too much for the great beast that had never seen anything like it. With one last defiant roar, it turned and fled. He would later tell his grand-cubs of the insane scarecrow that had appeared from out of thin air, flying and breathing fire (he'd added the fire bit when asked why the King of the jungle had run from a mere scarecrow).

The man was still lying on the ground, looking on in amazement, as Pistor passed him in hot pursuit of the beast. This continued when Pistor stopped at the edge of the clearing and turned, grinning madly. The man was still staring goggled eyed when Pistor's grin disappeared and he collapsed face first beside him on the ground. It had been at this point that Pistor had noticed the man's legs were missing.

It was several minutes before Pistor came round. When he did a heavily tanned face was peering down at him.

'I Jungle Man,' stated the face.

Pistor then remembered who what and where he was. 'Your legs! The beast!' He sat up and nervously looked across to where the beast had left the clearing.

'Beast Jungle Man's friend,' said Jungle Man.

'What?' muttered a bewildered Pistor.

'Beast and Jungle Man play. Jungle Man winning when madman come charging. Why man chase beast?'

'Your legs?'

'Jungle Man not have legs. Jungle Man never have legs. Jungle Man not need legs.'

Pistor had a discreet look. The jungle man was a mass of rippling muscles from head to foot, with no sign of injury. Strategically placed about his person were patches of hide. The like were on each knee.

'How do you get about?'

Jungle Man gave Pistor on indignant look. 'Jungle Man have strong arms. Jungle Man swing through jungle, no problem.' And to prove it, he crouched, then sprang like a coiled spring onto the nearest hanging vine and started to swing from one vine to another around the clearing until he was back where he started. The jungle man landed, surprisingly lightly, at an astounded Pistor's feet.

'Now you come home with Jungle Man. Tell Jungle Man why madman in jungle chasing friend.'

An eager Pistor, glad to be going anywhere away from where he was, couldn't wait. 'Which way?' he said, looking for a path.

Jungle Man pointed skyward. 'Jungle Man's home in tree.'

Turning pale, Pistor viewed the vines and creepers still swinging in the trees with sudden dread. 'I'm not very good at climbing,' he said. Up was a very long way.

'Madman not climb,' said Jungle Man, who then made Pistor jump by howling at the top of his lungs.

Moments later a giant ape descended from above and dropped into the clearing. Pistor, all of a sudden, felt very weak and dropped his belongings.

'Hairy Man too friend. He take you.'

Protesting, but to no avail Pistor and belongings were swept up into a giant arm and whisked at great speed into the tree tops, with close on their heels a howling Jungle Man. It took but a few minutes to reach Jungle Mans home.

'Madman open eyes now,' said Jungle Man.

Venturing a quick peep, Pistor immediately began to sway when he saw how high up he was. Jungle Man grabbed his arm and ushered him into the tree house where he lived.

'You will soon be good in tree,' said Jungle Man, attempting to reassure.

Pistor seriously doubted that, but nodded all the same and thankfully entered the safety of the tree house.

'Madman sit in Jungle Man's chair.'

When Pistor was sitting comfortably, Jungle Man emitted a short howl and the ape appeared at the door. More howls, intermingled with several grunts, set the ape scurrying.

'Jungle Man's friend get food,' explained Jungle Man, 'Now you tell why you here. Jungle Man listen. Jungle Man good listener.' Jungle Man settled down on a branch protruding through one of the tree house windows and gestured for Pistor to begin.

Pistor started with his name.

CHAPTER 28

Musca and the others had just settled at the wooden table to discuss their predicament when the tent flap flew open and Fornax made an undignified entrance.

Mouths gaped and dribble flowed when she stood up. She was actually wearing more than she had been, but it was the way she was wearing what she was wearing.

'All right, hands on your laps boys, I don't want to see how happy you are to see me. There are more important things to talk about.'

Hydrus and Equuleus, who had got up to help her, quickly sat back down.

Fornax dusted herself down and made her way to the table. 'Do any of you know what's going on?' No one did. 'Then you better listen, because I do.' She sat beside them her features stone. 'We've got to get away from here and quickly.'

'But the feast?' said Equuleus.

'The only feast they're interested in is the one afterwards,' said Fornax.

'The one afterwards?' said Equuleus, 'I don't understand. Why two feasts?'

'I'm coming to that,' said Fornax, drawing closer. 'We are to be fattened at the feast and then sacrificed to some sort of bug creatures they worship.'

'How could you know that?' said Musca, ready to dismiss what Fornax was saying.

'One of the guards thought it better to stand guard *in* my tent rather than outside it. His tongue quickly loosened when I changed my clothes.' Musca could understand that and apologised for doubting her. Fornax nodded and continued with her story. 'It seems these creatures, scarabs they call them, are seven in number and every seven years they come to feed on seven poor souls who

198

are thrown to them.' This was met by several gulps; three from Musca, who's imagination was back and ready to get the better of him. 'With Pistor missed for whatever reason they now haven't got enough of us to sacrifice. They're out looking for him right now.'

'What if they don't find him?' said Cetus.

'They'll let us go,' said Equuleus, more in hope than in knowledge.

'No, they won't,' said Fornax, dashing Equuleus' hopes, 'if they can't find him the head of the tribe will take his place.'

'I thought you said they always sacrificed strangers,' said Cetus, hoping he had found a flaw in their plan.'

'I did, they adopt a stranger as their leader from time to time, don't ask I don't know, so if there's a short fall come the time of the ceremony, as there is now, he gets it as well.'

'What if there's more missing?'

'Who knows? Perhaps they disown the odd one or seven of their own.'

'So Fatidic's for the chop if they can't find Pistor,' said Musca, feeling he was getting the gist of it.

'Would seem so,' said Fornax, 'but I for one don't want to be around when the time comes.'

If there was a way out without being discovered no one found it. All night they looked without success and now it was too late. The sun was up and the flap of the tent had been thrown open. Akneed appeared accompanied by two guards carrying food and water.

Food and water placed on the table, Akneed clapped his hands and the guards swiftly left. Alone with the captives he unsheathed his sword and laid it on the table. He fingered it nervously.

Anxious eyes went from sword to Akneed. He wasn't smiling, or if he was no one could tell. He had a face like thunder; black and puffy and ready to crash. He spoke, spitting out each word as he did.

'My face is like this because of you accursed infidels. I have been beaten with the bones of an ass as befits my crime. If I fail again my brother will be beaten with *my* bones.'

A deathly hush fell on the tent, no one daring to breathe, as fingers curled and tightened round the sword's hilt.

'If I had my way you would all be buried alive in the sands this very minute, but the high priest has spoken and so you are to be honoured with a feast tonight.' He attempted a sneering grin, but the pain proved too much. 'Until tonight then!' said Akneed, through gritted teeth and, with a flourish of his sword, left the tent.'

Kneeling, Fornax lifted something from the floor and handed it to Musca. It was a tuft of hair, his hair, cut from his head without him feeling it. Colour drained from him.

'We must escape tonight,' said Fornax, 'whatever.'

Her words sent a shiver down their spines.

It was nearing dusk and still they were short of any concrete plans of escape. Except one perhaps; a long shot conceived by Equuleus. It had formed in his mind from what Fornax had said regarding her loose tongued guard. It involved a sexy dance – Fornax had given it a try to everyone's approval – crossed legs, and the overpowering of said crossed legged guard while his mind was elsewhere. It was a very long shot. It was all they had.

Time passed and when the stars began to make their appearance and no other plan had come to light it was decided to put all they had into action. Fornax called to the guard on duty.

The guard entered. All got ready. Fornax did the sexiest dance ever seen. The tension was unbearable. The guard was enthralled. Then smiled and spent the next ten minutes asking Musca if he came there often and if he was free for a minute or so. It had ended in disaster.

A flustered Musca thanked the guard, but said he would be spending the evening in. The guard sighed, winked, mumbled something about, "didn't know what he was missing", and left.

The next time the flap opened it was time for the feast.

As they were led from the tent, thoughts of escape began to rapidly diminish amongst the throng of sword wielding thugs. If the chance came they would still try, but now they needed a miracle.

'Move, infidels,' it was Akneed, standing beside tables bowing under the weight of food, the sword in his hand gleaming cruelly in the light of a huge campfire. 'Sit and enjoy your meal. It will be a long while before you enjoy such a feast again.' The evil chuckle that followed sounded more like a throttled gurgle.

Akneed left them and made his way to the head table which was standing on a raised platform in front of where Musca and the others had been led. Sitting at it already were Magus Fatidic and the high priest. Akneed nodded to them and sat. The high priest then nodded to Fatidic who rose.

Fatidic spent the next ten minutes or so speaking on the virtues of togetherness and feasting and how under his leadership they had prospered and would continue to prosper in the coming years. Ominously no one at the top table appeared to be listening.

He concluded, 'And now my friends and honoured guests,' Fatidic gestured to the lower table, 'let the feast begin!'

On the lower table the six guests were prompted to eat. A seventh seat stood empty.

'Doesn't look like they found Pistor,' whispered Cetus, grabbing a leg of something.

'Then why does Fatidic sound so happy? Going on about the future like that,' said Hydra.

'Perhaps he doesn't know yet,' said Fornax.

They looked as one at the top table. The little man was tucking into his food as if he didn't have a care in the world.

'I've a feeling you could be right,' agreed Cetus.

'Perhaps we could use him somehow?'

A guard intervened. 'Stop your mumblings and eat,' he said, digging Musca between the shoulder blades with a gnarled and bony knuckle.

The feast itself was sumptuous; a multitude of meats and fruits, the like none of them had ever seen before. Cetus tucked in. If this was going to be his last meal he was determined to make the most of it. Around him the others followed suit, all bar Fornax that is, who toyed with the food she had taken and smouldered silently like a sleeping volcano looking for a reason to erupt.

To make matters worse dancing girls had appeared wearing just enough to keep the imagination interested. Fornax seethed and glowered at the semi-circle of guards who sat leering and dribbling at the dancers. She wondered, were all men pigs? Then looked at her own. They were stuffing their faces and ogling the girls with the same interest as the guards. Didn't they care? Fornax became scathing in her mind and not a little bit bewildered. Didn't they realise this was their last meal? She decided she couldn't stand it any longer and made to stand but a strong pair of hands, one with a thumb missing, forced her back to her seat.

'Feast not finished yet. Ramblest told no one to leave until feast is finished.'

Fornax fell back into her seat, returned to her thoughts and playing with her food. She felt useless; perhaps this is how the others felt? Fornax looked closer at her friends and discovered something she hadn't noticed earlier. Forgetting the food they were stuffing in their mouths, forgetting the cheers and ogling looks, she looked deeper into their eyes, and saw fear. Perhaps she was being too harsh. Perhaps they were dealing with fate the only way they could. She took a piece of meat and took a bite; it was good. Fornax took another bite and chewed on it thoughtfully. She then drank some of the clear liquid that had been provided. It went down well. She hadn't realised she was so hungry; so thirsty. Fornax drank some more and without realising it resigned herself to her own fate.

At a quarter to midnight hush was called for and Magus Fatidic stood up to give another speech. 'Dear friends and honoured guests may I say what an honour it has been for me to be your host and now as the feast draws to an end may I invite you all to one last celebration, the honouring of the Seven Sacred Scarabs! Guards!'

The guards swiftly descended on Musca and the others; there was no struggle.

Fatidic spoke again, 'Take them to the pit!'

But this time the guards didn't move.

'I, Magus Fatidic, your leader has spoken,' said Fatidic, too full of self importance to notice the guards weren't looking at him. 'Take them to the pit!'

The high priest nodded and Akneed knocked Fatidic's hat to the ground and hauled him aloft by his shoulders.

'*Now* take them to the pit!' squeaked the high priest in his peculiarly shrill voice.

'What the hell?' demanded a wriggling Fatidic as he was removed from the top table.

On the top table the high priest was squealing with manic delight, 'Take them! Take them all away!'

The prisoners, led by Akneed, were dragged to a barely visible patch of dark amidst an oasis of rock and centuries old ruins. Only Fatidic struggled. Fornax reached across a hand to Equuleus who gripped it tightly. Tears glistened in his eyes but none fell. Fornax suddenly became incredibly proud of the small group of survivors who had come so far in search of a place called Ohm. They were much braver than she could ever give them credit for, she after all, was a warrior, they but ordinary folk. They reached the edge of the dark patch which could now be seen for what it was; a deep dark pit.

'Ramblest throw them in now?' asked an eager Ramblest, who for all his faults was never backward in coming forward when death and destruction was to be meted out.

'No,' said Akneed, raising his hand, 'not yet brother, we must wait for the high priest.'

So they waited. Fornax, Musca, the brothers, Equuleus, Cetus and a bewildered Fatidic stared into the pit before them; each with a guard's hand placed on their shoulder and another in the small of their backs, ready to push the moment the order was given.

'Akneed?'

'Yes, Ramblest.'

'Where are the stars?'

Sometimes Akneed couldn't believe his brother's stupidity. 'In the sky…' he started, but the sight that met his skyward glance stalled him. He looked behind him. The stars were still there twinkling as ever but, he returned his gaze forward, there were none ahead. Then the shout went up.

'Simoom!' screamed a guard, 'Simoom!' Before fleeing back towards the camp.

All around panic now started to set in. Within seconds panic turned to terror. It swept through the remaining guards and within seconds only Akneed, Ramblest and the prisoners remained at the edge of the pit.

Akneed looked from the prisoners to Ramblest and back again. He had a choice to make; he made it. To hell with the prisoners, they had caused him enough grief. 'Run Ramblest, run,' he shouted, 'Simoom!' Together they disappeared into the night.

'What's happening?' demanded Fornax, quick to regain her wits and grab Fatidic's throat.

He just stared at her looking shocked.

Fornax slapped him hard across the face. 'Tell me what's happening,' she said, ready to administer another slap should it be needed.

'It's a Simoom,' he replied flatly.

'What the hell is a Simoom?' screamed Fornax.

'A sandstorm. The worst. Rip the skin off your back in seconds.'

Dropping Fatidic, she watched with horror as the oncoming storm raced towards them. It appeared they had survived the frying pan only to have jumped into one hell of a fire.

CHAPTER 29

It was thought better to drug Bootes. For their plan to work everything would have to be in place before he awoke.

Lupus dragged Bootes across the threshold of the silver saucer's exterior door and headed along the path Musca and the others had recently travelled on. Tee Hee had taken Draco on ahead to set the scene for the beginning of the plan. The old man murmured something inaudible and Lupus, not for the first time, grew concerned for his health. He had been out for quite a while now, but Tee Hee had assured Lupus that the old man would not suffer any lasting side affects from the drugs, or his time spent unconscious. A short while later Lupus met up with a still beaming Tee Hee.

'I take it by your smile all is in place,' said Lupus, through a mouthful of Bootes.

'The basket is in the clump of bushes to your left and supplies and a suitable note is hidden with it. You shouldn't have any problems, but make sure the note is only read at the end of your journey,' said Tee Hee, the smile threatening to remove the top of his head.

Lupus raised his bushy eyebrows. It was true he harboured certain misgivings about the venture he was about to undertake, but Tee Hee seemed more than happy that all would be all right. 'What about the sandstorm your instruments picked up?' he said, counting it as one of those worries on his list.

'Not a problem, it's heading away from you, towards the lower mountains. Could turn into a tornado,' replied Tee Hee, attempting a shrug of non existent shoulders, 'wouldn't want to be around when that hits.' He then waddled over to Bootes and removing an instrument from a pouch around his waist and placed it against the old man's throat.

When he was finished Tee Hee gave Lupus a serious look. 'I must apologise. I read your mind as you approached. He will be all right just a little groggy when he wakes.' Tee Hee now took from the pouch another instrument resembling a hypodermic. 'I'll give him a neutralising agent. No need for him to be under any longer than necessary. He'll be up and on his feet again quite soon.'

Lupus felt a little better as Tee Hee returned the hypo to his pouch.

'There, now I fear I must go and leave everything in your capable hands or paws, as is in your case,' said Tee Hee, suddenly distracted. He turned away and called for Draco who appeared overhead. 'Now remember, once Draco has freed my craft I will have only enough fuel to visit you once. Then I will have to leave this planet.' Tee Hee paused for a moment, as if searching for what he wanted to say next. 'Whether I will ever return, I do not know.'

Lupus couldn't help but feel the sadness building in the strange little creature.

Then, as if shaking himself down, Tee Hee became business like once more. 'You have the emitter?' he said.

Lupus nodded.

'Good. I now leave you to get on with things.' Tee Hee signalled to Draco that he was ready to go. Draco swooped and grasping Tee Hee by the belt, whisked him into the air. Soon they were just a distant dot.

Lupus watched them until they disappeared from sight, then had a look behind the bushes. All was as Tee Hee said it would be; he never doubted it wouldn't. Now it was time for the old man to play his part.

Bootes was snoring happily. Lupus sniffed him – from a distance – and decided he was no longer under the influence of drugs, but naturally soundly asleep. Time to wake him up. Lupus howled.

Dragged from a dream of nothing in particular, Bootes woke screaming, his eyelids fluttering crazily over staring yellow orbs. He began to thrash about like a thing possessed, his hands reaching for something that wasn't there. 'Where's me bone? I'll flatten yer, yer big flappy oik!'

Smiling, he couldn't help it, Lupus backed out of harm's way as Bootes staggered this way and that, his fists flailing violently. Eventually he toppled sideways and vanished headlong into the clump of bushes.

Bounding over to the crumpled bush Bootes had fallen on to and over, Lupus peered beyond. Bootes was lying on his back, arms stretched forward and staring upwards, through a stunned expression, at something happily gurgling in his hands. Lupus quietly backtracked and sat down to wait. The plan had started better than he could have expected.

'Fluffy! Fluffy!' yelled Bootes, appearing at great haste from the bushes. He was carrying the baby under one arm and the basket under the other. 'Look Fluffy. Look wot I found hiding in them there bushes, a tiny bab!'

Lupus dutifully trotted over to him.

'Look Fluffy boy, a bab.' Bootes knelt down and gently placed the baby in the basket. 'There be a note too, but me ol' eyes ain't wot they used.'

That's a relief, thought Lupus, it could have complicated things no end. Lupus barked and licked the baby and wagged his tail. He thought he had better make some sort of gesture.

'Good boy Fluffy,' said Bootes, patting Lupus on the head. 'Now, go get us a coney or two for ours dinner, for sum reason I'm mighty hungry.' Lupus hesitated a moment; no point rousing the old man's suspicions by doing as he was told. 'Go on then boy,' said Bootes, waving a hand in the general direction of the path, 'an' then I'll tell yer 'bout me dream and the giant firefly and talking tree that wuz in it.'

Wondering how the old man could possibly have had a dream about Tee Hee a frowning Lupus did as he was told this time and sped off down the track, a scent already reaching his keen nostrils.

* * *

'And that's 'ow ol' Bootes saved the day,' ended Bootes, dramatically.

Lupus half-heartedly lifted a heavy eyelid and yawned, it was late and the stars filled the night sky; Bootes had gone on and on.

'So Fluffy ol' boy, it's a good thing I found yer when I did. Wiv me to protect yer, yer'll come to no 'arm.' Bootes started to wave and swish – he made the noises – an imaginary sword out in front of him.

Lupus sniffed loudly and closed his eyes. The story had certainly started off as a dream; where it became reality for the old man he didn't know.

After another couple of swish noises Bootes flopped exhausted beside his Fluffy. His imaginary exploits had taken a sudden toll on him. He sat for a moment in silence, then lay back and rolled on his side. ''Night boy,' said Bootes, sounding weary.

Goodnight old man, thought Lupus, sleep tight and don't let the monster fireflies bite. He smiled a contented smile. The plan was working thus far; now he only had to get Bootes to deliver the baby to its rightful owner and hey presto that would be it; mission accomplished. If only it was that easy.

A glorious clear blue sky above and a warmth that caressed the very air below, greeted Lupus when he woke next morning; that and Bootes shouting at him.

Slightly fuddled as waking from deep sleep can sometimes take you, Lupus could have been forgiven for thinking he had not actually woken but was still asleep and dreaming. Above him, glinting in the morning sun, stood a vision in silver. Lupus blinked as the vision moved closer.

'Wot d'yer think boy?' said Bootes, somewhere distant to Lupus' hearing. 'Found 'em in yon bushes where the bab wuz.'

It was Bootes, the silver thing, and he was holding something in his hands. Something that wavered with the effort Bootes was using to hold it up. Just in time Lupus came to his senses and dived out of the way, as a huge sword fell from Bootes' grip and embedded itself in the ground where Lupus had been lying.

Now that Lupus was wide awake and he was sure it wasn't a dream, he didn't know what to think. Tee Hee hadn't said anything about such regalia in his plan. Lupus rounded on Bootes, getting a better look at just what Bootes had found. A silver suit. A silver sword. It certainly smacked of Tee Hee. Perhaps it had been an afterthought on the creature's part; a measure of security, but for who? Surely he hadn't meant it for the old man. The old man, looking a lot like a shrivelled roast wrapped in too much foil, was at that moment trying to free a hand from a sleeve so he could point to the bushes. And giving the old man a sword was akin to giving the baby a razor blade to play with. Holding that thought Lupus decided he had better check on the baby.

When the baby saw Lupus it started gurgled happily. Lupus wrinkled his brow. Surely the baby had been smaller? Still, if it was happy. He left the razor free baby and went to check if anything else had been added. More supplies, enough to last at least a couple of weeks, but nothing else of note. Lupus picked them up in his mouth and trotted over to Bootes who had the baby's basket in his hands. He was cooing into it.

'Quite a big feller, ain't yer,' said Bootes, playfully sticking a bony finger into the baby's ribs, 'but wot are we gonna to do with you?'

Surely there was no question, thought Lupus, quizzically cocking his head to one side. Bootes noticed.

'We can't take 'im wiv us boy, it'll be too dangerous wot wiv me swinging me sword in battle an' the like,' said Bootes, in all seriousness.

Lupus couldn't argue with that, but leaving the baby was not an option. He let out a low menacing growl.

'Bad dog,' said Bootes, sternly wagging a finger at Lupus.

Dropping the new bag of supplies, Lupus barked at Bootes and then retrieved the old one from yesterday picking it up and placing at Bootes' feet.

'Wot's got into yer boy?' said Bootes, scratching his head. Bootes put the baby down and picked up the bag. 'Wot is it boy? Yer want me to look?' He started to rummage through the bag's contents.

Encouraging the old man, Lupus barked again; louder.

Bootes got the wrong end of the stick. 'It's no gud yer yapping like that. I don't understand dog and that's that,' he snapped.

Loosing his patience, Lupus snatched the bag from an aghast Bootes and started emptying its contents on the ground.

'Bad Fluffy!' Bootes, chastised angrily, 'Someone won't be 'aving any grub t'day.'

Ignoring the old man, Lupus found what he was looking for and held out a contraption consisting of leather straps and buckles for Bootes to see. To Lupus' relief a glimmer of understanding flickered on Bootes' face.

'You want me to strap something?' said Bootes, taking the harness from Lupus.

It was hard work, but a rolling eyed Lupus persevered and picked up the basket which he offered to the old man.

'You want me to strap yon bab to you?' said Bootes, wide eyed. 'Well I'll be. You want the bab to cum with us.'

At last, thought Lupus, barking and furiously wagging his tail.

Bootes still wasn't sure. He stood for a moment looking thoughtfully at the harness. 'Well I suppose it'll be all right for now, but the first village we cum to the bab stays. Do yer hear me?'

He heard all right, but Lupus was sure it wouldn't be too hard to steer the old man clear of any villages that happened to be in their way. For now though, it was time to make tracks and move on.

CHAPTER 30

Someone had to act quickly, the storm was almost on them; that someone would have to be Fornax. Scooping up an array of weapons that had been dropped in the panic, she pointed to the pit. 'Quick into the pit, it's our only chance,' shouted Fornax, trying to make her voice heard above the noise of the ensuing storm.

Nearly everyone else stood rooted to the spot, staring into the black depths of the pit as if hypnotised. Only Fatidic retained the use of his feet, but as he turned to run Fornax grabbed him by an arm.

'The more of us there are, the better our chances,' she shouted, her eyes burning with an intensity that had Fatidic shying away.

A hand reached out to Fornax. Cetus had snapped from his stupor. 'I'll take a sword,' he said smiling, 'you never know, those scarabs might be good eating.'

It was a weak attempt at humour, but it had an effect. The others finally awoke to what Fornax was saying and grabbing what weapons they could, leapt after her as she dragged the reluctant Fatidic with her into the inky depths.

If they had been expecting shelter then they were to be sadly disappointed. The pit wasn't as deep as they thought it would be. Clinging desperately together they waited for what fate was about to throw at them.

'What's that?' said a near invisible Hydra.

The others listened and could just make out above the top of the approaching roar a faint clicking noise. Knuckles grew white around weapons as the sound drew closer; the beetles to the fore in all their minds. Suddenly the clicking stopped and they were bathed in light. Standing a couple of yards from them was Fatidic holding a flaming torch. 'I might not be a warrior,' he said, a wry look on his face, 'but I am a thinker. I thought this might come in handy.'

It was Fornax's turn to smile; a wry one. The short man might prove his worth after all.

'This way, quick as you can,' said Fatidic, urgently

He hurried them, to what looked at first sight, to be a cave entrance, but which upon closer inspection proved to be an ancient gaping doorway. Strange and peculiar etchings and writings adorned the surrounding stone frame.

'We shouldn't trust him,' whispered Musca, as Fatidic beckoned them on, 'he was quite happy to see us all die not so long ago.'

'I haven't forgotten, but I really don't think we have a choice right now,' replied Fornax, who would be watching the small man like a hawk however useful he was proving.

In the end they made it beyond the doorway none too soon as the storm arrived hard on their heels. Inside they found a dank and musty passageway big enough to get three horses along side by side. They quickly pushed on, Fatidic leading the way, until Fornax, decided it was safe enough to stop .

Sword raised just high enough to be perceived as a threat, Fornax decided it was time to confront Fatidic, 'Right little man, what are we going to do with you?'

'I never meant you any harm. I never meant anyone any harm. I'm sorry, I had no choice,' cried Fatidic, falling on his knees eyes fixed on the sword. 'I was their leader yes, but only a figurehead. The high priest gave the orders. It was expected; what they did,' groaned Fatidic, expecting any moment soon to be his last.

'Why should we trust you now?'

'I got the torch didn't I? I could have run when you dropped me in the pit but I didn't. Please don't kill me, give me a chance to prove you can trust me.'

Never for one moment had Fornax entertained the idea of killing the little man, but as a little fear in the right place was sometimes useful she wasn't about to tell Fatidic that. Besides, he had already proved useful having had the presence of mind to grab the torch. And he had led them to the passageway when he could have disappeared in the dark and left them behind at the mercy of the storm.

'Tell us what you know and be quick about it.'

'About what?' said Fatidic.

The sword in Fornax's hand rose a little higher.

'Everything I know, yes of course. But it's only rumours you understand. I don't know for sure.'

'You don't know what for sure?' said Musca.

Fatidic appeared to falter, 'Can I get up?' Fornax nodded. 'Thank you.' Fatidic brushed dirt from his knees. 'I don't know where the passage leads. Some say it to be the way to hell. Others believe it's an ancient pathway to a lost city in the jungle.'

Looks were exchanged, as Tee Hee's words came back to them.

'And what do you say little man?' pushed Fornax.

'I don't know. I always thought of it as an escape route for just a day as today.'

Fornax gave Fatidic's words some thought before questioning him further, 'And the scarabs?'

'Those I'm afraid do exist and somewhere within I should imagine.'

They couldn't go back, that was decided. Trusting Fatidic? They would have to, but watch his every movement; besides where could he go? Onwards it was then.

The air in the passage grew staler and thinner the further they travelled, making the going increasingly harder. Several times the torch flickered as if to die, but each time holding on and coming back to life.

'How much further?' moaned Cetus, sweating; suffering from the amount of food he had managed to put away during the feast.

'Don't ask stupid questions,' snapped Fornax, the closeness fraying her temper.

Up ahead the light they were following stopped. Fatidic called for Fornax.

'It looks like we have come to the end of the passage,' said Fatidic, as Fornax drew beside him.

Stretching out before them was a vast hall, circular in shape, with a high domed ceiling decorated with what must have been, in another day and time, a beautiful display of ornate carvings and paintings. Now sadly, the carvings were worn and broken and the paintings mostly faded colour and bare plaster.

The light from the flame flickered across the hall casting shadows, but just able to illuminate the far walls and floor. The floor, in contrast to the ceiling, was far from beautiful or at least what was lying on it could hardly be described as such. Littered from wall to wall lay the bones and skulls of ancient and not so ancient human skeletons. Behind her Fornax heard a sharp intake of breath as Equuleus took in the sight.

'Who?' stammered Equuleus.

Fornax, with Musca now holding the torch, his height throwing more light, stepped into the massive chamber. The light danced on the nearest skulls, distorting their blank looks into something more sinister; grinning monsters smug in the knowledge they held. Doing their best to ignore them they carefully stepped deeper into the hall, interested now by what faced them on the far wall. Several archways, their depths shrouded in darkness.

'More passages?' said Musca.

'Let's take a look.'

While the others watched from across the hall, Musca and Fornax began to explore beyond the arches. The first search bore fruit. Musca appeared carrying two more torches, one of which he carried over and gave to Cetus.

'Where did it lead to?' asked Cetus, arriving at the archway where Musca had found the torches and looking in.

'A small room not ten yards away,' said Fornax. 'One of the others has to be the way out.'

To save time it was decided to split into smaller groups. Musca, nervous of what he might find next, wasn't so sure that it was a good idea, but Fornax got her own way. To add to his pains he was given Fatidic. Fornax took Equuleus and the brothers went with Cetus. They entered the next three arches.

It didn't take long to discover they were the same as the first except they were totally empty. Down to three. Not much later Fornax and Equuleus were back quickly followed by Cetus's group. The same story. They moved to the arch Musca and Fatidic had taken.

Musca had given Fatidic the torch, mainly because he wanted to know where the little man was, secondly because he didn't want to be the first to see something he didn't want to. The passageway this time went further than just a few yards. It had to be the way out.

'I think we should get the others,' said Musca, keeping close to Fatidic.

'But we don't know what's down here,' argued Fatidic.

It was a fair point, but Musca would rather it stayed that way until they got re-enforcements, 'We could be going on for ages.'

'I think I can see something.'

'Where?'

'Dead ahead.'

It wasn't a sentence Musca found endearing, but if it was just ahead. 'What is it?'

'It looks big.'

Another wording Musca didn't like the sound of and one sadly he usually didn't hear when it concerned him. 'What does?' Why did he have to ask? Fatidic, because of Musca dragging his feet, was now a little way ahead.

'Wait, I'm nearly there.'

'I'll get the others.'

'Waagh!' The torch dropped to the floor.

'Fatidic? FATIDIC!' Did he stay, or did he go?

The passage filled with several grunts and groans and then Fatidic spoke, 'I'm all right. Tripped on something. Wait a second.' Musca wasn't going anywhere. 'There,' the torch was back hovering in the air, 'it's a wall.'

'What?'

'The big thing I saw. It's a dead end.'

'It can't be,' said Musca.

'Look for yourself.'

Musca did. 'Then how are we going to get out of here?'

More heads were needed. They hurried back to the others and met them coming the other way.

'Fatidic,' growled Fornax on hearing the news.

'I said it was only rumours,' Fatidic defended.

'Damn the rumours!' roared Fornax, 'you've led us on a wild goose chase.' She raised her sword; the old Fornax was back.

'Wait,' said Cetus, bravely stepping between Fornax and her quivering victim, 'there must be a way out or how else could that have happened back there,' he pointed to the domed hall and its underweight occupants. 'We must have missed something.'

The voice of reason had Fornax slowly lowering her sword; the bloodlust ebbing from her veins.

'Maybe there's a secret doorway or hidden passageway,' said Equuleus, eager to help, 'or perhaps you have to say a magic password.'

'Or you've been listening to too many fairy tales round the fireside,' said Fornax, glowering at him. She disapproved of such nonsense.

'Yes,' agreed Musca, whose own thoughts had been travelling along the same tracks as Equuleus, 'nonsense.'

'Then what do we do?' asked Cetus, relieved to see the sword return to Fornax's side.

'Do?' snapped Fornax, looking daggers at Fatidic. 'We look again I suppose, it's possible we missed something, but it'll be more likely we've been led on a fool's errand and we'll end up back at the pit.'

The idea of going back to the pit held little appeal so, determined to leave no stone unturned this time, they started back to the hall; to the sound of clicking.

'Fatidic,' said Fornax, short with the little man, 'we've enough torches for now so put your little toy away.'

'I'm not making any noise,' protested Fatidic, showing her his palms.

The hairs on the back of Fornax's neck immediately raised a warning. 'Then what…?' Before she could finish her question a sudden gust of wind swept past her, extinguishing the torches, but not before the last of their light illuminated a large dark shape in the passage close behind them; too close to be any wall.

The clicking started to build in crescendo. Panic as realisation of just what was with them in the passage ensued, but frantic scrambling to get away turned to disaster as first Hydra, then

216

Hydrus stumbled in the race to escape. Someone screamed as more bodies piled on top of the fallen and the sound of steel on stone mingled with the clicking, that now, almost purring with excitement, reverberated through the ancient chambers and passageways. Then, for a moment, there was sudden and total silence.

Nothing stirred for a full minute then, speaking in a whisper, Musca's voice broke the silence, 'Fornax?'

'Over here.'

'You all right?'

'I think so, but I can't move my leg.'

'I'm coming over to you.' Musca blindly stumbled over to where he thought Fornax was until he literally fell across her.

'My ankles trapped,' said Fornax.

'Does it hurt?'

'No,' she lied.

Musca felt his way to her ankle and found something smooth and cold resting on it. No prizes for guessing what, he thought. He was just glad it wasn't moving or making that damned clicking noise. It gave him the creeps. One of the reasons why he gave short shrift to any thoughts he might have had as to why it was no longer doing either. Finding places to get a good grip, Musca heaved with all his might. It didn't move an inch. He needed help. It was then his blood ran cold. Something had started clicking up and to his right.

'Quick, my sword,' yelled Fornax. She wasn't going to let her present predicament stop her doing battle.

Desperately scrabbling on the ground for a weapon, Musca almost missed the clicking stop. The next thing he knew, he was bathed in the yellow glow of a torch. Crammed in a small niche in the wall sat a shaken Fatidic, the burning torch quivering in his hand. At the same time Hydrus and Cetus appeared from their hiding places.

'What is that?' exclaimed Hydrus, skidding to a halt.

'I think it's a scarab,' said Musca.

'Is it dead?' said Cetus, gingerly prodding it.

'I hope so,' said a muffled voice emanating from somewhere beneath the creature.

'Hydra, is that you?' said a stunned Hydrus, 'Where are you?'

'Down here.'

Together Musca, Cetus and Hydrus moved to the opposite side of the beetle carcass to where Fornax lay, got down on their knees and peered beneath the stricken monster. Hydra was on his back covered in a foul smelling liquid that had to be the scarab's blood; the only thing stopping him from being crushed was the sword half embedded in the beetle's guts.

'What's going on?' said Fornax, squirming to get a better view.

'It's Hydra, he's trapped under the beetle,' said Musca and then to Hydra. 'We'll get you out, but Fornax is trapped by its shell so we will have to try and free her first. By now Fatidic had clambered from his hiding place and the light from his torch fully illuminated the unfortunate Hydra, who nodded that he understood.

'No you don't,' yelled Fornax, 'Hydra's in more danger than I am. Get him out first,' she ordered even though her foot was hurting like hell.

You didn't argue with Fornax so they silently returned to her side and began to lift.

'What did I just say?' said Fornax.

Ignoring her, Musca told Fatidic to pull her out once she was free of the shell. Together the three of them heaved just enough for Fatidic to pull Fornax clear, but the shift in weight caused the carcass to embed itself completely on Hydra's sword, its weight crushing down on him.

'Quick,' yelled Musca, 'push. Fatidic!'

Leaving Fornax, Fatidic helped them tip the beetle on its side and then with one last mighty shove onto its back. The sword in its centre now swallowed to the hilt.

'Hydra?' whispered Hydrus at the sight of his brother, now completely covered in smelly liquid and unmentionable goo.

'Quick,' said Fornax, holding the torch as high as she was able, 'before he drowns in it.' The thought that he may already be dead not allowed to enter her head.

They dragged Hydra clear and cheered their relief when he showed signs of life. The middle underside of the scarab had been soft so enveloped him instead of crushing him, but left any longer he would have been smothered.

Leaving Hydra to the others to look after, Musca grabbed a discarded torch and lighting it on Fatidic's went over to where Fornax was sitting nursing her ankle.

'You all right?' said Musca, kneeling.

'And if he had died?' she said, referring to them ignoring her.

'He didn't,' said Musca, just a tad defiant.

Fornax wasn't sure she was happy with the new Musca so she gave him a look that had the marrow in his bones freeze a little, then smiled. It wouldn't last, she thought.

'Just as well, I don't think Hydrus would have been too happy if he hadn't,' whispered Fornax, the smile lingering, 'How is he?'

'A bit bloody, but thankfully it's not his. Your foot?'

'Cut and bruised but not broken,' said Fornax, picking dirt from one of the cuts, 'but we do have another problem.' Musca gave her a quizzical look. 'Equuleus isn't with us.'

As if to verify what Fornax was saying, Musca turned and raised his torch. The others were coming over to where he knelt; a messy Hydra with them, but no Equuleus.

'What's wrong?' said Cetus, guessing by the way Musca was looking that something was up.

'Equuleus is missing,' said Musca.

Everyone took a turn looking at each other.

'Perhaps he's hiding,' proffered Fatidic, 'if so he couldn't have gone far.'

'He would have heard us,' said Hydrus.

'Heard us screaming and shouting,' said Fornax. 'He might be too frightened to come out even if we called him.'

Lighting the last torch Cetus had freed from underneath one of the scarab's legs and checking Hydra was fit enough to join in, they split into two groups and began to search, but first they helped Fornax back to the domed hall and propped her against the wall facing the passageway from the pit. She wasn't able to help, but she would be able to shout a warning if something came that way. The desert storms, so Fatidic had said, were unpredictable. If it had passed would their captors be brave enough to come looking for them?

Back to where they had been before the appearance of the scarab, with no sign of Equuleus, Musca, Cetus and Fatidic headed down the final passageway back towards the wall Fatidic had discovered. Hydra, winded by the scarab falling on him and now showing signs of being a little worse for wear was sent to sit with Fornax, Hydrus went with him.

'You could have missed something,' said Cetus to Musca, 'a secret door the like Equuleus was going on about.'

'We saw no door,' Musca replied stonily, he wasn't happy. What if another scarab appeared?

'Then a hole in the ground. A mine shaft or well,' said Cetus.

'We saw nothing did we Fatidic?'

'The man's right. Nothing but walls unless…'

'Unless what?' said Musca, quickening his pace to keep up with Fatidic who had suddenly put a spurt on, but finding time to keep well wide of the dead scarab as he passed.

'Unless one of the walls isn't a wall,' said Fatidic, sounding all of a sudden quite excited. 'Perhaps your young friend was right.'

'Right about what?'

'A secret door, of course,' said Fatidic.

'We'd have seen it,' said Musca, frowning, 'there would have been runes and the like around it or on it. There was nothing like that.' Musca looked at Cetus and twirled his finger by the side of his head.

'Never could understand that,' muttered Fatidic, stopping, 'if I wanted a door kept secret I'd want it well… secret.'

'But…'

But Fatidic wasn't listening. 'Sssch,' he said, getting down on all fours.

'What are you doing?'

Standing Fatidic held up a finger. 'One,' he said, 'the torches blew out. Where did the draught strong enough to do that come from? It had to be quite a blast and sudden.' He held up another finger, 'Two, where did the scarab come from? I'm guessing not from thin air.'

The screwed up features gave away the arrival of Musca's thought process. 'Then,' he said, while chewing his bottom lip, 'where did it come from?'

'Come down here,' said Fatidic, on all fours again, 'there's a draught.'

Reluctantly Musca and Cetus did.

'See how the flame flickers?' said Fatidic, holding the torch to the ground.

'So you've found a hole, whoopee-do,' said Musca, missing the significance of Fatidic's find. 'What we should be finding is Equuleus. Come on Cetus, we've wasted enough time here. Equuleus must have headed back to the pit.'

'It's not a hole,' said Fatidic, getting somewhat exasperated, 'it's a gap; a gap that runs the length of the wall.'

CHAPTER 31

Serpens was feeling pleased, although the loss of contact with Draco was worrying him more than he cared to admit, the journey through the lower mountains was nearly over. He congratulated himself. The detour from the upper range, through the pass he had found, was going to cut the travelling time to the desert by half. Smugly content he kicked his heels into Ophiuchus' back and gave him the hurry-up. He felt things were going right for once.

'Stop,' ordered Serpens, as the desert at last came in sight. Ophiuchus obeyed so sharply Lyra didn't have time to stop and walked straight into one of his tree trunk legs. 'Put me down here. We will rest and continue our journey at first light.'

Ophiuchus knelt, narrowly missing Lyra who recovered enough wits to scrabble clear in the nick of time, and waited for Serpens to alight. Serpens climbed down and surveyed what was left of the pass. He didn't need to rest, Ophiuchus did all the work. It was time for a gloat.

Gloat over, Serpens called for Lyra.

'Yes, O Dark One,' said Lyra, bowing low now that he was able to do so since he was no longer plate shaped. The walk had done him good.

'I'm going to send you looking for Lupus again. Try not to fail me.'

'Yes, O Dark One,' said Lyra.

'And Lyra.'

'Yes, O Dark One?'

'Call me Master. Dark One sounds a little too familiar.'

'Yes, O Dark One, Sire, One Master One.'

Determined nothing was going to spoil the moment Serpens ignored the irksome imp. 'Now be gone.' And with a flick of his wrist Lyra headed for the ether.

*   *   *

It's funny what goes through your mind when travelling at the speed of sound. With Lyra it was an unsettling feeling that gnawed at his tiny mind. Since the latest incident with Serpens' foot, secret longings had started to manifest themselves and rise to the surface of his consciousness. He found he was wishing for simpler times, like putting the finishing touches to the odd disaster. Or even, when he was a newly formed, attached to the inkling nursery and his only worries were whether to add the "I don't remember eating that" carrots to the new batch of vomit or not. It seemed he had a longing for the good old days.

Lyra arrived back at the big pit* and hovered above. To his dismay and surprise Lupus was no longer there. This hadn't happened before, usually he arrived and there he was. Lyra's mind began to fizzle and spark as he tried to think. What now? He couldn't go back empty handed. He had to take back some news, and no news was definitely not good news. Lying was no good either, Serpens had a knack of seeing right through you; unless you ripped before fully stretched. Lyra began to frantically search the area for a clue to Lupus' whereabouts.

But it was to no avail. He had even tried barking. Lyra fell to the ground and began to cry. His wet, boggling, pop eyes swivelling hopelessly in their sockets as his small bony shoulders rocked with each raking blubber. He couldn't ever remember crying in anguish, only with laughter after one or another cruel jape had gone hilariously right. He took several deep breaths to try and control the sobbing and humming that had started in his ears. After a while the crying stopped, but annoyingly the humming remained. He cupped his hands over his ears. The humming stopped. Hands off; it started again. It wasn't in his head. Something else was making it. Taking a tissue from his tutu, Lyra dried his eyes and, anguish forgotten for the moment, set off to investigate. Maybe he would have something to report after all. Either way he wasn't in

* Not to be confused with the one in Wales that wasn't created by a crash landing spaceship. *SJ*

223

much of a mood to go back just yet. He was going to take his time. He was going to walk. It had done him good before.

Dawn was doing what it always did this time of the day; dawning as Lyra wriggled on his belly atop the brow of a small hillock. The humming was now deafening and emanating from an area bathed in an eerie bluish pulsating glow.

Boggle eyes peeping over the brow were sent fairly spinning by the scene on the other side.

'Draco!' yelled Lyra, standing and waving, but he was drowned out by the humming.

'Draco!' Forgetting he could hover, Lyra was now running as fast as his little legs could carry him. 'Draco!' he shouted, waving. He was so excited.

He was nearly at the saucer now. 'Dracooooooo!' He never got there. Just as Draco started to turn in his direction Lyra's second tail, the one with the ribbons, grew taut and he was away and gone in an instant. Draco frowned, wiggled a finger in an ear and, satisfied he must have been hearing things, continued with his work.

The sun was just appearing over the horizon as Serpens stretched and sniffed the morning air. Evil he may be, but there was, even for him, something about a warm summery morning. He stretched some more and watched, with middling interest, something that had appeared in the desert some distance from the end of the pass. Strange, he thought, it appears to be moving this way. Middling was replaced by intense and then panic as Serpens realised just what he was looking at. And it was moving fast, very fast.

'Ophiuchus! My throne, quickly!' He tugged on Lyra's rope. 'We have to move.'

But it was all too late. As Ophiuchus made a grab for the throne the tornado struck.

'NO!' screamed Serpens, as he and Ophiuchus were thrown into the air. 'NOoooo!'

When Lyra arrived the pass was empty but for pieces of broken throne lying strewn about the ground. The pass was as quiet as the grave.

'Master?' said Lyra. 'Ophiuchus?' He noticed the shattered throne and went over to the largest piece. Sitting on it Lyra took what was left of his rope and examined its frayed end. 'Oh dear,' he said.

CHAPTER 32

Pistor closed his eyes tight and held his breath as the great ape wrapped a massive arm round his waist and flung them both into space. He couldn't believe, as he whizzed through the tree tops in death defying leaps, that he had actually asked for it to happen, but when last night the jungle man had mentioned the old buildings he had found in the jungle he just had to go see them for himself.

A grunt from Jungle Man somewhere ahead signalled it was time to descend. The great ape slowed and headed down. Pistor chanced a glimpse at his surroundings but only succeeded in getting an eyeful of matted fur.

'Pisser Man open eyes now he on ground.'

Pistor wasn't happy with the jungle man's new name for him, but as he had returned to good old terra firma in one piece he felt forgiving.

'Pisser Man now follow. Follow close, not all creatures here Jungle Man's friend.'

The journey by foot was a brief one, and soon Pistor was standing before a magnificent wall, almost as tall as the trees he had swung through; in it stood an open gateway which Pistor immediately started to head for.

Excitement building, he covered the ground between in no time, but as he drew closer the distant magnificence and grandeur quickly turned to a picture of ruin and decay. The giant gateposts of stone still stood, but were crumbling with time and all that was left of the gates, that would have barred the way of any unwanted intruder, were its twisted hinges. It still had an air about it though and as Pistor, shallow man that he was, crossed the threshold of this long lost kingdom he couldn't help but feel humbled by it all.

Jungle Man, who had followed a few steps behind, now stood at the gates reluctant to go any further. 'Pisser Man be careful. It said go in no come out. Place taboo.'

'Taboo?' said Pistor, absentmindedly as he took in the buildings stretching as far as the eye could see, 'What's taboo?' He had never heard of the word before.

'Jungle Man not know, but word is bad.' Jungle Man took a chance and bounced along the ground to where Pistor stood. 'Pisser Man go now. Come with Jungle Man. Have food and drink. More talk.' He was almost pleading.

But Pistor had other things on his mind and ignoring Jungle Man's pleas stepped further into the great courtyard that the gateway led into. Outside the walls he could hear agitated grunts from the great ape that had carried him there.

'Jungle Man's friend worried. So too Jungle Man. You come now.' Jungle Man beckoned for Pistor to follow him.

'No,' said Pistor bluntly, 'I want to see what treasures this place holds. 'I'm staying to look around.'

'Jungle Man may not be able to help Pisser Man if he find trouble.' Jungle Man now had hold of Pistor's shirt sleeve.

Pistor shrugged his arm loose. 'I'll take my chance,' he said dismissively.

Fear was not an issue in Pistor's mind as he clambered over fallen masonry heading for the nearest building. He was as sure as ever that this was the lost city Tee Hee had spoken of and greed had stolen a long march on reason and sense, taking him away from safety and the only friend he had in the jungle.

More grunts, intermingled now with the occasional pathetic whine, entered the emptiness of the lost city and Jungle Man's ears as he watched Pistor moving away. Jungle Man, head bowed, decided he could do no more. He turned with heavy heart and headed back out to the jungle where his friend, the great ape awaited him. The mad Pisser Man was on his own.

Without so much as a glance behind him, Pistor reached the ruined building and stepped inside. The sudden coolness was welcoming as he carefully navigated the crumbling interior to claim his imagined prizes. He was to be disappointed. As he grew accustomed to the gloom he saw he was wasting his time; in there anyway. The place was nothing but a rotting, near empty shell. But he wasn't to be deterred. In fact he began to whistle happily as he kicked aside the odd bit of rubble in his path. His reason; even though the building he was in and those in close proximity were grander than any he had ever seen, he was obviously in the city's poorer district. He needed to find the palace; there was always a palace in a big city. There he would find his treasure.

Back outside, blinking in the renewed harshness of a downward sun, Pistor took in his surroundings with a different eye. The buildings looked the same, big, but not grand after all. If he wanted grand he decided, he would have to travel deeper into the city.

To his satisfaction they became just that, bigger and grander the further in he travelled. He was going the right way, he knew it. Now and again curiosity got the better of him and he would pay a visit to one of the buildings just to make sure they weren't playing host to the odd valuable or two. And each time he returned to the path empty handed, but all the more confident the real treasures he sought waited for him up ahead.

How far he travelled he didn't know, but as the sun was looking to rest for the night his thoughts turned to shelter from the creatures that thought of night as their domain. He wasn't tired; at least he didn't feel tired, but if there was one thing he had learnt in his trek through the jungle was that night was filled with too many things that wanted to bite or eat you. The trouble was though, although the buildings were getting larger they were still only a single story high; he needed to find shelter off the ground.

The sun was casting shadows to frighten the bravest of men when at last Pistor found what he was looking for. Steadily gaining pace he first walked, then trotted, then ran as his mind began to play tricks on him. Shadows shimmered, buildings appeared to groan and growl. He no longer wanted to be on the streets of the lost city however much treasure there was waiting for him. Greed now gave way to self preservation.

He arrived at the foot of the watchtower he had seen in the distance and prayed the stairs had been hewn from stone and not from the abundance of timber that lay at hand. The stars were kind to him. With renewed effort he attacked the first step and never looked back until he reached the top where he slumped to the floor looking at the first stars. The tower had no roof, but that little mattered. What did matter though was the gaping hole he had just come through. He would have to somehow block it if he didn't want his night disturbed by a curious carnivore interested by his scent.

Pistor took off his pack and went to get up, but he must have been more tired than he first thought and sat back down again. His legs were stiff; cramping. He would rest a moment.

Pistor woke with a start. Wide-eyed and sweating from forgotten nightmares, he reached for and drew his knife. It was morning. He had slept the night away. The hatch had remained a gaping inviting hole all night. Ignoring the water Jungle Man had given him, he took a long hard swig of potato juice. He had been fortunate; the stars had indeed been looking after him. He took another swig and decided to ride the crest of his fortune's wave. Hurriedly placing his pack back on his back he made for the stairs; treasure awaited him; he could taste it.

But halfway down he stopped; something nagging at him. He tried to ignore it and took another couple of steps, but it was no good. The nagging persisted, he had to go back up. He had seen something up top that had barely registered, but it was something his mind was telling him was important. Reluctantly he gave in and returned to the top.

Leaning on the tower's parapet he scanned the horizon, first in the direction he had travelled, then followed it round so he wouldn't miss anything. And there it was. Standing some distance away from the city stood the tallest building he had ever seen. Of course, thought Pistor, the chieftain of such a city would hardly see fit to live within its confines. Each side, and he thought there were at least four of them, rose smooth and sheer from the ground to meet in a point at their highest. To an archaeologist it would count as the find of a lifetime, to Pistor it said, "look at me, I'm filled to the rafters with treasure".

Waiting just long enough to get his bearings, Pistor headed again for the stairs and this time didn't stop until he was at the bottom. At last fortune was really smiling on him. At last he, Pistor, would be somebody; would live like a chieftain. He headed at speed for the shortest route; a route that would take him back into the jungle.

Moments later, as Pistor disappeared from view into its depths, wispy smoke, hidden from him and anyone lower than the trees or watchtower, started to float into the air not far from where Pistor was heading.

In the jungle Pistors march was one of relentless purpose. Focused on one thing and one thing only he hacked at all that lay in his way. No overgrown weeds were going to stop him. The shirt on his back soon turned into a sodden rag as the effort squeezed moisture from every pore in his body. It didn't matter. On he advanced, his blade sweeping his way clear; each effort accompanied by growing grunts and groans, loud enough to wake the dead, or alert anyone who might be listening.

By mid morning Pistor could just make out the beginnings of a clearing. Grinning widely he pushed on not wanting to waste a moment. Finally the jungle relented and Pistor burst from its confines into the space. He stood there in triumph, his aches and pains forgotten in the moment. The building that he had spied from the tower was even more magnificent than he had imagined and now there it was, standing no more than fifty feet away. The sides he now saw were not smooth but made up of hundreds of steps and the top didn't end in a point but at a small building. He got closer. He now stood at the bottom of one of these sides looking up in wonder at the immenseness of it climbing high above him. He took his first step.

He didn't take a second.

CHAPTER 33

The desert loomed.

'Well Fluffy boy, looks like we've cum to the end of the trail. I'll never be able to track them across all that there sand,' said Bootes, wiping sweat from his brow with a baggy, silver sleeve.

Lupus never thought otherwise, but across they still had to go. He decided to make his point using a pathetic doggy whine.

'And it's no gud yer looking at me like that neither. We'll 'ave to turn back.'

Lupus barked.

'Now now, Fluffy that's enough of that, bad dog.'

Lupus, sniffing as he went, crossed to an outcrop of rock not far from where they had stopped. The monkey man's scent was strong here. He howled into the desert wind. They had to go on. Luckily he had expected the old man to play up when they got to the desert so had already conceived a plan to get him across.

Hands to ears Bootes shouted at Lupus to stop, 'Will yer quit yer complaining an' go get us sum food.' Lupus stopped and Bootes let his hands drop. 'That stuff wiv yon bab is awful,' he snorted, 'all watery an' there's no salt in it.' Bootes kicked at the ground, 'An' I think we'll camp 'ere for the night before going back on the morrow.'

So that's where the baby's food been going, thought Lupus as he climbed down from the rocks to put his plan into action. The plan went like this. Lupus would change shape; grab a rag, draw the old man's attention with it and lure him into the desert where the old man would be led a merry dance until he was so lost and tired he wouldn't know what day it was. Then Lupus would come back; collect the baby and no more arguments. He padded over to the baby's basket shaking his head. On the other hand, it was hot, it would be hard work and...

231

Sod that, thought Lupus and as Bootes bent to collect firewood Lupus crept up behind him and whacked him across the back of the head.

The sun was beating down hard enough to fry an egg and sausage and bacon.

Bootes, bewildered, but recovered from his latest bout of unconsciousness, walked beside Lupus who marvelled at the old man's resilience as he marched along with the vigour of someone half his age.

'I wish yer could talk, Fluffy,' said Bootes, suddenly, 'I sure would like to know how cum I got so far in the desert without knowing 'bout it.'

Lupus gave a bark cum cough.

'Yer know boy, I'd 'ave thought the desert would 'ave been 'otter than this, I'd 'eard stories yer see,' said Bootes, knowingly.

Lupus raised an eyebrow. He had been in many a hot place, some he didn't want to think about, but right now the heat in this desert ranked right up there with the best of them. He cocked his head and gave the old man the once over as Bootes ambled along as if on a Sunday stroll in the park. It had to be something to do with the suit but for now he could only surmise and as it seemed to be aiding the cause why worry?

'Look Fluffy,' said Bootes, pointing ahead, 'I think I've found a place for yer to rest, yer look plumb worn out.'

So would you if you'd dragged yourself, an old man, a flaming great sword and a baby across twenty odd miles of scorching desert, thought Lupus. Biting his lip, Lupus tagged behind as Bootes led him to a large outcrop of sandblasted rock. Once there, though he was loath to admit it, the respite he found in the rock's shadows was more than welcoming.

Wriggling free from the basket Lupus lay down to snatch what rest he could.

'Gud boy, Fluffy,' said Bootes, who was standing on top of the rock. 'Yer get yer 'ead down and I'll stand and watch. Yer never know wot kinda monster yer'll find lurking in the desert.'

He now assumed a sitting position. 'I'll wake yer when the sun goes down.'

Huffing and puffing under his breath, Lupus put his head down and prepared to leave the old man to his own devices. Let the fool play, thought Lupus grumpily, what possible harm can he come to way out here?

It wasn't quite sundown when Lupus found out. As he lay snoozing in the lengthening shadows of the rock a faraway noise brought a twitch to his ears. At first it was just a mumbled jumble of clatter, but as sleep fell from him he realised what he was hearing was exchanges of heated words. His ears pricked up. Unless the old man was arguing with himself – and he wouldn't put that past him – they were no longer alone.

'I say yer stay away from me yer funny looking beggars!' threatened Bootes.

Keeping low Lupus peeped through a gap in the rocks. There were five or six swarthy men atop creatures the like he had never seen before. Each of the creatures had an uncomfortable looking lump in the middle of their backs. Some of Lyra's doing I'll be bound, thought Lupus. Between the swarthy men was a skinny man with a gaunt look dressed in black, sitting astride a mule. Lupus took him to be the leader.

'Yer cum near me an' yer'll wish yer'd never been born,' shouted Bootes, with as much venom as he could muster.

His threat was met by howls of laughter. Lupus needed to get Bootes in his sight so crept silently from the gap. From his new vantage point he could see why the men were in fits of hysterics. In his silver suit Bootes had the appearance of an ancient crazed tortoise.

'And what will you do to make us worry so much, eh infidel?' shrilled the man on the mule.

For a very long second an uncertain Bootes didn't answer. Monsters were one thing, he knew monsters, could deal with monsters and the like but men, big men with nasty looking swords, was something else. He didn't have to explain his words or actions to monsters.

Bootes finally mustered together a threat and shouted back at the man, 'Why I'll mish yer and mash yer wiv me sword, that's wot.'

The men started laughing again making Bootes all the angrier. Monsters didn't laugh, they had manners. With all the strength he could muster he began to move the great sword. Slowly at first, just skimming the rock, swinging it in a low arc, but as the weight of it took over, the momentum started to build taking it higher, turning Bootes with it.

'Enough!' squealed the man on the mule, 'I've no time for this stupidity. The scarabs await. Seize him!'

Things now took a serious turn as the laughing stopped and the men on the camels moved their steeds menacingly forward. Lupus the wolf, crouched low and made ready to attack, his teeth and claws bared, a deep growl growing in his throat. He would if he could try to knock the old man clear before the carnage began.

Meanwhile on the rock the speed and the weight of the sword became too much for Bootes to handle and both he and the sword shot from it. The scream from Bootes was closely followed by another, this one high pitched and bloodcurdling to the ears.

Instead of leaping Lupus held back, waiting to see what happened next. Bootes, not looking to be in any immediate danger, was lying face down in the sand, the sword still clasped in his hands, deep in the skinny man's chest. Around them the men on camels looked on, dumbstruck. Finally one of them spoke, 'It not Ramblest's fault this time.'

The largest of the swarthy men turned in his saddle. 'No, not this time brother,' he said. The man called for everyone to dismount, then dismounted himself and inspected the dead high priest. Once satisfied the priest had truly passed on and was therefore in no position to exact any sort of retaliation, he kicked him as hard as he could and laughed out loud. He began to dance round the priest's head. 'Hear me!' he cried, 'I am Akneed the new leader of our people.' At last things were going his way. He stopped his dancing and pointed to Bootes. 'Put the old one in a sack and tomorrow he will be sacrificed in place of the others.'

Not on my watch he isn't, thought Lupus, steeling silently to the top of the rocks where Bootes had been standing. He now looked down on the new leader.

'The sack Ramblest, quickly,' ordered Akneed.

But as stupid as Ramblest might be he wasn't about to move.

'Well? Have I got to do everything myself?'

Ramblest didn't answer, he was too busy staring at what had appeared on the rock. Akneed turned angrily to find the rest of his men doing likewise.

'Fools! What are you doing?'

A deep, guttural growl answered him from behind.

Spinning back Akneed went for his sword. It was the last thing he ever did.

Lupus now stood beside Bootes, snarling at Akneed's men, the bloody remains of Akneed's throat hanging from his jaws.

This was more than enough for the desert men. With their sight firmly fixed on Lupus and his dripping trophy they started to slowly back away, feeling for their camels as they did, but the camels being infinitely brighter than their riders had already left. Lupus dropped Akneed's throat and howled at the men as they stood there groping at thin air. It was the invite to leave they had been waiting for. The men scattered and disappeared like scalded cats into the growing darkness. Lupus stepped forward a couple of paces to make certain they had all got the message and no one was having second thoughts. They had, no one did. He listened. In the distance someone could be heard screaming the same words over and over again, 'Not Ramblest's fault! Not Ramblest's fault!'

Satisfied all was well again Lupus returned to the guise of obedient sheepdog and went to check on the old man.

Bootes was sitting up in a dazed state, mumbling something that made no sense, but then he did have a lump the size of a goose egg on his head. Lupus went to lick him but thought better of it and barked instead.

'Quiet boy,' said Bootes, putting a gnarled finger to his lips, 'I can't 'ear the bells wiv you going on.'

Lupus backed away and ran to the bag of supplies. He returned with a small silver bottle that Tee Hee had made a point of showing him in the spaceship, saying it would prove useful in the event of any cuts or bruises. Lupus dropped it into Bootes' lap and whined at the old man until he picked it up. Behind the rocks the baby started to cry. Torn for a moment Lupus decided on the baby and went to check on him.

Bootes unscrewed the bottle's lid and took a swig from it. 'Ah! That's better,' he said, he took another one.

By the time Lupus returned, the baby had lost its blanket over the side of the basket, Bootes had finished the bottle and was laying on his back dead to the world, the last signs of its contents sticky on his lips. Lupus couldn't believe it as he nudged the empty bottle, the old fool was supposed to rub the stuff on his bump not drink it. He rolled the bottle over so he could read the label. Under the application instructions it read:

IN THE EVENT OF ACCIDENTAL COMSUMPTION PLEASE EVACUATE THE PATIENT'S STOMACH (or stomachs) IMMEDIATELY

Just short of panic, Lupus raised his paws into the air and brought them down hard on Bootes' stomach. Bootes' mouth instantly flew open and a bubbling eruption of hot vomit shot through the air, landing with a sizzle on the sand between his feet. Lupus, having the presence of mind to bring a canteen of water with him poured the liquid down the open sewer Bootes called a throat. Lupus then had the presence of mind to get out of the way as a build up of pressure saw Bootes spring upright and let rip a belch that would have stripped paint.

'Way-hay-hay,' said Bootes, blinking, 'that stuff's well gud, but we can't sit 'ere all night, time's a wasting; we got friends to find.'

Lupus couldn't believe it. One minute the old man's knocking at death's door, the next, he's up and pulling swords from a dead priest's body. Lupus watched Bootes stick a foot on the priest's chest and pull. The sword held for a moment but then, with the most grotesque of sucking noises, it came free. Bootes proceeded to wipe the blade on the sand which was a bad idea as now it looked like a child's lolly covered in sandy coloured hundreds and thousands. He started to walk away from the rock dragging the sword behind him.

'Cum on Fluffy,' said Bootes, his silver suit shining in the now full starlight, 'I feels another adventure cuming on.'

Lupus sat, dumbfounded for a moment, but as the old man was showing willing for once he snapped out of it and started gathering the gear together as fast as he could, including the baby, who he now noticed had its feet hanging over the edge of the basket. But there was no time to ponder on this as Bootes was already veering off a true path. Gear gathered, baby strapped, Lupus set off after him and this time he was adamant all thoughts of, "what could possibly go wrong", would be firmly stowed away.

CHAPTER 34

'Come on, Cetus, let's go.'

But Cetus was curious. 'How can the wall...?'

'Wait... I hear something,' said Fatidic. He got lower to the floor to see if he could see under the wall.

'Cetus,' said Musca, giving him the hurry up, now hearing the noise himself.

This time Cetus was with his chieftain. 'I think Musca's right,' he said, 'we don't know what's making the noise.'

'Something's coming,' said Fatidic.

'Let's go.'

Fatidic was now with the majority and made to join them.

'Wait.'

'What now?' said Musca, already heading for the hall with or without the light from the torch Fatidic was carrying.

'We run,' said Cetus.

'Fatidic said wait.'

'I didn't.'

'Here.'

As all three were now gathered close together it was obvious someone else was doing the talking.

'Who's there?' said Musca, asking the most stupid question the passageway had been privy to in a long while.

'Equuleus.'

'Equuleus! Where are you?' said Musca, this question claiming the mantle from his last one.

'Behind the wall.'

Fatidic, already there and peering underneath, was surprised to see the gap had widened; Equuleus, dirty and frightened peeped back.

'How did you get there?' said Fatidic.

Equuleus began to babble franticly.

'Whoa, slow down we can't understand you,' said Musca, who had joined Fatidic.

The other side of the wall went quiet as Equuleus collected himself together. A deep breath and Equuleus tried again. He told how he had been thrown through the air and then nothing until he had heard Fatidic and seen the light under the wall.

'Can you see any way of opening the wall further?' said Fatidic, his brain whirring furiously.

'I can't see anything, it's too dark.'

But, thought Fatidic, the wall has moved. 'Have you touched anything?'

'I don't think so.'

'What are you thinking?' said Cetus.

'Yes?' said Musca.

'I'm thinking there must be a way to move the wall on each side of it. Equuleus, can you see a lever or something like?' said Fatidic.

'How could they use a lever?' said Musca, proving he wasn't a complete idiot.

'Anything that looks like it might move the wall.'

'I'll try, but it's dark in here,' said Equuleus.

As he moved away from the wall there was a feint creaking noise and Fatidic nearly lost his nose. The wall had lowered back to the original gap.

'What was that?' said Musca, jumping when Fatidic did.

'The gap narrowed. Equuleus?'

'Yes.'

'Come back to the wall again.'

Equuleus did as asked and the gap widened again.

'Pressure pads,' said Fatidic, jumping to his feet, 'they use pressure to move the wall.'

Musca didn't like the sound of what Fatidic was saying. 'You mean the beetles are intelligent?'

'Perhaps,' said Fatidic, raising the torch and looking around, 'but more likely the people who built the passages were. The beetles I should imagine don't even know they exist.'

'Then…?' The question was there, but it was way over Musca's head so he didn't finish it.

Fatidic, back on the floor, nose to the gap, called to Equuleus, 'Can you see any rocks or rubble lying about?'

'I think so,' said Equuleus.

'Then get them and pile them where you're standing.'

There was a moment's hesitation, but Equuleus did as he was asked. Four rocks, a hand full of stones, plus Equuleus' weight later the gap had widened to nearly four inches.

'It's not enough,' said Fatidic, managing to get no more than an arm underneath the gap.

Equuleus started to whimper, 'But it's all I could find.' He sounded close to tears.

'You said pads?' said Cetus, remembering what Fatidic had concluded earlier.

'Did I? I did,' said Fatidic. 'One there and one on this side; it must be close by. Of course!' he said slapping a thigh, 'we're on it.'

'We are?'

'Yes. One directly before and after the wall, it makes sense; we need the others.'

A short while later everyone was gathered either side of the wall and the gap had risen to six inches.

'We need more weight,' said Fatidic.

'We haven't got anymore.'

'I know a room that has,' said Fatidic.

Reluctantly, they gathered bones along with what rubble they could find and brought it back to the pad. The result: a gap they could crawl under.

Glad to be finally escaping the horrors behind them they took it in turns to roll, one by one, beneath the wall until only Musca was left. On his back and preparing to follow he caught a fleeting glance of the dead scarab. A shiver promptly ran down his spine, but it wasn't what he saw that had caused the involuntary shudder; it was the thought of what might be waiting for them beyond the wall.

CHAPTER 35

'Oh dear, oh dear, oh dear,' muttered Lyra, pacing frantically.

It was almost nightfall and Lyra had fretted the day away. There had not been seen hide nor hair, nor scale, of Serpens and Ophiuchus since he arrived back. What did he do? Look for Lupus as Serpens had ordered or try to find them? Or wait and do nothing? Choices, choices, choices. He felt like the filling in a rock and hard place sandwich. He paused by a remnant of Serpens' throne. Why was it broken? He hadn't the faintest idea, so kicked out at it and continued with his mobile fretting.

As time continued the stress built twisting his already twisted little face. Lyra was sure all the thinking he was trying to do would culminate in his eyeballs bursting and his head exploding. He stopped at another piece of throne. What if Serpens had lost his temper and flown into a rage, smashing the throne and disposing of Ophiuchus in some horrible way? Maybe it wasn't temper, perhaps he had gone mad; a homicidal anarchist on the loose looking for his next victim. Lyra shuddered; he couldn't help but think the worst at that thought. He then brightened up; maybe the creators had exacted some terrible punishment on Serpens. Lyra suddenly fell to his knees and looked skyward. But it wasn't an act of repentance that had Lyra on his knees, it was the considerably sized rock that had done it; the one which sat on the back of his legs, wedged firmly between his shoulder blades and which the back of his head now rested upon.

Lyra, through self preservation, instinctively played dead.

'Lyra!' thundered a misshapen figure bearing down on him.

Lyra had the feeling he ought to recognise the voice, but there was something not quite right about it. He decided it was safer to stay where he was for the time being; that and not being able to move because of the rock.

The misshapen figure drew beside Lyra and ordered another misshapen figure that had played the dark silent type of misshapen figure pretty well up to now to remove the rock. 'Opens, un-wedge him,' he said.

A massive clawed hand grasped the rock and removed it while another hand, this one slightly smaller and not so clawed, shook Lyra straight.

'Good,' said the first misshapen figure when Lyra was upright, 'do... you... know... who... I... am?' The figure was kneeling and staring into Lyra's blank, playing dead eyes. There was no response. The figure was not happy.

'Opens you fool. Why did you have to throw the rock so hard? This useless dolt is my only chance.'

Your only hope, thought Opens, what about me?

The figure stood up. 'See if you can bring him round while I find somewhere to sit, that walk was exhausting.'

Opens begrudgingly did what he was told and carried Lyra to a small stream where he dunked him into its icy depths.

A short while later Lyra sat shivering on a piece of throne, wondering what was going on. The figure was sat looking down at him.

'He is well now, Sire,' said Opens.

'About time, now get me something more befitting my rank to sit on,' said the figure, waving a dismissive hand.

'Yes, Sire,' said Opens, saluting. This rang a bell with Lyra.

'Now Lyra,' said the figure, hesitantly, 'it pains me to say this, but needs dictate, I need your help.' There was a cough from somewhere distant. 'We need your help.'

Through water logged eyes Lyra squinted up at the creature. Did he know him? Something was familiar, but no he didn't think so. 'Who are you? What do you want from me?' whined Lyra. But what about the tutu?

'Do you not recognise me? The Master of Darkness; your master, soon to be master of all the universe,' said the figure.

Lyra's eyes grew wide. It couldn't be, but the creature did in some peculiar way bear some resemblance to the Dark Lord, but in another peculiar way he didn't.

'Well,' said the figure growing impatient, 'has the Pathtor Hopsheer* got your tongue?' The figure struck a dramatic pose. His best side facing Lyra. 'It's me, Serphiuchus.'

Lyra fell backwards. It *was* him; sort of. 'Do you mean Serpens?' he said hesitantly.

'Yes, yes, that's the fellow, Serpens,' said Serphiuchus. Serphiuchus was standing with his hands clasped together by the side of his head and fluttering his eyelashes. 'Now, will you give an old mucker a helping hand? Because if you don't, I think I shall go quite mad.'

And he won't be the only one, thought Lyra; quite certain in his mind that he wouldn't be alone in seeking the comfort of a rubber room in the immediate future.

'What happened to you?' ventured Lyra, warming to the idea that maybe this creature was indeed Serpens; even with the display of increasingly odd behaviour.

'It was a tornado. I was just bringing you in when it hit and turned me into this monstrosity.' Serphiuchus dragged the back of his hand across his brow to emphasise the distress he was feeling.

Ah! It clicked in Lyra's mind, they got mixed up.

Serphiuchus was now slumped across a boulder in an over boiled act of desperation. 'If you don't help I'll stay this way forever, degenerating until I'm at a level I cannot return from. His level.' He narrowed his eyes and nodded at Opens. 'I don't want to be that stupid. I want my body and mind back as it was before the transition has gone too far.' A tear trickled down one of his cheeks; it had teeth.

'But what can I do?' asked Lyra, chewing on the ham that was flying around.

Serphiuchus sprang into a sitting position. 'You have to separate our present bodies and reassemble them as they should be. Please.'

Lyra wasn't sure. An air of caution had blown into the space between his ears. He looked perplexed. What did he do? On the one hand he would be elbow deep in smelly gore rebuilding a

* Amazing what they call cats on other worlds. *SJ*

243

monstrous bully who would most certainly carry on making his wretched little life a misery or he could leave things as they were and have a pleasant, well mannered, slightly creepy Serphiuchus as a travelling companion. Serphiuchus meanwhile was slumped backwards over the boulder again, fluttering his eyelids at Lyra as if his life depended on it.

'Please,' he said, 'pretty please.' Serphiuchus now had both hands linked beneath his chin.

There was really no choice.

'I'll get something sharp,' said Lyra, jumping down from the piece of throne.

It took Lyra a while, but he found just what he needed, something sharp edged, but also smooth in just the right way so as not to damage any vital organs, too much, then returned to where the two twisted figures patiently waited. Serphiuchus was smiling, Opens wasn't when he arrived.

'You have the implement needed?' said Serphiuchus.

'Yes.'

'Then if Opens here is sitting comfortably you may begin.'

Lyra clambered onto a large boulder placed between and slightly behind the two by Opens and began the operation. The rock in Lyra's hand slammed down hard without the slightest trace of surgical precision onto Opens' skull splitting it in two.

'Good shot, old chap, hurrah,' cheered Serphiuchus, his hands tightly clasped and pressed with glee against his chin. 'I say, is that a piece of brain. Oh! I feel quite faint.'

Giving Serphiuchus a sideways glance Lyra realised the operation was going to take place not a moment too soon. Then, with a speed that belied his natural neural impulses, he made a sudden change of plan. Before Serphiuchus had a chance to utter, "oh I say", Lyra brought the rock crashing down on his skull cleaving it open in much the same way as he had Opens.

The plan had been to have Opens glistening and pulsating on the ground in a neat organised pile so Serphiuchus could pick over the best bits, but because of the degree of deterioration he was displaying Lyra thought it better to be safe than sorry. He didn't think he could stand an eternity with whatever it was Serpens was turning into. Besides, he hated having someone looking over his shoulder when he was working. He quickly brought the rock crashing down again, this time onto Serphiuchus' neck, severing head from body.

And so the butchery continued. Lyra, whistling while he worked, whacked and hacked until all that remained of the two creatures were two mashed and mutilated steaming piles. Lyra flicked gore from his fingers and surveyed his work. The easy bit was over, now for the hard part. Rolling up imaginary sleeves Lyra dived head first into the pile that was Serphiuchus.

Working steadily through the night Lyra sorted and re-sorted each pile into two new ones. And as the first light of a new day dawned the second stage was complete. He stood glistening in the sunshine, dripping with gore. It was time for the third and final stage; the reassembling.

But some hours later, as the sun reached its zenith, Lyra still hadn't started. He had moved to shoo the odd interested carrion, but he had not touched so much as a toenail; he was in a quandary. The putting together wasn't the problem. He had done it before. All inklings were given compulsory courses on first aid, dismemberment and rebuild, but that only covered singles. Something he had a proven record in. Had he not helped out on project Frank… Frankie? Whatever; had something to do with a beer mug. And that had been from scratch. He had been top of his class for Creators' sake; he was a natural. Yet here he was dithering. The problem: who did he rebuild first?

If he put Ophiuchus together first, Serpens would surely be angry at being left to last and do something nasty to him. But if he started with Serpens he would surely complain about having to wait around while Ophiuchus was being built and get angry and do something nasty to him. Dread lay heavy on his bony little shoulders.

Then it came to him; an idea that had him sweating. Lyra's constipated little brain was pushing out a big one. He couldn't, could he? Sweat beaded on his forehead. It was an option, but could he get away with it. His lips trembled, the idea wanted to

245

tumble forth. He needed to hear it out loud. Finally it came. Lyra grunted and groaned with the effort, 'Unless I don't rebuild either of them,' he shouted aloud, triumphant. There it was out and Lyra lay exhausted where he fell. He could do it. He knew he could.

'NO YOU COULDN'T!'

The sudden new thought dug deep into his brain raking his nervous system with pain.

'AND IF I WAS YOU I'D THINK VERY CAREFULLY BEFORE THINKING ANOTHER THOUGHT LIKE THAT!'

Lyra's feeble brain was again pummelled by the deep dark force of the thoughts invading his mind. His body, equally shown no quarter, was thrown with considerable force to the ground. The invading thought came again, but this time with less power.

'Now, I think it's time you put us back together again, *don't you*?' Less power, but painful none the less.

On the ground Lyra was nodding uncontrollably into the dirt. Nodding at an end he slowly rose and looked at the Serpens pile.

'Yes it's me,' said the bloody mess. 'Did you think I wouldn't know what was going on in that minuscule dumping ground you call a mind even in this condition?'

Stupidly Lyra hadn't, but why had Serpens waited until now to punish him?

'Wait until now?' said Serpens.

Drat, thought Lyra.

'What time is it?'

'Noon, Master,' said Lyra, cringing.

Noon, thought Serpens, shocked. It was a good thing he had attained consciousness when he had or who knows what would have befallen him.

'Then I think it's about time you got on with the job.'

Lyra didn't need telling twice, he hurried across to the pile and got stuck in.

'Good. I'm glad we have our understanding back,' said the pile. 'Ouch! Careful.' It added.

CHAPTER 36

'Ah! So you awake. 'Good, yes-no?' said someone, in a particularly bad attempt at a French accent.

Pistor was showing signs of coming round.

'Well?' stabbed the voice, 'Are you to say somezing, yes-no?'

Against his heavy eyelids' better judgement, Pistor prised them open to see who was adding to his headache.

'Ah ha!'

'Where am I?' managed Pistor, through a wave of nausea. Head bowed, he took in a pair of knee length, black boots.

'*Where am I? Where am I?*' mimicked, quite childishly, the bad French accent. 'I am 'ere to ask ze questions not you. So if you please it will be I who ask zem, yes-no?'

Not feeling in any position to argue, Pistor nodded in agreement and winced as a sharp pain rolled from the back of his head and rested moaning and groaning behind his eyes. If it wasn't for the lump he could feel tightening the skin on the back of his head, he would swear he was in the hands of a gigantic hangover.

'Who are you? Zere, is zat not a good question, yes-no?'

Good question or not the man's verbal tirade was grating on Pistor. To combat this he gently raised his head and for the first time saw his questioner in all his glory. A giant of a man sprouting a profusion of frills and mighty cuffs that fell almost to his knees from a coat that would once have taken pride of place in any tailor's window. His eyes began to clear now his head was tilted up and Pistor, rid of spots and mist, saw clearer now. The man did indeed cut a dashing figure, but now he could see the man and his clothes had seen better days. The frills and cuffs, once white and stiff, now hung yellow and stained. The man was grizzled in appearance, a patch of black covered his left eye and a beard that would have been glorious in its red heyday now grew heavily speckled with a dirty yellow grey. His fingers were almost orange from the rigours of tobacco. On his head he wore a black tricorne hat. Though tatty, it sat cockily on his head; a reminder of his youth perhaps.

'Well? 'as ze so called furry animal got your tongue, yes-no?'

Pistor went to answer, but faltered as his tongue stuck to the roof of his mouth.

The man shouted to someone out of Pistor's area of vision. 'Voussoir! Bring our guest some water so he can wet 'is so called instrument of noise.'

An older man with bowed legs approached carrying a bucket. Pistor tried to sit up but the bonds strapped round his arms and chest restricted his movement to a slight shuffle.

'Sorry, Cap'n but we seem to be short of mugs,' said the bow legged man.

'A drink and a wash zen, eh Voussoir, yes-no?'

Grinning evilly the bow legged man emptied the bucket's contents over Pistor's head causing him to cough and splutter as the water entered his mouth and nose. But it was cool and did go some way to soothing his aching head. He even managed to swallow some between the snorting and choking.

'Good man, Voussoir, it would appear you 'ave brought a little relief to our guest. Zough I am thinking your bedside manner is not all zat it could be.' Both men started to laugh.

'What do you want?' snapped Pistor, as his aches and pains lessened enough for anger to show itself.

'Ah, ze little man asks ze questions again.' The captain drew a scarred and pitted cutlass from his belt and bent forwards menacingly. 'I 'ave told you once. Do not let me 'ave to say it again or my friend 'ere will cut short our conversation.' He sliced the air in front of Pistor to emphasise his point.

Pistor got the message and clammed up, pressing his back against whatever it was he was tied to.

'I zink, as zey say, we 'ave come to an understanding.' Replacing his cutlass, the captain stood up, his face suddenly brightening. 'Let me introduce myself. I am Captain Pluperfect and zis rapscallion is First Mate Voussoir.' The bow legged man bowed, 'And zere,' Pluperfect pointed away to his right to a fair

248

haired boy tending a large cooking pot, 'is Caudal. 'e is the ship's cabin boy.' The boy turned and gave Pistor a smile that made his skin crawl. Pluperfect bent conspiratorially low and whispered in Pistor's ear. ''e is quite mad you know, but we 'ave to 'ave one. It is tradition, yes-no?' He waved at the boy who waved back. ''e is terribly loyal. Loyal, but mad.' Pluperfect spat on the floor and stood up. 'And zis rabble you see milling around pretending to do somezing useful is ze rest of ze crew. A finer bunch of cut-throats and buccaneers you will never see.' He moved aside to give Pistor a better view. 'I call zem by number. It is easier you see as zere are so many of zem,' he explained. 'Zere, by that barrel, that is 3a and 3b. Zey are brothers.'

There were perhaps ten men scurrying back and forth. Not that many, but Pistor didn't like the look of any of them. They all appeared to exude craziness to a certain degree.

'And now zat I have introduced you to myself and my men, I zink it only polite you do ze same.' Pluperfect suddenly reached down and grabbed Pistor by the shirt pinching the skin beneath. 'Or I will 'ave Caudal zere cook something special. Special to you zat is. I make myself clear, yes-no?'

What could he do? Pistor nodded, at least the pain in his head was lessening.

Pluperfect let go of Pistor and for no obvious reason did a little jig. 'What is your name?'

'Pistor,' muttered Pistor.

'What? What is it you say? Are you talking to me or to your boots, no-yes?'

Lifting his head, Pistor repeated his name with as much venom as he thought healthy.

Pluperfect stopped his jigging and smiled. 'Good, Mister Pistor. Now perhaps we are on, how you say, the same wave-width yes-no?' He perched on a handy barrel and took a dagger from his belt. This he held loosely at Pistor's throat. 'So Mister Pistor, pray tell why you were snooping where you 'ave no business?'

The touch of the cold metal on his skin worked where the water had failed. Pistor had regained his senses and they were telling him, the wrong answer here and you are dead meat. He had to think. Think quickly.

'I... er...' The point of the dagger dug a little deeper. 'I can't... talk... with that thing pressing on my throat.'

A momentary reluctance that had Pistor fearing the worst followed, but Pluperfect eventually relented and the blade was withdrawn, but not far.

'I wait,' said Pluperfect, with the undertones of someone who didn't usually.

It was now or never. It was just another lie and he was good at them, Pistor assured himself. 'I was looking for water. Check my bag. My bottle's nearly empty.' It sounded convincing, even to Pistor. Trouble was it was Pluperfect who had to swallow it.

Pluperfect stared at Pistor, studying him. The man in the fancy clothes was now his judge, jury and prosecution. Pistor felt the man to be fickle and Pistor the problem, could easily become Pistor the very dead solution.

For Pistor the next few seconds seemed suspended in time. He felt a trickle of sweat between his shoulder blades. He could hear a bird somewhere in the distance. He thought he would be able to hear the man's heartbeat if he tried. He had never felt so alive. Pistor came to the conclusion that life and death were akin to night and day and, as it was darkest before the dawn, so you were more alive before your death.

Pluperfect got up so quickly Pistor thought the man had stabbed him and he hadn't felt it yet. But the man was placing the dagger in his belt and there was no sign of blood on it. 'I believe you, Mister Pistor, but I feel you have more to tell. Later, perhaps?' Pluperfect called to the cabin boy, 'Lay an extra place boy, we have ze guest.'

The boy, Caudal, nodded and smiled and for a second time Pistor felt his skin crawl. The boy's smile was most definitely not that of a sane person.

'Voussior! Cut him loose.'

* * *

Free to join Captain Pluperfect and his men for food Pistor wasn't afforded the same luxury afterwards when Pluperfect and his men settled down for a siesta. Once more bound hand and foot to the same tree Pistor watched as the men surrounding him gradually drifted into whatever world it was drunken cut-throats went to when asleep. Even the boy had had his fill of booze. Only Pistor, for once in his life, hadn't had a drop pass his lips, but that wasn't because he abstained; they simply didn't offer him any. That, thought Pistor, as he wrestled with his ropes, might be what saves him.

He had told his story and for the moment Pluperfect was happy enough, but Pistor wasn't stupid enough to think that that was that. He had an uneasy feeling in his gut that had nothing to do with the food. He had been spared, but for how long? He made another sweep of the men; if he was going to try and make an escape now was the time to do it.

It hurt, his wrists were weeping and bloody, but the ropes were giving; a drunken man ties loose knots. Grimacing through the pain and stopping only for the occasional grunt or fart from the sleeping men, Pistor continued his struggle. Finally, with tears in his eyes, the ropes slipped away. With no time to congratulate himself and eyes never leaving his sleeping companions he started on the binding holding his ankles.

Loose and up, Pistor kicked away the ropes and made for the edge of the clearing. Treasure was in his mind, but for another day maybe. His hunger for it had been dulled by the captain's blade. He touched the nick on his neck.

The plan was to run as fast as he could, once out of the clearing and head for the city; not stopping until he was past its boundaries. There he hoped he might get help from the jungle man. But plans, like promises, sometimes fall to the wayside when something else comes along.

Standing on the edge of the clearing and he didn't know why he did it, he took a last look behind him. He stared hard then patted his trouser leg; the one where his potato drink should have been. They'd taken it. Of course they would. Now he saw it propped against the bottom step of the building; alongside it his bag. The bag that had Tee Hee's recipe in it. Pistors step faltered. The bag that had his gizmo in it. More importantly, did he want to be without alcohol for who knows how long? This last thought was too much to bear and the falter became an about turn. He could get it; he had got this far.

Carefully watching where he stepped Pistor made his way over to where his bag and bottle had been stacked. He just prayed that whoever had taken it hadn't emptied it. To his relief the stars were smiling on him once again. Half full. He took a small swig from it before putting it back where it belonged. Anxiously sweeping the clearing for movement Pistor grabbed his bag, but was surprised to find it heavier than when he had had it last. Closer inspection showed he had made a mistake, the bag wasn't his; obviously one of them had taken a shine to his bottle and stowed it with his gear.

Pistor should have put it back and made swift tracks there and then; he had what he held most dear, but he couldn't help himself, curiosity getting the better of him he peered inside. There was something about the way the bag clinked.

A gasp later, Pistor shoved his hand in the bag and pulled it back fairly dripping with gold and jewels. He dropped them back in and pulled out a gold coin. He bit it; it was real. Pistor's legs almost gave way below him. He had found his treasure after all. He was going to be rich.

The next thing Pistor did was proof as to why his life never went quite how he thought it should. He whooped for joy. Not a quiet whoop you understand, a whoop that might say – I'm rich, but let's get out of here as quietly as possible before someone wakes up – but rather a – Yahoo! Wake up and look at me you bunch of psychopathic cut-throats I'm stealing your treasure – kind of whoop.

At first nothing happened and Pistor, under some kind of self imposed delusional state, had the idea he was going to get away with it. Then in the space of a breath all hell broke loose. Captain Pluperfect and his men awoke, rose, grabbed their weapons and rounded on Pistor in one fluid movement that would have had any group of synchronised swimmers green with envy.

'There me hearties,' cried Pluperfect, all sign of an accent dropped, 'grub and water's not good enough for him don't yer know. He'd steal the pension from under yer pillow. Get him!'

Frantically looking for a way out, Pistor backed away from the advancing cut-throats. He could see the boy, Caudal, giggling and dribbling, insanity reigning. Pistor shivered and then stumbled. He looked up; the building. It was his only chance. Clutching the bag tightly to his chest he started to climb. Behind him he could hear his pursuers. He had to reach the top.

But what then? Only the stars knew. For now Pistor could only cross his fingers and run as fast as he could.

CHAPTER 37

'Cum on boy, we're nearly there,' encouraged Bootes.

Behind, struggled Lupus who in any other form would have coped better, but as a dog, big as he was, he was having difficulty. The problem was, since the run in with the men in the desert the baby had grown at a phenomenal rate and now only its bottom was able to rest in the basket.

Lupus gave Bootes the evil eye as the old man waved him on. Couldn't the old fool see? Or maybe he didn't want to. Or… and this was a totally feasible idea… Tee Hee had had something to do with it. Who knows what was in that serum he had given him? But whatever the reason, enough was enough! The baby was now the size of a teenage youth. The baby was a teenage youth. Lupus released the basket and the big baby and all fell out onto the sand.

With the terrain about to change from sand to rock, Bootes turned to announce its arrival and was horrified to see the baby on the ground. 'Bad dog!' hollered Bootes, hurrying towards them. Obviously oblivious to the change the baby had gone through, he shouted at Lupus to pick the baby up.

Barking at the strewn contents of the basket Lupus ignored the advancing Bootes. The strewn contents were likewise ignoring Lupus.

'Come on you ungrateful little sprog, I know you can hear me,' hissed Lupus in his mind, 'it's about time you carried your own basket.' Lupus glowered down at the youth who was still doing his utmost to ignore him. 'Don't make me nip you!'

The threat was rewarded with a response, but not one Lupus had been expecting. The youth showed no anger, but instead started to quietly weep.

Taken aback, Lupus instantly felt a pang of regret at his actions. 'Please don't cry,' he found himself thinking, 'I'm sorry. I'm tired and a bit grumpy because of it.' Then, and keeping this thought from the youth, 'Grief I'm getting soft in my old age.'

The youth sat up and blinked away the tears that had been welling. He pointed at Bootes who was still advancing. 'He's got my clothes.' Lupus swung a glance in Bootes' direction. He was still advancing. 'How would you like to walk around with a nappy wrapped round your backside? For goodness sake, I'm nearly a man. It's not going to do my street cred a lot of good being seen like this.'

Although Lupus didn't understand all that the youth had placed in his mind, he did get the general gist. The problem now of course was how was he going to get the old man out of the silver suit? Maybe?

'Start shivering,' popped into the youth's mind.

'Why?'

'Don't argue, just do it before he gets here,' said Lupus, as Bootes bore down on them.

'Well, I'll be. The babs...' Bootes wavered in mid sentence as he arrived. He's going to notice how big he is at last, thought Lupus. 'Shivering,' finished Bootes.

Why Lupus was surprised at the old man missing how big the baby had got he didn't know, but at least he had noticed the shivering.

'Now, why would yon bab be a shivering in all this lovely sunshine?' said Bootes, rubbing his chin thoughtfully. 'Never mind, if the bab's cold the bab's cold. Fluffy, get me the civilian clothes will yer?'

He has to be shielded, thought Lupus, definitely something to do with Tee Hee.

'Well go on, Fluffy, the bab's freezing.'

Snapped from his musings Lupus dutifully went to get what Bootes had asked for from the bags. Halfway there, he realised what the old man had in mind for the baby. The only civilian clothes, as Bootes had put it, were his own. Lupus shuddered; surely he didn't mean to put the youth in those smelly rags. There had to be something he could do to get the old man out of the silver suit. Thinking hard, he continued to the bag with Bootes' clothes in and tentatively reached out a paw. The instant he touched it a small cloud of flies flew from its depths. Lupus heroically held back the contents of his stomach. No way was he picking it up with his mouth.

'Gud boy,' said Bootes, patting Lupus and retrieving the bag he had dragged over to him with his paw.

'Now,' said Bootes, holding out an item of yellowing underwear above the youth, 'don't yer worry bab we'll soon have yer dressed.'

The youth's eyes grew large with fear at the sight of them. 'Help me,' he sent to Lupus' mind.

But Lupus, lying with his paws resting over his snout, could only suggest the youth stay calm and relax. It would soon be over.

It was. Bootes had won even though the baby had managed to get upright and taken its first wobbly steps in an attempt to escape. At the arrival of soft sobbing in his mind Lupus removed his paws from his snout and opened his eyes. The youth would have looked at home in a field as the worst most misbegotten scarecrow you could ever imagine. Lupus felt sorry for him and whined. The six feet, one hundred and fifty pound baby scratched at the wool his bottom half was encased in.

'It's for the best,' said Lupus, offering little in the way of comfort.

'You don't have to wear this,' said the youth, pouting.

'Pick up the basket.'

The youth did and together they trailed after Bootes who was already on rocky ground.

Both Lupus and the youth fell to the ground as the trio reached the spot where Musca and the others had been ambushed days before. Lupus because he was exhausted, the youth because of the terrible onslaught his nasal passages were under. Worried, Lupus probed his mind; it wasn't a pretty sight.

'What's wrong?' said Lupus.

'It's the ammonia,' explained the youth, 'my body can't take it. It's poisonous to us.'

By "us" Lupus figured the youth included Tee Hee. As for the ammonia Lupus didn't think it that strong, but then he wasn't wearing the clothes and had only occasionally had the misfortune to catch a whiff and then in the open air.

'What do we do?'

'I need to remove the clothes, but I don't think I have the… the strength,' said the youth, trying to raise his head, but failing. 'I didn't realise. My memories, information, only grows a small piece at a time.'

That prompted another question Lupus would look to ask later, now though the youth was teetering on the verge of unconsciousness; he had to do something. Ripping for all he was worth, Lupus tore the clothing from the youth's body until he had a ragged pile. The youth reacted to the fresh air caressing his skin and filling his lungs and started to recover.

'Thank you,' said the youth, 'I thought I'd be more resilient as I'm half monkey man, as my father put it.'

An intrigued Lupus cocked his head to one side. Not long ago this youth had been nothing more than a tiny pooping sprog, but now it was as if the youth had always been this way. Talking as if he had been around for as long as the age he looked.

'You look at me in puzzlement,' said the youth, 'Surely my father explained to you our growth rate.'

'Not in so many words,' said Lupus, remembering his bewilderment at finding the silver suit.

Rejuvenated, the youth stood up, stretched and smiled. 'That, from what my newly acquired memories tell me, sounds like my father.' A snore caught his attention. Bootes was asleep. 'I must have my suit. It is designed to protect me until I attain my full growth. Will you help me?' With Bootes sleeping he had reverted to normal speech.

Lupus and the youth crept to the sleeping Bootes and gently eased him from the suit. Bootes carried on snoring. But the youth didn't put the suit straight on, instead going to the bag Tee Hee had left with it. From it he withdrew an aerosol spray and a vial of green liquid. The liquid he said was for Bootes.

Slightly perturbed, Lupus knew what Tee Hee's liquids could do, he put his body between that of Bootes and the youth and waited for an explanation.

The youth smiled at him. 'Please, there is no need to worry. It will simply erase his memory from when we left the saucer. Father, it would appear, thinks of everything.' Lupus hesitated. 'It will save a lot of explaining.'

It would be helpful. Lupus stepped aside.

Tilting Bootes' head forward, the youth emptied the vial down Bootes' throat. 'It is done,' said the youth, replacing the top. 'He will sleep until the effect of the liquid takes place.' The youth gently laid Bootes' head on the ground. 'While we wait, perhaps you can tell me why the Serpens creature stalks the idiot my mother travels with; putting her in so much danger?'

The hackles rose on Lupus' neck. His tongue had been too loose with Tee Hee.

'You're upset,' said the youth, 'then let me tell you something of my people and you can tell me about yourself and yonder sleeping beauty.'

This was different. No one, not even the creators, had ever taken an interest in him. He began to feel the same warm glow building inside he had felt with the old man. The youth ruffled his hair.

'And as I already know your name, let me tell you mine.' The youth picked up his suit and sat on the ground away from Bootes and his clothes with his back to a tree and started spraying the suit's interior. He saw that Lupus was again looking puzzled. 'Disinfectant, you can't be too careful. Nothing personal, you understand.'

'Fair enough,' said Lupus.

'It's Telaesthesia.'

'What is?'

'My name, but you can call me Tee See.'

They talked well into the night. Bootes slept on, just waking once when he thought he heard his dog talking to a stranger. He passed it off as a dream and fell back to sleep.

Morning came and with it a commotion that brought Lupus from his slumber. Cripes, he thought, as a naked Bootes, not the most pleasant sight first thing in the morning – or any time for that matter – tore past him shouting and screaming at Tee See as he chased him round and round the trees, a sword held aloft in his hands, we forgot to dress him.

'Quick, Fluffy,' shouted Bootes, as he passed, 'I'm after a thief. He's stolen me clothes.'

Lupus flashed a thought Tee See's way.

'He means his own clothes,' came a frantic reply.

Diving in before someone got hurt; Lupus pushed the remains of Bootes' clothes in his path to draw his attention. The old man duly fell over them; the sword nearly impaling him as he did.

'Me clothes!' shouted Bootes, in triumph. Forgetting the chase, he scooped them up and held them aloft. They're still 'ere.'

With a bemused Bootes poking a finger in holes that weren't there yesterday, at least he thought it was yesterday, Lupus took the opportunity to move the sword he had dropped to a safer place. A sword that, it materialised, wasn't the one he had expected. Lupus sniffed at it. It held an unfamiliar yet familiar scent, a female one; a female scent that matched that of Tee See. Lupus picked it up with the idea of showing it to Tee See who was a short distance off, to see what he made of it.

He didn't get that far, as he passed the now half dressed Bootes, the old man snatched it from him. 'Give that 'ere boy. A hero needs a sword.' Bootes then thrust it towards an imaginary foe and got it stuck in a tree. The liquid didn't manage to rid him of his skills then, thought Lupus. ''ang about a mo. Let me... wait a minute... I can do this... ah!' Bootes fell over backwards as the tree released the sword. He sat there for a moment, then swore. 'Well I'll be,' he said examining the sword as if seeing it for the first time, 'yer can wrap me up in dung and let the flies at me if this ain't Fornax's sword.'

'My mothers?' said Tee See, who had started to come back when he saw the sword was safely embedded in the tree.

'Yer wot?' said Bootes, suspiciously eyeing the stranger in their midst, who he had forgotten about again until then.

'The others,' said Tee See, attempting to cover his tracks. 'I heard some others were lost and I came to find them.' He wondered if Lupus thought it sounded as flimsy an excuse for him being there as he did. Lupus let him know he did. Bootes on the other hand sucked it in, hook, line and sinker.

'Then yer shall join us, good knight on our quest for I, Bootes, the killer of fiery creatures 'as spoken.' Bootes raised Fornax's sword aloft once more and ran at another tree, hacking at it when he got there.

'I thought you said he'd forget?' said Lupus.

'From the saucer,' Tee See replied, 'memories from when you set out.'

Great, thought Lupus, who thought he had seen and heard the last of Bootes' heroics.

While Bootes played, Lupus and Tee See got down to discussing what the discovery of Fornax's sword meant.

'Can you pick anything up?' asked Tee See, meaning in the way of scents.

'Good news and bad news,' said Lupus, grimly. 'I can only find one. It belongs to one of them we seek, but it's not your mother's. There are other scents here of a creature I met in the desert; a strange one with a lump on its back.' Tee See said he thought Lupus was describing a camel. 'Whatever they are, they've masked all scents but one with their own which is very strong.'

'Why do you think the one lingers?'

'Whoever the other scent belongs to appears to have been away from the others and so didn't befall their fate.'

'Then what do we do?' said a worried Tee See.

'Do the only thing we can. Follow my nose.'

Without knowing what may have befallen his mother, the decision for Tee See was a hard one, but he knew the only chance they had of finding her before Serpens did, was to find whoever the remaining scent belonged to and ask him what he knew.

The jungle beckoned.

CHAPTER 38

'It's no good, I've got to stop,' said Fornax. She hated to say it, but she had to admit defeat. Her foot was killing her.

The brothers, who had been supporting her, gently eased her to the floor.

'But we can't stay here,' said Musca, warily scanning the passage behind them.

Fornax scowled at him. 'I know that, but my foot. I think it's worse than I thought. I may have sprained something.'

Cetus, the closest they had to someone medical; he knew about herbs, bent to have a look at it. 'It looks pretty swollen. I think we should strap it up.'

'Will this do?' Musca offered up a sash; part of the get up he had been given to put on for the feast.

'That will do nicely.'

When Cetus finished strapping Fornax's foot she went to get up, but Cetus stopped her. 'I think five or so minutes rest wouldn't go amiss,' he advised. Fornax thought otherwise, but when she tried to put weight on the foot her mind was changed for her.

'Perhaps ten minutes,' she said.

'I'll go and tell the others,' said Cetus. Equuleus and Fatidic had gone on ahead; their torch could just be seen flickering some way distant.

'I'll go with you,' said Musca. He cast a quick glance at Fornax, but she was busy tending to her foot.

They set off and caught up with Fatidic and Equuleus who had already stopped, but not because of anything happening behind them.

'What's going on?' asked Musca.

'Fatidic thinks he heard voices,' said Equuleus, shrugging.

'You didn't?'

'No,' said Equuleus.

'He was behind me,' said Fatidic, 'and it was definitely voices from somewhere up ahead. I couldn't guess how far, noise carries in here.'

As Fatidic had proved his salt so far, the general consensus was to listen to him.

'We better find out how far and who,' said Musca, 'I'll go back and send the brothers. It will be better the more there are in case of trouble.'

'What will you be doing?' asked Fatidic, a relative newcomer to Musca's style of leadership.

Both Cetus and Equuleus looked away.

'I'll be protecting Fornax of course.'

'Shouldn't a leader lead from the front?' said Fatidic, in all earnestness.

'Well... yes... I just... Equuleus, tell the brothers to get down here with their weapons, you protect Fornax.' Equuleus went to go. 'And take Fatidic here with you.'

'Are you sure?' said Fatidic.

'Of course I am. Better to have two protecting her,' said Musca. Better you out of the way than here interfering, he was thinking.

Fatidic and Equuleus headed back.

'I didn't realise your leader was such a coward,' whispered Fatidic, when he felt sure Musca was out of earshot.

'Please don't tell him that,' smiled Equuleus, 'he doesn't know.'

'Then why is he your leader?'

'He's the chieftain's son,' explained Equuleus, 'and as the chieftain isn't here...'

'Ah.'

'Mostly though we listen to Fornax, but he is better when she isn't around.'

'So he isn't himself.'

'Who is?' said Equuleus, his wisdom far exceeding his age, 'I think we all try to be something we're not at some time.'

This got Fatidic thinking; he had something on his mind and something he wanted to get off his chest. 'If I tell you something, will you keep it a secret?'

'What do you mean?'

'Promise first.'

'I shall try; stick a needle in my eye.'

'What?'

'Nothing. What's your secret?'

There was a brief pause. 'Magus Fatidic isn't my real name.'

Equuleus stopped walking. 'What is it then?'

'Promise you won't laugh.'

Equuleus agreed.

'It's Timbrel Tittle.'

'What sort of name is that?' asked a feminine voice from down the passageway. Fatidic was mortified.

When they arrived Fornax and the brothers were involved in a battle against the giggles.

'I knew I shouldn't have said anything,' muttered Fatidic.

'No wonder you changed it,' said Hydrus.

'My father named me after his instrument,' said Fatidic, his face straighter than any ruler. Everyone else was trying hard not to laugh. 'His tambourine; Timbrel. He loved it.'

'And Tittle?' enquired Fornax.

'A name passed down through the generations. It has a meaning of little consequence.'

'Come now, Fatidic, or should I call you Timbrel?' said Fornax, sucking in her cheeks, 'don't put yourself down so. It's a fine name.'

With a face like thunder Fatidic explained. 'No, that is what it means.' He wasn't sure whether to be angry or embarrassed. He plumped for neither and slumped to the floor. 'Musca says the brothers should go up ahead. I thought I heard somebody talking.'

The complexion of the mood in the passage immediately changed as the brothers grabbed weapons.

'How many?' said Fornax.'

'I don't know. Two, I think.'

'Quickly,' said Fornax.

The brothers hurtled along the passage to find Musca.

As all but the faint glow of the torch disappeared from sight, Fornax turned to Fatidic. 'You know, I feel a lot better. They say laughter is a great healer.' Fatidic huffed. 'Come now. You know your secret's safe with us and if you want no one else to know, then so be it. Eh, Equuleus?'

Equuleus nodded.

A sulking Fatidic folded his arms and grunted. What else could he do, he only had his own big mouth to blame.

Joined by the brothers, Musca and Cetus inched forward.

'Shouldn't we douse the torches?' said Hydra.

'We won't be able to see where we're going,' said Musca.

'But the people Fatidic heard might see them and us coming.'

There was an abrupt halt in proceedings as the point Hydra had brought to their attention was mulled over.

'Hydra has a point,' said Cetus.

'But we'll be in the dark,' argued Musca, who was thinking the solution to the problem might be to go back, but didn't like to say.

'Musca has a point too,' said Hydrus, 'what if one of us gets lost? Who knows what might be lurking in the dark.'

The beetles, traps, the beetles and more beetles sprang to over active minds, with good cause.

'If Fatidic heard voices why didn't he see any light? Surely if someone else was in here they'd need a torch?' said Hydra.

'Perhaps he was hearing things,' said Musca.

'Perhaps a little further then with torches?' suggested Cetus.

It was agreed. They cautiously inched on.

'Maybe they were hiding round a corner,' said Hydrus, a little while later.

There was an instant slowing of step. A few steps later the torches were extinguished.

They fumbled and stumbled their way forward for another fifty yards or so before anything of note happened.

'I think the floor's starting to rise,' announced Hydra, who had been given point, as it was he who suggested they put out the torches. It had, to a small degree; above him the ceiling rose parallel.

Climbing gradually it began to dawn on them why Fatidic would have failed to see any light from torches the voices may have been carrying, the slope having risen significantly enough to hide them.

'Stop,' said Hydra suddenly, causing a small pile up behind him.

'What is it?' said Musca, from the rear.

'Something's glowing up ahead.'

'Let me see,' said Musca, feeling his way past Hydrus and Cetus.

'I know what it is,' said Cetus, peering over Hydra's shoulder, 'it's daylight.'

'What should we do?' asked Hydrus.

This time Musca had little doubt as to what was to be done and no one argued. 'Hydra – Hydrus you go back and get the others. Cetus and I will get closer and see if we can find where the light is coming from.'

As the brothers scampered away, Musca and Cetus crept steadily closer to the light source.

'Can you hear something?' said Cetus, as they neared the top of the slope.

'People talking,' said Musca, flattening against the wall, 'but I can't see anyone.' The slope ended not far from where they were standing, giving them a clear view of a flat area the slope levelled out onto. The daylight and noise were coming from above.

They inched closer until they were almost standing at the top of the slope, above them they could see a roof, housed within it an ancient contraption that looked suspiciously like a pulley, but it was way above and the daylight appeared to be streaming down from below it. They could, if pressed against the wall, just make out blue sky. Against the furthest of these walls stood a ladder that reached to the top.

'We had better wait for the others,' said Cetus. Musca readily agreed. Up above, the voices they had heard grew louder.

'So first you want ze food and water and zen you want ozer zings and make ze big mistake eh, yes-no?'

There was a brief silence as if whoever was above them waited for an answer. None came.

The man spoke again. 'I am zen zinking zat you, Mister Pistor are a dishonourable man and not to be trusted, yes-no?'

Way below, two astonished faces turned skyward.

CHAPTER 39

Dusk was fast approaching as Lyra started putting the finishing touches to Serpens, who was quietly brooding.

'How long?' said Serpens, shifting awkwardly on the makeshift throne the then Opens had hurriedly and roughly hewn from a large piece of granite.

'Not long now, Master. Just the odd bib bit and bob bits to go,' muttered Lyra, shaking. It had been a long afternoon.

'Bib bits?'

'Yes, Master,' said Lyra picking it up.

'Ah yes.' Serpens frowned. 'Are you sure that's mine? It looks a bit small.'

'Yes, Master. Ophiuchus' is over there.' Lyra walked over to his pile and picked it up. 'I can show you mine if you like.'

'Er... no, that won't be necessary. Carry on.'

Nervously wringing his hands, Lyra continued, but the end was close and he wasn't sure how Serpens would react when he'd finished. There had been that moment of indecision and he was certain it hadn't been forgotten.

'Will it take long to put that idiot together?' said Serpens, throwing a thumb in the direction of Ophiuchus' pile.

'Not long,' said Lyra, retrieving the errant digit and fixing it on more securely this time. If Lyra was good at anything it was grovelling and a good bit of it now would perhaps help his cause. 'Not as complex as you, O High One. A simple beast that Ophiuchus, Master; not like you. Not long at all.' Lyra fixed a claw to the thumb and winced as Serpens scraped it against the claws on his fingers causing a small spark.

If the grovelling had managed to pour oil, Lyra couldn't tell; Serpens' expression remaining broody with a sprinkling of stoniness about it. 'Ready yet?' said Serpens.

267

Checking the ground where the pile of Serpens had been, Lyra rose with something in his hand. 'Just this and that's that,' he said. Lyra lifted Serpens' foot and popped the corn on. 'There, good as new.' Lyra instinctively stepped out of kicking range.

Ignoring the imp, Serpens strode across to the stream and stood admiring his reflection. 'Perfect,' he proclaimed after a moment or two.

Lyra felt an invisible weight lift from his shoulders.

'Lyra!'

It quickly made a reappearance. 'Yes, Master?' said Lyra, hurrying half-heartedly at the sound of his master's voice. 'What is it, Master? O Great One. Darkest Lord of them all. How may I, your most humble of servants, be of service?' As grovelling goes Lyra was doing his capering, sidling best.

'DID YOU THINK I WOULD FORGET?' Serpens bellowed, as Lyra arrived. 'DID YOU *REALLY* THINK YOUR BELLY CRAWLING WOULD HELP YOU?'

Wallowing in hopeful delusion, Lyra had been so caught, *slightly* on the hop, he fell backwards into the stream. Serpens fished him out.

'AND DID YOU THINK THAT I WOULD JUST LEAVE THINGS WITH NO REPERCUSSIONS?'

Lyra had rather hoped he would, but even he could see as hopes went it was out there with the washing. Held aloft by the scruff of his neck Lyra shook much like that washing might do in a particularly blustery wind.

'DID *YOU*?' roared Serpens. Lyra instantly drip dried with the ferocity of it. 'WELL?' Back to bellowing. Serpens started to shake Lyra when the imp failed to answer. Shaking now himself with fury, Serpens raised Lyra above his head and threw him head first into the pile that was Ophiuchus. 'NOW LEAVE ME. I WANT TO BE ALONE.' Serpens stormed past the star seeing Lyra and scattered parts of Ophiuchus and made for his seat of granite, mumbling as he passed, 'Lucky for you, you have your uses.'

Unable to take succour from Serpens' passing comment, as he was star counting at the time, a dazed Lyra came to with the belief any moment soon could be his last. Rising unsteadily, with one eye open for Serpens who had mysteriously disappeared from view, he set about gathering together the pieces of Ophiuchus, scattered by his intrusion. This accomplished he took stock of the enormity of his task. It wasn't going to be easy. He had lied to Serpens about the simplicity of reconstructing Ophiuchus. Ophiuchus had a physiology like no other. For one thing pretty much all his internal bits were a tawny colour and looked the same in pile form. It wasn't until one bit was attached to the right other bit that things started to become recognisable. Also, unlike Serpens, none of the bits had numbers on them. Lyra scratched his head and decided the best strategy was to start with the corners.

The midnight hour had come and gone by the time Lyra had finished. He had worked overtime, undertime (it has something to do with time and the shortening of) and any other time he could find to finish building Ophiuchus quicker than it had taken to re-build Serpens. Happily he had succeeded and Ophiuchus was back in one piece.

Pressure off, Lyra afforded a rare happy smile and told Ophiuchus to stay where he was while he went to fetch Serpens.

'As you say, old boy, as you say.'

Grinding to a halt mid step, Lyra felt his old friend, the sinking feeling come visiting. 'What did you say?' said Lyra, eyes narrowing.

'I said, as you say, old chap, toodle pip.'

Even to Lyra's limited scope of intelligence this wasn't good. He gave Ophiuchus the old up and down. There was something wrong with his eyes. They were clear and glinted with... That can't be right, thought Lyra. He had a closer look. Glinted with intelligence. Oh dear, something was dreadfully wrong. This needed quick thinking. Where was Lupus when you needed him? Sadly he would have to make do with his own wits.

'Could you sit back down please,' said Lyra, looking for his rock, 'I don't think I've quite finished.' He found the rock and carefully took aim.

'If you attempt to hit me with that rock I'll shove it down your throat.'

Shocked, Lyra dropped the rock on his foot slicing his big toe clean off. He began to howl. Ophiuchus shot out a huge fist and clamped it over Lyra's mouth.

'Will you be quiet if I let go?' Lyra nodded. 'I think we need to talk.'

With an eye shifting nervously in its socket for any sign of Serpens and the other firmly fixed on Ophiuchus, Lyra sat down all ears beside him.

'It would appear I am no longer under Serpens' trance and, if I may be so bold, feel I have acquired a fair modicum of intellect to boot.'

The swift downward glance by Lyra to Ophiuchus' feet threw no light on this. He wasn't even wearing any.

After a furtive glance at his surroundings Ophiuchus bent forward and whispered in Lyra's ear. 'I also think that what is said here should remain our little secret. There's no reason Serpens or anyone else should be told any of this.'

'I suppose not,' agreed Lyra, doubtfully. Did he catch a hint of menace in Ophiuchus' words?

'Good,' said Ophiuchus, brightly, 'and from now on I shall be known as Bob.'

'But what about the master?' said Lyra. He possessed an uncanny sixth sense when it came to stupidity and its consequences, especially around Serpens. The latter was usually obtained after the event.

'You could have a point there,' agreed Ophiuchus, nodding sagely. He had a moments think. 'Got it, you can call me Bob when he's not about.'

'And you can call me Rocky,' said Lyra, getting in the spirit of it.

A look that could easily have belonged to Serpens spread across Ophiuchus' face. Lyra shrank from it.

'*One* day?' said Lyra, hopefully.

'Maybe,' offered Ophiuchus, returning to his former bright self. He had thought Lyra's name request uncannily apt for the little creature, but for now uncomplicated was the byword and he wanted it to stay that way. This in mind he had some second thoughts. 'On second thoughts,' said Ophiuchus, speaking his mind, 'maybe it would be better Lyra if you carried on calling me Ophiuchus, at least until Serpens is Master of the Universe.'

Lyra was a little puzzled and equally downhearted.

'Now off you go and tell Serpens you've finished me before he gets in a temper and remember, what was just said is our little secret.'

The clouds dispersed over Lyra on hearing the word secret. He liked secrets. Most of all he liked exposing them. This one though he was sure he would keep. Rocky was such a nice name. 'Okey dokey,' he said, then before scampering away to look for Serpens he added in a whispered knowing tone, 'Bob'.

Watching Lyra go, a sighing Ophiuchus was already beginning to regret their little *tête-à-tête*.

'Master!' shouted Lyra, 'Where are you?' He stumbled over a slippery terrain of shale to a clump of high gorse bushes. 'Can you hear me?'

'What do you want?' said a sleepy eyed Serpens, appearing from amongst them. 'And why have you got that stupid grin on your face?'

'Well me and…'Lyra's voice trailed off as a rather dull alarm bell ringing for all it was worth in the recesses of his mind got his attention.

'Me and? What are you talking about?' Serpens at once sensed something was up.

The smile quickly dissolved as Lyra tried to think. 'Me and…' he faltered.

'Yes I get that, me and. I'm waiting.' Serpens' eyes had taken on that rosy glow that said someone soon was going to get theirs. Breathe.

'Me and… and.' Lyra was treading water with only a lead ring for company. 'Me and…' He was getting there, all he needed was a little help. It came in the shape of Serpens' gnarled fist curling around his body. Serpens squeezed. 'Ophiuchus,' said Lyra at last, the words squirting forth.

'You've finished him?'

'Yes, Master and we await your commands.'

'And that is all?' Breathe.

'Yes, Master.'

Serpens gazed thoughtfully at the little imp encased in his fist. There was something Lyra wasn't telling him. Breathe. He released his grip on him and let him fall into the gorse bushes below. For now though he would let it lie. He didn't have the time or inclination to go rummaging through the imp's jumbled mind for an answer. Breathe. Besides, he doubted anything Lyra might think he was scheming mattered. No, he had better things to do and issues to resolve. One of which was *why* did he keep telling himself to breathe? Serpens went to retrieve his makeshift throne.

CHAPTER 40

Bootes, energy abounding thanks to side effects, was cutting a relentless swathe through the jungle with Fornax's sword, behind him Lupus and Tee See were struggling to keep up.

'Is he going the right way?' said Tee See, sweat pouring.

'So far, no thanks to that green stuff you gave him. I thought you said it would wear off when he woke.' Lupus didn't like the look of his young companion. No one should sweat that much, even in a sweltering jungle. 'You all right? I thought that suit was supposed to protect you.'

'I will be when we stop. It's a bit hot that's all.'

Lupus shot Tee See a look that said he didn't believe him.

'Okay, I'm lying. If you must know it's the growth cycle. It's the stage before adulthood and the most difficult transition. I should be resting, but I can manage.'

Lupus didn't think so. The boy looked ill; very ill. He would have to stop the old man before the boy keeled over. Bootes meanwhile had done just that.

'Where is he?' said Lupus, noticing the lack of old man.

'Is that his feet?'

It was; Bootes was lying on the ground. Side effects instantly came to Lupus' mind and he sprang forward expecting problems. He was right, but this time it was nothing to do with Bootes or alien liquid.

'Sssch boy,' whispered Bootes, as Lupus arrived, 'we've got trouble.'

Senses kicked in and Lupus felt the fur rise on his back. A faint scent he hadn't picked up before now tickled sensors in his nostrils, sending warnings to his brain. He dropped to his belly and wriggled forward.

'What's going on?' asked a panting Tee See arriving on the scene.

Without a word Bootes reached up and pulled Tee See to the ground, then pointed to something in the distance.

Both Tee See and Lupus struggled at first to see what Bootes was pointing at, but they finally focused on some sort of fracas taking place in a clearing some way distant.

'How in the worlds did he see that?' thought Lupus.

'Side effect?' Tee See thought back.

'We'll have to get closer, could be the old man's friend in trouble.'

As if reading Lupus' mind Bootes got up and echoed them. 'Could be someone in trouble; someone needing me 'elp.' Bootes picked himself up and started off at a trot.

Here we go again, thought Lupus. 'Come on we had better keep close.'

With Tee See doing his best to keep up, they moved swiftly through the jungle until they were on the edge of the clearing. Bootes dropped to the ground, Lupus and Tee See hung back a little.

'It's a huge beast,' said Bootes, all agog, 'an' its attacking that poor man.' With the energy and speed of a teenager, Bootes sprang into action. 'I, the monster firefly killer an' scatterer of swarthy no guds will save yer!' Bootes began to charge.

'Grief,' thought Lupus, as Bootes sped off.

'Sweet Jee See,' thought Tee See.

'Yarrrgh!' screamed Bootes.

At the sound of Bootes' battle cry the fight in the clearing ceased and the combatants stared on in disbelief at the wrinkled old man charging at them.

'Not again,' sighed the man lying on the floor.

Well I'm not running this time, thought the beast standing over the man; I'll be a laughing stock. He faced Bootes and gave one of his more impressive roars.

The charging Bootes wavered at the noise, stopped at the sight of so many sharp teeth and turning in a spiral, fell in a dead faint to the ground.

Close on his tail, but not close enough to catch him, Tee See knelt by the old man's side.

'Is he hurt?' thought Lupus.

'No. Thankfully it looks as though the serum's side effects have finally worn off,' said Tee See, feeling the old man's pulse.

'About time.'

The lion, tail up fresh from his triumph, was squaring up to the gangly youth and the oversized dog. It had a determined gleam in its eye.

'I think we've got trouble,' said Tee See, reaching for his sword.

'Leave this to me.'

Tee See moved aside to let Lupus pass.

'Cover your ears,' advised Lupus.

The roar had creatures for miles around running for cover. The lion stood his ground for a split second then, self preservation taking control, turned and bolted deep into the jungle.

Happy the danger was over and that Bootes wasn't seriously or even slightly hurt Tee See went to check on the man the beast had been attacking.

'By all that's silver, your legs!' exclaimed a shocked Tee See on noticing the lack of them, 'Stay still, you're badly hurt.' He reached for his bag.

'WHAT?' said the man; he was holding his hands over his ears.

'You are badly hurt. Please lie still.'

'WHAT?'

Tee See removed one of the man's hands. 'I said you should lie still.'

'WHAT?'

'LIE DOWN!' shouted Tee See.

Lupus left Bootes' side to see what all the noise was about.

'It's his legs,' explained Tee See.

'You sure he's injured? I can't smell any blood.'

'Look at him. He's got no legs.'

The man struggled free of Tee See's restraining hand and sat up.

'JUNGLE MAN NOT HAVE LEGS. JUNGLE MAN JUST HAVE NOISE IN HEAD,' said Jungle Man.

'You're not hurt?'

'ONLY EARS. JUNGLE MAN HEAR BELL NOISES.' Jungle Man seemed to notice for the first time his friend was no longer around. 'WHERE FRIEND? WHY YOU FRIGHTEN FRIEND AWAY? JUNGLE MAN WINNING AGAIN.'

'Sounds like there are a few bats in the belfry with those bells,' thought Tee See.

'PISSER MAN DO IT. NOW YOU. JUNGLE MAN NOT HAPPY.' Jungle Man tapped the side of his head; the bells were lessening. 'JUNGLE.' Jungle Man shook his head. 'Jungle Man go now. Bells gone. Find friend.' He reached for a vine.

'Wait,' said Tee See, 'who is Pisser Man?'

'You thinking what I'm thinking?' thought Lupus.

'Who do you think put the thought in your head?'

Lupus scowled at Tee See, his mind was private property.

'Sorry,' thought Tee See, 'but this Pisser Man could be the scent we've been following; one of mother's friends.'

Lupus let the scowl drop.

'Pisser Man dead,' said Jungle Man, now hanging from a vine.

'Dead? How?'

'Pisser Man go to place of stone, not come back. Place taboo.' Taboo?'

'Jungle Man not know what taboo means, but it bad. No one come from city again. Clickers.'

'Clickers?'

'Jungle Man not know what clickers are, but Jungle Man's friend say they are bad mothers. He not seen them, but heard them and smell them. Jungle Man not know why clickers make bad mothers.

Mothers? thought Lupus.

'Did Pisser Man know about the clickers?' said Tee See.

'Jungle Man not tell him. Jungle Man not want scare Pisser Man.'

'Did he say Pistor?' said a groggy Bootes, who had come round without anyone noticing. He wandered over to the others.

'Yes. That what Pisser Man say name is. Pisser.' Jungle Man wrinkled his nose and climbed a little higher. 'There water in city. Old man need it.'

'Can you take us there?' said Tee See, sensing a breakthrough in their search.

'What about the clicking mothers?' thought Lupus.

'Who cares if I can find my own,' Tee See sent back.

'Maybe. If old man stay far away,' said Jungle Man, eyeing Bootes suspiciously.

'Can you take me?' said Tee See.

'Jungle Man take shiny one. Smelly one and friend scarer no.'

Before Tee See could protest, 'tell him you agree', popped into his head.

Sure Lupus must have a plan, Tee See agreed. Jungle Man put his hands to his mouth and hollered. Not long after a great ape appeared.

'Jungle Man's friend. We go now.'

With introductions short and sweet Jungle Man and the ape, with Tee See tucked under his arm, swiftly climbed and were soon lost in the dense canopy above.

'Well I'll be knocked out cold,' said Bootes, staring up after them.

Yes you will, thought Lupus.

Lupus, now in an ape shape, was soon swinging through the trees after them; Bootes hanging limply over one of his broad, hairy, muscular shoulders swayed with the motion.

Keeping out of sight, but close enough to keep tabs, Lupus tracked Tee See and the jungle man through the trees. A couple of hundred trees later Lupus descended a discreet distance from where the others had landed. He waited until he was sure Tee See was on his own before contacting him.

'They've gone,' confirmed Tee See.

Still in ape form, Tee See had been pre-warned as to his shape, Lupus appeared carrying Bootes.

'It would seem "Pisser" went in there,' said Tee See, thumbing at a high wall behind him, 'Any sign of his scent?'

Lupus gently placed Bootes on the ground and changed back to Fluffy; he sniffed the air. 'Not that you'd notice.' Tee See looked downcast so Lupus quickly added, 'But that doesn't mean he isn't in there somewhere. Looks a big place.'

'Do you think he's dead?'

'I don't think that jungle man knows for sure.'

Tee See cheered up a little. 'What now?'

'We go in and find Pisser. You got anything in your bag that will bring him round?' Lupus nodded at Bootes.

Tee See rummaged through his bag and brought out a small vial with a label that read "Smelling salts. Please keep away from infants". Tee See assumed that had meant him. He removed its lid and gave the vial a cautious sniff. His eyes instantly watered.

'Got something?'

'I thought I had, but it almost smells the same as he does.' He offered Lupus a sniff but he declined. Tee See replaced the lid.

'Who yer talking to mister?'

Tee See almost dropped the vial in surprise. Bootes was awake and surveying his surroundings. Wonders will never cease, thought Lupus, shaking his head.

Up and looking puzzled, Bootes started to ask further questions, 'And where's the bab?'

Tee See shot Lupus a thought, 'I think the serum's reactivated. What now?'

'Yer better speak up mister or you'll 'ave me sword and dog to contend with, 'ere Fluffy.'

Lupus ran to Bootes' side; the safest place considering the way the sword was wavering in his hand. The old man was back to as normal as he would ever get.

'I... er...' Tee See was at a loss until Lupus entered his mind and told him to repeat everything he said. Ten minutes later a sceptical Bootes was still pointing the sword at him or rather the ground in Tee See's general direction; normal Bootes was no match for gravity.

'So the babs is with a family wot you cum across in the jungle?'

Tee See nodded, but had trouble believing what he had just said himself.

'An' you 'ad to carry me through it after I wus knocked out saving Fluffy from a golden monster?' Lupus had thrown that in for good measure.

'A giant, two headed golden monster,' Tee See elaborated.

Chest gradually expanding from pigeon to chicken, Bootes looked to be finally on his way to believing Tee See.

'An' I did it all on me jack?'

'Yes. I don't know what we would 'ave… I mean we would have done if you hadn't been so brave.'

'Not too much now,' thought Lupus, 'he'll think he's invincible.'

'An' yer couldn't have dun it without me?'

'No.' Mental nudge. 'I mean yes… No.'

Bootes gave Tee See a funny look.

'I think you should shut up now,' urged Lupus, through their mental channel.

A pained expression, that could have only been thought, shrivelled Bootes' nose until it nearly disappeared. 'Well it sounds the truth to me. Wot do yer think Fluffy?'

Lupus wasn't about to tell Bootes what he thought, but he did run up to Tee See and lay on his back for a tummy rub; trying cute for the first time.

'Well mister, looks like me dog likes yer so yer can't be all that bad,' Bootes conceded. He held out a hand which Tee See grasped by the fingertips. 'Gud to meet yer stranger. Me name's Bootes and I'm or used to be a shepherd. Guess I'm a hero now.'

'Told you you'd overdone it,' thought Lupus.

'Me an' me dog are looking for me friends, you can come along too if yer want to.'

'Glad to.'

'Gud, now where wuz we.'

'I believe the people who have the babs suggested we look in the lost city.'

'Lost city?' Tee See who had been towering over Bootes stepped aside. 'Ye stars!' said Bootes, eyes widening as he saw

279

the massive wall and gates for the first time, 'Whoever lost it must 'ave been really stupid to lose something that big.' He began to walk away from the gate in the opposite direction.

'I think the gate's this way,' said Tee See.

'Ah, so it is. Couldn't even put the gate in the right place, no wonder they lost it.' Bootes headed for the gap.

'How you feeling, any better?' thought Lupus as Bootes strode on. Tee See wasn't sweating so much and a little colour had returned to his cheeks, but as with the old man, Lupus didn't know what side of normal that fell.

'Better. Think the suit's kicked up a notch.'

Lupus didn't believe him, but didn't say. First chance they got they were going to rest and find something in his dad's bag of tricks that would help him.

'Cum on you two!' yelled Bootes, standing on the gate's threshold.

Tee See broke into a slow trot and caught him up.

'A giant, *five* headed golden monster yer say?' said Bootes.

CHAPTER 41

They hadn't been able to hear exactly what had been said, but they had heard Pistor's name clearly enough. And that had led to Musca throwing caution to the wind and climbing the ladder. Cetus had argued against it, but the usually cautious to the point of running away Musca, had it in his head that Pistor was amongst friends. Hadn't they heard Pistor being offered food? Cetus had argued they hadn't at all, but as Musca was having none of it he thought he better tag along.

'What can you see?' whispered Cetus, his head a rung below Musca's feet.

'Wait a minute,' said Musca, eyebrows only just breaking the floor line, 'I'm not quite there yet.'

And then quite suddenly he was and Cetus was left staring up at the bottom of Musca's speedily rising feet and into several snarling faces that didn't look the least bit friendly.

'Up yer come,' said one of them. Cetus didn't argue; the heavily tattooed arm belonging to it was waving a sword at him.

'So, what is it we are 'aving 'ere, eh?' Pluperfect was pacing back and forth and looking from Musca to Cetus and back again like a hungry dog that hadn't seen a meal in quite some little while and was now spoilt for choice. 'Spies I am zinking, yes-no?' Pluperfect stopped in front of Musca, 'Robbers perhaps, waiting to slit our throats while we sleep, yes-no?' Pluperfect grabbed Musca's sleeve, 'You dress like the desert men, yet you are not one of them I zink.' He turned to Pistor, who was being held by Voussoir. 'What do you zink, Mister Pistor? Funny zese men should turn up as you attempt to leave. I am zinking it cosy, yes-no? Take them down. Voussoir.'

'Yes, Cap'n.'

'Take some men and see if zere are any ozer rats lurking below.'

'Six, Seven, Eight and Eleven, come with me,' shouted Voussoir.

Voussoir grabbed the extinguished torch from Cetus and prepared to climb down the ladder.

Pluperfect snatched it from him. 'No light, if zere are rats down zere we don't want zem to see you coming.'

'Cap'n,' said Voussoir, as he disappeared over the edge.

Musca and Cetus were dragged unceremoniously down the side of the stepped building and thrown to the ground beside a bewildered Pistor. The space they occupied becoming claustrophobic as the remaining pirates closed in.

'So, Mister Pistor, what 'ave you got to tell me, eh?' Pluperfect reached down and took from Pistor the bag he was holding, 'Ours I zink, yes-no?'

Pistor released it without a struggle and pushed closer to Musca and Cetus as the pirates pushed even closer.

Pluperfect suddenly laughed out loud and moved his men away from the trio, giving them room. 'I zink I must apologise for my men, zey are too eager to kill you perhaps and forget zeir manners. I 'ave questions before zat 'appens.' He noticed the blood had drained from Musca. 'You,' he said, pointing his cutlass at Musca, 'how many others are zere?'

Musca gulped and opened his mouth, but nothing came out.

'You 'ave no words for me, yes-no?' Pluperfect moved closer to Musca, 'I zink you are maybe like a fish out of ze so called wet stuff, yes-no?' He laughed at his little joke, but there the joviality ended and he became deadly serious. 'But zen maybe I 'ave no time for a dying fish and should put you out of your misery.' Pluperfect raised his cutlass preparing to bring it crashing down onto the head of the petrified Musca.

'No!' cried Cetus, as the cutlass began its downward arc.

Brought to his senses by Cetus' cry, Musca found his voice in the nick of time. 'I won't tell you,' he shouted, covering his head with his hands.

The cutlass continued its downward journey, but instead of splitting Musca's skull it sliced the soft earth between his legs.

'So ze fish 'as ze tongue after all, yes-no?' Staring hard at the cowering Musca, Pluperfect pulled his cutlass from the ground and wiped it on Musca's clothes. 'Tie zem up. We will wait for Voussoir to return.' Pluperfect backed away as his orders were followed. 'Zen we shall 'ave more questions to ask I zink, no-yes?'

First Mate Voussoir inched his way along the pitch blackness of the passageway with his men in stony silence until a faint glimmer of light signalled the oncoming approach of company.

'How far is this light?' asked Fornax, as she hobbled along supported by Equuleus.

'Not far,' said Hydra, 'at least I don't think it is.'

Fornax was about to grumble, but was interrupted by Voussoir stepping into the light of their torch.

'The boy's right,' said Voussoir, grinning inanely at the sight of Fornax, 'perhaps you would like to accompany me the rest of the way?' He held out his arm, his eyes not leaving Fornax's charms for a moment.

It was an invite Fornax was not about to accept; not without a fight. She sprang towards Voussoir, her sword already scything through the air, but the sudden pressure on her ankle caused it to collapse under her weight sending her crashing to the ground.

Voussoir grin broadened. 'See how women throw themselves at my feet lads?' He made a grab at Fornax who twisted out of reach.

'The torches,' screamed Fornax, before a knee crashing into her back managed to push all the air from her lungs, 'put them out!'

The passage erupted in violence and confusion. Hydra managed to extinguish the one he was carrying, but the pirates grabbed the other one from Fatidic's hand before he could do likewise. Cursing his stupidity, Fatidic ran towards the pirate who had taken it. The pirate easily dodged him, but failed to miss the flailing leg that struck him in the back of his knee. Fornax. Fatidic smothered the torch and threw it. Someone threw him. The melee now continued in total darkness for a short while then, save for the occasional

283

groan quiet fell on the passage. The seasoned pirates had been too much, even for Fornax, in the dark and once she had been restrained the others had soon capitulated. Voussoir broke the silence with an order to find the torches.

Fatidic, on his own, on all fours and fearing the worst, felt for a wall. He had a bad feeling, but he also had an idea to avoid capture. He started to run alongside the wall away from the bawling pirate, feeling as he went for one of the arched niches in the wall he had noticed on the way up. They were intermittent and perhaps a foot above his head. If he could find one he might be able to hide. He remembered wondering when he had first seen them if they had once been filled with statues as the corridors of grand houses did. But there was no time for such thoughts now. He doubled his effort and at last his hand made out a hollow just as a recognisable clicking resounded through the passageway behind him.

Ducking into the niche, only six inches deep, but enough room to stand in, Fatidic flattened his body against the wall. Twenty yards away the passage glowed in the light of a recovered torch.

'Stand up you!' ordered the far from dulcet tones of Voussoir, 'and give her a hand.' Funnily enough he had dropped his warped ideas of romance when Fornax had sunk her teeth into his left ear robbing it of its earring and the lobe it was attached to. 'Bring them.' He was keeping his distance.

'What about the midget?' said Seven. In a niche not far away Fatidic quietly snorted his disapproval.

Holding his ear and cutlass with one hand, Voussoir grabbed Seven round his throat with his other. 'If you'd lit the torch quicker the dog wouldn't have got away.' Voussoir pushed Seven away, causing him to trip and fall to the ground.

It was a heavy landing, but Seven managed to lash out with his sword. Voussoir however parried the stroke and stuck the fallen man a mortal blow in the chest. Both the cutlass and the torch slipped from Seven's hands. Voussoir picked the torch up and aimed its light down the passage. Fatidic breathed in.

There was the slightest of hesitations, but Voussoir shook this off and made a decision. He knew the scent of fresh blood would have them running and running fast from wherever it was they

284

were hiding, so he wasn't about to waste his life looking for a worthless midget who would undoubtedly soon be an entrée to his fallen shipmate. 'Move it,' he snarled, pushing the brothers forward, 'I want to see daylight.'

Barely daring to breathe Fatidic waited until the torches' light had diminished to a small dot then clambered from his plaster eyrie. Back on solid ground he started to blindly follow the wall again using the small glimmer of light ahead as his point of focus. As he reached the place the pirates had attacked more clicking noises started.

Not sure from which direction they were coming, but certain no one was preparing to light his way, panic set in and, stifling a cry of alarm, Fatidic decided to run. He had only got a couple of paces when to his horror something gripped his ankle. This time the scream wasn't held back.

'Help me,' pleaded Seven. The pirate wasn't yet dead.

Almost rigid with fear Fatidic kicked out, but the pirate's grip was laced tight with approaching death.

'Don't let the beetles get me.'

'I can't help you,' Fatidic shrieked.

The clicking was getting closer. The man's grip tightened; Fatidic could feel his toes going numb.

'Help me,' begged the pirate.

There was no time Fatidic was telling himself. He wanted to help; really he did but. Fatidic started to feel for something to hit the pirate with. His fingers felt something cold. Iron? Steel. He grabbed for it and even though it was heavy he swung it with all his might at the pirate's arm. Seven howled in agony, but Fatidic was free. The clicking heightened. Fatidic ran for his life.

The clicking stopped. Fatidic fearing he might be running in the wrong direction slowed and clung to the wall. Sweat ran down his face. His heart wanted out of his chest. Was this to be his last moments? He expected them. He waited for them as he now inched along the wall. A blood curdling scream filled the passageway. Fatidic stopped still. Had that been him? Was he dead but didn't know it yet? No. Reason, logic, the real Fatidic took back control and ran; ran as if hell itself had opened it's gates.

His heart beating a rhythm Fatidic's father would have been proud of, he continued running until at last he could see the light at the end of the tunnel.* Fatidic fairly flew up the ladder.

Resting a few rungs from the top, Fatidic, trying not to look down, tried to listen above the blood hammering through his veins for any sign of life above. He waited. When sure he could hear nothing but his own blood and breathing, he gingerly popped his head out of the shaft. It was clear; he crawled out.

Still shaking from the horror below Fatidic pushed on to the edge of the building and in the shadow of one of the pillars looked out. The pirates were below; the man who had led the attack on them had wasted little time getting out. He was talking to a large man wearing flamboyant attire. The man pointed up. Fatidic ducked behind the pillar. Had they seen him? He waited; heart notching back up a gear, then chanced another look. No, they were walking away, taking Fornax and the others with them. He had to help them, he had grown to like them, but not now; he needed to rest. Fatidic crept from his vantage point to the other side of the wall-less room and looked down. There were steps this side too. A plan started to formulate in his mind. First though he needed to rest; time to regain sufficient senses. He moved a couple of steps down the side of the pyramid building and sat getting his breath back; he would climb down when he had. He had been lucky. Fatidic allowed a smile to form. Perhaps he had a charmed life? His ankle itched where the pirate had grabbed him. Still smiling at his good fortune Fatidic reached down to scratch at it. Funny, he thought, as he did, he'd swear the man was still holding on. It wasn't long after that that Fatidic's limp body rolled down the rest of the steps and landed with a bump at the bottom. Seven's hand, grimly holding on, went with him.

* Well it was, wasn't it? *SJ*

CHAPTER 42

Serpens was uncomfortable. A combination of the new throne Ophiuchus had built for him after dropping the granite one and the extra spring in the ogre's step. He was sure he would soon be sharing his morning meal with the world. Moreover, he felt certain Ophiuchus was doing it all on purpose. Serpens made a mental note: When Master of Universe have all purpose throne built. Comfortable all purpose throne. Also: Get new minions.

'Will... you... stop... bouncing!' snapped Serpens, as the first breakfast rabbit tickled his tonsils.

At the command Ophiuchus stopped dead in his tracks, catching Serpens unawares and sending him shooting into the branches of his new throne that a certain someone had failed to remove. Serpens disentangled and dropped to the sand below.

'What is wrong with you?' demanded Serpens. Ophiuchus stared straight ahead and said nothing. 'I command you to answer me!' stormed Serpens, fast losing his temper. The storm together with the last couple of days in relentlessly unforgiving heat, Serpens shifted uncomfortably in his nylon tutu, and the constant nagging that all was not right with his minions of darkness, was taking its toll on his nerves. He aimed a frustrated kick at Ophiuchus who, belying his size, deftly side stepped it. Serpens' momentum spun him on the spot and he fell in a cross legged heap.

He stayed put until steam coursed from his nostrils. Furious, steaming and a dangerous shade of purple Serpens caressed his horns, stood up and charged headlong at Ophiuchus.

Waiting until the very last second Ophiuchus, with all the grace of a ballerina, which was ironic as he wasn't the one wearing a tutu, dodged the charging Dark Lord. He even threw in a "breathe" for good luck, as Serpens tore past.

Unable to stop Serpens hurtled head first into a massive sand dune, instantly fusing it into a massive dome of glass. Ophiuchus watched as Serpens rose in the centre of it, the glass encasing him beginning to crack under the intense pressure building inside from the intensifying anger. The dome exploded hurtling millions of lethal shards of glass speeding into the air. Ophiuchus accepted gravity; hands over his head.

'OPHIUCHUS!!'

Moving his hands, Ophiuchus was horrified to find a double sized, ten fold meaner than he had ever seen before, Serpens bearing down on him. The sight was awesome; fearsome; downright underpants filling. Shaking, Ophiuchus stood up thinking that he may have pushed his luck just that little bit too far. Serpens closed in; each footprint in the sand turning to glass as he did. He stopped inches short of the quaking Ophiuchus who, expecting the worse, found to his amazement he wasn't in the least bit smote.

'I know what's going on. That idiot Lyra has left a piece of me inside that worthless body of yours hasn't he?' said Serpens, calmly. It had dawned when the dome had exploded; whether it was all that pent up anger and the power that triggered it he didn't know, but clarity had come to him in a rush, slapping him squarely between the niggles.

Taken aback by this sudden change in developments, but ever aware it was never a one way thing with Serpens, Ophiuchus backed away.

Serpens held up an appeasing hand. 'Now, now Ophiuchus, you know I'd never hurt my own flesh and blood.'

What about what's surrounding it? thought Ophiuchus.

'Or should I call you Bob?'

Ophiuchus couldn't disguise his look of shock.

'Don't look so shocked, Ophiuchus. Isn't it obvious that if you are part of me I am part of you.' It was also useful that in his moment of terror at seeing the bigger, improved Serpens, the idiot had left his mind open.

Suddenly Serpens was feeling a whole lot better. 'Now Bob. No, only joking. Where is that useless piece of imp dung?' Yes, a whole, whole lot better. He was even returning to normal size. 'Well?'

Slack jawed Ophiuchus was lost in confusion.

'You can talk, can't you?'

'Ye…yes, Sire.'

'Good, glad to hear it. Hate to think that piece of me you possess somewhere in that mind of yours is being wasted.

'No, Sire – I mean yes, Sire.'

'Right then, where is he?'

'He's…er still in the tree-throne, Sire.'

'Then get him down.'

Ophiuchus undid the strap holding the throne and shook it. A small lump fell to the ground.

'What's wrong with him?'

'I don't think he's recovered yet.'

'Recovered?'

'From being your cushion.'

'I'll leave him in your capable hands then. I'm going to walk for a while.' Serpens wanted to stretch his legs before travelling on the throne again. A throne that he was sure would be a lot more comfortable to ride on when next he sat in it. He did feel a whole lot better.

Ophiuchus gave Lyra a shake. 'Lyra, you with me yet?' He gave him another shake, 'Lyra?'

He got a mumbled reply about being very "conkfortaple fank oo".

This time Lyra got a slap across his head. It worked.

'Wazzup? Where the hell am I?'

'You're in the desert.'

'Still?' said Lyra, astounded. Cushions had no idea of time. His boggling eyes, still coming to terms with life outside of the cushioning circles, fell on the empty throne lying on the sand. 'What happened?'

With ever widening eyes, Lyra was filled in on what had recently transpired.

'And you're still in one piece?'

'That is what is most disconcerting,' Ophiuchus confided.

'Most disconcerting?'

'Worrying.'

'Oh!'

'*Why* am I still in one piece? *Why* didn't he take back what belongs to him?'

Together they watched Serpens as he disappeared over the brow of a sand dune and wondered.

What sinister plan, apart from ruling the universe and subjecting its millions of hapless victims to slavery did he have in that evil mind of his? pondered Ophiuchus.

Will he still be in need of a cushion? mulled Lyra.

CHAPTER 43

Bootes gawped in continuous wonder at the buildings that stood either side of him as they strode down the lost city's main thoroughfare. As dilapidated and overgrown as they were, to Bootes, each was a palace; he had never seen such splendour. He stopped to admire a larger roofless one.

'We could keep a lot o' sheep in there, Fluffy,' he said, peering in through a window, 'and still 'ave plenty o' room for us.'

Lupus gave the building and the old man a despairing look. As fond of the old man as he had surprisingly become, he doubted he would hang around for long once they reached their journey's end.

'Let's take a closer look-see.'

Bootes started over the house's rubble strewn path and headed for the door, but Lupus stayed put. He didn't like the place; the city. Its crumbling buildings, echoing streets, they gave him the creeps. Something wasn't right with the place, he could smell ancient fear, evil and death clinging to everything. The sooner they were out of the place the better, but until then he would have to be at his sharpest; he had a feeling the *something* may still be around.

'Cum on boy,' shouted Bootes, from the doorway he was entering.

The sense of foreboding Lupus had carried since entering the city temporarily drifted from him as he focused on the old man and became aware that there could be a problem closer to home. Where was Tee See? When had he last seen him? Lupus had been so engrossed in the city's brooding malevolence he had wandered oblivious to all else around him. He used a mind link, but got no answer. All of a sudden the city and its something seemed somehow trivial. Lupus barked; perhaps Tee See was somehow shielded from him. He tried again, but the only response came from Bootes who came to a window to see what all the barking was about.

Lupus started to backtrack giving an occasional bark here and there. Bootes, fearing the return of the *seven* headed golden monster now appeared at the door; sword at the ready.

Worry weighing heavier with each step, Lupus upped his pace. He couldn't check all the houses they had passed; not on his own. Lupus now upped his bark rate; getting louder with each one; he needed the old man to home in on his worries and help.

'Wot is it boy?' called Bootes, hurrying down the street, his eyes darting skyward, 'more fireflies?'

Lupus waited for Bootes to catch up.

'I don't see any,' said Bootes, viewing the heavens. His gander was up and he was back in hero mode. Hero mode it seemed heightened his sense of what wasn't there. 'Where's the boy?' he said, 'if there's trouble we may need 'im an' that big sword of 'is.' But now Bootes came to think of it, he hadn't seen the young whippersnapper for a little while now.

Lupus gave another bark and wandered over to a half demolished wall. He had got a whiff of Tee See's scent. His nostrils flared; something was terribly wrong. It was terribly disjointed in a way he couldn't explain. It was coming and going. Lupus howled in anger and frustration, he should have kept a closer eye on him, he knew the boy had been suffering more than he had been letting on.

The anxiety Lupus was feeling spread to Bootes who began to call Tee See's name; or a version of. 'Teepee! Where is yer boy?'

Another time Lupus would have rolled his eyes, but now instead his body grew rigid; ears pricked. Had he heard a response to the old man's calling? He barked as loud as he could; not wanting to damage the old man's hearing any more than it was. There it was; a reply, faint but definitely Tee See.

'Teepee!' shouted Bootes again; unable to hear the reply Lupus' doggy hearing had picked up.

Leaving Bootes behind, Lupus found a gap in the wall and walked through. On the other side he concentrated his senses. It was feeble, but he was rewarded as Tee See's voice entered his mind. He was in a building. No help there; Lupus was surrounded by them. Straining with the effort Lupus now pushed his senses to the limit. No voice this time, just an overpowering sensation of hopelessness; of time running short. He picked up his pace, working on instinct; without any particular direction to head for, it was all he had. He had to find out which building Tee See was in. Lupus called out. A snatched word: table. Table? No, not table, *stable*. Tee See was in a stable somewhere. Lupus hoped there weren't too many.

Running back to the street, Lupus passed Bootes coming the other way. No time to stop, Tee See was out there somewhere and fading fast.

'Where yer going boy?' Bootes shouted after him, as he scooted past into the middle of the thoroughfare. Ignored, Bootes huffed and began climbing a crumbling stone stairway leading to one of the building's roofs. His feet hurt. They'd hurt worse stumbling in the buildings looking for that fool boy. He sat halfway up and proceeded to inspect his sandals; they weren't going to last much longer. He removed one.

'Yer know what, Fluffy,' said Bootes, examining his toes and showing a total lack of concern towards Lupus' frantic toing and froing, 'me ol' bunions ain't 'alf giving me gyp.'

Lupus had not the time or the inclination to listen to the old man's moans as he desperately scanned this way and that. Didn't the old fool realise Tee See was in trouble?

Gingerly prodding at a bunion, Bootes blew dust from between his toes and continued his drivelling, 'I bet the posh folk that lived 'ere never 'ad to walk.'

Lupus didn't know what to do. How could he help Tee See if he couldn't find him? Time was shortening fast, he could feel it ebbing away. Didn't the old fool ever shut up? He screamed Tee See's name in his mind.

'Oh no, not them, bet they 'ad great big 'orses to park their backsides on and carts an' fings.' Bootes stood up and stretched. No horses there; not any more, thought Bootes, but mayhap there could still be some good leather lying around. Good leather lasted forever. Bootes came back down to the thoroughfare and walked past the frantic Lupus who was still trying desperately to contact Tee See. 'Gud Fluffy,' said Bootes, patting Lupus on the way past, 'I'll be back in a mo, gonna see if that old stable over there 'as any leather left lying about in it.'

Bootes didn't realise just how close he had come to losing a hand. Lupus was fast losing his temper with the old man. His inane ramblings going on and on while he was locked in a life or death struggle to find Tee Hee's son. *What did he say?*

Across the road Bootes was squeezing between two walls. The stable, out of Lupus' sight but not Bootes' as he sat on the stairs, lay behind; its main entrance facing a side street beyond. By the time Lupus had reached the wall Bootes was preparing to enter through a space where its back door used to hang. Lupus rushed past him, knocking the old man against the wall.

'Tee See?' Lupus' mind filled the stable. Nothing. Grief, thought Lupus, it's the wrong stable. Or worse, his mind filled with dread, he could be too late. He called again, screamed Tee See's name.

'Here.' It was faint, barely audible, but it was a reply.

'Where are you?' Lupus, felt like somersaulting.

'In the corner.'

Lupus saw him, propped against a wall.

'Good to see you, old friend,' said Tee See, managing a weak smile, 'but I don't know how much longer I can hold on.'

'The bag?' whispered Lupus, noticing Bootes enter.

'There.' Tee See lifted a finger and motioned to where it lay, 'But I don't think there's anything in there that can help.'

That wasn't going to stop Lupus from looking. He tipped the bag's contents on the floor. 'The serum you gave the old man?' he said hopefully, grabbing at straws he knew weren't there.

'So I forget I'm here,' said Tee See. 'Good idea, but I don't think it will work.' He forced another weak smile.

'There must be something.' What was he saying? He was a shape changer, a minion of darkness, according to Serpens, a thoroughly bad egg. What did he care if someone lived or died? Truth was, not long ago he wouldn't have. He had changed and not just shape. He did care. Perhaps he had been cursed.

'There's nothing.'

'The suit?'

'No. Father said things would be different for me. I guess he didn't know how different.'

Bootes arrived and knelt beside Tee See. 'What's going on?'

Lupus wanted to say something. *Help him. Do something!* But it wouldn't help. Instead he whined and nuzzled at Tee See.

Bootes raised Tee See's hand and felt his wrist. 'Well I'll be,' he said, 'I think the young whippersnapper's passed on.'

That, Lupus already knew. Tee See's last thought had come and gone. He had begged Lupus to find his mother and tell her what had happened to him. Lupus had agreed, but would he be able to? Hadn't he already broken one promise he had made. He left Bootes and Tee See and ran into the side street. There he howled as he had never howled before.

CHAPTER 44

'What by all zat swims in ze sea is zat?' exclaimed Captain Pluperfect. He and the pirates stopped what they were doing and listened. None of them had ever heard anything like it. It near froze the blood in their veins.

'I don't like it Cap'n. It bodes of bad omens,' said Voussoir, his ear swathed in bandage.

'You and your so called items zat bump in ze night,' Pluperfect gave Voussoir an uneasy grin, 'you would 'ave us looking under our 'ammocks at every opportunity, yes-no?' The noise had unnerved him, none the less. 'Still, I zink we will double the guards tonight and leave at ze first light.'

'But we haven't all the treasure yet,' Voussoir protested.

'Maybe you would perhaps rather stay and greet your omens, no-yes?'

Voussoir grunted and started packing.

Next morning, before the cock had a chance to crow, the uneasy pirates, in most part thanks to stories whispered by Voussoir around the campfire, had started to load what treasure they had onto a large cockboat. Pluperfect was with the prisoners. With one less body now to board ship he had room for a passenger and he knew who that was going to be. He was about to break the good news.

Wounds still weeping from the previous evening's interrogation, Musca and the others watched him approach with loathing trepidation.

'We've told you everything we know,' spat Fornax.

Pluperfect gave her his most handsome smile. 'And for zat we are truly zankful, but I am not 'ere for zat. I only want to wish you bon voyage. We are leaving.'

'What about us?'

'Ah... zat is how you say an awkward question. We have room for one. The others I'm afraid...' Pluperfect shrugged his shoulders.

'You can't do it.'

'Ah, madame but we can.' Pluperfect meant business, which meant no witnesses. He drew his cutlass. 'Now... who would like to travel the eight seas with me and the lads?'

The interrupting scream of agony was horrific, but mercifully short.

'Cap'n!' screamed Voussoir, 'the pyramid.'

A dark gap, the size of the passageways running beneath the pyramid, had opened up on the nearest side and a scarab stood half in, half out, its head swaying to and fro above the remains of its victim. Behind it others fought to push past, spurred on by the scent of fresh blood.

Matters taking an unexpected turn for the worse, Pluperfect's time had lapsed for silly accents. 'Bring the girl to the boat damn you!' yelled Pluperfect, as further beetles poured into the daylight in search of food. Something they had never done before; dangerous yes, but usually shy creatures drawn only by the scent of blood. Something had upset them. Pluperfect's thoughts returned to the howling he had heard the previous evening. It hadn't been natural. Perhaps it was the cause. Whatever; there was no time for further thought on the matter. The beetles were moving; moving fast, pouring from the gap. A feeding frenzy was sure to ensue. He was not about to be part of it. He started running for the boat.

Another scream filled the air, as pirates began fighting for their lives. Voussoir grabbed Fornax by the arm and tried to pull her to her feet. He couldn't. In their wisdom the pirates had tied the prisoners together. He had a decision to make and, as before, he would come first. He turned in time to see the back of Pluperfect disappearing into the jungle. Blow the girl and curse Pluperfect, thought Voussoir, there will be plenty more women. Voussoir pushed Fornax away and began to run himself.

'What do we do?' yelled Equuleus, struggling with his ropes.

Fornax struggled, but the ropes were well knotted. 'Keep trying,' she shouted back, but she knew they would need a miracle to escape and time was fast running out. Once the beetles were finished with the pirates they would come for them; an easy meal that couldn't fight back.

That miracle was on its way. While they struggled with their ropes and the pirates fought to stay off the menu no one noticed the small figure ducking in and out of the shadows as it skirted the clearing and chaos.

Despair getting the upper hand, Fornax was about to give up and give in to her fate when a voice she recognised whispered in her ear.

'Where is ze girl?' demanded Pluperfect, feeling safe enough to use his accent again, now he was standing in the boat.

Voussoir shrugged his shoulders. 'The beetles were everywhere,' was his simple answer.

Pluperfect growled in his throat, but now was not the time for arguements. He instead barked orders at his remaining men, telling them to go for more treasure.

'But the beetles?' Eleven protested.

'Stay and you will be ze fish food, go and you have ze chance,' was Pluperfect's blunt response, 'each zat returns can keep half zat zey carry.' It was an incentive his men couldn't resist and he knew it.

'But the boat, Cap'n,' whispered Voussoir, 'how will we get it into the sea if none of them make it back?'

'Someone will 'ave to swim to ze ship to get help,' said Pluperfect, leaving Voussoir under no illusion as to whom that person might be.

'Fatidic,' whispered Fornax, 'where have you been?'

'Let's just say I didn't want to show my hand too soon,' said Fatidic.

Fornax frowned, but said nothing, it was enough that he was here now. The ropes binding her wrists fell to the ground. 'The others, quickly,' she whispered, her eye on the battle being fought. A battle that wasn't going well for the pirates, who were badly outnumbered; the end for them wouldn't be long in coming.

Working feverishly between them all the ropes were soon on the ground.

'Where now?' said Hydra, as they huddled low on the edge of the clearing.

'We can't go back the way we came, that's for sure,' said Musca.

'Pistor.'

Pistor was sat a little way apart from them, thinking. The others had explained what had happened under the trees, they hadn't abandoned him, so they said. He didn't know what to believe. They could have got the clothes from anywhere. 'What?'

'What about the city?' asked Fornax.

'What about it,' replied Pistor, awkward as ever.

'Can we go that way?'

Pistor shuffled to face her. 'I don't think that would be wise. There's a smell. I didn't know what it was until they arrived.' He nodded towards the beetles.

Some shuddered. Fornax thought of the boat.

'It's bound to be protected,' said Musca.

'It looks like being our only chance.'

It was agreed, just as the last of the pirates fell dying. Motivated by his screams they headed as fast as they could for the boat.

Pluperfect was loosening the boat's moorings when Caudal, bleeding from a cut to the arm, came running. He had a crazy look in his eye; crazier than normal. 'They're dead. All dead,' he gasped.

'All!' said Voussoir. He snapped an accusing look towards his captain.

Rope in hand Pluperfect returned to the boat and threw it aboard. 'Time for ze swim I zink,' he said, staring at Voussoir.

'We should try and push it first,' said Voussoir, thinking of the shark infested waters.

'We can try,' said Pluperfect, keeping his back turned well away from his first mate who he knew only too well, 'but zen ze swimming, yes-no?'

* * *

299

Without realising it they had followed close in the cabin boy's footsteps.

'What did you see?' said Fornax, as Fatidic slithered back from the treeline on the edge of the beach where Pluperfect and Voussoir were swapping glares.

'Just the three of them,' said Fatidic, 'the fancy man, the bandy one and a boy.'

'We should be able to handle just the three of them,' said Musca.

'Don't be so sure,' said Pistor, 'they are the worst of the bunch and we have no weapons.'

He was right. They needed a plan. It was Fornax that came up with it.

'It'll never work,' said Pistor, when she finished telling her idea.

'You got a better one?' she said. Pistor shook his head. 'Then unless someone has, I think we should try.

'They'll kill you,' said Pistor.

'Want to take my place then?' Pistor looked away. 'Thought not.' With a helping hand from Cetus and Musca, Fornax was pulled to her feet. Her ankle was still giving her gyp. She beckoned for the brothers to come forward. 'You know what to do?' They did. 'Remember, wait until you see us leave the trees before you start for the water. May the stars go with you.' Fornax was slipping back into the world that suited her best; that of the warrior.

The brothers started through the jungle. Part one of her plan was underway.

Part two. 'You ready Cetus… Fatidic?'

They were ready as they were ever going to be.

'Can you see the brothers yet Musca?'

He could. 'They're in position, but I still think I should be the one to go.'

'I thought we discussed that?' They had and it was decided it best they send someone the pirates might think twice about killing there and then on the spot.

Musca ground his teeth together and sat back out of sight.

'Then let's go.' Fornax wrapped an arm round Cetus' neck, who in turn slipped a steadying arm about her waist. Together they stepped from the uneasy sanctuary of the jungle and onto the beach.

'It'll never work,' whispered Pistor, as he watched them walk towards the boat.

'If it doesn't you had better be ready to run, we're the only chance they've got if there's trouble.'

A sudden rustle from behind tested their nerves. They weren't good, but it was only Equuleus carrying three heavy sticks. 'It's all I could find,' he said, handing one each to Musca and Pistor.

'It will have to do then,' smiled Musca, nervously as he took one. He settled back down to watch and hope.

They were halfway to the boat before the pirates realised they were no longer alone.

'We have visitors,' said Voussoir, placing a discreet hand on the knife in his belt.

A flushed Pluperfect stopped pushing and faced them. 'So,' he said, a glint in his eye when he saw Fornax, 'it would seem zat someone is looking for a ride, yes-no?' He flashed a smile that was nearer a leer at her. Caudal was no where to be seen.

Fornax and Cetus stepped closer.

This made Voussoir uneasy, they were planning something, he could feel it and his fool of a captain was going to be blind to it because of the girl. 'Stop where you are,' he ordered. 'Take another step and I'll cut you down where you stand.' He took his hand from the dagger and placed it on his cutlass. Where were the others?

'Now now, is zat the way to treat visitors?' Pluperfect waved a hand at Voussoir to stand down. 'I apologise for Voussoir 'e is a good man, but sometimes ze manners… you know.' He brushed dust from his coat and straightened his hat. 'Please,' he held out a hand to Fornax, 'we have ze room for one more.' He turned to Cetus, 'You, I'm afraid will have to be ze man and take ze so called way of things, yes-no?'

Fornax chanced another step forward with the help of Cetus. Voussoir returned his hand to his sword, but said nothing. 'If he doesn't go neither do I,' said Fornax pouting. Her features softened. She, believe it or not, was attempting to play the little girl lost card.

A nervous Voussoir glanced at his captain, who was thoughtfully stroking his beard. 'The fool – couldn't he see?

'Well,' said Pluperfect at length, 'perhaps I am being ze hasty host. We could use ze extra muscle, yes-no?'

The fool, thought Voussoir, but as Pluperfect motioned for Fornax and Cetus to come forward he gave his first mate a sly wink.

'What say you give ze young lady a hand aboard Voussoir? She'll make little difference to ze weight.'

Inwardly chastising his doubt for his captain, Voussoir moved from the boat and held out a hand.

It was now or never. As Voussoir moved within a pace of her Fornax let go of Cetus and fell to the ground. A surprised Voussoir never saw it coming. Cetus swung into action catching the unsuspecting first mate full on the chin with a heavy right hook.

As Voussoir crumpled, Pluperfect went for his cutlass. This is where Fatidic came into the picture. Cetus, following the arc of his swing with his body turned to reveal Fatidic strapped to his back. Pluperfect had only time to pull his cutlass half from its scabbard and no time to defend against the heavy branch Fatidic wielded. It caught Pluperfect across the ear, knocking him senseless to the ground.

'We did it,' yelled a jubilant Fatidic, as Pluperfect landed across the back of his unconscious first mate.

Fatidic's joyful shout brought Musca, Pistor and Equuleus running, but the celebrations were short as the cabin boy, forgotten until then, popped up from where he had been bandaging his arm.

'Not so fast!' said Caudal, his features twisted and ugly; his voice cold and evil. In his hands he held a wicked triple bolted crossbow; its deadly bolts aimed at Fornax's head. In her prone position she would be hard pressed to dodge anything that came her way.

Fornax cursed under her breath. She thought the boy would be no trouble and had ignored him. Pistor had been right. Fornax hoped the brothers realised what was going on.

'Pick them up and put them in the boat,' the boy snarled. 'You three help them.' Caudal pointed the crossbow in Musca's direction 'Then you can push us out to sea.'

'You won't be able to row that big boat all by yourself,' said Fornax, trying to buy time. Where were Hydra and Hydrus? Anytime now would be good.

An impish grin replaced the snarl. 'Won't 'ave to,' said Caudal, a glimmer of triumph lighting up his otherwise cold stare, ''cause soon as the ship sees the boat they'll come and pick me and the captain up.'

Fornax was shocked; she had never given thought to the idea that there might be a ship. How could she have been so stupid? Where had she thought the pirates were going in their boat? If they had set out they would have more than likely run straight into them.

'Now 'urry up or the lady gets an airing.' He watched closely as Fatidic was unhitched and Pluperfect was plucked from the ground. ''urry I said.'

Where were they? Fornax tried to see past the boat for any sign of the brothers, but from where she lay that was impossible. Then a foot appeared followed by its owner's head popping round the stern of the boat. Hydra had a finger to his lips. Did they know the boy was armed? She would have to help them. Draw the boy's attention.

'What about me?' said Fornax.

'What about you?' sneered Caudal.

'I thought I was coming along too?'

'You were,' snapped Caudal, somewhat shaken by her remark. Why did she still want to come?

'Were? Don't you think your captain will have something to say about that when he comes round?' As Fornax spoke, Pluperfect's limp body was dropped into the boat, gently rocking it.

Caudal kept his feet as any good sailor would, but he was hesitant. He didn't trust the woman. 'Now Voussoir,' he ordered.

Fornax persisted. 'You haven't answered my question,' she said, the idea to goad him, a dangerous move considering the boy's obvious mental instability, 'or are you frightened of being overpowered by a mere woman?' Around her breaths were held.

'No!' said Caudal, his voice on the verge of breaking. 'Now put him on.' He would kill the woman; he would, but for now he had to stay calm, bide his time, control the hate burning up inside him.

'I think he's afraid.'

'Shut up. Shut UP! SHUT UP!' Caudal aimed the crossbow with shaking hands. 'I'll kill you. I'm not afraid to.'

He wasn't; they could all see that. What was Fornax playing at? Equuleus decided to take a hand.

'She doesn't mean it, it's her foot. She's not well. Don't take any notice,' Equuleus begged.

'He's right,' agreed Fatidic, thinking she was pushing the little maniac just a little too hard, 'she's not herself.'

Caudal, beads of sweat dotting his forehead looked from face to face. The woman was playing him. They all were. She had to die. His finger tightened on the trigger.

CHAPTER 45

Tee See was given as good a burial as Bootes was able under the circumstances. This of course didn't help ease the pain Lupus was feeling in that new heart of his, but he had enough of his old one left to know there was no point in moping around. He had a job to do and was going to finish it. Deliver the note to Tee See's mother and then... Truth was he didn't know, but he wasn't going to hang around and turn into everyone's favourite collie dog when the job was done. He needed to... he never thought he would ever say it... find himself. These new feelings were complicated. Not as simple as life and death. Not black and white. There was more to it all than he understood. Perhaps he would return to the creators, tail between his legs and ask them to explain, but that was for the future. Other things were calling now and one of those was Bootes.

''ere Fluff,' said Bootes, slapping his knees, 'where yer been all night?'

Not visiting any queen, thought Lupus, a sliver of humour slipping into the confused blackness that was for the moment his mind. But he had visited someone or rather something - some things. He had sniffed out and found a whole nest of them and judging by the noise they made when they saw him, he figured they must be the "clickers" the jungle man had been going on about. He killed four of them before it sunk into their tiny little minds he was too much for them to handle. He had released a lot of pent up tension. They had released a lot of gaseous smells in their hurry to escape. He had let them go, why not? They weren't going to cause any problems for him unless he wanted to be adopted by them. The jungle man had been right, there didn't appear to be a single decent mother amongst them.

'Gud boy, Fluffy.' Bootes ran a gnarled old hand through Lupus' fur. 'Let's be off shall we?' Bootes shouldered the bags, his and Tee See's, he buried Tee See's sword with him and started to move off along the city's main thoroughfare.

For a moment Lupus felt the old man was attempting to empathise with him. Could there be hidden depths to the man? Pure conjecture that the jury would have to take a rain check on, as Lupus nudged Bootes in the opposite direction to where he was headed. Some things happily never changed.

During his incursion into the world of the beetle and before they noticed him, Lupus had sensed excitement coming from them and had smelled the scent of fresh blood. He now had the smell of freshly spilled blood in his nostrils again; to his right, through the jungle. He led Bootes towards it. Thankfully it was not the blood of Tee See's mother, nor did it belong to the scent they had been trailing from the edge of the jungle. A scent he had found again leading back into the jungle on his night time foray. It was on this path, made easier to follow by Pistor's earlier hacking, that Lupus was "led" by Bootes.

'Someone's been through 'ere,' said Bootes, using all of his deductive skills, 'mayhap it wuz Musca an' the others.'

The old man's tracking skills never failed to amaze Lupus who sighed, then stopped. He was picking up a commotion from somewhere up ahead. Cautiously he walked on taking the lead from Bootes. He didn't want the old man in the firing line if there was one.

He now picked up on shouting... no... screaming and the excited clicking of the beetles. Was there a way to skirt round? Too late, the clearing opened out in front of him.

It was mayhem and the beetles were getting the better of it. Behind him, Bootes looked on in horror, clutching at his sword, but with no inclination, hero that he was, to join in. Something caught the corner of Lupus' eye and he saw her for the first time. Tee See's mother, it could be no one else.

But it was only a glimpse. Tee See's mother and her companions were already melting into the greenery as the last scream echoed in his ears. Shepherding Bootes quickly in that direction they skirted the clearing avoiding the bloodshed. Lupus didn't fear the beetles, but neither did he want to attract their attention. Across the way the beetles' fun had finished and a frenzied feast was taking place.

Except for one, a smaller one, a runt. Having been pushed and squeezed from the meal, it was alone and without the taste of the kill flooding its senses it picked up on Lupus. It quickly turned, a spark of recollection flickering in its tiny brain, fear to the fore, but there was nothing there, Lupus had already gone. Now something else. The scent of food, young food. It had picked up on the blood of the fleeing Caudal. It raised its head, its mandibles clicking. It wanted to give chase and would have if not for a lingering primeval doubt. The killer had been there, it sensed it. The creature wanted food, not to be food. The creature dallied, its senses duelling. Food. It would get none here. Self preservation faltered. The creature clicked its mandibles and slowly, begrudgingly, gave in to its needs.

CHAPTER 46

'It's so nice of you to join me,' said Serpens, with just a soupçon of sarcasm as his minions caught up with him, 'I thought I was going to have to walk the rest of the way through my conquest of the universe.'

A heavily puzzled Ophiuchus stood stiffly to attention. Lyra tried, but his heavily heaving chest wouldn't allow it.

'I suppose you must be wondering why you are both still in one piece,' said Serpens, inspecting his troops. As he waited for an answer he breathed on and buffed Ophiuchus' breast plate. A couple of er's, um's and evasive eye movements later he decided he would tell them anyway. Well at least tell them something to keep them sweet until he no longer needed them. He didn't want his minions going AWOL at this stage of the proceedings and he still didn't know what they were up to. Mind reading was out of the question; Ophiuchus too dense, Lyra too stupid and cluttered. No, it had to be done softly, softly until he knew what they were up to.

He spoke to Ophiuchus first, 'Ophiuchus, my most faithful of minions, losing you would be like losing my own right arm.' If it was dumb, flabby and useless, he was thinking, 'A perfect soldier. An order follower, who never thinks of himself.' There, thought Serpens, that should do it, flattery always works; especially with halfwits like these two.

Ophiuchus took it on the chin, but there was more to him than that now. It was time to get things off his chest. Tell Serpens what he thought; how he wanted to leave and find a new life somewhere away from all this, a new start, the chance to spread his wings and have adventures of his own; to be called Bob. This was his time. This was his chance to speak out and be free. Frightened, but determined, Ophiuchus prepared to get things off his chest.

He was bitterly disappointed then to hear himself say 'Thank you, Sire.'

Job done. Serpens' attention now alighted on Lyra.

'Lyra-Lyra-Lyra, what can I say?' said Serpens, grasping the imp by his shoulders. And for some considerable time he didn't say anything. He stood there thinking, gripping Lyra's shoulders, his eyes glowing red. He sifted his mind to find the imp's good points; some; one. Ah! No. There wasn't any; the imp was completely useless. A total waste of space. Drat! He was supposed to be making them feel at ease. Frightened, the fools would clam up. Put at ease, if only falsely, one would sooner or later make a slip and reveal all. He would have to make something up; use his imagination. How hard could that be? No, he couldn't do it. Only one thing for it then, no one would miss him. Frustrated, he grabbed Lyra by the throat and began to throttle him.

'Glurg,' said Lyra.

Drat, thought Serpens, feeling Ophiuchus' gaze on him, I have to try. 'Give me one good reason why I shouldn't reach down your throat and remove your immortality?'

Seeing a chance to escape his fate Lyra said, 'Glurg!'

'Not good enough!' snarled Serpens, pushing his free hand down Lyra's throat. What was he doing? He couldn't help himself. The hand stopped at Lyra's tonsils, impeded by his throttling hand.

'Wait!' said Ophiuchus, finding a smidgeon of courage from somewhere. It also helped that Serpens had his hands full.

In a blind fury at Lyra's lack of usefulness and to a certain extent his own lack of imagination, Serpens ignored him and attempted to push one hand past the other.

Accruing ten points for heroic persistence Ophiuchus pushed on, 'He has got some uses.'

This time Serpens stopped his assault on Lyra and glared at Ophiuchus. Lyra dangled from his fist.

'He has?'

A way out. 'Yes, Sire.'

'Then what are you waiting for? And it had better be good.'

Suddenly the cushion idea didn't seem so solid. There had to be something else. He didn't like it when Serpens looked at him like that. What would Draco or Lupus have said? *That's it.*

'Lupus, Sire.'

'Lupus?'

'Yes, Sire. It's been a while since you contacted Lupus. You use Lyra.'

Serpens tapped his foot on the sand as he thought this over. He had a point. That was lucky. Obviously the part of him in Ophiuchus was playing a part. He couldn't have thought of that otherwise. Good old me. 'Um... I suppose so.' Serpens let go of the, now blue in the face, imp, but as his temper hadn't quite subsided he couldn't resist aiming a kick at him on the way down. Lyra landed some dunes distant. And talking of Lupus it was about time they made contact again. They were fast running out of desert and not a monkey man or sack in sight. So much for Ophiuchus' visions. But what else did he have? Trees it was then.

'Now that we all know where we stand,' said Serpens, rubbing his hands together, 'I think we should push on. I've a universe to conquer.' He waited for Ophiuchus to kneel so he could climb aboard his throne, 'and, if I'm not mistaken, it looks like the desert ends just over there. Giddy-up!'

A few dunes distant, a recovering Lyra watched as Ophiuchus with Serpens on his back set off. He wasn't a happy imp. For one thing he was having a bit of a job finding his neck. It, like most of his head, being buried deep between his shoulders. He also had an almighty concussion. Lyra sat stewing. It just wasn't right the way he was treated; he being a class one imp. It was the most important non-thinking job the creators dished out and he was one of the best; one of the most mischievous. They had even told him it was his forte*. He wasn't going to take this lying down. Someone was going to pay for belittling his profession. Him, he suspected. Well for one thing he wasn't going to tell Serpens he had seen Draco. There, that served him right. His head hurt.

* On long cold lonely winter nights he sometimes wondered what had happened to the other thirty-nine.

'Pohickory.'

It was about time he stood up for himself.

'Dickory.'

Take a leaf out of Ophiuchus' book.

'Dock.'

Yes indeed. Lyra stood up, brushed sand from his tutu and peeped from between his shoulders. 'You're as thick as a rock,' slipped from his lips. His head really hurt.

The nursery rhyme the creators' nursery division used to sing to him when he was new drifted through the draughty corridors of his mind and out through his mouth which was somewhere near his breastbone. Lyra started walking, his thumb prodding and probing his forehead as it tried to find his mouth. Was that what was making his head hurt?

And they would all pay. Who would?

'Pohickory Dickory.'

He would. What would?

'Dock.'

It had been a long time since the last time he'd sung the rhyme.

'You've a head as dense as a rock.'

A long time ago. The tip of his thumb found its way to his lips. Lyra began to suck on it.

'What was I going to do?' Lyra watched his feet for a moment. 'I know. Find some vinegar and brown paper.'

CHAPTER 47

The bolt hit the sand less than six inches from Fornax's head. She would thank the stars later, but for now something more dangerous than Caudal was occupying her thoughts; the cause of her survival. The beetle trailing the cabin boy had entered the fray. Smaller than the rest yes, but still as big as the boat, it stood and swayed its head as if deep in thought; weighing its options perhaps.

With the surprise entrance of the beetle, Voussoir had been dropped. Caudal chose to ignore the beetle and concentrate on his shipmates, he ordered him picked up again and put in the boat, warning that this time he wouldn't miss as he aimed his crossbow once again at Fornax.

'But it'll kill us before we can,' Cetus tried to reason.

'I'll kill you if you don't,' said Caudal coldly.

The beetle continued to sway its head. The scent of the killer was back. Where was it? It swung its bulk towards the break in the treeline where Fornax and Cetus had walked onto the beach. It seemed to be listening; looking for something.

'Quickly.'

Voussoir was manhandled, almost rolled against the side of the boat, until he dropped into it.

'Now push.'

Come on Hydra, thought Fornax, staring at the back of the boat, where are you?

Behind the boat, the brothers were undecided as to their next move. They had seen the bolt just miss Fornax. One false move and the next one could be her last; or one of theirs. What did they do?

The beetle now moved until it was sideways on to the boat and looking directly at the gap. It clicked. It couldn't see anything. Food was so close. Caudal's blood seeping through the bandage putting the creature on edge. It could almost taste it. It could wait

312

no more. Swiftly changing direction it charged at the boat; drawn to Caudal and the life blood dripping on the treasure below his feet.

'Ah ha!' said Bootes, bursting from the jungle at exactly the same time, Fornax's sword held aloft. 'I Bootes the killer of ten headed monsters am 'ere to save yer. He started towards the beetle. Hidden behind him a cursing Lupus had again just been a mite too slow to stop him.

All on the beach, including the beetle, turned at the sudden interruption. A vision to behold was charging uncontrollably towards it. It was Bootes! It was some mad geriatric from hell. The sword in his hands started waving dangerously above his head.

'Aargh!' screamed Bootes.

Oh oh, thought Lupus.

The weight of the sword was tipping Bootes forward; propelling him to the sand. He fell. He rolled. Nearly everyone closed their eyes. Those that didn't couldn't believe what they saw. He careered down the beach into the beetle slicing its two front legs off at its knees. The beetle stood for a moment as if not quite sure what had happened, then teetered forward, much in the same way Bootes had done, as the weight of its fearsome mandibles became too much for its other legs to hold up and pitched head first into the sand. It was all too much for such a small brain; food, so close, the killer, the geriatric lunatic. All too much. The beetle fell into a shock induced deep sleep never to wake again.

'Hurrah for Bootes,' shouted Equuleus, unable to contain his joy.

'Shut up or-'

'Or nothing,' said Hydra, standing over the prostrate cabin boy. The branch he had used to knock Caudal senseless hanging by his side.

'You took your time didn't you?' said Fornax who, like Equuleus, was finding it hard not to show her relief.

Musca and Cetus ran to help her up while Equuleus went to see what he could do for Bootes. Pistor sidled up to the boat to relieve Voussoir and Pluperfect of their weapons.

'What about these three?' Hydrus asked, as he helped Pistor.

'Drop them onto the sand,' said Fornax, hobbling alongside, 'the boat's ours.'

Smiling broadly, Hydra threw his branch into the sea and helped his brother unload the dead weight.

'Shouldn't we kill them?' said Pistor, handing Fornax a cutlass.

'If you like,' said Fornax, handing it back.

'But I…' said Pistor, his colour draining.

'Thought I would do it?' finished Fornax. 'Well think again. There's been enough bloodshed.'

'But they'll kill us,' spluttered Pistor.

'They've got to catch us first,' said Fornax, brightly. 'Now come on, put your backs into it. We've a boat to launch and an Ohm to get to, in case you'd forgotten.' A cheer went up and Fornax turned to Musca. 'Help me over to that old rogue Bootes; I've a few words I want to say to him.' Oh dear, thought Musca.

Bootes was standing with Equuleus who was hugging him. He looked sheepish as Fornax approached. But Musca needn't have worried. The mud rain and slippery slope had been long forgotten. Fornax gave Bootes a hug which surprised the hell out of him and thanked him for saving them; which he had. She told him he was a hero. Of course Bootes already knew that, but didn't want to say.

'Now help us get the boat afloat,' said Fornax, accepting Musca's support again while whispering to him, 'and when we are well out to sea you and Cetus make sure he has a bath in it.'

Equuleus rushed to help the others, but Bootes hung back.

'What's wrong?' said Fornax.

'It's me Fluffy. I can't go wivout me ol' Fluff.'

Fornax gave Musca a look that said what is he on about?

'Did you knock your head?' said Musca, looking concerned.

'Wot? No, it's me dog.'

'Dog?' They couldn't see one. 'You sure you didn't bump your head?'

Bootes cupped his hands to his mouth and started shouting, 'Fluffy! Here boy!'

The shouting drew the attention of the boat pushers who were near to achieving their goal.

314

'What's he going on about?' yelled Cetus.

'Seems he's lost his dog,' explained Musca, winking at Cetus.

'Not the only thing by the looks of it,' said Pistor, who received an annoyed frown from Equuleus for his pains.

'When did you last see your dog?' asked Fornax, attempting to humour the old man.

'In the jungle,' said Bootes.

A call from the boat told Fornax the boat was almost afloat. She waved back. 'We've got to go,' she said, 'the beetles.'

'I'm not leaving Fluffy,' said Bootes, digging his heels in.

Fornax waved her hand discreetly behind Musca's back and motioned for Cetus to come across. He tapped the brothers on their shoulders and nodded to Bootes. They nodded back.

'There 'e is,' shouted Bootes, suddenly, 'there's me Fluffy. Gud boy!'

Heads turned. Chins dropped. Mouths gaped. Cetus and the brothers came to a halt midway between the boat and Bootes.

Lupus had trotted through the break in the trees. When seeing Bootes was safe he had gone back and cleared the clearing. Now for introductions, he thought, as he came forward. Someone was acting furtively in the boat. Lupus showed his teeth and Pistor who had been greedily sifting through the treasure before Lupus turned up now had second thoughts about the crossbow.

'This is Fluffy,' said Bootes, happily tousling the fur between Lupus' ears, 'me dog.'

A dog to Bootes. To everyone else, a great slavering beast of a beast.

'This is Fluffy,' said Bootes, introducing him, 'an' Fluffy boy these are me friends.' With Fluffy by his side Bootes took him on an introductory tour culminating at Fornax and Musca. 'An' these two is Fornax and Musca,' said Bootes, proudly. He bent down and whispered just loud enough in Lupus' ear for Musca to hear, 'you 'ave to be nice to 'im; 'e's our new chieftain.'

So this is Musca, thought Lupus, giving him the once over. The idiot that Serpens is chasing, that is putting Tee See's mother in so much danger.

Musca pushed out his chest and put out a hand which was quickly withdrawn when Lupus treated him to a close up of his teeth.

'Bad dog, Fluffy,' said a horrified Bootes, 'bad dog.'

But it's not time for the letter or news of her child just yet, thought Lupus, or the signal, there's still danger. The beetles were gone for now but they would be back. He pushed his head at Fornax whom he allowed a tentative pat.

At the boat which now bobbed occasionally as small waves found the strength to lift it at its stern, Cetus and the others, especially Pistor, were anxious to be on their way. They didn't know what Lupus knew about the beetles.

'Can I bring 'im?' said Bootes.

'I can't see why not,' said Fornax, 'but he'll have to sit in the back.'

Away from us, thought Musca.

'He'll be a gud dog. Won't yer boy?'

Lupus managed a wag of his tail.

'There, told yer.'

A final shove set the boat bobbing amongst the small breakers heading for the shore. Fornax settled at the stern beside Lupus and Bootes and mindful of Caudal's words about the waiting ship suggested to Musca he order they keep as close to land as was safe.

CHAPTER 48

If pacing was a sport, Tee Hee would be a champion. He had been back and forth across his main living quarter's non-stop for nearly half a day. He was impatient. He was racked with grief. Tee Hee knew of Tee See's demise but there was nothing he could or would have done about it. He blamed himself of course, but on his home planet nothing was caged, all were free spirits, which is why he had had to let Tee See go. Tee See belonged to this planet, to take him away would have been cruel. But he knew no amount of reasoning was going to lessen the anguish. Instead he put all his energies into worrying about his fuel situation; the lack of and the danger Fornax and the others were in. To make things worse his spacecraft had been free and ready to go for a couple of days now. Where were Lupus and the signal?

Temptation building to leave before the signal Tee Hee tried to take his mind off it by wandering over to a portal to see what Draco was doing. He had been flapping around aimlessly like a spare part since the spacecraft had been freed. It was as good a time as any to ask Draco the question he wanted to ask. He reached across and touched the wall; the exterior door slid open.

'Will you please come in?' said Tee Hee, as Draco swooped overhead.

Draco flipped and landed by the open door.

'I have a question I want to ask.'

Draco followed Tee Hee into the craft and stood in the main living quarters waiting, his blank eyes not shifting from that far off place they had been intent on staring after since arriving.

'Do you mind me asking you a question?' said Tee Hee, sitting down.

'No, Master,' said Draco, in his best monotone.

'I want the truth when you answer.'

'Yes, Master.'

'Do you know Lupus?' The shift in blankness was almost imperceptible. A pause before Draco went to answer.

'But before you answer,' said Tee Hee, interrupting, 'be warned. If you wish to travel with me, as I believe you do, it *must* be the truth.'

Draco closed his mouth.

'Well,' Tee Hee demanded.

Draco opened and closed his mouth a couple of times before he finally answered. 'Yes,' he said, 'we...'

'There's no need to go on, I know everything. Well, almost everything.'

The blankness fell from Draco. 'You do?' he said, astonished.

'Since the day you arrived and may I say what a fine actor you are, Draco my friend. You totally fooled Lupus with your act and if it wasn't for my own telepathic skills I would undoubtedly have been taken in as well.'

A flustered Draco flushed a multicoloured blush.

'I know all about your real master and your journey to this planet.' Tee Hee studied Draco's reaction closely. He appeared fearful. 'And a few things a mere mortal as me should never be privy to.' Draco's blush deepened.

'He will come after me,' said Draco, his lips hardly moving.

'If he does, he'll have me to contend with,' said Tee Hee, with resolute conviction.

This surprised Draco as much as it did Tee Hee himself who wondered at his bravado and how he could ever stand up to the power Serpens possessed if Draco's mind was to be believed; which he did. No time to dwell though, now the lid was off he had other questions.

'Why didn't Lupus read your mind? He's got the capability.' Draco frowned, but Tee Hee ploughed on, 'And if this Serpens has so much power why doesn't he use it to get himself off the planet instead of chasing the humanoids?' Tee Hee stopped for breath and wondered if he had pressed too hard. Things were getting to him.

'I don't know,' said Draco, in answer to Tee Hee's first question.

Fair enough, thought Tee Hee. 'And my other question?'

'I don't know,' said Draco, a little perturbed. 'I haven't thought about it. But once he gets a bee in his bonnet.'

The Serpens creature doesn't know either, thought Tee Hee, that's useful. He wants power but he's already got it, could be more dangerous that way. Tee Hee got up from the seat. He had come to a decision.

'Prepare yourself, Draco my friend, we go to meet destiny.' The blank look Tee Hee received in return was genuine this time. 'With this Serpens on the warpath, fuel or no fuel, signal or no signal, we have to move now or it maybe too late. Come with me.'

Draco did, but he was worried. Did Tee Hee mean they were going to look for Serpens? He was afraid to ask. The colour drained from his face. He certainly hoped not.

CHAPTER 49

The boat had been drifting aimlessly for two days thanks to the loss of the oars; a combination of tiredness and lack of thought on the first night afloat. Its course now dictated by the wind and currents. Its position, somewhere out at sea. On the third morning the storm broke, tossing the boat like a cow in a tornado. By mid afternoon the boat was driftwood. Come night on that third day everyone clung to what they could. Miraculously they had all survived. No – not a miracle, but down to a very busy shape-changer doing the wolfie paddle for all he was worth with – you've guessed it – an unconscious Bootes gripped tightly in his teeth.

It was dawn on the fourth day and Pistor was moaning. 'So Musca, *O Great Leader*, it looks like we'll not be finding this wonderful land of yours; unless it's on the bottom of the ocean that is. And mark my words, that's where we're going.'

'Shut up Pistor!' yelled Fornax. The situation was bad enough without that whining fool adding his pennyworth and scaring everyone. 'You all right?' she asked Equuleus, who was sharing the huge empty chest she was clinging to. He said he was, but others fed on Pistor's words.

'We're going to die, aren't we?' said Hydrus.

'No little brother,' comforted Hydra, 'as long as we keep moving we'll be fine.' If he thought otherwise he didn't show it.

'Hydra's right,' said Fornax, managing a sunny smile at Hydrus while glaring daggers at Pistor, 'we've come this far, haven't we?'

All took a degree of heart from Fornax's words except Pistor who continued to tut and grumble under his breath. All was lost to his mind. The treasure he'd worked so hard to discover was gone. His belongings, which he imagined were somewhere below. Everything that he held important was gone. He patted his shirt.

Make that nearly everything; he still had the gizmo he'd stolen from Tee Hee. He'd found it along with his bag that first night afloat and had hidden it away from any prying eyes. Pity he hadn't put more in with it. He suddenly remembered where he was and shifted a look to see if anyone had seen him pat his shirt. He didn't think they had and why should they; they didn't care a fig about Pistor and his moaning and groaning. But they would; when the gizmo proved to be valuable. Then they'd want to be his friends; he'd bet on that. Pistor sneered. It was his though; his secret and it would stay that way and they could all take a great running leap. But the truth was he was stuck with the bunch of terminal no-hopers and the gizmo was worthless while he was here. Odds were he'd soon be at the bottom of the ocean anyway, sadly with them for company; all grinning inanely at each other as the fishes moved in for lunch. Pistor couldn't think of anything that could possibly be worse. Five minutes later he found there could.

Cetus was first to notice. 'What's that?' he shouted.

'Where?'

'There, in front of us.'

Those that weren't facing the direction Cetus was, paddled round until they were.

A dark triangular shape moved ominously on the not so distant horizon.

'There's another one!' shouted Equuleus, pointing.

Lupus sniffed and the fur on his neck bristled. Predators; he knew that scent well. They would need his help again. Lupus swam up to Pistor and nudged at his arm. He would rather leave the old man with someone else than this bad tempered creature, but he was adrift on the largest piece of wreckage; enough room for two.

'Get away from me you overgrown mutt,' snapped Pistor, trying to push away.

'I think he wants you to look after the old man,' said Fatidic, 'the poor thing must be tired.' Only Fatidic and Bootes saw nothing unusual about Lupus' size. Then again everything was big compared to Fatidic.

To show Fatidic was right and to dissuade him from otherwise, Lupus showed Pistor his teeth. Pistor knew he had little choice so grudgingly wrapped an arm around Bootes and hauled him half onto his piece of boat.

'But I'll not be doing it for long,' moaned Pistor, as Lupus swam away.

Waiting until attention was on anything but him Lupus took the opportunity and disappeared beneath the waves. Up front several more triangles had now joined the original two.

'What are they?' said Equuleus, peering over Fornax's shoulder.

'I don't know, but I think we all should pull closer together.' Like Lupus, Fornax knew a predator when she saw one and the one thing she knew for sure about predators was that they always went for the weakest or straggler first.

Fornax shouted to the others to move their bits of wreckage closer together; safety in numbers. Using Fornax as the hub they slowly formed a rough circle. Only Pistor, who was struggling to move with any purpose because of Bootes' dead weight, now remained adrift.

'Pistor!' shouted Fornax. The triangles were on the move forming a circle of their own.

'I'm coming as fast as I can,' replied Pistor, 'but he's heavier than he looks.'

'Cetus, you're nearest.'

Cetus was already on his way, guiding his piece of boat alongside the struggling Pistor.

'I'm losing him.'

'Here, help me shift him onto mine and I'll share yours.'

Pistor was ready to say "but only for a while" but instead yelped in pain.

'What's wrong?'

'I've cut my hand on something.'

'Dip it in the water. The salt will do it good.'

Pistor grimaced as the salt stung his wound. Now he was going to bleed to death thank you very much. What had he done to deserve his fate?

'Come on. One more push and he'll be on.'

'All right, all right,' said Pistor. Grief, can't a man bleed in peace?

As Pistor heaved his wound opened and more blood mingled with the sea. It floated away, tangled in what currents saw fit to bear it. On it drifted, following the blood that had already bled, past Cetus, past the others and on to the circling triangles.

Senses heightened. Like the beetles, these new predators could smell the blood; taste it. Something good was on the menu. The triangles tightened their circle, drawing closer until one could wait no longer. The shark followed its nose and made straight for Pistor, its fin cutting through the sea's surface like a hot knife through butter.

'Pistor! Behind you!' But the warning, from Fornax, came too late. She could only watch in horror as the great dark shape beneath the waves reached him.

Open mouthed but voiceless Pistor's face froze in a mask of terror. Then he was gone.

Cetus, left alone and clinging tightly to Pistor's piece of wreckage pushed it as fast as he could to join Fatidic who was closest of the circle. Behind him the sea where Pistor had disappeared was now a foaming red mass. Other sharks were quickly on the scene thrashing and churning the bloody waters in their frenzied attack.

'Where is he?' screamed Equuleus.

Fornax was quick to block his view. Nearby Musca gave up what food he had left in his stomach to the smaller fishes.

'We've got to move away,' shouted Hydra.

'We'll never outrun them. We'll have to fight!' Fornax yelled back. The idea she knew was hopeless, but what other chance did they have? She pulled her sword from her belt. 'Quickly, your weapons,' she ordered.

The response was poor. Only three other weapons were produced and of those one was only a letter opener shaped as a dagger that Fatidic had kept from better days.

'It's no good,' said Musca, staring at the haul, 'we've got to try and get away.' The situation was looking more and more useless.

If they stayed to fight they would certainly die. If they moved away they would surely be picked off one by one. 'We have to try,' he repeated quietly.

Fornax weighed up the options. With what weaponry they had, fighting, she admitted to herself, was out of the question. This left retreat. She hated the word. 'All right, but if one of them attacks we fight. It's all or no one.' She said it in a "do I make myself clear" tone. 'Let's go while they're still busy.'

Manoeuvring their scraps of wreckage together, with Bootes still oblivious to their plight and balanced at their centre, they moved away and towards the climbing sun, an orange arc in the distance.

Nothing was said and hardly a breath was exhaled as they gradually moved further and further away putting space between themselves and the triangles. No one dare look back and each prayed for their lives as they pushed on. Did they dare hope?

An eternity passed and hope grew. The sun, fat and round, now appeared to float on the sea's surface. They had travelled without incident thus far; surely they were safe now? Were going to see the sun high in its heavens? Find Ohm?

'Look!' It was the first time any of them had spoken since they made their run for it.

Everyone looked. Another triangle had appeared, bearing down on them. It would appear their prayers were going to go unanswered.

'It's bigger than the others,' gulped Equuleus. Its dark shape silhouetted against the sun.

This time they would fight; would have to, thought Fornax. She told the others to ready their weapons. 'We'll meet it here,' she said.

All stopped swimming. Musca and Hydra drew their weapons; a sword and a knife. Fatidic drew his letter opener. It was going to be a fight to the death. The huge shape came closer, the sunlight dancing on the sea before and behind it making it difficult to make out, as eyes screwed up against the sun's brightness. Knuckles whitened. It was nearly upon them. It was a monster. This was it. Do or die; probably die.

'Ahoy there! I say, you in the water.'

It took a moment or two for what they had heard to sink in. Knuckles were still white. Those without weapons were still praying.

When it did and it was Equuleus who first realised their prayers may well have been answered, the relief that was felt could have borne them high amongst the clouds. 'It's a boat,' he yelled, 'it's a boat.'

The craft drifted up to them. 'May I be of service to you?' asked its only occupant.

Suddenly the sea was alive with laughter and cheers and numerous yeses.

'Then I suggest you climb aboard sharpish now before those sea devils come back this way.'

One by one, the lone sailor hauled them aboard his craft, a raft not a boat. Job done he introduced himself.

'My name is Pyxis,' he said, bowing slightly, 'it is an honour to have you aboard.'

'Pleased to meet you too,' said Fornax, squinting up at her rescuer, a man; a foreigner the like she had never seen before; skin the colour of jet, his head a mass of tight dark curls dotted with grey, 'but how did you know we were out here?'

'Serendipity really, I saw the sharks heading this way and as I had nothing better to do, the fish weren't biting you see, I decided to follow them to see what they were up to,' Pyxis explained. 'They lost me of course, the old girl's not very fast,' he patted the raft's mast, 'but lucky I did or I wouldn't have found you. Someone might have got hurt.'

'Someone did,' said Equuleus, sadly, 'we lost Pistor.'

'Sorry to hear about that, but we really must be going, haven't had breakfast you see,' said Pyxis, somewhat cheerily. It was sad, but it really wasn't any of his business. He moved the sail and set his raft on course for home.

Just then Bootes rejoined the ranks of the conscious. He moaned groaned sat up spied his surrounding had changed and called for his Fluffy.

'Fluffy?' said Pyxis.

'His dog,' said Fatidic.

'Where is it?' said Pyxis, scanning the debris bobbing on the ripples.

'Back there,' said Hydra, thumbing the open sea behind him.

'Then there is nothing more we can do.'

'Where's Fluffy?' groaned Bootes.

'He's gone,' said Fornax, shuffling beside the old man, she explained what had happened while Bootes had been out of it.

'Not me Fluffy,' wailed Bootes, 'not me poor ol' Fluffy.'

Fornax put a comforting arm round the old man's shoulders.

The raft moved off. On board all but one of its passengers were silent; an old shepherd who struggled to understand why, as he sobbed for his lost best friend.

CHAPTER 50

'What *is* he going on about?' said Serpens, as Lyra at last arrived at the edge of the jungle where he and Ophiuchus were stood waiting.

'It's a nursery rhyme, Sire,' explained Ophiuchus, 'from when we were inklings.'

'I can't recall being an inkling,' said Serpens, his brow crinkling as he tried to remember being in that state once upon a time. Then dismissing it as fantasy, he produced Lyra's rope. It was time for Lyra to contact Lupus again. 'Lyra!' he commanded, 'get your sorry little bag of bones over here.'

'Your head's as thick as a *rock*.'

Ophiuchus winced, but the expected thud of large scaly fist against soft greenie-grey flesh didn't come. Instead Lyra now floated several feet above his head and Serpens was giving him his orders.

'Now I want you to make contact with Lupus. You are to find out where he is and what he is doing... oh... and find out if he has seen anything of that deserter Draco. Do I make myself clear?' said Serpens to the bobbing Lyra.

A look of serenity mixed with a sprinkling of insanity flourished on Lyra's impish features. He nodded and thought of Draco desserts. Draco! The name drifted through his mind. I know that name, but I'm not telling him, he thought, oh no. Nah-nah-neh-nah-nah!

'Go then,' said Serpens, frowning quizzically at his deranged minion.

A quick salute and Lyra shot skyward and away.

Serpens noticed Ophiuchus staring at him. 'What?'

'I... er...' he stammered, as he realised he'd been caught.

'If you're wondering why Lyra's still in one piece after his insubordinate remark the answer's easy, I haven't the time right

327

now. Perhaps later I shall mete out appropriate punishment,' Serpens glared at Ophiuchus, 'to *those* who deserve it, but for now there is a job at hand and I think we draw near to its conclusion.' Serpens faced the jungle, his arms raised aloft. 'Soon I Serpens will be Master of the UNIVERSE!'

Ophiuchus was amazed by the outburst. He had only wanted to point out that Serpens had his tutu on back to front. Serpens clambered aboard his throne. 'Onward Ophiuchus, the monkey man is close.'

Ophiuchus, the ogre, stepped into the jungle.

Lyra flashed through the air with the flappiest of knees, totally oblivious to all including the trees.

Birds squawked their disdain and ducked for cover, some with the odd scorched feather were left feeling how wonderful it was to still be alive, as he tore past. He was still singing his little song.

'Pohickory dickory dock. You've a head as thick as a rock.'

The same words rolled over and over again, like dandelion clocks caught in a breeze through the draughty corridors of his mind. He was remembering the happy days and for now that was all that counted to him.

The green of the jungle canopy passed beneath him. On he went, past the scarab temple in the lost city, over the beach where Musca and the others had fought the pirates. On he went; carefree. He swooped low over the ocean and looped and skimmed over the waves until he came within sight of the wreckage and the survivors of the storm clinging to it. Lyra climbed higher. He could see the sharks now, heading for the people bobbing like corks in the water. He watched impassively as they circled them. Idly he drifted closer for a better look. Down he went, his mind and body gliding as one but separated by different times. Still lower he went until he skimmed the waves which reached out and tickled him. He laughed; he couldn't remember the last time he felt so happy. Pohickory dickory....

Dock! The water closed over Lyra as his skimming found a wave that wasn't content with just tickling him; it wanted a hug. He crashed beneath it. Luckily none of the bobbing corks noticed his crash into the sea. They were otherwise occupied. Under the sea it was another story.

As he sank into the sea's salty depths he caught the attention of one of the marauding sharks. Maybe it was the way Lyra was wriggling as he attempted to free the rope that was wrapped around his neck that brought it tearing through the water. Maybe it was because he was the shark equivalent to bite size; a precursor to the main meal perhaps. Whatever the reason, the shark made a beeline for Lyra and swallowed him whole in one swift movement.

What happened next surprised everyone concerned, but who the most, we shall never know. It may have been Lyra who had been well and truly knocked from his cradle as he travelled down the shark's throat. It could have been Lupus, who had been moving in for a kill of his own on that very shark who now had a tummy full of Lyra snack, but the smart money was on the shark as it suddenly found it had snagged a free ride on an unscheduled non-stop flight to a jungle somewhere not remotely near him.

CHAPTER 51

'Home sweet home,' announced Pyxis, proudly as he guided the raft through shallow waters to a small island, lush with green vegetation.

'You live here on your own?' asked an excited Equuleus, all thoughts of Pistor and his fate for the moment washed away by the sight of dry land.

'Sadly, but not always,' replied Pyxis, a tinge of regret in his voice, 'I lived here with a friend, but he died when the meat ran out.'

This drew puzzled looks. 'He starved to death?' inquired Fornax, wondering how, if indeed that was true, Pyxis had survived.

'Oh no my dear lady,' said Pyxis, smiling, 'I ate him.' Then noticing the horrified looks he was getting went on to stress how he preferred pork. This didn't totally reassure the raft's majority, who were now assembled as far away as possible from Pyxis, causing it to tilt dangerously.

Pyxis raised his hands in an appeasing gesture. 'Please – please, I'm a vegetarian now,' blank looks, 'a plant eater, admittedly the sort that likes to eat fish, but a non meat-eater all the same. Here, I've something for you.' Pyxis rummaged in his shirt which caused the majority to take another step back and Musca, who was standing at the rear of the majority, to hold on tight as his heel dipped in the briny. Fornax had a hand on her sword. 'Here,' said Pyxis, offering a carrot, 'it's all I've left of my breakfast.' He threw it to Equuleus who sniffed it then took a bite. 'There's plenty more on the island.'

A general consensus of uneasy relief was heard as the carrot was passed round, but he had still eaten his friend, so an air of distrust lingered amongst the carrot munching non-cannibals.

* * *

Pyxis secured the raft to a rickety jetty then led the way to his humble desert island abode. As he went he told how he came to end up on the island, in a terrible storm many years ago that wrecked the fishing boat he was in and washed him, barely alive, onto its shores. He'd survived alone for many years after that until one day a white man with a long grey beard was put ashore and marooned by a gang of rough looking cut-throats; their leader, a large man covered in white frills. Captain Pluperfect immediately sprang to mind amongst Musca and the others. Pyxis continued his tale and told how he and the white man had become good friends, but when the island's wild pigs died from a mysterious sickness and the meat ran out, the white man went suddenly crazy and attacked him. Pyxis stopped and showed everyone a scar on his leg where the white man had bitten him; he had tried to eat Pyxis while he slept.

They walked on and Pyxis told them that in the following struggle the white man had struck his head on a rock* and died. It was a sad time for him and he had meant to give the old fellow a decent burial, but he was what he was and old habits died hard, so he ate him. Afterwards he felt such strong remorse he vowed never to eat meat again.

'Well this is it,' said Pyxis. They had arrived at the dilapidated shack he called home. He ushered his guests in.

It was dark, dank and smelled strongly of vegetables. This strangely had a soothing effect on everyone.

'Please excuse me while I open a window or two,' said Pyxis, pushing aside ancient wooden shutters. One fell off and clattered to the ground outside. 'Sorry about that,' said Pyxis, embarrassed, 'needs a little work doing on the place, but you know how it is, where does the time go?'

No one did, so they just stared at him.

'Er... yes... where was I?' Pyxis patted a wall which shook slightly, 'Sadly I've never been one for the manual side of things. Old Sextans built it. I wouldn't know where to start,' he admitted.

'What did you say?' said a suddenly animated Cetus.

* Pyxis omitted to say that he happened to have the rock in his hand at the time.

331

'I'm no good with my hands, all right. I can cook. I can grow vegetables. I can catch fish, but when it comes to a hammer and nails I'm useless. Never had the schooling for it. Never would have had the skill anyway. Happy now? Even the raft and jetty was built by him. If something goes wrong with it I don't know what I'll do. Become a proper veggie I expect. There, you have me laid bare.'

'I meant the name,' said Cetus, raising his eyebrows at the others, 'what name did you say?'

'Oh…,' said Pyxis, now feeling a tad foolish, 'Sextans.'

Cetus couldn't believe his ears. He had said Sextans and he knew a Sextans; they all did. But surely it couldn't be the same man; could it?

When Cetus was but a small lad, a man from the village had left to explore the world. He'd been given a hero's send-off, but sadly was never heard of again. That is if you ignored the rumours. Cetus grabbed Pyxis by the arm. 'Did he have any belongings?' he said.

Pyxis nodded and pointed to a small chest standing in the corner. Cetus went to it and pulled the lid open. The chest was plain and old with rusting hinges, but inside it the contents were as good as new.

'He took good care of them,' said Pyxis, peering over Cetus' shoulder as he retrieved a bone handled knife; its edge as keen as the first day it was honed.

'I'm sure it's the same Sextans,' said Cetus, handing the knife to Fornax, 'I remember this.'

All gathered round in amazement as Fornax carefully turned the knife over in her hands. If true, the thing was a relic. Sextan's story went down as folklore in their village. Did. On each side of the handle was carved an S with a long squiggle trailing underneath. It was Sextan's all right.

''Ere, let the dog see the coney,' said Bootes, who if the least bit sensitive would have wilted at his own words, but Bootes being Bootes, it passed right over him without incident. He took the knife from Fornax and turned it upside down. 'I'll know if it's 'is.' On the base of the handle was scratched a spidery X.

332

'What's it mean?' said Fornax, as Bootes thrust it under her nose.

'It's me name,' exclaimed Bootes.

'It's just an X.'

'It's 'ow I writes me name,' said Bootes, 'Sextans wuz a pal. He tol' me to write it. Said it would bring 'im luck so 'e did.' Bootes was beaming as the memory flooded back.

'When was that?' asked Cetus, sure he already knew the answer.

'Now let me fink,' said Bootes, rubbing his chin thoughtfully. 'Ah yes. I remember now. It wuz just before 'e left on 'is world jaunt.' Bootes' mind wandered again, back to that fateful day. When he came out of his little reminiscing daydream Bootes asked Pyxis why Sextans had ended up on the island.

Puzzled and sure he had already cleared that up Pyxis reiterated.

'No,' said Bootes, 'I mean, where wuz 'e going to end up 'ere?'

Pyxis' smile broadened and he laughed. 'I believe he was going "'ome", as he put it.'

A sudden deathly hush descended on the room.

'Was it something I said?' said Pyxis, the smile for once dropping, 'because if it was I'm sorry…'

'Did you say "Ohm"?' said Musca, finding his voice, but hardly daring to believe his ears.

'I did,' said Pyxis, warily, 'is there something wrong?'

'What else did he say about Ohm?' said Musca. Behind him the questions started to build, then gushed forward, hard and fast. So hard and fast in fact that Pyxis was corralled into the corner where the chest had stood.

'Wait… wait!' shouted Pyxis, when he could retreat no further without serious damage to the shack, 'one question at a time, *please*!'

As Musca was asking loudest, his was the first answered. 'Did he tell you where it was?' he asked, hardly able to hide his excitement.

'He said there was no place like it,' said Pyxis, raising a murmur amongst the massed ranks of interrogators and much nodding of confirming heads.

'But where did he say it was?' said Hydra, impatience growing.

'He didn't,' said Pyxis, 'but he was going to take me with him and pointed out its general direction.'

Disappointment was hardly able to establish a toehold as Pyxis's last words were greedily seized upon.

'Which way?' said Fornax, ankle well and truly forgotten about.

Pyxis went to point, but that was not enough. They wanted to see from the shore. This was what they were searching for. Perhaps they wouldn't get as good a chance again.

Both woman and manhandled Pyxis was pushed to the door, but there they stopped. Their exit barred. Lying in their way, draped across the threshold was a soggy bundle of rags. Standing over the rags was a soggy, bedraggled mass. It said, 'Woof.'

Fur bloodstained, matted and wet, Lupus looked a sorry sight, but to someone it was the best one in the world.

'Fluffy!' Bootes shouted with joy, 'where yer been boy? I thought yer wuz fish food.' Bootes ran forward and draped his arms around Lupus' neck, his tears mingling with the pink-red droplets already dripping on the floor from Lupus' coat.

'Well, would you believe it,' said Fatidic, hands on hips, 'the dog's still alive and found us.'

Everyone else stayed quiet, standing their ground, all staring at Lupus. If they thought the dog looked menacing the first time they had seen him he now appeared ten times worse. Sensing their fear Lupus began to back away. At the same time the bundle in the doorway started to move. Fatidic went and took a look.

'Grief,' said Fatidic when he got there, 'it's your friend,' he turned the rags over, 'and he's still alive.'

* * *

Considering what Pistor had been through, he was in surprisingly fine fettle and was soon sufficiently recovered to recount what he remembered of his adventure. It was little, but he told what he could. How one of the killer fish had tried to take a bite out of him, but had only succeeded in snagging his shirt on some of its teeth before it dived deep below the surface taking him with it. He thought he was a goner as the pressure of the dive pushed the air out of his lungs. He thought he was going to drown; worse be eaten alive. But as he drifted between consciousness and unconsciousness, life and death, he saw a larger darker shape appear from nowhere and attack the fish that held him in its killer teeth, tearing it apart.

'And that's all I remember until I woke up in yon doorway.' Pistor took a sip of the water Pyxis had given him and gave each of the onlookers a wry inquisitive glance. 'Who is it then? Who do I thank for saving my miserable hide?'

Bootes stepped proudly forward. 'It wuz Fluffy that dun it,' he said. 'I trained 'im me self yer know.'

Lupus, who was lying on the floor of the shack, raised an eyebrow towards Bootes.

'The dog?' said Pistor, surprised.

'That's right,' said Bootes, who was smiling fit to burst.

Pistor held up his mug of water and toasted Lupus. 'To you dog,' he said and finished off what was left in the bottom.

With Pistor and Lupus' miraculous appearance the subject of *Ohm* was, for a short while, forgotten but it continued to bubble just beneath the surface and Musca, when it finally seeped back up, was the first to tell Pistor. How he loved doing that. Pistor, happy for the moment because he was alive, took it on board with a half smile, but said nothing; he even joined everyone on the beach where a beleaguered Pyxis indicated to them the *rough* area Sextans had determined "'*ome*" lay.

That evening, before everyone turned in for a surprisingly sound sleep considering the excitement building, it was agreed they would make modifications to the raft – Fatidic to take charge of that – and set sail for Ohm at the first opportunity.

Happy they were, at last, on their way, the shack was soon filled with snores, other bodily noises and the tip toing of Pistor as he stepped between and over the sleeping bodies. He made his way to the door and crept outside. It was the first opportunity he'd had to check if something was still in one piece.

One last look to check all was quiet Pistor went to remove the gizmo.

'It's still there,' said a voice in his head just as he reached inside.

'Who's there?' said Pistor, eyes darting here and there.

But the night remained silent.

'Show yourself.' Pistor popped a head in through the shutter-less window to see which one of them knew of his secret. Goose bumps appeared on his skin as he realised they were all still asleep.

With one eye on the surrounding vegetation, Pistor slipped back inside the shack. He would be the only one that didn't sleep that night.

Outside a dark shape appeared noiselessly from the vegetation and lingered momentarily by the door of the shack. All inside was quiet again. That was good. It moved away and lay on the ground; the stars shining on the clean again fur. That one will have to be watched closely, thought Lupus, settling down.

Next morning was filled with the happy toing and froing of people on a mission. Even Fornax was able give a hand after Bootes had produced a salve to rub on her ankle from a bag he had managed to salvage that, when applied, reduced the swelling and pain enough for her to stand on it without too much difficulty. Where Bootes had come across such an item he either couldn't or wouldn't say, but she suspected it was something Tee Hee may have had lying around. Fornax hadn't pressed Bootes further as, and as was the case when anyone mentioned anything regarding his adventures since they had last seen him, his faithful mutt would invariably make its presence known and interrupt, but she was in no hurry to hear of Tee Hee or anything to do with him just yet, if indeed the salve was of his doing; the wound of her time with him and the baby were still too tender by far to be touched.

With everyone working together for once, the raft was soon finished. All that was left was to gather enough supplies for the journey. How much that might be no one knew, but it didn't hinder them. Pyxis led them to his garden and a supply of fresh water and by mid afternoon everything was ready.

'Everyone ready?' asked Pyxis, after he had double checked for the umpteenth time that there was enough carrots on board.

The answer was loud and affirmative with one exception.

'Pistor?' said Fornax.

Pistor had been quiet and withdrawn all morning, but as he was a perpetual misery-gut no one had taken any notice.

'What?' he said, drawn from another mental re-run of last night. He must have dreamt it, he had told himself all morning and would have been more than happy to believe that, if the fact he hadn't slept a wink all night wasn't the glaring fly in the ointment that said otherwise.

'Are you ready?'

Pistor, arms wrapped tightly about his chest, sauntered over to the raft and climbed aboard.

'Let's go then.'

A cheer rose from the raft.

'Wait,' shouted Cetus, 'I've forgotten Sextans' chest.' Cetus jumped from the raft and made his way back to the shack as fast as he was able.

The shack was quite dark inside, even with the shutters open so it took a hard puffing Cetus a second or two to grow accustomed to the gloom and find the chest; put back on the floor by Pyxis. He saw it, bent to pick it up, but as he reached for it he was forced to pull up short as a sudden pain shot across his chest. What the...? Cetus gasped and clutched at his heart. Another bolt of pain, its intensity bringing Cetus to his knees. He tried to call out but couldn't; had no breath. A third stabbed at him. He needed help. Cetus tried to stand, but the effort caused him to overbalance and with nothing within reach to hold onto he crashed to the floor.

This wasn't supposed to happen; not with the end of the journey in sight. The world around Cetus started to dim. A noise. With what strength he had left Cetus managed to turn his head in time to see Sextans' chest lifted from the floor. Who? He tried again to call out but the light was failing too fast. He didn't have time. His life was quickly passing before his eyes. He now saw the shack again. He was entering it to get Sextans' chest. Why was it so dark…?

'Where's he got to?' said Fornax, wondering what could be taking Cetus so long.

'Call of nature I suspect,' said Fatidic.

'I'll go and get him,' offered Musca, eager to get going.

'There he is,' said Equuleus, spying a large bulk disengaging from the shadows thrown by the trees at the edge of the shoreline. 'Slow as ever,' he laughed.

'What kept you?' said Fornax, as he ambled over. If she didn't know better she would have sworn he was drunk.

Cetus mumbled something no one really caught and climbed onto the raft. After roughly stowing the chest amongst the supplies, he sat down as far away as was possible from everyone else and stared out to sea.

'Manners,' grumbled Musca.

'Are we ready now?' asked the perpetually smiling Pyxis.

It appeared they were.

'Good.' Pyxis let go the rope holding them to the island and pushed off. This was it, he thought, as he took a long last look at the place that had been his home for so many years. The raft gently drifted from the jetty.

Seconds later that jetty crumpled and collapsed into the sea.

CHAPTER 52

'Thank you Lyra, that was most gracious of you,' said Serpens, smacking his lips and picking the last remnant of shark from between his teeth. 'I must remember to give my compliments to the creator responsible the next time I'm in Creators Hall. That was absolutely delicious.'

Good humour abounding, Serpens ambled over to the stepped pyramid, also known as the scarab temple and stepped amongst the remains of the pirates at its gore spattered base. 'Ah, carnage,' he said, picking up a skull, 'I know it well.' He smiled and tossed it back where he had got it from. The smiled widened when the crack of breaking bone reached his ear. But enough of play, he had work to do. Where was that Lyra?

The imp was being stitched back together by Ophiuchus. 'Stop fidgeting, I haven't finished yet,' warned Ophiuchus, as the slither of dead pirate's bone he was using as a needle snagged Lyra's spinal cord threatening to snap it in half.

Not that it mattered to Lyra; he was much too busy being in shock to notice anything as trivial as that. A deep shock that was brought about, not as you might imagine, from the suddenness of the shark attack or the swallowing by. Nor was the cause the heavy handed retrieval from within the shark at the hands of Serpens that had ripped him apart as he brushed against its razor sharp teeth on exit. It was something far worse than any of those. Lyra had realised he had forgotten the next line of his nursery rhyme.

'And you say they are only a few miles away from here?' said Serpens, ambling back.

Lyra didn't answer; he was too busy being shocked.

'I said…'

'He can't answer, Sire, I think he's in shock,' said Ophiuchus, tugging at the needle as it struggled against gristle.

'Shock?' said Serpens, rounding the impromptu sewing circle. He studied Lyra and didn't like what he saw. Sheer unadulterated gormlessness was staring back at him; and just when he was getting so close. Now how was he going to find out where the monkey man was? The ocean he'd paddled in earlier was vast. It would be like finding a haystack in a needle.*

Many "ums" and "what to do's" later, Serpens was left with only one option: a mind link. Normally this was an easy thing to do, but he had found to his cost – headaches nausea etc – that dealing with Lyra was not in any shape or form the least bit normal. Mind linking with Lyra was the equivalent of taking your own brain out and giving it to a group of two year olds and telling them to do something constructive with it. But it *had* to be done. He snatched the needle Ophiuchus was using and stuffed it through Lyra's nose; in and out via the nostrils.

'Hold him,' ordered Serpens.

Being the recipient of a small part of Serpens, Ophiuchus caught on quickly to Serpens' intentions. He was glad he didn't have to do it; he knew how dangerous it was linking with Lyra.

Serpens placed a hand on the side of Lyra's face and then, quick as a flash, he placed one on Ophiuchus'. Before Ophiuchus could do anything they were hit by the first wave of nonsense; a wall of interlocking teddies standing firm on a wall of icebergs. Serpens stood his ground and deflected most of it into Ophiuchus' shocked brain. Worse was to come.

As the first line of defence disintegrated the second was upon them; pink things with little purple flowers embossed on them. It was so cruel. Soft things, pretty things, Serpens began to sweat profusely, but again he sent them the way of Ophiuchus who was now on bended knee and crying.

Now the big one; the third wave. Once Serpens was past this he would be free to rummage in the dusty cupboards of Lyra's mind. He steeled against the expected onslaught of whatever it may be, happy in the knowledge Ophiuchus was going to take the brunt of it. He waited. And waited.

* Much harder to do than finding a needle in a haystack. *SJ*

It didn't come. Serpens opened a tentative mind's eye to see what was going on. To say what he saw was a surprise was an understatement. Sat all alone on a pink potty in the middle of nowhere was a smaller and younger version of Lyra. The small figure saw Serpens and smiled. Um, thought Serpens, his defences lowered a little by the significant lack of nausea or brain pain.

'Who am I?' asked the small Lyra.

Serpens grew a tad confused.

'Can you help me?' said the potty sitting imp.

As Serpens ventured a little closer his inner defences nagged at him to be careful. He ignored them and drew even closer.

'Why?' asked Serpens. Caution was now discarded wholesale as curiosity got the better of him. He was now standing over the tiny Lyra.

'BECAUSE I'VE LOST SOMETHING IN MY POTTY!' screamed the imp, a hand shooting forward and growing in size to envelope Serpens' head. 'MAYBE YOU CAN FIND IT?'

Serpens was forced head first into the potty. Down he went; deeper and deeper, all the time trying to regain control of his mind. He hit water and bobbed, gasping to the surface. Up above, the tiny Lyra, a minute speck in the distance, was leaning over the potty's edge pointing and laughing. Then he was gone and Serpens was alone floating in a vast ocean.

Trying to get some sort of bearings Serpens turned this way and that. Was all this real? Was he still in the grip of Lyra's twisted mind? Something drifted into view. Some *things* drifted into view. Pieces of wreckage. They drew closer. Now, to his horror, he could see that each piece of wreckage carried a tiny passenger, a tiny pointing and laughing Lyra. He had to get away before he went insane. His rescue came in the form of a raft. Asking no questions he climbed aboard and watched with some relief as he gradually drifted away from the insanity that was now waving their tiny little hands. What next? thought Serpens, not realising *next* was already happening.

The raft was gone and he was now floating high above the ocean and homing in on a small island. As he hung there in mid air, an idea suddenly came to him. Lyra was no longer in control and this was real time. Something had changed. Ophiuchus? No – not Ophiuchus – well not completely; a mixture of Lyra, Ophiuchus and the small part of him that was Serpens. All coming together somehow to bring about this out of body experience he was experiencing; turning it into real time. That or he was now stark raving bonkers and well and truly up dirty creek without a paddle.

He began to slowly descend; drifting towards a ramshackle hut. Someone was struggling up a path making for it. Didn't he know the fat creature from somewhere? Of course he did; he was one of the humanoids Lyra had described at the hole. Serpens landed beside the hut. But what now? The fat humanoid had entered the hut. Did he follow? How could he, he was twice the size of the hut. But he wasn't. Serpens was no longer restricted to the confines of flesh and bone. Whatever was happening had put him beyond that. Neither did he have to use the door. Serpens slid through the wall of the hut and stood behind Cetus. It did have its drawbacks though. In his current form Serpens wasn't as powerful. All he could do for now was follow; hitch a lift. Then another idea came to him.

The fat humanoid was looking for something; now reaching for something, a chest in the corner. Enough. Serpens put his latest idea into action and reached through Cetus until he found his heart. He squeezed. He squeezed again. Three times he squeezed. The humanoid collapsed to the floor. Serpens left him, went to the corner and picked up the chest. What was so interesting? He opened it. Nothing he could see. Could be important though, he thought, better take it with me. Now for the second part of his plan. 'Move over fat boy,' whispered Serpens, 'I'm coming in.'

Back at the scarab temple, Ophiuchus, suddenly free of the mind link, staggered backwards.

'Ow!' cried Lyra, as he too came round, 'what yer doing to me?'

Swinging from Ophiuchus' hand by his nose, a puzzled Lyra was struggling to get free.

'Oh,' said Ophiuchus, some modicum of senses returning. He let go.

'Ow-ow!' said Lyra, rubbing his backside, 'what are you playing at?'

Ophiuchus was staring past Lyra open mouthed and pointing.

'What?' said Lyra.

'Lo… look,' stuttered Ophiuchus.

Lyra did. Serpens was lying on the ground in a crumpled heap. Lyra frowned. Something was forming in his mind. He was remembering something. 'Oh yes,' he said, 'the master wants you to look after his body while he's away.' It was said almost matter of fact. Gone was the gibbering of before. Lyra pulled the bone from his nose.

'But… what?' said Ophiuchus, wondering what the hell was going on. He remembered nothing. Only that Serpens had touched him as…. *now* the headache started; *now* he remembered the little teddies that had floated before his eyes. 'Drat,' he said.

'Well, come on,' said Lyra, who had already started for the beach, 'we haven't got all eternity you know. The master will be waiting.'

Head thumping, perplexed beyond all reason, stunned by Lyra's lucidity and resigned to what Serpens had done to him, Ophiuchus plucked Serpens' body from the ground and staggered from the clearing.

CHAPTER 53

Lift-off had been achieved slowly, but without a hitch and now the huge silver saucer hovered high over the mountainside that had for so long been its prison.

'Can I look now?' said Draco, trying *not* to peep between his claws.

'Check,' said Tee Hee.

'What?' said Draco.

'Check,' said Tee Hee, again.

Draco decided to peep. Tee Hee was bent over a console pressing buttons. He unclasped the belt Tee Hee had tied round him for take-off and sidled over to see what Tee See was doing. 'What are you doing?' Draco asked.

'It's this game, the computer always wins. Drat!' A red CHECK MATE flashed on the VDU. 'Supposed to help me relax during a take-off; never does. I think the thing cheats.'

Draco hadn't the faintest idea what Tee Hee was going on about so chanced a peek through one of the portholes. 'We've taken-off then?' He said this rather nervously as it was the first time he had ever flown. If you didn't count the time he spent in the comet or the fact he was a fully fledged dragon.

'Yes,' said Tee Hee, switching the computer game off and moving to another console where he started to press more buttons.

'Another game?' said Draco.

'No, systems check,' said Tee Hee, 'light switch on – check.'

Bored with watching Tee Hee flicking this switch and flipping that one, Draco returned to the porthole. 'Can't it go any faster?' he asked idly, as the ground below slipped slowly past.

'Propulsion jets not at full max yet,' said Tee Hee, not looking up from his latest console.

It meant nothing to Draco who was now bored of looking out of the porthole, but not with his questions. 'Won't they see us from below?' he asked.

'Who?'

'The natives. Read somewhere that higher beings should never interact or attempt discourse with lower forms, in the event said lower forms perceive said higher forms as deities or, said higher forms should disrupt the natural lines of lower forms' evolution,' said Draco.

This time Tee Hee raised his eyes from said earlier console. 'Not in my manual it doesn't, besides the Manowski brothers' principle will kick in. Their invention, the bi-pole-ar transfixing unit, should deflect any prying eyes.'

Draco thought about this for a moment or two and decided not to ask. He did have another question though. 'What does this button do?'

CHAPTER 54

Something was wrong and Lupus just couldn't put his claw on it. He studied each of the raft's occupants in turn until his gaze fell on Cetus who had distanced himself from everyone else. Lupus discreetly sniffed in his direction. He couldn't sense anything out of the ordinary, but that didn't stop the fur on his neck telling him otherwise. The wrong he felt, was definitely coming from the fat one, but there was no hard evidence for it and that was what bothered him most.

'Biscuit, Cetus?' asked Pyxis.

Cetus shook his head to say no.

'They are pretty damn fine biscuits if I do say so myself,' said Pyxis, still offering one, 'made them myself; coconut and carrot.'

But Cetus could not be tempted and waved Pyxis away.

'Okay, but don't say I didn't offer when they are all gone,' said Pyxis, who then shrugged and walked away to join the others.

'I cannot believe your friend refused my biscuit,' said Pyxis, sitting down.

'Maybe he's sickening for something,' said Equuleus.

'He is very quiet,' said Fornax.

'It's since he went back for that box,' said Musca, 'I reckon he's put his appetite in it along with his manners.'

'You'd need a bigger box than that,' said Pistor.

No one laughed.

Watching this with interest Lupus added it to the fuel he had already gathered for this particular fire. The man was acting strangely; his friends were saying so. Vigilance was called for. Lupus returned his gaze to the man called Cetus who was again sitting with his back to all and staring out to sea.

As Lupus watched and the others wondered at Cetus' refusal of food, Cetus' eyes clouded over and started to glow a faint red. Soon, thought Serpens, soon he would be the master of everything, but until then he would have to stay in control and suffer the tiresome witterings of those on the raft. 'One… two… three…' he whispered, as quietly as he could. And how he hated the feel of the bloated soft pink flesh he was encased in. 'Four… five… ' He reached five and five was enough for now. Enough to calm the wrath he would soon let loose. The red glow gradually diminished.

So the journey continued. Each day the horizon was continually scanned for the first sight of Ohm. Each day Cetus ignored those around him and in turn was ignored more and more by them. The raft drifted on. One day. Two days. Three days came and went. Surrounded by nothing but green, hope would sag by nightfall but rise again at sunrise. Four days passed.

It was on the morning of the fifth day and Equuleus, always the first to rise, was the first to notice the dark spot on the otherwise unblemished horizon.

'Land!' yelled an excited Equuleus, 'I see land!'

Through sleep encrusted eyes the others peered towards the horizon. Sure enough it was blessed with a distant dark shape. Soon, with the exception of Cetus and Lupus, the raft was a shouting, cheering bedlam of celebration and congratulations.

'I knew you could do it,' said a grinning Hydra, shaking Musca by the hand. 'We've nearly reached Ohm.'

'I said I would,' said Musca, modestly accepting the praise that had started to fly in his direction, but colouring when his eyes met those belonging to Fornax.

Fornax smiled. 'Well done,' she said, gently squeezing his arm, 'I knew you would do it.'

Bootes, who had woken up a little behind the others and missed the gist of what was going on, but had been cheering along with the best of them anyway; now felt it might be a good idea to ask why. 'Wuz up?' he said into the nearest ear.

'It's land,' said Hydrus, pointing out to sea, 'we've found Ohm.'

Bootes narrowed his eyes to slits and squinted at the horizon. The dot in the distance was already a lot closer and even he, after a moment or two of peering this way and that, managed to make it out. Now excited for a reason, Bootes reached over to Lupus and ruffled the fur on his head. 'Look Fluffy, land.'

But Lupus didn't need to be told; he had already spotted it and didn't like the look of it. It was getting too big too fast. And unless they were travelling a lot faster than it looked like they were, that meant the dot was also moving; towards them, and at speed. Lupus gave a low growl.

'What's wrong with your dog?' asked Fatidic.

'Dunno,' said a mystified Bootes, 'but summit's got 'is back up.'

The dot grew closer; the growling turned to barking. Lupus tugged at Bootes' sleeve.

'Wot is it boy?' said Bootes.

'I expect he's getting excited at the thought of a good tree,' said Pistor, dryly, his remark generating the odd laugh.

They won't be laughing soon, thought Lupus who could now make out exactly what the dark shape on the horizon was.

At first it appeared the ship was going to ram the raft, sending it and all on board to the bottom of the ocean, but it slowed enough to stop just short; its momentum carrying it the rest of the way until it settled alongside the raft. It wasn't a big ship by any stretch of the imagination, but it dwarfed the raft that bobbed perilously close to its hull. From somewhere above someone called for the anchor to be dropped.

'Anchor away!' The anchor fell and splashed into the sea, rocking the raft in its wake.

On the raft emotions that had run a gauntlet of change from excitement to disappointment, to fear to self deluding hope; hope that the ship would perhaps be their salvation and take them on to Ohm, veered back to fear again as a familiar voice boomed down at them, shattering the fragile illusion they were clinging to.

'So we meet again, yes-no?' Captain Pluperfect grinned down at the raft. 'What, no greetings for an old friend? I zink perhaps the proverbial furry creature 'as got your tongue, yes-no?'

'What do you want from us?' shouted Fornax.

'Me? I zink you have ze wrong idea,' said Pluperfect, 'I want nothing. Except my treasure perhaps, but as I see you are travelling light...' He was joined by someone else they knew. 'Ah, Voussoir,' said Pluperfect, as the first mate appeared by his side, 'we have 'appened on old acquaintances. Zey zink we want somezing. Do you want somezing?'

'Not me, Cap'n,' said Voussoir, peering menacingly over the side of the ship.

'You see,' said Pluperfect, 'we want nozing from you.'

'Then we'll be on our way,' said Fornax.

A laugh rang out from above her. 'I see you 'ave lost none of your fight young mistress, yes-no? But I am of the bitter opinion that that is somezing I cannot allow. You see zere is someone aboard who does want somezing from you.' Pluperfect and Voussoir parted and someone smaller filled the void. 'You remember Caudal, yes-no?' The boy stood on tiptoe and looked over, he was wearing a black patch over one eye. 'He lost somezing very important to 'im the last time you met and now he wants, how you say, an eye for ze eye.' As Pluperfect spoke, Caudal whispered something to him. Pluperfect let out a roar of laughter. 'Ha, ze boy becomes ze man. It would seem Caudal here is willing to forgive and forget where you are concerned young lady. Myself I am zinking 'e is too young to be taking a bride, but he does insist. Will you come aboard?'

Fornax took no time in giving a response and in no uncertain terms.

The down turned face of Pluperfect took on a look of thunder at the crude gesture. 'Then you die!' he stormed, 'you insult my crew, you insult me. Voussoir! The cannon.' He slammed an angry fist on the ship's rail and disappeared from sight. Down below panic became the emotion of the moment as the blackened snouts of three cannon poked through the ship's side.

'Up anchor!' The anchor began to rise.

'Quickly,' yelled Pyxis, handing out paddles, 'it's our only chance.'

He was wrong; they didn't have one and all knew it, but still they took the oars and frantically dipped them in the water. Even

Lupus, who had transformed his front paws into flippers amid the panic, paddled for all he was worth. He could escape at any time, but the old man? Tee See's mother?

The ship lurched away from the raft and circled it until its cannon held it in their sights.

'Steady lads!' ordered Pluperfect, 'Steady I say. On my word. FIRE!!'

A thunderous roar which had the majority of the raft's inhabitants diving into the sea met Pluperfect's command and never again would their paths cross.

CHAPTER 55

Draco was deep in serious thought. He should have learned from his first mistake. Tee Hee had not been happy. "Could have destroyed a city", he had said. As it was the weapon had not been at full power so only half the forest had gone. "Don't press any other buttons", he had said. But curiosity had got the better of him. He had wanted to know what a "BEME UP" button did. Should have asked in hindsight. Shouldn't have pressed it. A "lion" Tee Hee had called it when it arrived. A lion whose mind made disturbing reading.

It had been a while since it had happened and Draco, watching the world go by at a snail pace, decided it was a long enough space to resume his questions. Tee Hee didn't look so angry now.

'What do you think the scarecrow apparition it saw was?' asked Draco, chancing it.

Tee Hee didn't answer at first; instead doubling his effort at the console he was standing at, re-flicking and re-twiddling various ergonomic switches and knobs. But he wasn't the type of alien that could be angry for long.

'I don't know,' said Tee Hee, stopping mid knob, 'but obviously the poor soul was near demented by the thought of it.'

Draco thought this over. 'And the mad man with the sword?'

'The result of a rather over active imagination brought on by previous trauma,' said Tee Hee, who really didn't have time for all this. 'And don't forget his "brush" with the big red, horned, scaly one.' This Tee Hee felt sure was something the lion had not imagined.

'And this was what finally sent him over the edge?' said Draco.

'I think you know the answer to that Draco. I believe he may have seen an old friend of yours.'

Yes-yes-yes, thought Draco, seeing him could most certainly send anyone over the edge. He gave this some thought. Could send anyone. He now shifted uneasily and wandered from the porthole he had adopted as his own since take-off. The idea of heading to and not away from Serpens would have made his blood run cold if it wasn't already the norm.

'What about the man-thing? He wasn't very happy screaming "not again, not again" like that.'

'He'll get over it,' said Tee Hee.

'The potions you gave them, will they really work?'

'Of course. All memories as far back as a season will be lost to them when they wake up.'

Draco didn't know how long a season was to Tee Hee, but in his experience that could be quite a time. The lion and man-thing could be in for a shock when they woke up. But that wasn't his problem so he didn't broach the subject.

At the console Tee Hee was watching Draco closely. He felt Draco had not quite finished with his questions, but he didn't have the time to answer any more so decided to cut him off at the pass. 'And now Draco, old friend, I must get on. I've a mission to complete and a craft to tweak.' Tee Hee returned to his knobs and buttons. 'Oh, and just one thing; please don't touch any more buttons. There's a good fellow.'

To Tee Hee's growing annoyance the ship continued with its reluctance to respond to his furtive mechanical or mental urgings. It was slow work not helped by a thumb twiddling Draco who still insisted on throwing the odd question at him. Couldn't he see he was busy?

'Shouldn't we be going a little faster by now?' said Draco, who had returned to his favourite porthole.

Obviously he couldn't, thought Tee Hee. Enough was enough. The ship was taking its time; he would have to live with that, but not with Draco's constant interruptions. It wasn't his fault, he knew that, but there was only so much someone could take. Problem was Draco was big and also had an uncanny knack of getting out of locked rooms. There was only one thing for it.

The M.C.E. That would bring him down to size. He could pop him in one of the specimen cases. He wouldn't like it, but the thermal locks would stop him from getting out. Drastic yes, but these were drastic times that were calling for drastic measures. Tee Hee waddled to a panel of drawers and opened one. From it he removed what appeared to be a wooden box. Tee Hee clicked a button and the lid opened.

'DRACO!' screamed Tee Hee, when he saw the box was empty, 'Have you taken the M.C.E?'

Draco didn't know what Tee Hee was talking about. He looked at the box Tee Hee was holding out to him. Inside was a depression made by something that had lain there.

'Well?'

Not counting the button pressing episodes, Draco had never seen Tee Hee so animated or agitated. He dropped the shield surrounding his mind and let Tee Hee in. It was free of guilt. 'What was it?' said Draco.

Calming a little, Tee Hee closed the box. A Molecular Compressor Expander. I collect samples with it that otherwise wouldn't fit in the hold. It also doubled as a weapon should the need arise. In the wrong hands it can be dangerous; very dangerous indeed.'

'Who could have taken it?'

'I don't know... unless.' Tee Hee's mind wandered back to the last time he had seen it. He remembered; he had told Fornax about it; had shown it to her while Musca waited outside. She had wanted to see his weapon before she went. She had touched it and smiled. He had wept a little. She...

'Tee Hee?'

'Er... yes?'

'Do you know who could have taken it?'

It wasn't Fornax or Musca, he remembered replacing it and then walking them to the outer portal. Tee Hee concentrated. There had been someone else; someone lurking in the shadows as they left the room. He had thought nothing of it at the time.

'Pistor.'

'Pistor?'

'One of the men travelling with Fornax.' Tee Hee threw the box back into the drawer. It was worse than he thought. The need for speed was all the more imperative.

Across the room Draco wasn't saying so, but he was a little miffed. He had picked up on the reason Tee Hee had looked for the M.C.E in the first place. Surely he hadn't been so irksome as to warrant what Tee Hee had planned for him? Had he? Draco frowned and leaned against the wall. Well, serves Tee Hee right if he doesn't say anything ever again. He'll be sorry then. Draco looked from Tee Hee to the console behind him; the one with the madly flashing red light. Yes, serve him right if he didn't.

'Tee Hee?' ventured Draco, after a full five minute's of heavy silence.

All quiet on the console front, apart from the frantic noise of clicking and flicking buttons.

Draco tried again to get Tee Hee's attention using a nonchalant cough.

It didn't work; Tee Hee was turning a blind one.

Draco pouted. If he didn't want to know then why should he tell him? But what if it was something important?

'Tee Hee?'

'What?' snapped Tee Hee, 'can't you see I'm busy here?'

'There's a light flashing,' said Draco, 'a red one.'

Only half listening, an exasperated Tee Hee was going tell Draco to find something useful to do, when the flashing light caught his eye. He hurried over to it.

'Why didn't you tell me?' said Tee Hee, bending over it. 'It's Lupus; he's switched the transmitter on.' The look of distress on Tee Hee's face brought Draco a pang of regret. 'What am I to do? He'll think I'm not coming, the speed we're travelling.

'Can I help?' offered Draco, the pang now full blown guilt at not saying something sooner.

Tee Hee, dithering between consoles was slow to answer, but it came in the positive. 'Yes. Watch this panel below the flashing light while I see if I can't do more to increase our speed. Tell me when a small white pulse starts flashing in the centre of the circle.'

Glad to be doing something useful Draco moved to the flashing console, as Tee Hee waddled back to the other one. He stared hard at the screen. 'In the centre you say?'

'Yes.'

'Like this?'

Tee Hee tutted and waddled back.

'When the bleep gets...' Tee Hee couldn't believe his eyes. The pulse was in dead centre.

'What does it mean?'

'It means we are right over him.' As quick as he could waddle, Tee Hee raced back to the console he had been working on and pushed a button. The craft juddered to an unimpressive stop. 'Is the pulse still in the same position?' Draco confirmed it was. 'Then follow me.'

Tee Hee led Draco to a small hanger cum hold where a single seat shuttlecraft sat waiting. Tee Hee climbed aboard.

'What about me?' said Draco.

'Er-hum,' said Tee Hee, nodding at Draco's wings.

'Oh yes.'

'See you down below.' Tee Hee got in, adjusted the seat, closed the shuttle's canopy after him and pressed a switch on a large panel set out in front of him. A large section of the wall slid away to reveal blue sky and the odd cotton wool cloud. The shuttle's engine roared into life and Tee Hee disappeared through the gap.

Now it was Draco's turn. He moved to the open panel and peered outside. It was a long way down. He could do this.

'There's an island.' It was Tee Hee communicating telepathically, 'He must be on it.'

Draco edged closer to the edge. He could just make out the island below. It was a long way down.

'Come on.' The shuttle started down.

A deep breath. Draco stopped on the edge. I'll be okay. I'm a dragon for goodness sake. No he couldn't. He couldn't do this. Suddenly the world around him took on a different angle. The spacecraft had tilted making Draco's mind up for him. He started

355

to fall. He was going to die. No he wasn't; he was immortal, but it was going to hurt a lot. Now he could hear voices. No, one voice. It was saying sorry. Sorry! Draco opened his eyes in time to see Tee Hee waving to him from the shuttle craft.

'Sorry about that,' said Tee Hee, 'but time is of the essence.'

Why the little… Draco could feel his temper rising.

'Good,' said Tee Hee, 'now let's get going.' The shuttle craft headed for the island leaving a small vapour trail behind it.

It was only as Draco watched it go, did he realise he was no longer falling. 'What?'

'Just needed a little stoking that's all,' said Tee Hee, his telepathic voice rising from below.

'Why I-you….'

When Draco finally arrived Tee Hee was already on the ground trying to pinpoint the transmitter's exact location. 'It's coming from over there,' he said, pointing to a path leading from the beach he had landed on, 'it's not far.'

Tee Hee went to go, but Draco grabbed him by a shoulder and pulled him back. He sniffed the air, but what he sensed wasn't carried on it. 'He's been here,' he said.

'Who has?'

'The Dark One,' said Draco, pushing past Tee Hee, 'we need to be careful.'

'Is he still here?'

'I don't think so. I don't think he ever was.'

'You're not making sense,' said Tee Hee.

'His body was never here.'

'So what was?'

'His mind, I think.'

'He can do that?'

'Not as far as I know, but things change.'

Was he making any sense? Tee Hee had his doubts, but as Draco looked decidedly more frightened now than when he was tipped from the spacecraft he thought it better to err on the side of caution. He let Draco lead the way. Not all aliens were arse kicking deviants.

They reached Pyxis' shack without drama and Tee Hee found the transmitter amongst bushes not far from its door. He suspected Lupus was ignorant of its loss.

'We have to go,' said Tee Hee, holding the transmitter in his hand, 'without this Lupus can't signal us if there's trouble and with your master up to no good and so close that could be sometime very soon.'

'But how are we going to find him?'

Up until then Tee Hee had had a good idea of Lupus' whereabouts. He hadn't told Lupus, but the transmitter was also a tracking device. From now on it would be guess work. 'They can't be far away, I'll set the scanners on full sweep.' Tee Hee started for the path.

'Wait,' said Draco, suddenly.

'Serpens?' said Tee Hee, stopping, hearts thumping.

'No, something else, I think there's someone in the shack.'

CHAPTER 56

'And you say he knows where the monkey man is going?' said Ophiuchus. Since leaving the lost city, Ophiuchus had been trying to get it straight in his mind just what it was Serpens had told Lyra.

'Yes,' said a beleaguered Lyra.

'And we are to round up other monkey men and wait for him to arrive?'

'Yes.'

'Why doesn't he just go straight there and wait for us?'

Enough was enough. Lyra called a halt. The tiny sliver of intelligent stability Serpens had seen necessary to endow him with, for the purpose of the mission, was growing impatient.

'Because-he-wants-to-keep-an-eye-on-him,' said Lyra, hoping that if he said it deliberate enough, it might just sink into Ophiuchus' thick head and he would stop asking his stupid questions. 'Now, if you've quite finished questioning the Dark Lord's bidding, I suggest we get on our way.'

He didn't like it. Something bad was going to happen very soon and he didn't think he was going to like it. No... scrub that. He *knew* he wasn't going to like it. Ophiuchus thought of dragging his feet, but had second thoughts when a mental picture popped into his mind of an ogre, him, trying to drag his feet. Only in this picture they weren't attached to him. But he had to do something. He knew he was different now. Since landing on this damn planet they had all changed in some way. Add to that, the piece of Serpens he was host to and; a whole new perspective. Funny that the bit of Serpens inside of him didn't try to stop his thoughts of dissent, unless that's just what it was; a piece that encouraged those sort of ideas. But what would happen to him when Serpens had his monkey man and wanted all his bits back? Where would that leave him? Back to being a mindless moron that possessed nothing more than the ambition to be called Bob. He didn't want that. Bob he did. He wanted out and away.

'I'm not going,' said Ophiuchus, planting his feet firmly on the sand.

'What?'

'I'm not coming. I quit!'

'You can't quit. You're not employed, you're owned. Owned by the Dark Lord.'

Lyra was, of course, right, but he would have to catch him first. Ophiuchus dropped Serpens body and made a run for it.

He didn't get far. A bluish light, quite beautiful in its way, flashed through the air and struck the sand at Ophiuchus' feet scorching it and the ends of his toes.

'Serpens said you might try something like this,' said Lyra, blowing smoke from a smouldering finger tip.

Ophiuchus waited for the flash that would be his last. Instead he heard the flump flump of Lyra's feet crossing the sand between them.

When Lyra reached Ophiuchus he wore the mark of Serpens; glowing eyes like red hot embers and an evil grin that any homicidal clown would happily pay a small fortune for. He reached behind him and pulled from a hidden something or other a scroll of yellowing parchment. This he unfurled and showed to Ophiuchus. It was his contract.

'Serpens told me to show you this and to remind you what would happen to you should it be torn asunder.'

Ophiuchus nodded. He did. He would lose his immortality and all the rights that went with them; pension etc. Oh, and his life. Damn that small print.

'That's better,' smiled Lyra, 'now go pick up the Master's body and we'll say no more about it.'

Ophiuchus reluctantly did as he was told.

Much mind numbing, unnerving, tuneless whistling from the lips of Lyra later, he and Ophiuchus found themselves free of the jungle and looking out over miles of open savannah and beyond that, miles of open scrubland that led to a range of distant hills or mountains. Ophiuchus would admit to being a little vague on the difference; feet and inches he thought. It was these mountains/ hills that Lyra now gestured to.

'We must be on the other side by noon tomorrow,' said Lyra. It was already late afternoon.

'That's impossible,' said Ophiuchus, before he could hush his mouth.

'Not if we run.'

So run they did and by the time the stars had reclaimed the space above, they stood at the base of the mountains immersed in the shadows that lay like huge dark pools amongst them.

His breaths coming in long painful rasps, Ophiuchus stood fruitlessly searching for the peaks way above. There was no way they were going to get over them by tomorrow.

'We don't have to,' said Lyra, stealing Ophiuchus' thoughts, 'follow me.'

A short walk later they stood at the mouth of a gully that split the mountain range in two.

'How did you know?' said Ophiuchus. It was in all honesty a question he needn't have asked and he knew it.

Lyra scrambled down a small slope and melted into the gully's shadows.

CHAPTER 57

Heads bobbed to the surface. Attached to each of them a face etched in disbelief.

The raft, with only Cetus and Fatidic still aboard, was still there unscathed, floating on an otherwise empty sea. The whereabouts of Captain Pluperfect and his ship a burgeoning mystery.

Bodies began to squirm onto the raft; Fornax the first, all wanting to know what had happened. Cetus, still staring at nothing in particular chose to ignore them. Fatidic, lying face down, hunched, bottom up, gibbered something intelligible and appeared to point at the sky. He was pulled upright and asked again, but his answer amounted to nothing more than gibberish utterances. And that is how Fatidic remained for the duration of his time on the raft. When finally he did find a voice with reason attached to it he found he couldn't remember what it was he had been gibbering about.

The next couple of days passed without incident, but the atmosphere on the raft instead of being jubilant and excited because of their escape had become one of subdued melancholy. No one could put a finger on why, they just did. The other feeling they had in common was that things weren't right with the world either. The feeling strengthened when dawn on the third day since Pluperfect's mysterious disappearance introduced them to a rapidly approaching storm of biblical proportions that inexplicably veered around them at the very last moment. Something was indeed terribly amiss. To make matters worse, Cetus had taken to whistling very badly.

Lupus meanwhile had watched and noted everything with growing concern and now had enough to put two and two together and arrive at an answer he didn't particularly like. But there was nothing he could about it at the moment, not on his own; he needed help for that. All he could do for the moment was to continue watching and waiting.

Time passed wearily and when, later that third day something else, another dot, appeared on the horizon it went unnoticed; unheeded. It was a heavy-hearted Equuleus that was again first to notice this new dot on the horizon, but in his state of mind he took it to be a figment of his longing imagination and tried to ignore it. It was only when it wouldn't go away, no matter how many times he closed his eyes, that Equuleus started to believe what he was indeed seeing. Better still this dot was closing at a more sedate speed and had not, as yet, sprouted sails.

Slowly, but surely the fog that had hung over Equuleus since the incident with Pluperfect's ship lifted inch by inch from his spirit the closer the dot came. He could see… was that…?

'Trees!' shouted Equuleus, 'trees!' And not just trees, but mountains in the distance and a shoreline that didn't fade away on either side. This was not just land; not an island. This was mainland. The edge of some country or continent.

The others muttered, but didn't stir; the shared torpor deeper in their bones. Only Lupus bothered to cock a wary eye past the edge of the raft. He raised his head. The boy was right; it was land, proper land. Lupus began to bark. As each turned so the fog started lifting from their shoulders. They began to stand. Shout. Cheer. Even Pistor was on his feet shouting and waving as if the fog had taken with it the mist that usually clouded his heart and mind.

The wind was taking them straight to it, but Pyxis handed out the oars anyway. This wasn't the time to take chances. They were soon paddling for all they were worth towards the cliffs that seemed to grow before their eyes. It didn't take long, with the wind at their backs, for the raft to reach shallow water. Pyxis gave the call to head for the small cove to their left. They glided in and ran aground on a small pebble strewn length of beach.

The land that rose from that shoreline looked familiar, but not recognisable. Bedecked with trees, oaks and sycamores mingled with birch, all showing the first touches of autumn, were native to the land they had left so long ago, but the terrain was different.

When the raft was safely ashore Musca, under the watchful eye of Fornax to name but one interested party, put together a scouting party consisting of him and the brothers and scurried inland. It wasn't long before they were back.

'The wood thins quite quickly just beyond,' said Hydra, hands on knees getting his breath back, 'and beyond that…'

'Are fields and copses and rolling countryside,' Hydrus finished.

Equuleus sidled up to Musca. 'Is it Ohm?' he asked.

'I think it is,' said Musca, smiling.

Equuleus let forth a triumphant whoop of joy and cartwheeled across the pebbles. When he stopped he began to shout at the top of his voice. 'Ohm at last! Ohm at last!'

While Equuleus jigged Musca turned to Fornax and asked how Cetus was faring.

'Well he got off the raft without any help which I suppose is a good thing, but he's still not talking. I'm worried,' Fornax cast a glance in Cetus' direction, 'and he seems to be waiting for something. Don't ask me how I know, it's a feeling. Like the ones we had on the raft.'

Cetus was standing several yards away staring as he did on the raft, but now at the treeline. Occasionally a smile would appear fleetingly on his lips; indeed, so fleet that unless you were studying him closely you would be apt to miss it.

One that *was* watching him closely hadn't. Since they had spied land Lupus had been watching Cetus like a hawk. Something was going to happen and soon. His mind turned to Tee Hee. He couldn't save anyone on his own, he needed help. It was time to make contact. Lupus tilted his head to one side and shook it. He couldn't feel the transmitter. He would have to change. Lupus waited for the right moment then trotted into the trees. With one eye on the beach he changed the shape of his left foreleg to that of a human hand and arm and poked a finger in his ear. It wasn't there. The transmitter was gone and there was no point in looking for it, it could be anywhere; most likely the bottom of the ocean.

Things had just turned from bad to worse. It looked like he would have to face Serpens on his own.

CHAPTER 58

Tee Hee flicked open an intercom and asked how the patient was doing.

Draco, given the job of nursemaid, flicked the intercom on in the infirmary and reported back that the patient was as well as could be expected and that he would report back if anything changed.

Tee Hee closed the connection and hoped nothing would. If the patient showed any signs of fading away he doubted they would be close enough to do anything for him. He returned his focus to the scanners. So far there had been nothing to see but sea, sea and nothing but sea, so help him. But Tee Hee was not about to throw in the towel just yet. They had to be out there somewhere and as long as their patient remained as he was there was still hope.

The silver craft started to descend to sea level and an observation panel the size of the far wall appeared giving Tee Hee a panoramic view of the ocean. He had decided he wanted to see what was out there. Not that he didn't trust his scanners; on the contrary, they were the best any serious space jockey could wish for, what he wanted was to see with his own two eyes, to feel he was physically doing something himself. He thought of Fornax and wondered if he would ever see her again; wondered how he was going to tell her about Tee See. He was becoming maudlin and may have become worse if not for Draco suddenly yelling hysterically into the intercom for him to get to the infirmary as quickly as he could.

When Tee Hee arrived Draco raced up to him and pointed to the far corner. 'We've got a visitor,' he whispered.

'Where?' said Tee Hee. Apart from Draco and the patient whom he couldn't see anyway the room was empty.

Draco explained. 'He's talking to Cetus.' Cetus was the patient. At least his spirit was. Draco had found him in a corner of the shack, shocked and afraid. Not that Draco could ordinarily communicate with or see spirits, but for some reason with Cetus he could. Tee Hee thought it had something to do with the link between body and spirit not being broken yet; Cetus' body technically still being used, so not dead; a supernatural thing.

'Who is?'

At this point Draco became a little coy and pushed small puffs of white smoke from his nostrils; a sign amongst dragons showing anguish or discomfort. 'He say's he's your son.'

'What!' Tee Hee swayed for a moment then rallied; collecting his senses. 'But that can't be. Show yourself!' he bellowed. It had to be a trick. Something conjured up by Serpens to slow them down. But Serpens didn't know they were following; did he? He cast Draco a suspicious glance, but the shock and sorrow in Draco's expression sent that thought where it belonged; oblivion. Tee Hee now spoke in a whisper, 'My son? Where?'

'Close,' Tee See left Cetus and stood by Draco's side, 'he says he has a lot to tell you.'

'He can talk to me?'

'Yes, Father.'

Tee Hee, aided by Draco, staggered to a chair and when he was ready Tee See told his story.

'Pulled up with the lion, eh?' said Tee Hee, throwing a glance in Draco's direction. Perhaps he could be forgiven for that one now. 'That was indeed lucky. You have Draco here to thank for that.' Draco managed an awkward smile. 'So now you are like Cetus?' said Tee Hee.

'Yes and no,' said Tee See, who was finding it just as hard to explain as it was for everyone to understand. 'I believe I have successfully transferred to the humans' next stage of evolution, something they call death, but unlike them perhaps because of the mix of our and their genera, I have a little more control so haven't yet completely ascended. I only managed this state a short while ago so didn't realise I could make contact until I overheard Draco talking to Cetus.'

No it didn't explain everything; not clearly, but what the heck, thought Tee Hee beaming inside, my boy's back. But time was short. 'Whatever,' said Tee Hee, rising from his chair, 'just glad to have you back, but now I'm afraid the time for talking is over, we have people to save and one of those is your mother.'

CHAPTER 59

It was happy times, why even Cetus had acquired a spring to his step. And why shouldn't he? They were walking through a land of beauty that promised an end to their journey. Somewhere near lay Ohm; they all knew it, they could all feel it. The pot of gold at the end of the rainbow each sought was close; so close.

'Look, a jack,' shouted Equuleus, as a large rabbit bounded startled from their path. He started to give chase, but Fornax was quick to call him back.

'Careful, Equuleus,' warned Fornax, 'we don't know the land.'

'But it's Ohm, isn't it?' Equuleus argued, 'we're safe.'

Fornax had to smile. 'Not yet. We haven't found the valley Musca's father spoke of. Until then I think we should be careful.'

Careful of what? thought Equuleus, frowning and pouting at being pulled up, he slowed to sulking pace and fell in alongside the brothers who were bringing up the rear.

Lupus, who since leaving the raft was never far from Fornax's side, discretion allowing, picked up on what Equuleus' was thinking and thought it a good question? He threw a glance at Cetus who was walking apart from everyone else. What indeed?

They left the cover of the woods and followed the slope of a small hill leading down to the meadows the brothers and Musca had seen earlier on their scouting mission. What they had failed to see on that foray was the well worn path that ran around the bottom of the hill. Fornax called a halt and knelt down to inspect it.

'It's been used regularly and quite recently,' she said, bringing murmurs from those crowding round her. They had spoken of Ohm often enough, but until now none of them had given a second thought that Ohm might be inhabited. Everyone looked at Musca.

'Did your father ever mention people?' said Fornax, standing.

'People?' said Musca.

'People living, in Ohm or near Ohm?'

Musca shifted uncomfortably. 'Not that I remember,' he said, 'but we're not there yet. Ohm's a valley.'

It was no real answer, but it was enough to satisfy most, not Fornax though. Ohm may or may not be inhabited, but someone was around and she didn't want any nasty surprises springing out at them. Erring on the side of caution she decided it might be wise to scout the path in both directions. Hydrus and Equuleus were sent to explore the path away from them. Musca took Hydra the way they were heading; everyone else would wait.

It wasn't long before she got some answers. Hydrus and Equuleus returned quite quickly. The direction they took led to nothing as the path meandered away into the distance with no buildings or people in sight. Musca and Hydra who arrived back five minutes later had a different story to tell. They had seen smoke billowing from the other side of a small rise. Hydra had wanted to investigate further, but Musca had thought better of it. This time Fornax had to agree with him.

'What type of smoke,' grilled Fornax.

'Chimney smoke I think,' said Musca. Hydra agreed.

'There,' shouted Tee See, excitedly, 'a raft. It must be theirs. They're safe.'

Tee Hee didn't share his optimism. It may well be their raft from the description Cetus had supplied, but that didn't mean they had been on it when it came ashore. 'I'll take a closer look.' He pushed a button and the window was replaced by a viewing screen that magnified the area surrounding the raft. 'See anything?'

Both Tee See and Draco shook their heads. The pebbled beach showed no indication that anyone had walked on it.

'We'll have to travel further inland,' said Tee Hee. The hovering spacecraft started to move. And hope we're not too late, he thought, shielding it from the others.

'What do you think they'll find?' said Equuleus, crouching beside Fornax amongst trees in a small copse not far from the rise.

Alerted by approaching footfalls Fornax readied her sword, but relaxed it again as Pyxis and Fatidic ambled into view. 'I don't know, but I imagine we shall soon find out.' She had suggested Pyxis and Fatidic were sent to investigate the source of the smoke thinking it better to send outsiders who wouldn't so easily have their judgements blighted by unhelpful sentiment.

'Well?' asked Fornax, emerging from the copse to greet them.

'Huts,' said Fatidic, 'lying at the mouth of a small valley.'

'Quite a few of them,' said Pyxis, 'but no people.'

'Ohm,' said Musca, 'we should get going.'

And this was exactly why Fornax had sent Pyxis and Fatidic. 'No one goes anywhere,' she said, grabbing Musca by the shoulder, 'until we find out why there's no one about.' Granted it was getting late, but dusk was still a long way off. People, children, should still be out and about doing whatever it was they did. Something was wrong and she had the feeling it involved them somehow. Call it warrior's instinct. But danger or no danger something had to be done if they were going to journey on; nothing would be achieved just sitting there among the trees. She made her decision and told Pyxis and Fatidic to lead the way. The others she told to follow as quietly as possible.

They reached the rise with hearts racing and breasted it. Pyxis and Fatidic had scouted well. Over it, hiding them from view, ran a hedge of gorse and hawthorn bushes. From this vantage point they were able to see right into the village; a village that caused breaths to be caught in throats. They were looking at a place that stirred familiar memories within. A village that could almost be the same one they had left razed to the ground all those months ago.

Everything that could be used to observe the land below was being utilised.

'Anything?' said Tee Hee, for the umpteenth time as they skimmed the tree tops.

Tee See was staring down at the scanners without success. 'It's no good. The leaves are blocking them.'*

'I'm going to take us to the other side of the trees, perhaps we'll be able to pick up any signs of them there.'

Tee See intensified the scanners and concentrated. He didn't want to miss anything if it was there. A foot print, a torn piece of cloth. Even a broken twig could prove important. Even smoke.

It was Draco that spotted it through the reverted viewing screen.

'Where?' said Tee Hee.

'I see it,' said Tee See, 'nine o'clock, father.' Tee See left the scanners and joined Draco at the window.

Tee Hee was already on it and changing course.

'Do you think it's them?'

'We shall see, son. We shall soon see.'

'Can anyone see anything?' whispered someone, as they crept as one, closer to the village.

'No.' Came replies from at least four different sources.

They inched closer. Apart from the occasional bird call from somewhere distant, they heard and saw no sign of life. Fornax didn't like it. Nor did Lupus, the fur standing on his back, he could smell a rat; two if he were being honest and had done since they had come over the rise, but as yet the scent of the biggest still eluded him. He cast a glance at Cetus. The man was grinning. That couldn't be good. Lupus had a growing feeling in his water that whatever was going to happen was going to happen pretty soon.

His timing was impeccable. The moment they reached the outskirts of the village the doors on a large barn flew open with such force they broke in two and as the dust settled the ugliest,

* Believe it or not leaves when they put their mind to it can be disruptive little so and so's. It's rumoured that on one planet of so called higher life forms they on numerous occasions caused havoc by congregating on railway lines. No, I too find that hard to believe. *SJ*

371

craziest, little critter that you could ever have the misfortune to meet stepped over the broken pieces and into the open.

Lyra, donning the grin of the homicidally insane, confronted them; he was dragging something. 'Well, well,' he said, stopping and letting go of whatever it was he'd had in his hand, 'it's so nice to finally meet you.' The creature appeared to be looking at Musca, but with his boggle eyes it was hard to tell. All but Lupus and Cetus, took a hurried couple of horrified steps away. 'And Lupus, or should I call you Fluffy,' sneered Lyra, 'how are you?' He started to giggle insanely as the spotlight of horror found another player to shine on.

'Told you the thing wasn't right,' whispered Pistor.

'Whoops!' said Lyra, coyly poking a finger in his mouth, 'did I accidentally reveal your little secret?'

Lupus growled, but not at Lyra, he knew he was being controlled and by whom; his teeth were shown to Cetus.

Cetus took a horrified step back from those razor sharp fangs, but then started to laugh. Walk and laugh. Walk towards the crazily grinning monster standing by the barn.

'Nor him,' said Pistor.

'Cetus... no!' yelled Fornax, stepping forward, 'you don't know what you're doing.'

Cetus stopped and turned. 'Oh, but I do,' he said, in a voice no one but Lupus and the mad Lyra knew. 'TELL THEM LYRA. TELL THEM *OUR* LITTLE SECRET.' Cetus began to laugh again.

Stepping away from the barn, Lyra stooped low in a theatrical sweeping bow. 'Lords, ladies, fellow inklings and soon to be subjugated humanoid dross, may I introduce my master,' Lyra pointed both hands at Cetus. 'He who will soon be the master of all the universe. His most regal, his most... darkest, his most... highest,' drums started to roll from somewhere, 'LORD SERPENS, *th-eeee* one and only... ANARCHIST!'

Cetus waved, bowed and stepped behind Lyra onto whatever it was the imp had been dragging. Moments later Cetus' body lay on the ground and Serpens had risen in all his glory and body again. He nonchalantly rested an elbow on the roof of the barn and leaning casually, admired the claws on his other hand. It was enough to have the bravest of men running for the hills. Luckily there was none of such ilk in sight so what were there, together with a brave woman and a brave estranged inkling shape-changer called Fluffy, stood their ground.

'Thank you, Lyra,' said Serpens, 'but if you don't mind I'll take it from here.' The evil grin instantly fell away from the imp's lips who then staggered for a couple of steps before falling on his knees. Serpens stepped over him. 'Now, monkey man, tell me *your* secret.' His eyes glowed red and focused on Musca.

Musca felt suddenly faint.

Serpens grew impatient. The seconds passed. The end of a very long tunnel was now within sight and he wanted to reach it. 'Well?' he said, 'Do you DEFY ME?'

Musca didn't mean to, would have told Serpens every secret he could think of, including the embarrassing fight with the rabbit, but as his mouth had ceased to operate properly and his body wasn't far from doing likewise it looked as if, for once, he was being the stoic heroic figure that folklore expected.

'YOU *DO* DEFY ME!' stormed Serpens, standing straight, steam escaping from nostrils and ears, but only slightly as he had secretly been ready for this. He had read story books in his youth and knew all about how stubborn, so called heroes, could be. He was impatient to rule the universe yes, but that didn't mean you couldn't have a little bit of fun along the way. 'OPHIUCHUS! BRING THEM FORTH!'

From around the side of the barn appeared Ophiuchus carrying with him a huge drum in one hand and in his other a trailing rope.

'You can lose the drum now,' sighed Serpens, who couldn't wait to have in his ranks a better class of minion, but until then...

Ophiuchus obediently dropped the drum and tugged on the rope. Slowly other creatures began to stumble from behind the barn; sad pathetic creatures whose appearance brought gasps of horror, surprise and fear from the gathered humans.

'Father?' whispered Musca, as a man dressed in rags and smeared with dirt appeared. The man hearing Musca's voice looked up. It was indeed Musca's father. Musca, confused, his mind pounding, his heart keeping pace, drew his knife as he now recognised others in the line bound by the rope Ophiuchus held; others from the village. Amongst them were also strangers. Those that hadn't been unconscious at the time would have recognised the gypsies that had taken Musca in. One of them was sobbing softly; a young woman. The sound of her crying stirred a memory deep within, but he couldn't quite catch it; pull it from the depths. Did he know her? Anger built. Did it matter? Anger began to rise. No it didn't. Anger spilt.

'What have you done to them?' screamed Musca, brandishing his blade, tears stinging his eyes.

Serpens looked shocked, hurt even. 'Me? Why nothing,' he said, posturing disbelief at Musca's accusation. But then the grin reappeared. 'But that can change if you don't tell me what I want to KNOW!' He leaned down to the young woman who had stirred something in Musca and placed a claw under her chin. 'YOUR CHOICE.'

Watching and motivated by something he still didn't understand, Lupus decided he could no longer stand by and do nothing. He had had enough. He wanted no more to do with this. Lupus sprang into action, aiming for Serpens' throat, but in his fury had given no thought to the shape he still adopted. Serpens easily dodged the oversized sheepdog hurtling at him – a werewolf may have been a different proposition – and swatted him as he would a fly. Lupus whined as ribs broke; the wind forced from him. Serpens swiftly made a grab for this wind; Lupus' breath; the breath of the immortal and ripped it from him. Lupus, now mortal, fell to the ground with a wound he would never recover from.

If that wasn't enough Serpens now poured scorn on top of Lupus' pain, 'You think to attack your master. Dare to disobey ME! I made you what you are, Lupus, and you repay me THUS! Goodbye Lupus, you have ceased to be useful to me.' Serpens raised his foot, ready to snuff the last breath from Lupus' broken body.

'No!' screamed a voice, cracked with age and heavy with emotion, 'not me Fluffy.' A pain shot through Serpens' left ankle as Bootes, who had dashed forward when Lupus had flown through the air, with a speed that belied his age, hit home with the pitchfork he had taken from its place against the barn wall.

Glaring at the pitchfork Serpens pulled it from his leg and crushed it between his fingers. That same glare now beat down on Lyra. Serpens was furious and bellowed at the cowering imp, 'WHY DIDN'T YOU STOP HIM?'

Whimpering and simpering on the ground Lyra, sitting arms round his knees, stared at the ground. He had wanted to, but he hadn't wanted to. He was… poor Lupus. Lyra started to cry.

'Oh, never mind,' growled Serpens. He would have to do everything himself. Always did. He now turned his venom on the old humanoid that had had the audacity to stab him. It was staring back at him, defiant, tears running down its cheeks. He had no time for this. 'ENOUGH!' he roared and coldly swept Bootes aside, sending him crashing against the barn.

Unseen or sensed by those on the ground the silver spacecraft glided to a stop high over the village.

'Quick Father, bring him up,' said Tee See, urgently.

Tee Hee locked on and pressed the button Draco had earlier mistakenly pushed to bring the lion, Jungle Man and Tee See aboard. He spoke into the intercom.

'He's here,' confirmed Draco, sent to wait for Cetus' body to materialise. Tee Hee and Tee See dashed to the infirmary.

'Where is he?' said Tee Hee, heading for a tray.

'On the bed,' said Draco.

Tee Hee could see that. 'I mean his spirit.'

'Over here,' said Tee See, 'he's huddled in the corner.'

'Can you get him over here?' said Tee Hee, anxiously examining Cetus' corporeal body, 'there's not much time. He's starting to close off to the world.'

Tee See took Cetus by the hand and coaxed him over to the bed. Cetus knew what he had to do, but seeing his body like that, appearing from nowhere, had shaken him. 'You'll be all right once you join again,' said Tee See, reassuringly.

Cetus climbed up.

'Is he there yet?' said Tee Hee. Tee See relayed that Cetus was standing on the bed. 'Please lie down.'

Cetus lay down and levitated just inches above his body.

'It's time,' said Tee Hee, 'you just have to relax.'

It wasn't easy, but Cetus managed to and slowly he and his body began to merge until there was only one of him lying on the bed. Nothing happened at first then Cetus suddenly sat bolt upright clutching at his chest, his eyes wide with fear. 'What's happening?' he cried, startled and confused.

It was the cue for Tee Hee to step forward and administer what was in the hypo he had in his hand. He pressed it into Cetus' neck, there was a slight hissing sound and Cetus slumped backwards.

'Right,' said Tee Hee, 'back to the control room.'

But as they reached the door Draco suddenly stopped dead.

'What's wrong?' said Tee Hee.

The dragon's face had taken on a deathly pallor. 'It's Lupus,' said Draco, 'he... he's dying.'

Tee See, a step behind, caught up as Draco dropped his bombshell. 'Lupus? You must be wrong. He can't, he's immortal.' But the look Draco gave him had him faltering. 'Can he?' Tee See was mortified. 'I've got to see him.'

'But-'

'Now, Father, you've got to send me down there.'

'The Serpens creature,' Tee Hee protested.

'I'm dead, what can he do?'

The answer to that no one knew for sure.

They continued on, Tee See's urgent step now leading the way.

'Are you sure?' said Tee Hee, on reaching the control room, although he knew he would do the same if he were in his son's position.

'Where do you want me?'

'There will be fine.'

Nanoseconds later Tee See was in the village by Lupus' side.

'Lupus,' said Tee See. Tears, or the feeling of them, were building as he looked down at his friend's broken body.

'Tee See?' Lupus tried to lift head, but the pain was too much.

'Here, old friend.' Tee See crouched low so his friend could see him.

'But I saw you die.'

'You did, I'm a spirit.'

'Ah!' said Lupus, he had heard of this. A mortal thing. Perhaps he…? But this was not the time for the wondering of such things. Time was short. 'Are you alone?' he asked.

'Father's ship is above us.'

'You must get him to help them. I've failed.'

'You haven't…'

'Promise me.'

'I promise, but…'

Lupus closed his eyes. His breathing grew shallow.

'Lupus?'

But Lupus was gone.

With nerveless steel Fornax edged forward, her sword moving in controlled arcs above her head. She was in warrior mode and someone was going to pay for hurting one of her people.

'Big against dogs and old men, monster, let's see how you do against a warrior!' she challenged.

Now a monkey woman threatened him. It was all getting rather tedious. Serpens made a grab at her, but Fornax easily sidestepped the attempt and brought her sword down on his fist, drawing a deep gouge across the back of it. Serpens roared in anger more than pain. Enough really was enough. As Fornax swung her sword for another strike Serpens grabbed the blade with his other hand. It started to glow. Fornax screamed and the sword fell from her blistered hands, sizzling before becoming a molten puddle on the ground.

'NOW WE SHALL SEE HOW YOU DO AGAINST THE NEW MASTER OF THE UNIVERSE!' roared Serpens.

'No!' Musca ran between them, brandishing his knife.

The monkey man. He had almost forgotten him. Serpens checked his advance. The pathetic creature he had followed for so long. Chased for so long for the secret he held. Within his grasp. So puny yet with so much power… Only had to reach out

377

and... power? He hesitated. Why was he hesitating? Something in Serpens' mind shifted; was lifted. He reeled. What power? asked a voice. What? What power? it asked again. He felt odd. Something... Then it came. Not slowly. Suddenly, like a curtain being pulled across to reveal... Ta-ra... Realization! It poured into him; from him. The blind removed, he saw the monkey man as he truly was; nothing. *Had* always been nothing. It was he, Serpens who had the power, had *always* had the power. The chase had been for nothing. But why had it taken him until now to see it? Because the only power the monkey man wielded was the power of illumination and he had to see that for himself. Serpens roared with demonic delight. The monkey man was nothing more than a pathetic light of dawning that now barely shone against the greater power towering over him. He didn't need him. He didn't need anyone. He was the master. It was time to take his rightful place.

'FINISH THEM,' he thundered, 'FINISH THEM ALL!'

Help them, how could he help them? He had no weapons. The spacecraft was not a battle ship, it was for exploring. The only thing that could have been used as a weapon had been drained of power when Draco had inadvertently flicked it into life and destroyed that forest with it. There was no way to recharge it while the ship lacked vital power. There was nothing he could do. Tee Hee started to pace. There *was* one thing. If the thief still had it that was. But *he* couldn't go, he was needed up here. He couldn't send Draco; who knows what confusion that would add. For the same reason he couldn't see Tee See being able to help. That left... but he was a human. He was their only chance; he would have to try. But how could he contact him and could he be trusted? He had no choice. It would have to be a mind meet. But not here, he had to concentrate. Tee Hee told Draco what he intended and left the control room, after a short hurried pace down one of the corridors he came to a small room he used for meditation and entered. Now thief Pistor, let's see what you're made of.

On the ground strange things began to happen to Pistor as he watched Fornax attacking the monster. His thoughts of a second ago that were primarily run, forest, hide, had suddenly blanked out leaving him in a state of confusion. His ears were ringing. He felt sick; was surely going to be sick, if the spinning didn't stop.

It wasn't working. The harder Tee Hee tried the worse the link between he and Pistor became. It was no good. He would have to concede defeat or Pistor's brain would become more pickled than it sometimes was; permanently perhaps. He would have to try something else, but what, his choices were limited if not already exhausted.

'Perhaps I can help?'

A contact just as he was about to break the link. Tee Hee couldn't believe it. 'Pistor?'

'No, but I want to help.'

Not Pistor. Then who? 'Draco?' The wave signal was similar, but not quite.

'It's not Draco, but I am one of Serpens' minions.' Tee Hee immediately tried to break the link but couldn't, whoever it was, was powerful and wouldn't let him go. 'I think I may be your only chance.'

Tee Hee stopped his wrestling he had no choice but to listen. If the creature was an enemy he had already won. 'How can you help?'

'Tell me what to do?'

'What about Serpens?'

'He's occupied. Trust me.'

What could Tee Hee do but divulge to this minion the secret Pistor held upon his person.

Lyra staggered, his thoughts confused and twitching in their draughty shell of a mind. The plug had been pulled on the confidence he had been bathing in. Serpens had taken it back. Serpens had always taken, never given.

'KILL THEM!' roared Serpens.

Lyra bore down on the group of monkey men who had surrounded the fallen female. Weapons were raised against him. Feeble weapons, but Lyra hesitated.

'WHAT ARE YOU WAITING FOR!' growled Serpens, 'DO MY BIDDING OR SUFFER LUPUS' FATE.'

'I'll do it, Sire,' shouted Ophiuchus, leaving his prisoners tethered to a rail.

Serpens was impressed. But of course Ophiuchus did possess something of him inside him. Which, he thought, I'll have to remember to take back when all this messiness is over. Serpens ushered Ophiuchus forward and prepared to enjoy the show.

Pushing Lyra aside, Ophiuchus charged at the huddle of frightened humanoids. He knew what he had to do. Ignoring the screams and attempts to stop him with their woeful weapons he made straight for Pistor.

Pistor for his part had not yet recovered from Tee Hee's attempted mind link and was standing alone with his hands over his ears wishing the ringing in them would stop. He never saw Ophiuchus until it was too late. Whisked aloft in Ophiuchus' massive fist Pistor, the swinging doing nothing for the nausea he felt, did the only thing he was able and vomited down Ophiuchus' back.

Ignoring this, Ophiuchus turned to Serpens and held Pistor out in front of him.

'For me?' said Serpens. And why not, he thought, it's no more than I deserve. Haven't I always been the best of masters? Serpens held out his hand. 'You shouldn't, but as you are I shall receive your offering. I have to admit I am feeling a tad peckish. Give it to me.'

But as Serpens went to take the monkey man snack from Ophiuchus' outstretched hand the ogre took a step back and pulled his own hand away, gently rolling Pistor across the ground out of harm's way. Ophiuchus did want to give Serpens something, but it wasn't the monkey man. Serpens, hardly believing what he was seeing, howled his outrage.

'Isn't this where I'm supposed to say "breathe"?' said Ophiuchus, coldly.

'WHAT?' bellowed Serpens, now hardly believing what he was hearing. Serpens' glare returned to Ophiuchus who was pointing something at him.

'So another worm turns,' growled Serpens, 'well Ophiuchus, what are you waiting for? Do your worst and then prepare to face MINE!' Serpens began to laugh.

Ophiuchus found the tiny firing mechanism with the tip of one of his claws and fired. A stream of molecular disruption particles, unseen by the naked eye, flowed from the M.C.E. hitting Serpens in the chest.

Laughing louder still Serpens spouted his contempt, 'IS THAT IT? IS THAT YOUR WORST?'

Ophiuchus fired again, and again the M.C.E. found its mark.

Still Serpens laughed; laughed to the heavens above, but he was growing tired of this new game. It was time Ophiuchus was taught a lesson; a permanent one. The terrible power he now knew he possessed was going to be unleashed with full fury; without mercy. His eyes glowed as the power within built. Poor Ophiuchus wouldn't know what hit him and the universe would tremble.

'NOW OPHIUCHUS! NOW YOU WILL FEEL THE POWER OF THE DARK LORD!' screamed Serpens, looking for the fear in his minion's eye so that he could drink deep with satisfaction from it.

He didn't find it. He didn't even find Ophiuchus' eyes. Nor did he find his face. What trickery was this, thought Serpens, as he stared at Ophiuchus' knees? He looked down at his feet expecting to find he had stepped into some unseen trap the monkey men had set for lesser beings than he. There was none, he was still standing on the ground but... whose footprints were those he stood in? Puzzled, confused, he stared up at a towering Ophiuchus who fired the M.C.E. again and again. Then the confusion lifted just enough to allow the second notable realization of Serpens' day to peep through.

'NO!' screamed Serpens, now aware of what was happening to him. 'NO!'

'Yes,' said Ophiuchus, through gritted teeth.

'BUT I AM THE DARK ONE. MASTER OF ALL.'

Ophiuchus fired again.

'YOU CAN'T!'

And again.

Serpens tried to muster his power, but it was all too little too late. His power was shrinking as fast as he was. 'YOU WILL PAY FOR THIS. MARK MY WORDS. ALL OF YOU WILL!'

Again and again Ophiuchus fired.

Smaller and smaller Serpens shrank. Thumb size. Pea size. Ant size. Until he could shrink no more within the vision of the naked eye. Here he lingered for a moment and managed to utter a last word before oblivion.

'DRAT!'

With the merest of red flashes and the faintest of pops, Serpens was no more.

CHAPTER 60

Chaos gave way to order. Ophiuchus was hailed a hero, but given a wide berth. Lyra was tied with the rope holding the prisoners; he hadn't put up a fight. Bootes cried for his friend while beside him another, unseen by him, did likewise. Reunions were made. Corvus bound Fornax's blistered hands. Tee Hee popped some seriously old champagne and Draco burped a few times, causing a mild burn here and there. Pistor's ears finally stopped ringing and he fell over.

They had reached Ohm and it was in a valley very much like the one they had left behind, but not burnt and not the same one. From a hill opposite the crest they had climbed and followed down into the village, they could, if they wanted to; which none did for a very long time, see that very valley they had left so long ago.

Musca never did. He freed his father and told him of the journey they had undertaken to find Ohm and of his surprise of finding him already there. Musca's father told him the secret of Ohm and, not surprisingly, it was never mentioned again.

The adventure was over.

Well… almost.

In the weeks and months that followed friendships were forged and animosities forgotten. Stories were swapped, tales told. Life went on; alien, inkling and human.

* * *

Tee Hee managed to talk to Fornax and say his goodbyes before leaving Apomas forever. Draco who wanted to travel further than his wings could ever take him went with him.

* * *

Tee See sadly never met his mother, but knew she knew he was close and so bade farewell to the living world and all in it to explore the new plane he now existed in. But not before helping an old friend find a new home.

* * *

Bootes found a new flock of sheep to herd and thanks to a new sheepdog puppy that seemed overly large to everyone but he and Fatidic, he managed to get over the loss of Fluffy, but never lose the memory.

* * *

Lupus, thanks to help from Tee See, breathed new life into a stillborn puppy, who would grew up to become a sheepdog with very special powers and, with just the smallest of mental nudges, be called Prince. Sadly he never did deliver the note.

* * *

Cetus never quite got over his out of body experience and after losing several stone in weight sought refuge in a monastery where he was hired as a short order fryer.

* * *

Hydra and Hydrus also left the village. They wanted to explore the new world they had discovered and would return frequently with stories of their adventures.

* * *

Pyxis was made welcome and told there would always be a home for him in the village, but he too had itchy feet and left with the brothers.

* * *

Equuleus, his eyes widened by all he had seen, decided he wanted to travel the world and fight evil wherever it lurked. Once he had finished his apprenticeship at the bakery that is.

* * *

Magus Fatidic didn't change his name back to Timbrel Tittle and became the village soothsayer when the old one mysteriously drowned whilst having an illicit taste of Pistor's wares. How you drowned in mashed potato was anyone's guess. Nothing was ever proved.

* * *

Pistor became teetotal and remained sober the rest of his days. Believe that and you'll believe anything. But he did become the biggest potato baron this side of Sir Walter Raleigh.

* * *

Ophiuchus and Lyra went their separate ways. Ophiuchus headed for the hills after having his wish come true at an official naming ceremony at which he changed his name to Bob. Some say he's still there, waiting and watching for new dangers that may one day threaten the village. And to this day the village and its people hold an annual holiday, Bob-day, to celebrate Bob's courageous deed.

Lyra disappeared, but there are stories. One of which told of someone answering his description ringing bells in a far off church called Notta Dam. It was also reported that he wore a chain of daisies around his neck. It is only a story though.

* * *

As for Musca and Fornax, well, they got married. No, not to each other, that would be too much. Musca took Columba, the gypsy girl that had tended him, for his bride and Fornax got hitched to Aquila. And while Musca and Columba were happy to stay in the village Fornax took Aquila's hand and took to the open road with the other gypsies.

* * *

And the others? There are stories of course, but for another time maybe.

* * *

And now, before you close the book and hie it down the road to the nearest bookshop for my other titles, I think we should take a moment and travel back to the beginning. The very beginning.

* * *

BACK AT THE BEGINNING.

There was a tentative knock on the Chief Creator's door.

'Ah, Creator Brown. Do please come in,' said the Chief Creator, without looking up.

Creator Brown shuffled through the open door. He was in trouble. He had to be to be called into the Chief Creator's office at this time of the millennia.

'Please be seated.' The Chief Creator tidied a ream of papyrus; he hated the new fangled paper and looked up, 'We seem to have a problem.'

Brown tugged at the throat of his robe. Was it hot in here or was it just him? 'What problem is that then?' he asked.

The Chief slammed both his hands onto his desk, making Creator Brown jump. 'APOMAS, Brown. Do I need to say more?'

Brown tugged harder at his robe. 'It was only a couple of years. I'll get straight back to it now.' He went to rise, but was stayed by the Chief who looked slightly puzzled.

'A couple of years?' The Chief stood up and walked round to where Brown was sitting, 'What are you talking about?'

'Lunch.'

'Lunch?'

'I left early to have lunch. I should really be getting back.' Creator Brown went to get up, but the Chief Creator placed his hands on his shoulders and pushed him back down.'

'Then you don't know.'

'Don't know what?'

The Chief sighed and went back to his chair. 'We've a problem.'

This was it, he was going to get the sack. 'I'll work harder,' wailed Creator Brown.

'No need, Creator Smith is taking up your duties as we speak.'

Creator Brown gulped and began to fidget.

On the other side of the desk the Chief Creator was also feeling slightly hot under the collar. He didn't want to do it, but he had no choice. Creator Brown had an irrevocable link to the problem. He had indeed caused it. He took a deep breath. Here goes.

'I have another job for you.' The Chief Creator ignored the murmur of relief that emanated from the other side of the desk. He wiped sweaty palms on his robe. 'Now, listen carefully, the fate of the universe is in *your* hands.'

ONE YEAR LATER

The dark clad, mysterious figure moved stealthily through the shadows to the hut. Light from inside poured through cracks in the badly made door. The figure pulled his cloak to him and his hood fell across his forehead putting his face into shadow. He knocked on the rickety door.

'Musca dear, it's the door. Be a love and get it will you, I've got my hands full with baby Auriga.'

Musca, slightly more rotund than a year ago and coughing slightly, downed the pipe he had recently taken to sucking on, slipped into his slippers and left his comfy armchair. Things were good for Musca. Very good in fact. But sometimes, in a quiet moment, he found the yearning for another adventure smouldering away inside him. He opened the door and looked outside.

'Yes?' he said, into the dark beyond.

The mysterious figure detached itself from the shadows. 'Are you Musca,' he asked.

'Yes.'

'Good,' said the cloaked figure, dramatically throwing back his hood, 'for I am Randolf the Magician!'

'Never heard of you,' said Musca and slammed the door shut.

'Who was it dear?' called Columba.

'No one,' said Musca, returning to his chair, 'just another bloody salesman.' He leaned back and took a long thoughtful puff of his pipe. Just a little adventure would be nice.

Outside the mysterious figure staggered from Musca's door in painful retreat and into the night, holding a not so mysterious bruised and bloodied nose. He wandered over to a grassy knoll and sat down, head tilted back. Creator Brown took a hanky from his robe and dabbed at the blood. Saving the universe wasn't going to be as easy as he thought.

Other titles by
Stefan Jakubowski

DEAD PECULIAR

You're dead – end of story. At least that's how Richard Ross saw it.

But he knows different now. Now that he's dead that is!

When Richard Ross entered the afterlife he thought his worries were well and truly over. When will he ever learn? Trapped, with all hell breaking loose around him he needs help; the living kind.

Can Marvo, a hapless hypnotist, and Rosemary Bloom, a plant psychic, really come to his rescue? Who knows!

With his dead relatives beside him Richard sets out on a dangerous journey that will take them deep into their past. For Richard things are about to change from strange to peculiar. Dead Peculiar.

The Chaplain swallowed hard, he knew he had no chance if the beast attacked. 'What do I do?'

'Flutter your eyelids would be my guess.'

'Be serious, I'm in trouble here.'

'I was, I think he likes you.'

The Chaplain gulped. A moment ago he was worried about being ripped apart but now the ball was in a totally different and very worrying court.

'What do I do?' repeated the Chaplain.

'Keep still,' advised Sammy.

'I can't, I'm shaking too much.'

'I think he likes it.'

'What?'

'The submissive bit. Look he's sniffing, he wants to sniff you.'

It was all too much for the Chaplain. Blown cover or no blown cover, he was not about to stand there and have his bits sniffed by some great slavering beast.

Published by ZYGMUNT STANLEY
ISBN 978-0-9554244-0-3

Other titles by
Stefan Jakubowski

STRANGE RELATIONS

Truly original, intriguing, amusing and touching –
altogether a compelling read.

Richard Ross, joiner, part-time local football referee, ordinary man, is
about to get a shock. It's time to meet the relatives. But guess what?
They're all dead. Even worse, they are his past lives and all share the
same soul - his!

With help from his Strange Relations, an angel named Joe, and Roberta
(Australopithecus Robustus), Richard has to learn the last lesson of life
so all will be allowed to journey towards the Light. Richard is the last of
a very long line and everyone's last chance.

One small problem though; Richard is in a coma and time is fast running
out.

   'Impossible!' blurted the Chaplain.
   'Why?' said Geoff, 'thirty-nine years ago I'd have said it impossible
for me to be sitting in a room talking to three ghosts. Let alone be one.'
   'That was improbable, not impossible,' argued the Chaplain. 'What
I mean is that it's impossible for a ghost to occupy a mortal's dead body,
even if they do share the same Soul.'
   'But Richard isn't dead,' Laura pointed out a gently as possible.

Published by ZYGMUNT STANLEY
ISBN 1-9-051702-0-3